SAVAGE HEARTS

OTHER BOOKS BY J.T. GEISSINGER

Queens and Monsters Series

Ruthless Creatures

Carnal Urges

Savage Hearts

Brutal Vows

Standalone

Pen Pal

SAVAGE HEARTS

J.T. GEISSINGER

BRAMBLE

TOR PUBLISHING GROUP | NEW YORK

SAVAGE HEARTS

Copyright © 2021 by J.T. Geissinger, Inc.

A Bramble Book

Published by Tom Doherty Associates / Tor Publishing Group
120 Broadway
New York, NY 10271

www.torpublishinggroup.com

Bramble™ is a trademark of Macmillan Publishing Group, LLC.

The Library of Congress Cataloging-in-Publication
Data is available upon request.

ISBN 978-1-250-38826-1 (trade paperback)
ISBN 978-1-250-34673-5 (ebook)

Our books may be purchased in bulk for promotional, educational, or business use. Please contact your local bookseller or the Macmillan Corporate and Premium Sales Department at 1-800-221-7945, extension 5442, or by email at MacmillanSpecialMarkets@macmillan.com.

Previously self-published by the author in 2021

First Bramble Trade Paperback Edition: 2025

Printed in the United States of America

0 9 8 7 6 5 4 3 2 1

For Jay, my reason for everything

And though she be but little, she is fierce.

—WILLIAM SHAKESPEARE, *A MIDSUMMER NIGHT'S DREAM*

ONE

RILEY

*W*hen my phone rings, I'm in the middle of editing a manuscript I'm behind on, so I ignore it and let the machine pick up.

Answering machines and landlines are old-school, I know, but I don't own a cell phone. I hate the idea of my every movement being trackable. And that Siri thing is just straight-up creepy, if you ask me.

A phone that's smarter than I am? No, thank you.

After my outgoing message informs the caller that I'm currently on another astral plane and they should leave a message I'll return when I manifest into flesh again, there's a beep. It's followed by a heavy sigh.

"Riley. It's your sister."

I send the answering machine on my dresser across the room a look of shock. "Sister?" I think for a moment. "Nope. Pretty sure I don't have one of those."

Sloane's voice turns bossy. "I know you're listening, because you're the only person in the world who still owns an answering machine. Plus, you never leave the house. Pick up."

It's amazing she thinks barking insults and orders at me would work. It's like she doesn't even know me.

Oh, wait. Now I remember! She *doesn't* know me. Which is totally not my fault, but leave it to Sloane to call out of the blue and act like I owe her money.

Shaking my head in disgust, I turn back to the computer screen and get back to work.

"Riley. Seriously. This is important. I need to talk to you." There's a heavy pause, then her voice drops. "Please."

My fingers freeze over the keyboard.

Please? Sloane doesn't say please. I didn't think she knew the word. Divas don't have it in their vocabularies.

Something must be terribly wrong. "Oh, shit," I say, panicking. "Dad."

I rush over to the phone and yank the receiver up to my ear. "What's happened?" I shout. "What's wrong? Is it Dad? Which hospital is he in? How bad is it?"

After a short pause, Sloane says, "Gee, overreact much?"

I can tell by her tone that there's nothing wrong with our father. I'm relieved for half a second, then pissed.

I don't have time for her bullshit right now.

"I'm sorry, you've reached a disconnected number. Please hang up and try again."

"Ah, sarcasm. The last resort of the witless."

"Speaking of witless, I'm not in the mood to have a battle of wits with an unarmed opponent. Call me back when you grow a brain."

"Why do you insist on pretending I'm not a genius?"

"An idiot savant isn't the same thing as a genius."

"Just because you graduated *summa cum laude* from an Ivy League college doesn't mean you're smarter than me."

"This from a person who once asked me how many quarters there are in a dollar."

"If you're so smart, tell me again why you're a freelance editor with no health insurance, job security, or retirement savings?"

"Wow. Straight to money. It must be convenient, having no soul. Makes all those poor men you chew up and spit out that much easier to deal with, huh?"

We sit in tense silence for a while. Finally, Sloane clears her throat and says, "Actually, that's what I'm calling about."

"Money?"

"Men. One in particular."

I wait for an explanation. When it doesn't come, I say, "Are we going to play twenty questions, or are you going to tell me what the hell you're talking about?"

Sloane takes a deep breath. She blows it out. Then, in a tone like she almost can't believe it herself, she says, "I'm getting married."

I blink an unnecessary amount of times. It doesn't help clarify anything. "I'm sorry, I thought I just heard you say you're getting married."

"You did. I am."

I huff out a disbelieving laugh. "You. The cockaholic. *Married.*"

"Yes."

I say flatly, "Impossible."

Unexpectedly, she laughs. "I know, right? But it's true. Pinkie swear. I'm getting married to the most wonderful man in the world."

Her sigh is soft, satisfied, and totally fucking ridiculous.

"Are you high right now?"

"Nope."

"Am I being punked?"

"Nope."

I cast around for some other explanation for this bizarre turn of events, but can't come up with anything except, "Is someone holding a gun to your head and forcing you to tell me this? Have you been kidnapped or something?"

She bursts into raucous laughter.

"Why is that so funny?"

She laughs and laughs until she's sighing again. I imagine her on the other end of the line wiping tears of joy from her face. "I'll tell you later. The point is, I'm getting married, and I want you to meet him. The wedding will be spontaneous, not a big event or anything. I don't know the exact date yet, but it could happen any day, so we'd like you to come visit us as soon as you can."

Visit *us*? Not only is she getting married, she's obviously living with this guy, too. I open my mouth to respond, but nothing comes out.

"I know," she says sheepishly. "It's unexpected."

"Thank you for having the decency to realize how weird this is."

"It is weird. I know. For all the reasons. But . . ." She clears her throat again. "You're my sister. I want you to meet the man I'm going to spend the rest of my life with."

"Please hold. I'll be right back after I'm finished with this stroke I'm having."

"Don't be mean."

Oh, the things I could say to that. Ho ho *ho,* the things I could say. But I choose the higher road and ask the next obvious question. "What about Nat?"

"What about her?"

"Why aren't you calling her about this guy?"

"She's already met him."

There's something odd in her tone that makes me suspicious. "And she knows you're going to marry him?"

"Yeah."

"So what does she think about all this?"

"Probably the same things you do." Her voice gains an edge. "Except she's happy for me."

Man, this conversation is a minefield. I'll be lucky if I survive with all my limbs intact.

Trying to keep my tone civil, I say, "I'm not not happy for you, Sloane. I'm just in shock. Also confused, to be honest."

"That I'm finally settling down?"

"No. Well, yes, but not mainly that."

"What, then?"

"That you're reaching out to me. That you're telling me about it. That you're inviting me to visit you. I mean, we haven't exactly been close."

"I know," she says softly. "I think that's probably my fault. And I'd really like to see if we can fix that."

After a long pause, she says, "What are you doing right now?"

"Lying flat on my back on the floor, staring at the ceiling, wishing I'd never taken all that ecstasy at Burning Man last year."

She says drily, "You're not having a drug flashback."

"I beg to differ."

She runs out of the infinitesimal amount of patience she has, and snaps, "You're coming to visit us. It's settled. We'll send the jet for you—"

"Excuse me. *Jet?*"

"—on Friday night."

I sit up abruptly. The room starts to spin. She's dislodged my brain with all this nonsense talk of matrimony. "Wait, do you mean *this* Friday? As in, three days from now?"

"Yes."

"Sloane, I have a job! I can't just jet off to . . . Where would I be going in this jet you'd send?"

She hesitates. "I can't tell you that."

I deadpan, "I see. How illuminating."

"Quit being a pain in the ass, Riley, and say you'll come! I'm trying to be a good sister, here! I want us to be closer. I know after Mom died, things were rough, and we've never really been, you know . . ."

"'Friends' is the word you're looking for," I say acidly.

She draws a quiet breath. "Okay. That's fair. But I'd like to change that. Please give me a chance."

Another "please." I lie back down again, utterly confused.

Whoever this guy is that she's marrying, he must really be something else to morph the world's biggest ballbuster into such a softie.

I decide on a whim that I have to meet him. I bet he's putting Valium into her morning coffee, the evil genius! He's spiking her afternoon wine with Xanax!

God, why did I never think of that? "Okay, Sloane. I'm in. I'll see you Friday."

She squeals in excitement. I hold the phone away from my ear and stare at it.

I have no idea what's happening, other than that aliens have obviously abducted my sister and replaced her with an insane wifebot.

If nothing else, this trip should be interesting.

Friday night, I'm sitting inside the VIP waiting area of the private jet terminal at San Francisco International Airport, looking around. I'm in total awe, but trying to be low-key about it.

So far, I've had two celebrity sightings, drank as many Ketel One and OJs from the complimentary bar, accepted caviar and crème fraiche on blinis from a smiling lounge hostess, and enjoyed a full-body massage from this ridiculously huge leather chair I'm sitting in.

It vibrates all over at the touch of a button.

One more vodka OJ, and I'm liable to straddle the damn thing.

A limo picked me up at my apartment. When I arrived at the separate private jet building at the airport, I was whisked away into the VIP lounge by a pretty, uniformed young man.

There was no TSA, security line, or removal of shoes. My luggage was taken away and checked in for the flight without me having to do anything except give a nice lady behind a counter my name.

I've never been impressed by money, but I'm starting to think I might have been misguided.

The pretty young man returns and informs me with a dazzling smile that my flight has arrived. He gestures to a gleaming white jet taxiing to a stop in the middle of the tarmac outside.

"Please, follow me."

I trudge behind him as we exit the building and head to the jet, wondering if they'll kick me off the damn thing for wearing flip-flops and sweats.

If they do, whatever. Life's too short to wear uncomfortable pants.

The inside of the jet is nicer than any hotel I've ever stayed in. I settle into a butter-soft leather captain's chair and kick off my flippies. A beaming flight attendant approaches and leans over my chair.

"Good evening!"

"Hi."

"My name is Andrea. I'll be taking care of you tonight."

She's very attractive, this Andrea. If I were a dude, I'd already be thinking of ways she could "take care" of me.

The thought is appalling. Ten seconds on a private jet, and I'm already corrupted.

It's a good thing I don't have a dick. I'd probably be waving it in this poor woman's face before takeoff.

"Um . . . thank you?"

She smiles at my expression. "First time flying private?"

"Yep."

"Well, you're in for a treat. Anything you need, just let me know. We've got a full bar and a large variety of food and snacks available. Would you like a blanket?"

When I hesitate, she adds, "They're cashmere."

I snort. "Only cashmere? I was hoping for baby alpaca."

Without missing a beat, she says, "We do have vicuña, if you prefer."

"What's vicuña?"

"A llama-type animal from Peru. They look a little bit like a camel, but cuter. Their wool is the softest and most expensive in the world."

She's serious. This broad is literally not shitting me. I stare at her with my mouth open for a beat, then smile. "You know what? I'll just go with good, old-fashioned cashmere, thanks."

She smiles at me like I've just made her whole week. "Certainly! Anything to eat or drink before we depart?"

What the hell. I'm on vacation. "Do you have champagne?"

"Yes. Would you prefer Dom Perignon, Cristal, Taittinger, or Krug?"

She waits for me to decide, as if I have a clue, then suggests, "Mr. O'Donnell prefers the Krug Clos d'Ambonnay."

I furrow my brow. "Who's Mr. O'Donnell?"

"The owner of this aircraft."

Ah. My future brother-in-law. An Irishman, by the sound of it. A very *rich* Irishman, evidently. He's probably ninety years old with dementia and no teeth.

My sister is such a mercenary.

I tell the flight attendant I'll take the Krug, then ask where in the world we're going.

With a straight face, she says breezily, "I really have no idea."

Then she turns and walks away, as if this is all completely normal.

Nine hours later, I've polished off two bottles of champagne, watched three Bruce Willis movies and a documentary about famous drummers, enjoyed a nap of indeterminate length, and am slumped sideways in my chair, drooling on my sweatshirt, when Andrea returns to cheerfully inform me we'll be landing soon.

"Lemme guess. You still don't know where we are."

"Even if I did, Miss Keller, I couldn't tell you."

She says it kindly, but her expression conveys in no uncertain terms that her job would be at risk if she blabbed.

Or maybe something more important than her job . . . like her life.

Or maybe that's the two bottles of champagne talking.

When she disappears down the aisle, I slide up the window covering and peer out. Above are clear blue skies. Below are rolling green hills. Off in the distance, a long strip of blue water shimmers in the afternoon sun.

It's an ocean. The Atlantic? The Pacific? The Gulf of Mexico, perhaps?

The plane starts to descend for landing. It appears we're headed for an island off the coast.

Watching the ground rise up to meet us, I have a dark, powerful premonition that wherever I'm headed, there's no going back.

Later, I'll remember that feeling and marvel at its accuracy.

TWO

KAGE

The man standing across from my desk is tall, hulking, and silent.

Dressed entirely in black, including a heavy wool overcoat beaded with the evening rain, he stares at me with an emotionless look that somehow also conveys a capacity for extreme violence.

Or maybe I only think that because of his reputation. This is the first time we've met, but the man is a legend in the Bratva.

Almost as legendary as I am.

In Russian, I say, "Take a seat, Malek." I gesture to the chair beside him.

He shakes his head in refusal, which irritates me.

"It wasn't a suggestion."

His green eyes flash. A muscle slides in his jaw. His big hands form fists briefly, then flex open again, as if he needs to smash something. But he controls his anger quickly and sits.

Apparently, he likes being issued orders as little as I do.

We gaze at each other in silence for a while. The clock ticks ominously on the wall like the countdown to an explosion.

He offers no polite greeting. There's no pleasant small talk, no effort to get acquainted. He merely sits and waits, patient and mute as a sphinx.

I sense we could go on like this forever, so I start. "My condolences for your loss. Your brother was a good man."

He replies in English. "I don't want your sympathy. I want you to tell me where I can find the man who killed Mikhail."

I'm surprised that he doesn't have a trace of an accent. His voice is low and even, as emotionless as his eyes. Only the pulse pounding in the side of his neck gives any evidence of humanity.

I'm even more surprised that he'd dare to speak to me with such flat disregard.

Few people are that stupid.

My voice as cold as my stare, I say, "If you want permission to operate on my soil, I advise you to show me respect."

"I don't need your permission. I don't show respect unless it's earned. And I'm only here because I was told you're the one with the information I need. If that's incorrect, stop wasting my time and say so."

Bristling, I grind my molars and consider him.

I'd normally shoot a man for that kind of disrespect. But I've already got too many enemies. The last thing I need is an army of Bratva from Moscow descending on Manhattan with the intent of separating my head from my body because I buried the vicious Hangman who serves their king.

Not that they could. Even this enormous, bearded asshole sitting across from me is no match for my skills. If I decided to kill him, he wouldn't stand a chance.

Plus, if he does take out Declan O'Donnell, head of the Irish Mob and a man I'd very much like to see dead, Malek will be doing me a solid.

But still.

My house, my rules.

And rule number one is show me respect or bleed out on the rug, motherfucker.

My voice deadly soft, I hold his gaze and say, "The Irish murdered my parents and both my sisters. So, when I say I know how you feel, I'm not talking out my ass. But if you continue acting like a mannerless cunt, I'll send you back to Moscow in a thousand bloody pieces."

A brief silence follows. "You know what would happen if you did that."

"Yes. Ask me how many fucks I give."

He examines my expression. Weighs my words. A hint of warmth surfaces in his eyes, but dies a quick death, smothered by darkness.

Solemn, he nods. "My apologies. Mikhail was my only brother. The only family I had left."

He turns his head, looks out the window to the rainy night, swallows. When he glances back at me, his jaw is clenched and his gaze is murderous. His voice turns rough. "Now, all I have left is vengeance."

It's very clear: Malek is going to make Declan O'Donnell wish he were never born.

Cheered by that thought, I smile. "Apology accepted. Let's drink."

From the bottom drawer of my desk, I remove a bottle of vodka and two glasses. I pour a measure into each and offer one to Malek. He takes it and nods his thanks.

I raise my glass. *"Za zdorovie."*

He shoots the vodka down, swallowing it in a single gulp. Then he sets the glass on the edge of my desk and settles back into his chair, tattooed hands spread over his massive thighs.

"So. This Irish bastard. Where is he?"

"I'll give you his last known address, but he's cleared out since then. At the moment, he's a ghost."

I don't offer that my contact inside the FBI has no idea where Declan went, either. Or that I'm keeping Declan's former boss, Diego, hostage in one of my warehouses near the docks.

There's no need to show every card in my hand.

That stubborn bastard Diego has so far refused to disclose any useful information, anyway. But if anyone's going to get it out of him, it'll be me.

I'll be damned if I'll hand my captive over to this arrogant out-of-towner.

Malek says, "Not a problem. Just give me whatever you have. I'll find him."

I don't doubt that. He looks like he'd burn down every city on the face of the earth to locate Declan if he had to.

There's nothing more single-minded than a man out for blood.

We discuss a few more details that might be helpful in his search before I broach what I know will be a delicate subject.

"He's got a woman with him. Under no circumstances can she be harmed."

I watch him carefully for his reaction. He says nothing, but in his silence, I sense dissent.

"It's nonnegotiable. If she gets even a scratch, you're dead."

He knits his brows together. "Since when does the dreaded Reaper care about collateral damage?"

I hesitate, knowing exactly how bad what I'm going to say will sound. "She's family."

He digests that in unmoving silence for about thirty seconds, then repeats slowly, "Family."

"It's complicated."

"Uncomplicate it for me."

I ignore the urge to pull the Glock out of the top drawer of the desk and blow a nice big hole through his skull and pour us more vodka instead.

"My woman's tight with Declan's."

One of his dark brows forms a distinctly disbelieving arch.

I'd like to rip that eyebrow clean off and stuff it down his throat. Fuck, this prick's annoying.

Through gritted teeth, I say, "They were childhood friends. Obviously, it predates our present situation."

Malek pauses to drink his vodka before answering. "Inconvenient."

"You have no idea."

"What if it looks like an accident?"

"If the Irishman's woman doesn't live to an advanced old age, no matter the cause, I'll be held responsible."

We stare at each other. He says, "By your woman."

"Yes."

He pauses another beat. "She'd get over it eventually."

My smile is dark. "You don't know Natalie."

He's starting to look confused. "So, you're not the head of this family? She is?"

He's got about ten seconds of life left, and the clock is ticking.

I snap, "I take it you're not married."

He grimaces. "Of course not."

"In a relationship?"

"Is that a joke?"

"Then you couldn't possibly understand."

He looks around the room as if trying to find someone more reasonable to speak to.

"You don't have to comprehend, Malek. You just have to abide by the request."

"It sounded more like an order."

My smile is grim. "Call it what you like. The result of noncompliance will be the same: death. I'll make it slow and painful."

We gaze at each other in tense silence until he says, "It's been a long time since anyone threatened me."

"I believe you. It isn't personal."

"Of course it's personal."

"Like I said, you couldn't understand. Get yourself a fiancée, and it'll become clearer."

I have to admit, the expression of incredulity on his face is perversely satisfying.

He takes a moment to gather his thoughts. Stroking a hand over his dark beard, he watches me with calculating eyes. There's a distinct possibility he's debating how he'd like to kill me, but I simply wait for him to decide which way this conversation will go.

Eventually, he says, "A fiancée. I suppose congratulations are in order."

Knowing that's as close as he'll get to admitting he's decided not to bother with an attempt on my life and also will spare Sloane when he kills Declan, I smile. "Thank you. You'll come to the wedding, of course."

He looks like he'd rather be roasted alive and fed to wild dogs, but he finally shows some manners and says solemnly, "It would be my honor."

We drink another toast. We talk for a few more moments. I give him a picture of Declan and another of Sloane, both of which he tucks into his coat pocket. Then he rises unexpectedly and informs me he has to be on his way.

Without a farewell, he turns and heads to the door.

"Malek."

His hand on the door handle, he pauses to look back at me.

"Don't harm any other women while you're at it, either."

He gazes at me in that silent, annoying way he has that makes me want to grab the nearest machete and start hacking away at his neck, if only to get a reaction.

"Just don't kill any fucking females that might be around when you're taking care of your business, all right?"

"What difference does it make?"

"I'll be able to sleep better at night."

Contempt in his tone, he says, "This is why men in our line of work should be alone, Kazimir. Women make you soft." Before I can shoot him, he walks out the door and is gone.

On the desktop, my cell rings. The screen tells me it's Sergey, a trusted member of my crew. I answer the call and wait for him to speak. When he does, his voice is tense.

"We have a situation."

"Which is?"

"There's a fire." He pauses meaningfully. "At the warehouse."

The warehouse I'm keeping Diego captive in, he means. "How bad is it?"

"I don't know. I just got the call from the alarm company. I'm on my way now. Fire department's already been dispatched."

"Get there first and get him out. I want him alive, understood?"

"*Da.*"

"Call me when you've got him."

Sergey murmurs an acknowledgment and disconnects, leaving me to ponder the thousand ways this could go wrong.

And if perhaps Malek was onto something when he said women make men like us soft.

The old me would've put a bullet in Diego's head weeks ago. The old me also wouldn't feel a twinge of regret if one of his enemies died in a fire. The old me, the person I was before I met Natalie, would find the thought of Diego screaming in agony as he burned alive highly amusing.

The new me? Not so much.

I mutter, "Fuck. Next thing you know, I'll be running off to try to save Diego myself."

I chuckle at that idea.

I pour myself more vodka.

Then I grab my keys and head to the warehouse, cursing this horrible new conscience I've grown since falling in love.

THREE

RILEY

When the cabin door opens, I blink against the bright light.

We're at another airport, this one teeny-tiny compared to the one in San Francisco. There are a few outbuildings and a smattering of other private jets, but there's only one main runway, and no commercial planes.

Wherever we are, it's small and exclusive.

It's also humid as hell. My hair's up in a ponytail, but I can already feel it curling.

A sleek black Range Rover with tinted windows and shiny rims awaits on the runway. The driver steps out when he sees me at the top of the air stairs.

He's wearing a black suit so tight around the crotch area, it's almost pornographic.

Though, I suppose if I were packing that much heat between my legs, I'd get my suits tailored to show it off, too. Wowzers, this guy is *hung*.

Smiling, trying to maintain eye contact and not ogle his goodies,

I approach this well-endowed specimen of manhood and stick out my hand.

"Hi. I'm Riley."

The stud shakes my hand with such serious intent, it's as if we're two world leaders on a critical UN diplomatic meeting to save humanity.

He's got dark blond hair, gorgeous hazel eyes, a spiderweb tattoo on the side of his neck, and a jawline so glorious it could make angels weep.

He bears a striking resemblance to the Marvel comic book character Thor, Norse god of thunder.

"Hullo, Riley. It's a pleasure to meet you."

Okay, the world is totally an unfair place, because not only is Thor an ovulation-inducing stud, he's got a hot-as-fuck Irish accent to boot.

I bet Sloane's marrying the O'Donnell guy for the money, but banging this Thor dude on the side.

I hate to admit it, but it's a good plan.

"Nice to meet you, too. What's your name?"

"Spider."

I make a face. "Spider? No. Your mother didn't name you that. What's your real name?"

There's a beat of silence where it looks like he's trying not to smile. "Homer."

"Really? That's cool! I've never met anyone named after an ancient Greek poet."

He lowers his head and examines my expression with such intensity, I'm taken aback.

"Did I say something wrong?"

"No."

"Then why are you looking at me like that?"

"Your sister said exactly the same thing to me about my name when we met. Verbatim."

"Oh. Huh. Weird."

"Aye."

Oh my god, people from Ireland actually say "aye." That's so hot. Stop looking at his crotch.

"If you don't mind, I'd prefer if you called me Spider, though. Most of the lads don't know my real name."

My ears prick at the mention of "lads."

If there are more Spiders wherever we're headed, I'm extending this vacation indefinitely.

"Sure. You can count on me not to spill the beans. I'm good at keeping secrets."

I grin at him. He gives me an indecipherable look, then turns to take my bag from a worker carrying it over from the plane.

Spider throws the bag into the back of the SUV, opens the rear door for me, and waits for me to climb in. Then he slams the door shut behind me and slides behind the wheel.

We peel out with such force, I'm thrown back against the seat.

"Are we in a car chase I don't know about?"

"No. Why?"

The SUV careens around a corner, tires squealing. Now I'm thrown sideways, nearly banging my head on the window.

"Oh, no reason. It's just that a skull fracture isn't on my itinerary."

Glancing at me in the rearview mirror, he frowns. Then he takes another corner so fast, I have to cling to the door handle so I don't smash through the rear window and rocket off into space. "Dude, will you please cool it? I'm getting tossed around back here like a beach ball at the Electric Daisy Carnival!"

I can tell from the look on his face that he doesn't get the reference. But he does slow down to under a thousand miles per hour, so I guess he understands the general idea that I'm not one for aggressive shows of speed.

"Thank you. Sheesh."

We drive for a while without exchanging more conversation.

I resist the urge to pester him with questions, mostly because I'm afraid his Irish accent will make my panties go up in smoke.

After Spider has glanced curiously at me in the rearview mirror about four hundred times, I sigh heavily and adjust my glasses. "I know. My sister and I don't look alike."

"Same cheek, though."

"Cheek?"

"Sass. Confidence."

"Ha! Nobody on earth has Sloane's self-confidence."

He chuckles. "Aye. Except maybe her man."

I wasn't going to ask questions, but curiosity gets the better of me. "You mean her fiancé? The rich and elderly Mr. O'Donnell?"

He glowers. "Forty-two is hardly elderly, lass."

Okay, two things. First: he's right. Though it's quite a bit older than Sloane, forty-two isn't elderly.

More importantly, being called "lass" is my new favorite kink.

I drape myself over the back of the passenger seat and stare at Spider's beautiful profile. After a moment, he flashes me a quizzical look.

"Sorry, I'm just trying to imagine what it must be like to walk around looking like that."

"Like what?"

"You know." I wave a hand to indicate his general luminosity. *"That."*

"I don't know what you mean."

Bizarrely, he seems sincere. His expression is one of genuine confusion. But how is that possible? If I were gorgeous, I'm sure I'd know it.

Like Sloane does.

It occurs to me that maybe Spider's elevator doesn't go all the way to the top floor. I might need to clarify things for him.

"What I'm saying is that you're very good-looking."

I'm astonished when his cheeks turn bright red.

He sputters some kind of nonsensical denial, adjusts his tie, and stares straight ahead out the windshield, blinking comically.

Aw. He's bashful! Gorgeous, well-endowed, and bashful!

I want to crawl into his lap, but smile at him instead. "You must be very popular with the ladies, Spider."

More sputtering. He finally composes himself enough to say stiffly, "I don't have time for a relationship."

I laugh at that. "Gotcha. If I were you, I'd be a player, too. Why keep all those cookies in one jar when you can hand 'em out all over town and make *everyone* happy?"

He says gruffly, "You're off your rocker."

"Oh, don't be mad. I'm paying you a compliment."

"It doesn't feel like it."

"Would you prefer if I said you were homely and repulsive? Because I'm happy to indulge your charming delusion that you're not extraordinarily attractive. It's cute."

His entire face is now red. Bright red, from the top of his starched white collar to the tips of his ears.

This guy is ridiculously appealing.

I flop against the back passenger seat and heave a sigh. "Okay, we'll move on. How about if you tell me where we are?"

"Bermuda."

My eyes nearly pop out of my head. Bermuda? No wonder the air is so humid.

Noticing my expression, Spider says, "It's temporary. We were in Martha's Vineyard last, but there were some, ah . . ." He makes a strange face. "I'll let your sister explain."

Hmm. The plot thickens.

I say drily, "Were you run out of Martha's Vineyard by the daily stampede of Sloane's admirers beating down the door? I bet it must be hard for her fiancé to deal with the way every guy drops to his knees at her feet."

He pauses for a beat before saying quietly, "Jealousy doesn't suit you."

It takes my breath away. I look out the window at the passing scenery, my cheeks burning with shame.

We drive for a while in silence until I admit grudgingly, "Whenever she's around, people look right through me like I'm invisible."

"That's because people are bloody morons."

He's being nice to me because I gave him such effusive compliments.

Whatever. I'll take it.

I smile at him. "Thank you, Spider. In addition to being very hot, you're also very sweet."

His ears turn a darker shade of crimson.

Then we're turning onto a long private drive, and I'm distracted by the size of the iron gate we're going through. It's enormous, creaking open slowly to let us pass. The gate is flanked on either side by high stone walls and a grove of trees that obscure the view beyond.

When I spot the security cameras mounted on top of the walls and all the armed guards lurking under the trees, I frown.

"Spider?"

"Aye, lass?"

"Is my sister's fiancé famous?"

He quirks his lips. "Something like that."

"Don't be cryptic. I get nervous when people are cryptic."

"Mr. O'Donnell is . . . a powerful man."

The hesitation makes me even more nervous. "Like how powerful? Is he a politician or something?"

He scoffs. "Politicians wish they had his kind of power."

"Oh god. That sounds scary. Is he a supervillain?"

His smile is small and mysterious. "I wouldn't go that far."

"So, he's a good guy?"

He shrugs. "Depends on who you ask."

"*Seriously?* You're killing me!"

He must find my blossoming panic amusing, because he starts to chuckle. "It's not my place to tell you, lass. But don't worry. You'll be safe here."

We drive by a guy in a black suit holding a big black rifle. He's crouched in the bushes, watching us with narrowed eyes as we pass. He lifts a hand to his mouth and speaks into what looks like his wristwatch but is obviously some kind of communication device.

Like a spy would have. Or the henchman of a supervillain.

I say drily, "Oh, yeah, I feel totally safe already." Then I gasp. "Whoa. Is that our hotel? It's huge!"

When Spider only gives me another chuckle as an answer, I get it.

"Holy fuck nuggets. That's his *house?*"

"Aye."

I gape at the sprawling stone estate at the top of the hill. I've seen smaller castles. "That's *one* house? For *one* person?"

"Two, if you count Sloane."

I shoot him a sour look. "You're laughing at me."

"I would never."

He tries to pretend innocence, but totally fails. I smack him on the shoulder.

"Ow! There's no need for violence, lass! What a rabid wee badger!"

Now he's laughing even harder, the jerk. I mutter, "I'll shove a rabid wee badger right up your butt, mister."

His shoulders are shaking, his lips are pressed together, his eyes are bright, and I'm going to clobber him.

Except I'm not, because at that moment, I spot Sloane emerging from the huge wooden front doors of the house. She's followed by a man who makes my mouth drop open in shock.

Tall and broad-shouldered, with a Mick Jagger swagger, he's got hair as black as midnight, eyes as blue as cobalt, and the sly, cocky grin of a pirate king.

The man is so beautiful, the devil himself would be jealous. My voice comes out strangled. "*That's* the fiancé?"

Spider sounds proud when he answers. "Aye. The one and only Declan O'Donnell."

Declan O'Donnell.

Sweet Jesus, even his name is hot. He makes my last boyfriend look like Shrek.

As soon as this vacation is over, I'm getting on a plane headed straight for Ireland.

When the SUV pulls to a stop, Declan opens the back door for me before the engine is even off. I hop out and am immediately taken by his height. I have to crane my neck to look up at him. It makes his beauty even more impressive.

"Riley," he says. "At last we meet. Your sister has told me so much about you."

His voice is deep, his smile is brilliant, and my estrogen levels are surging.

Then, just to totally cross all the wires in my brain, he pulls me into a big bear hug, lifting me right off my feet in the process.

I wonder if my sister will mind when I start calling her fiancé Daddy?

When Declan sets me back onto my feet, I look at Sloane. She's standing a few feet away, watching us with a hesitant smile.

She says softly, "Hey, Smalls."

As always, she looks incredible. Perfect hair, perfect face, perfect body. My gorgeous older sister, fearless lion, effortless flirt, consumer of men's souls.

Life has always been easy for her. Even in her "awkward" teenage emo phase, she was the sun everyone else revolved around. She's never not been stunning.

Unlike me, who looks like one of the flying monkeys from *The Wizard of Oz*. At least according to her.

I say, "Hey, Hollywood. Thanks for inviting me. Your man is a toad, and this place is a dump."

"Wait until you see your bedroom."

"Let me guess. You put me in the attic with the ghosts?"

"No, we put you in the basement so you wouldn't scare the ghosts."

"Appreciate it, hooker."

"No problem, troll."

We smile at each other. I can tell Declan is disturbed by this exchange, which makes me think he doesn't have a sister.

Then I forget all about his siblings or lack thereof, because he picks me up and throws me over his shoulder.

He throws me over his shoulder!

I scream in delight then start to cackle like a madwoman.

An upside-down Sloane folds her arms over her chest and shakes her head in disapproval. "You'll make her throw up, honey."

"Are you kidding?" I shout, staring at Declan's ass, which is eye level and magnificent. "This is awesome! Declan, you have my permission to proceed!"

Declan chuckles, Sloane rolls her eyes, and I kick my feet in sheer happiness.

It's a good thing I packed enough of my favorite candy for this trip, because I might never leave.

FOUR

MAL

I'm about to pull the trigger and put a bullet in Declan's head when a female steps out of the car.

Through the crystal-clear magnification of the rifle's powerful scope, I take her in with one swift assessment.

Young and slight. Mousy blondish hair pulled into a sloppy ponytail. Baggy gray sweatpants and flip-flops. Eyeglasses and an ill-fitting sweatshirt.

Something about her appearance suggests she's homeless.

Or careless, at least. Her clothing is wrinkled. Her hair is scraggly. The way the sweatpants hang from her hips suggests malnourishment.

Perhaps Declan is adopting a refugee.

I watch with growing irritation as he embraces the slovenly waif. If she'd only get out of the way, I could get on with it. I've been crouched in this crumbling church belfry for hours already.

Sweat is pouring down my neck. My thighs are starting to cramp. The air reeks of mold and mouse droppings, intensified by the sweltering heat.

I can't wait to get back to Moscow. To the cold and the darkness, far away from this tropical hellhole. Everything is so bright here. So colorful. So cheerful. I hate it.

The woman standing off to one side of Declan and the new arrival is Sloane. I recognize her from the picture Kazimir gave me. She's tall, curvy, and unmistakable, watching the new girl with hesitancy.

Dismissing her, I turn my attention back to Declan.

He sets the waif back onto her feet, but I still don't have a clear shot. She's standing too close to him. Then he picks her up and . . .

I move my face away from the scope, blink to clear my vision, then squint into the scope again.

I wasn't mistaken.

He threw the waif over his shoulder.

Now he's swaggering back to the mansion, holding Sloane's hand while simultaneously carrying another woman upside down. The trio disappears inside together.

I sit back onto my heels and think.

The girl obviously isn't a refugee. Perhaps a domestic worker? A new maid? By the cool way Sloane greeted her, they didn't appear acquainted, so that would make sense. It seemed as if it were the first time they'd met.

But the way Declan embraced her with such distinct enthusiasm . . . The way he was so familiar in handling her, tossing her over his shoulder like a possession . . .

Ah.

She's a whore.

A girl so poor and disadvantaged, she has to sell herself to kinky rich couples for money to eat.

"Fucking Irish," I mutter, disgusted.

I think of my dead brother and the sad-looking waif in the baggy sweatpants, both of them victims of the vicious Mob king.

Then, seething, I settle in again to wait for another shot. That bastard can't stay inside forever.

FIVE

RILEY

The inside of the estate/castle/palace/whatever is even more impressive than the outside.

Everything is made of marble, crystal, or polished mahogany. Blank-eyed Grecian statues lurk in lit alcoves in the walls. Expensive bric-a-brac decorates every available surface. Plush Turkish rugs muffle our footsteps, while white linen curtains draped in front of floor-to-ceiling windows billow and fold in the languid sea breeze.

I gape at all the glamour right side up, because Declan set me back onto my feet as soon as we came indoors.

I still haven't forgiven him for it.

I trail behind him and Sloane as they lead me to the guest room where I'll be staying. It probably has its own pool. "So, Declan. What kind of work do you do?"

He and Sloane exchange a glance. He says, "International relations."

Outside the windows, a pair of armed guards prowl by. "Really? That's interesting. I saw this Denzel Washington movie one time where he told people he was in international relations, but he actually worked for the CIA. Do you work for the CIA?"

He scoffs. "They wish."

"The FBI?"

He lifts a muscular shoulder. "Occasionally."

"Yeah, me, too. Only when they twist my arm, though. I much prefer working for MI5."

"Six."

"Excuse me?"

"MI6 is foreign intelligence operating outside the UK. MI5 is domestic."

"Oh, right. I always forget. It's hard sometimes to remember all the different intelligence agencies I spy for."

"Tell me about it."

That makes me grin. I love it when people play along with my silly games.

At the end of a long corridor, we stop outside a closed door. Declan leans against the wall, folds his bulging arms over his chest, and smiles down at me. My ovaries sigh in contentment.

"I'll let you get settled in and give you girls a chance to catch up. If there's anything you need, just pick up the phone."

"I don't have a cell. I'm philosophically opposed to technology that can stalk me."

"I meant the phone next to your bed."

When I cock an eyebrow, Sloane says, "It's the house phone. Tell whoever answers what you want, and they'll bring it."

I look back and forth between the two of them. "Who is this person who'll answer?"

"Whoever's on shift," says Declan.

"So, you have *staff*, too, not just an army of bodyguards. Kinda like *Downton Abbey*, except with guns."

Declan chuckles. "You're a lot like your sister."

"Don't tell her that. She'll break off the engagement. Speaking of engagement, Sloane, why aren't you wearing a ring?"

Declan turns to her and says mildly, "Good question. I can't wait to hear the answer."

She rolls her eyes. "Technically, I haven't said yes yet."

I almost punch her in the face.

"What?" I holler. "Are you crazy?" I make spokesmodel hands at his overall gloriousness. "*He's* asked you to marry him, and you haven't said yes? What is *wrong* with you?"

Stifling a laugh, Declan says, "Amen."

"Also, hold on a minute, because did you or did you not say you wanted me to visit because you'd be getting married any day? To your *fiancé*?"

Exasperated, she says, "We *will* be getting married any day. When I finally say yes."

"You act like that makes any kind of sense. Spoiler alert! It doesn't."

"I ask her every day if she'll marry me," Declan interrupts, his voice throaty. "She always says not yet. But one day soon, she'll agree, and we'll go straight to the courthouse and make it official."

He looks at her with hot, half-lidded eyes.

How she manages to stay upright under that smoldering look and not melt into a flaming puddle of hormones is beyond me.

Indignant, I turn to her. "Are you deliberately leading him on? Because that's not cool."

"Not cool," agrees Declan, shaking his head.

She chews the inside of her lip and glances at the floor.

The hesitation is wildly uncharacteristic of her. She doesn't stop to think before she answers. It makes me worry. The Sloane I know would've already slapped me across the face by now.

Figuratively speaking. With scorn.

Looking at her feet, she says softly, "I'm not leading him on.

It's just so perfect right now, the way things are between us. There's no way it can get better than it already is. I don't want to ruin it."

Declan looks at her with so much need and devotion burning in his eyes, I'm embarrassed to be standing there. Then he grabs her and gives her a passionate kiss.

He pulls away and stares down into her eyes, all burning heat and hunger.

He growls, "Say yes, and I swear every day will be better than the last, you bloody stubborn woman. You have my heart. My soul. My life. I want you to have my name as well, and wear my ring so everyone who sees you knows you belong to me. I'm so proud to be your man, I want the whole goddamn world to know you're mine."

Sloane and I are both stunned and breathless. This man is just . . . wow.

I'll get back to you with an impressive adjective. Right now, I'm speechless.

If she doesn't marry him within twenty-four hours, she's dead to me forever.

I push past them into the room, close the door behind me, lean close to it and say loudly, "Great to meet you, Declan. Call me when it's suppertime. I'm gonna take a nap on this bed that's large enough for ten people. When I wake up, I expect to see a ring on that finger, Sloane. You idiot."

Then I lie face-down on the bed, feeling sorry for myself that I don't have even a quarter of my sister's beauty or style.

I fall asleep fantasizing that I'm a beautiful queen with a harem of virile Irishmen.

When I open my eyes, the sun is setting. Sloane is lying on the floor nearby with her long legs up on an overstuffed chintz chair, toying with a strand of her hair and staring at the ceiling.

I prop myself up onto my elbows and gaze down at her. "Ugh. I hate it that you can look so good when you're contemplative. When I have deep thoughts, I look like I need to take a dump."

She closes her eyes and starts laughing.

"You think I'm joking, but I'm not. It's one hundred percent legit."

"Oh, I know," she says, sitting up. Supple as a cat, she folds her legs underneath her and smiles at me. "I remember those faces you make. You take after Dad."

"He is strangely expressive for a military man, isn't he? You think they'd have militarized it out of him. All that marching and following orders and whatnot would definitely make my eyes glaze right over."

"Declan was in the military, and he's still very expressive."

As soon as she says it, two faint spots of pink appear high on her cheeks.

I can tell she's thinking of exactly how "expressive" he is. Now I'm thinking about it, and I'm getting all flustered, too. "Yuck. I don't need to picture my big sister having all kinds of excessively hot sex, thank you very much. Also, oh. My. *God,* dude. Where did you find him, and how many brothers does he have? I want two, at least!"

"He's amazing, isn't he?"

She bats her lashes and sighs like a crazy person. Or at least some *other* person, some romantic, sweet person with idealized notions of love, not her.

I swing my legs over the side of the bed, sit up, and squint at her. "You're really in love with him, aren't you?"

"Yes. It's horrible. I mean, it's *wonderful,* but also horrible, because . . ."

"You're not in control anymore."

She nods, cringing. "And I never had anything worth losing before. I never cared before, about anything but myself. Now, I care about everything. I'm one big sentimental ball of caring. I cried watching the sunset the other day, for fuck's sake!"

I try not to find her dismay so satisfying, but I do. I'm a terrible person.

"Anyway." She waves her hands to dispel that part of the conversation. "We need to do something about your hair."

"What's wrong with my hair?"

"It's hideous. You look like you lost a bet."

"Oh, thank goodness."

"What?"

"For a minute there, I thought you'd been replaced by a body snatcher."

Someone raps their knuckles softly on the door. At the same time, Sloane and I holler, "Come in!"

Spider sticks his head through. "Hullo. I have your luggage, lass. Is this a good time?"

Hot, hung, and polite. I swear, I'm going to find a scientist to clone him and Declan and make me the perfect male.

"C'mon in. You can drop it anywhere."

He walks inside, carrying my bag and my future children's chromosomes, and nods a hello to Sloane. He sets the bag on the floor next to the dresser, then turns to leave.

"Wait," says Sloane. "Where's the rest?"

"That was the only one, madam."

She makes a sour face. "What did I tell you about calling me that?"

He looks like he's trying not to smile. I like him even more now that I know he's been teasing her. It takes balls, which I already know he's not lacking.

I mean, I've got visual proof. It's staring me right in the face.

". . . Riley?"

"What?" I rip my gaze away from the substantial bulge in Spider's trousers and look at Sloane. "Sorry, I didn't hear what you said."

She says drily, "I wonder why."

I narrow my eyes and mentally telegraph a threat that she receives and smiles at condescendingly. "I asked where the rest of your luggage is."

"I don't have other luggage. That's it."

She stares in disbelief at my single carry-on, a beat-up duffel I bought before I went away to college years ago. "You brought one bag?"

"You say that like I just informed you it's filled with body parts."

Ignoring my sarcasm, she insists, "How can you travel with one piece of luggage? Where's your shoe bag? Your cosmetics bag? Your formal-wear bag? All your *clothes*?"

She gazes around the room as if expecting a set of monogrammed Louis Vuitton steamer trunks to appear from thin air, bursting with mink stoles and evening gowns.

Smiling, I say, "It's really gonna break your brain when I tell you my laptop's in there, too."

Spider catches my eye and winks. Then he leaves, closing the door behind him.

Sloane jumps up, crosses to the bag, bends over, rips the zipper open, and stares down at the contents. She rifles around in it for a moment, then straightens and looks at me.

"What's with all the boxes of candy?"

"I don't travel anywhere without Twizzlers. And you can't get those watermelon Sour Patch Kids everywhere, so because I didn't know where I was going . . ." I shrug. "Better safe than sorry."

She closes her eyes, draws a breath, gathers herself, then looks at me again.

"Do you have any other items of clothing that aren't gray or made of fleece?"

"Yeah. Duh. My undies."

"My god. I can't believe we're related."

She's so horrified, she's about to make the sign of the cross over her chest. Or maybe call for a priest and douse me with a vial of holy water. It makes me laugh.

"Oh, relax, Beyoncé. There's other stuff under the candy."

When she looks hopefully at the duffel, I say, "I also brought white T-shirts and jean shorts."

Her expression indicates she might be tasting the regurgitated remains of her lunch. "I can see we'll need to do some shopping while you're here, too."

"Too?"

"In addition to taming that feral skunk on top of your head."

"Excuse me, but not everyone thinks it's necessary to look like a fashion model."

"There has to be a happy medium between fashion model and hobo."

"If you mean people who don't have homes, Cruella, the correct term is 'unhoused.' 'Hobo' is super derogatory."

"You've been living in San Francisco too long."

"Can we table this discussion that's sure to devolve into a political shouting match for a sec so I can ask when we're going to eat? The last thing I had was a gross clot of slimy black fish eggs with some coagulated dairy product on a piece of bread the size of a quarter. I'm absolutely famished. You rich people eat like birds."

She pauses for a beat, then covers her face with her hands and dissolves into laughter.

I say drily, "I'm glad my starvation is amusing you."

"It's just that I forgot how funny you are."

"Funny as in ha-ha, or funny as in weird?"

"Ha-ha." She thinks for a moment. "And also weird."

"Thanks for that. Changing gears again: what does Declan do for a living? And don't lie to me. I'm not one of your bedazzled fuck boys. I know when you're not telling the truth."

Her smile fades. She walks slowly to the chair she had her feet propped up on, sits, and folds her hands demurely between her thighs. "I want to tell you, but I don't want you to judge."

My laugh is short and disbelieving. "*Judge?* Dude, I've been living in San Francisco for quite some time. There's literally nothing that can shock me anymore."

"Okay. Well, if you must know . . ." Hesitating, she takes a deep breath. "He's in the Mob. Actually, he *is* the Mob. He's, like, the main guy."

Several things click inside my head, and I nod thoughtfully. "Hmm. Makes sense. So, about the eating situation again. Are we doing that before or after I let you do something awful to my hair that I'm sure to regret?"

When she only sits there staring at me, her eyes welling with tears, I get panicky.

"Oh, shit. What's wrong? Please tell me he's not cheating on you. I'm not sure whose side I'd take."

She leaps from the chair and launches herself across the room, slamming into me and flinging her arms around my neck.

I'm almost thrown back onto the mattress. Despite my total shock and the force of her embrace, I manage to stay upright. Then she bursts into tears, leaving me at a complete loss.

I say tentatively, "Um. What's happening now?"

She wails, "I'm sorry is what's happening! I've been a terrible sister, and you're being so nice, and I can't believe we haven't seen each other since your birthday a few years ago!"

Three years ago, to be precise.

Not that I'll ever be able to forget it.

My boyfriend at the time took one look at Sloane and pronounced he was dating the wrong sister. He broke up with me on the spot.

In the middle of my friggin' birthday party.

When I heard through a friend a few weeks later that they'd been seen together and called Sloane to find out if it was true, she scoffed and said, "Who? Oh my god, that loser's already in the rearview mirror."

That "loser" she could barely remember had been my boyfriend for more than a year. He took my virginity. I thought we were madly in love.

After that, I started telling my dates I was an only child. I haven't seen Sloane since.

I pat her awkwardly on the back. "Okay, Hollywood. C'mon now. You'll ruin your mascara."

She pulls away, sniffling and gripping my upper arms like she's planning on holding me hostage. "Say you forgive me," she demands vehemently. "Please. Let's make this a new beginning. We'll start over from scratch."

I frown at her. Who is this person?

When her big pleading eyes get to be too much, I relent. "Fine. It's a new beginning. But I'm withholding forgiveness until after I see what you've got planned for my hair."

She bites her lower lip, tears spill over the edge of her bottom lids, and *what the fuck has happened to my sister?*

Daddy Declan must be laying some serious pipe to have turned this stone-cold savage into such a sweetheart.

Lucky bitch.

SIX

RILEY

I should've known it was going to be really bad when Sloane called up for booze.

A new hot Irishman arrived with a pitcher of skinny margaritas sweetened with monk fruit and infused with the juice of limes and jalapeños grown from the garden outside. The glasses were rimmed with a fine dusting of pink Himalayan sea salt and garnished with a spiral curl of lime peel so long and perfectly formed, it must've taken extreme concentration and probably like ten tries to get it right.

Because yeah, that's totally something one does.

The hot Irishman also brought warm tortilla chips and a delicious pineapple-mango salsa he said he made himself.

I was highly dubious of the claim and told him so. Imagine my surprise when he whipped out his cell phone and showed me a video as proof.

"Where do you *find* these guys?" I asked Sloane when he left.

She waved me off like I was being silly. "It's a gift. Now go sit in the chair I put in front of the sink in the bathroom and be quiet. I'll need to concentrate while I work."

Red flag number two: she needed to "concentrate." The last time that happened, a hole was ripped in the space-time continuum that still hasn't been repaired.

But I was starving, and the salsa was delicious, so I was an obedient subject and allowed her to paint some kind of foul-smelling goop onto my head that I wrongly assumed was deep conditioner. I sat as docile as a lamb as she washed, cut, and styled my hair, urging me to drink another of the tasty margaritas every so often.

When she finally spun me around in the chair to face the mirror, I saw why she was trying to get me drunk.

I cried in horror, "What the fuck have you done?"

She actually had the nerve to say smugly, "Saved you from that tragedy you called a hairstyle. You're welcome."

Then she sauntered out of the bathroom, leaving me to have my mental breakdown all by myself.

"I am *not* wearing that."

"Just put it on. You'll thank me later."

I stare indignantly at the tiny scrap of fabric Sloane is trying to pass off as the dress I should wear out to dinner. I've blown my nose into tissues with more substance than that.

"I'll thank you to stop trying to make me look like a sex worker. You've already done enough damage with the platinum catastrophe on top of my head."

"Are you kidding? Your hair is amazing!"

I say acidly, "Yes, if it's three o'clock in the morning, and I'm working in a Reno cabaret as a Marilyn Monroe impersonator old enough to have gone on tour with Frank Sinatra, and everyone in the audience is sight impaired or drunk, it's amazing. But in this dimension of reality, it's not."

Ignoring me, she turns to rummage deeper into the vault she calls a closet. "Do you still wear a size six shoe?"

I roll my eyes to the ceiling. "No. I wear a twelve now. I have this weird disease that causes massive foot growth."

Ignoring my sarcasm, she says, "Good. These will go perfectly with the dress."

She turns and tosses a pair of high heels at me. I refuse to catch them, so they bounce off my stomach and land onto the carpet near my feet. Next, she throws the dress. It lands on top of my head and hangs down in front of my face like a veil.

A minuscule, see-through veil with abdominal cutouts.

Sloane breezes past me out of the closet. "When you're dressed, I'll do your makeup."

Seething, I yank the dress off my head and stare at it. I could literally fold it up and put it into the pocket of my sweats.

Honestly, how does she expect me to wear this thing? I might as well just put on a thong and some pasties and call it a day!

Sloane calls from the other room, "Hurry up, Smalls, I'm hungry!"

I mutter, "Oh, now it's an emergency because *she's* hungry. The queen is hungry, y'all! Everybody giddyap!"

"I can hear you in there."

I holler over my shoulder, "How do you even fit into this thing? You couldn't get one of your boobs into it, much less that booty!"

"There's this interesting material called spandex. It's highly stretchable. You would've heard of it before if you hadn't been busy hoarding all that cotton fleece. Now *get dressed,* or I'll lock you in that closet without dinner."

I close my eyes and heave a sigh. *Should've brought less candy and more drugs.*

I spend five minutes wrestling with the stretchy nightmare of a dress until finally it's on. Barely covering my cooch, but on.

Then I shove my feet into the stripper heels and wobble out of the closet.

When Sloane turns to look at me, I throw my arms in the air.

"Here. Happy now? I'm Julia Roberts in *Pretty Woman,* only with a sluttier wardrobe and no happy ending."

Sloane stares at me silently, her eyes wide.

I'd rip off the stupid dress, but I think I'll need scissors to get out of it.

"Say something nice to me, Hollywood, or I swear to god, I'll cut you."

She says softly, "You look beautiful."

"Oh-ho! Good one. Go big or go home, right?"

"No, I mean it. You look beautiful."

I exhale hard in disgust. "Of course I do. I'm just a beautiful prostitute on her way out for an evening of romantic encounters in alleyways to earn fistfuls of sweaty dollar bills. Let's get this over with and go eat. My blood sugar is dangerously low right now." I glare at her. "I'm liable to stab the nearest person."

She says hopefully, "Did you bring contact lenses with you?"

"The glasses stay on."

She's crestfallen, but quickly recovers. "Okay, but let me just . . . a little swipe of lipstick and mascara . . ."

I'm too starving to have another argument, so I relent. "You have exactly sixty seconds. And none of that goopy foundation shit!"

Sloane runs gleefully back into the bathroom, emerging in a flash with one purple tube and one silver tube in her hand. She works quickly, one small mercy, then hops up and down in front of me, clapping in delight.

I say flatly, "Sister, you have totally lost your mind."

"So will every man who sets eyes on you tonight."

"I'll bet you a hundred bucks not even one man will look twice. Unless he's in the market for a sad and degrading sexual experience with a paid stranger, but that doesn't count."

Sloane tilts her head and smiles. "I'd take that bet, but I doubt you could come up with the cash."

"Fine. I'll bet you two boxes of Twizzlers and a watermelon Sour Patch. But when I win, you owe me . . ."

I look around the room for inspiration, then point to a round side table that's covered in expensive-looking baubles. "That cute little box with the peacock on top."

"That's a Swiss silver fusée singing bird box circa 1860. It's worth more than eighty thousand dollars."

I smile. "What're you, chicken?"

She sticks out her hand. We shake on it.

Then I march purposefully behind her as we head out of the room.

Halfway down the hallway, she has to grab my arm so I don't fall.

"When was the last time you wore heels?" she asks, steadying me.

"College graduation."

"I'm shocked you didn't fall flat onto your face on the stage when you went to accept your diploma."

"Who says I didn't?"

"God, you're hopeless."

"Please be quiet. My inner demons are demanding that I kill you, and I want to hear what they have to say."

"Okay, but before I'm quiet, I just have to add this one thing."

"Of course you do."

"Thank you."

She sounds so sincere, I have to shoot her a suspicious sideways glance so I can see what her face is doing. Surprisingly, she looks sincere, too.

"What're you thanking me for?"

"I know you're only doing this for me." She looks at my lady-of-the-evening costume. "You could've refused and put on more of your hideous gray athletic wear, but you didn't. So thank you."

Grr. She's being nice. I have no defense against my sister when she's nice.

It's like if Dracula took a moment before he ripped open your throat with his fangs and sucked out all your blood to say a few polite words about your lovely taste in interior design.

It's disorienting.

We're rounding the corner of the hallway and headed to the foyer when Sloane spots Spider, crossing the vast acreage of echoing marble she calls the "sitting room." It's so big, the weddings of future heirs to the throne of the House of Windsor could easily be held there in case Westminster Abbey burns down.

"Spider!" she calls. "Would you come here for a moment, please?"

He's holding a can of soda in his hand. In the middle of taking a swig, he turns his head and glances in our direction.

He looks at me.

Liquid sprays abruptly from his mouth in a huge geyser, as if he's just been punched hard in the gut. He stares at me, frozen and gaping, soda dripping from his chin.

Sloane stops and turns to me, smug. "You owe me two boxes of Twizzlers."

Cheeks burning, I mutter, "Give me a break. That wasn't a positive reaction. The poor man got such a fright, he nearly choked to death."

"What you don't know about men could fill all thirty-two volumes of the *Encyclopedia Britannica*."

"They have that online now, Grandma."

"Theory's the same. You know jack shit about men. Let's go eat."

"Can you give me a sec? I need a moment alone to mentally prepare myself for my forthcoming public humiliation."

Without waiting for her permission, I stalk off in the other direction, toward a set of open glass doors that lead to an outdoor patio.

I keep my gaze averted from Spider, who's still standing right where he was when I turned him into a pillar of stone in a tight black suit, and walk outside into the balmy evening air, vowing to myself that I won't let Sloane see me cry.

I've cried because of that heartless wench too many damn times in my life already.

SEVEN

MAL

*S*he emerges onto the patio in a burst of angry energy I feel all the way from where I'm sitting, fifteen hundred yards away.

Lying in wait, rather. Inside the same abandoned church belfry I scouted two days ago, when I arrived on the island.

It offers an excellent east-west view of the property. From this vantage point, I can see both the front and back of the estate. With a swing of my rifle's muzzle to the left or right, my sights can be on Declan's skull in either his driveway or his backyard.

Right now, they're on the woman stalking back and forth across the patio.

Her hair is platinum blond, cut to jaw length, sleek and swinging. Her clinging black cocktail dress is almost nonexistent. And she doesn't seem to be comfortable in the spiky heels she's wearing.

Several times as she spins to go the other direction, an ankle wobbles, and she has to throw out an arm to regain her balance.

She's young, slim, and extremely awkward. Something about her is fascinating. I can't look away.

Because of the hair and the dress, it takes me a while to recognize her. But then I note the glasses she's wearing and suck in a breath. It comes out in a furious hiss.

Poor baby. He wasn't satisfied with her simply *being* a whore.

He wanted her to look like one, too.

Clearly, she's upset about it. Or about something else he did to her.

Something much worse than a wardrobe change.

Anger boils in the pit of my stomach. *That son of a bitch.*

I knew he was ruthless when he killed all the leaders of the various American families. With the exception of Kazimir, which isn't surprising. He's notoriously hard to kill. Hundreds of men have died trying.

But to bring a girl from the streets to your home to fuck in front of your woman, then tart her up and parade her around so everyone can plainly see her humiliation . . .

That's beyond ruthless. It's sick.

My anger grows hotter as I continue to watch the girl. She stops pacing and leans against the curved stone balustrade of the patio, folding her arms over her chest and turning her face up to the full moon like she's trying to draw strength from its glow.

Dragging deep breaths into her lungs, she closes her eyes. After a moment, she bows her head, as if in prayer.

Furious, I decide that I won't kill him in front of her. She looks fragile enough already. She doesn't need more trauma.

I'll wait until he's finished with her and she leaves, then I'll put a bullet in his brain.

Mikhail would understand. He had a soft spot for girls like this. Abused, defenseless girls. A delay of a few hours or days won't make a difference in the end.

I'll still get what I'm coming for: my enemy's blood. Shoulders slumped, the girl pushes away from the balustrade and reluctantly returns inside. A few minutes later, a group exits the front door.

Declan and his woman are there, along with the girl and half a dozen bodyguards. They pile into a trio of SUVs and pull out of the driveway.

I watch the red glow of the vehicles' taillights, wrestling with myself.

Then I climb down out of the belfry and hop onto the motorcycle waiting outside the old church doors, knowing that what I'm about to do is both stupid and dangerous.

And also that my dead brother would approve.

EIGHT

RILEY

The restaurant Declan takes us to is so elegant and upscale, I feel like I should have a sign around my neck apologizing for my attire.

The sign would blame it all on Sloane, of course.

The three of us sit in a corner booth at the back of a large, candle-lit dining room. Spider and the other bodyguards sit at two separate tables nearby.

Every time I glance in Spider's direction, he's gazing at me with stern, unwavering focus, like he's judging my life choices.

That makes two of us.

"So, Riley. Tell me about yourself."

Lounging against the booth with one arm slung over Sloane's shoulders, king-of-the-jungle Declan smiles at me. How the man manages to ooze dominance and sexual prowess simply sitting there is one of life's great mysteries.

Meanwhile, Sloane gazes dreamily up at his chiseled profile with little red hearts in her eyes.

I swear, I never would've believed this shit if I wasn't seeing it for myself.

"Gee, where to start?" I muse, nibbling on a dinner roll.

Okay, nibbling is a lie. I'm gnawing on it like a farm animal. I'm so hungry, I could chew my own arm off. If the waitress doesn't arrive with our entrées soon, I'm going to barge straight into the kitchen and start threatening people with a meat cleaver.

"I work as a freelance editor, which I adore. Mainly because of how much I love books, but also because I get to work in my pajamas."

"And avoid all human contact," Sloane adds, smiling. "Yes. That's a major benefit."

Declan quirks a brow. "Not much of a people person, are you?"

"It's not that I hate people, I just feel better when they're not around."

Sloane laughs. *"Barfly."*

"I love that movie. Mickey Rourke was so dope when he was young."

Sloane makes a face at me. "Don't say 'dope.' It makes you sound so Generation Z."

"I am Gen Z."

"Ugh. That explains why you're so antisocial."

"At least I'm not a Millennial. You guys are all narcissists."

"We are not!" she says, indignant.

When I only stare at her with my lips quirked, she laughs again. "Okay. You got me."

Declan looks interested in the turn in the conversation. "What generation am I?"

Without thinking, I chuckle and say, "Generation Big D."

He cocks his head, Sloane lifts her brows, and I backpedal as fast as I can. "The D doesn't stand for dick!"

Sloane drawls, "What does it stand for then, Smalls?"

Cringing, face flaming, I lift my shoulders up to my ears and lie meekly, "Dude?"

"Uh-huh." She throws back her head and laughs. "Oh, god. If you only knew how right you are!"

Declan looks back and forth between us. "I'm lost."

Sloane reaches over and squeezes his thigh. "The D stands for daddy, honey."

He glances at her hand on his thigh, then looks at her mouth. His blue eyes grow hot. His smile comes on slow and heated.

And I am so out of here.

I stand abruptly, almost knocking over my water glass.

Yanking at the hem of my dress, I say, "Be right back."

"Where are you going?"

"Ladies' room."

"Spider." Declan snaps his fingers. Spider shoots to his feet.

"I think I can pee by myself, thanks."

Ignoring me, Declan makes a motion with his hand to indicate Spider is to follow wherever I go.

Knowing I don't have a say in the matter, I sigh and head toward the back of the restaurant, tugging self-consciously at my hem and hoping Spider isn't following too closely. He'll probably get an eyeful of one of my pasty butt cheeks.

Gah! Why did I agree to wear this stupid dress?

I burst through the bathroom door and lock myself into a stall. I sit on the toilet with my elbows propped on my thighs and my chin propped in my hands until it seems enough time has passed for Sloane to jerk off Declan under the table. Or whatever it was they were about to do.

Then I go to the sink to wash my hands. Even though I didn't pee, clean hands are always a good idea.

When I turn the water off and reach for a paper towel, I happen to glance into the mirror above the sinks. I freeze in horror.

A man is directly behind me. He's huge.

Frighteningly tall and broad, he stands with his legs spread open and his massive hands hanging by his sides. He's all in black, including a heavy wool overcoat with the collar turned up against his tattooed neck.

His hair and beard are thick and dark. A small silver hoop earring glints in one earlobe. Beneath lowered brows, his eyes are a startling shade of pale green.

A powerful energy of violence and darkness emanates from him.

It's like being in a room with a supermassive black hole. I'm about to be devoured and disappear for all eternity.

He's the most beautiful and the most terrifying thing I've ever seen.

His intense gaze locked on mine in the mirror, he murmurs, "You don't need to sell yourself, *malyutka*."

His voice is deep, rich, and hypnotic.

So is his scent. He smells like something that lives and hunts in the woods.

"You're better than that, no matter what he tells you."

He's speaking English, but I have no idea what he's saying. I can't think. I can't focus. All I can do is stare at him, seized with terror and fascination, my heart beating like mad. The rest of me is frozen solid.

"Take this."

Stepping closer, he removes an envelope from an inside pocket of his overcoat. It's a thick brown rectangle with a rubber band around the middle. He leans over and sets it noiselessly on the countertop beside the sink. He gazes down into my wide, unblinking eyes.

"Don't go back to him. Leave now. Make yourself a better life."

He reaches up and gently brushes his knuckles over my cheek. His voice drops even lower.

"I can tell it's not too late for you. There's still hope in those pretty eyes."

Swift and silent as smoke, he turns and vanishes out the door, leaving me stunned and breathless.

I'm a sweaty, shaking, disoriented mess.

What the hell just happened?

After several moments, I gather my last two living brain cells and look at the envelope. Turning it over, I pull off the rubber band, slide my finger under the flap, and stare in disbelief at the stack of crisp one-hundred-dollar bills looking back at me.

I say to the empty room, "Wait. Wait a second. *Wait just a fucking second.*"

Thumbing through the stack, I estimate I'm holding about a hundred thousand bucks in my trembling hands.

My brain does a series of complicated gymnastic flips, then presents me with a hilariously impossible scenario: a hot, scary, wealthy stranger just tried to save me from being my future brother-in-law's prostitute.

I run over the encounter again in my mind. Then again. Then once again for good measure. The only other possibility I can come up with is that Sloane is playing a bad joke on me.

Or she just doesn't want to lose our bet. Maybe that's it. Maybe she paid a guy to come in here and screw with my head.

No, wait. It's all mixed up in my mind. The bet was that *I* would win if a man thought I was a hooker because of the way I'm dressed. Wasn't it?

I don't know. I can't think. Giant Hot Dangerous Stranger ran off with my IQ.

Plus, how would she have found someone on such short notice? After we made the bet, I was only out on the patio before we left for like four minutes. Is that enough time for her to arrange this kind of prank?

Well, probably. This is Sloane we're talking about. And it seems like she has dozens of these big, dangerous guys hanging around.

And she probably carries that much cash in her bra.

But why would she make it so specific? There was no need for Giant Hot Dangerous Stranger to mention Declan. Not that GHDS mentioned him by name, but the implication was there.

Wouldn't it have made more sense if he simply approached me and said I didn't need to sell myself, his assumption that I'm a sex worker being based on the way I'm dressed?

And furthermore, why would a total stranger assume a woman is selling herself unless there was evidence? More evidence than a slutty dress and heels?

Plenty of girls my age dress like they're trying to mortify their fathers, and I've never heard of a single man approaching them in the ladies' room and telling them they still have hope in their eyes!

In their *pretty* eyes, specifically. My breath catches.

Wait . . . does GHDS think I'm pretty?

I ponder that for several seconds until I throw my hands in the air, irritated by my own stupidity.

"You all right in there, lass?"

I suck in a startled breath. It's Spider, from outside the ladies' room door. He must've heard me growling at myself in frustration.

I'm about to answer that I'm fine, but I'm stopped by the realization that if Spider's standing right outside the door, he would've seen GHDS as he left.

And if he *saw* GHDS . . . he definitely wouldn't have just let the guy mosey on past like he was out for a pleasant evening stroll.

I don't know much about men in the Mob, but I do know that if Declan put Spider on my security patrol and Spider saw that beast come out of the restroom I was in, Spider would've lost his mind.

I doubt he would've been quiet about it.

Holding the envelope of cash behind my back, I push the door open a few inches and look through.

Spider stands sentry two feet away. I peer cautiously up and down the hallway. Other than Spider, it's empty.

"Lass? You okay?"

"You already asked me that."

"I know, but your glasses are all steamy."

Of course they are. A large, handsome, terrifying man just set my endocrine system on fire. "I'm fine, thanks. Did you see someone come out of here a minute ago?"

"No. Why?"

"Oh, no reason. He just—"

"He?"

Spider bristles like Wolverine and steps forward, eyes blazing. He whips his hand around under his suit coat to the small of his back, where I suppose a large loaded gun is nesting.

I say quickly, "I meant she! Sorry. Um, she . . . whoever was last in here . . . left something on the counter."

"Oh. Right."

Like a light switch has been thrown, Spider settles back into his usual amiable, attractive self. He folds his hands in front of his crotch and smiles at me. "You ready to go back to the table, lass?"

The cash in my hand has gained considerable weight since I opened the door. I have no idea what I should do with it.

Leave it on the sink? Stuff it in my underwear? Try to find its owner?

I dismiss all those ideas as quickly as I think of them, but am still in a quandary. I don't want to leave this kind of cash lying around a ladies' room, but I can't keep it, either. And I can't exactly smuggle it out and devise a plan later on—a single bill would make a bulge under this obscene dress I'm wearing.

And what if it *does* belong to Sloane?

In that case, I should flush it down the damn toilet.

But I compromise with myself and ask Spider if he'd mind if I wore his suit jacket.

He hesitates a moment, his gaze unreadable.

"Sorry, it's just that my dress is air-conditioned. Sloane made me wear it. I think I've already caught pneumonia."

When he still hesitates, I understand. "Right. You need your jacket to camouflage all the weapons you've got stashed under it."

"None of us need to hide our weapons."

"Oh. Does Bermuda have an open carry law or something?"

His expression turns amused. "No, they have strict gun laws here. But who'd dare to challenge us?"

Wow. It must be nice to work for the king of the jungle. From the sound of it, anything goes.

"Here, lass."

Spider shrugs off his jacket and holds it out, waiting to help me put it on. I step through the door, my hands behind my back, then turn around, moving them to the front as he drapes his coat over my shoulders.

It's warm and smells like him, spice and musk. Must be the testosterone.

Tucking the envelope into a pocket inside the jacket, I turn back and smile at him. "Thank you. Handsome *and* a gentleman."

His cheeks turn ruddy. He clears his throat and says gruffly, "You're welcome. But do me a favor and tell Declan if he asks that it was your idea."

"It was my idea."

"Aye." Embarrassed, he runs a hand over his hair. "I just don't want him to think . . . you know . . . that I . . ."

I laugh. "Spider, he's not going to be mad because you let me wear your jacket. It's a nice thing to do!"

Shifting his weight from foot to foot, he shakes his head.

"There are protocols, lass. I can't . . ." He makes a vague gesture that includes the two of us.

I get what he's trying to say and am instantly horrified.

"Oh, shit! Oh my god, you're not allowed to flirt with me! Not that you *would*, I'm just saying. You'll get in trouble if you even look at Sloane's kid sister sideways. Ugh, no wonder I make you so uncomfortable."

He stares at me for a beat, then says softly, "That's not quite the word I'd use to describe it."

Taken off guard, I blink.

Before I can form a reply, Spider turns and walks away, shoulders stiff. He waits for me at the end of the hallway, acting as if he's desperate to look anywhere but in my direction.

O . . . kay.

Wondering if maybe I ate some THC gummies I forgot about, I walk down the hallway, then follow Spider back to the table.

When we arrive, the mood has changed. The tension is tangible. Sloane is pale, Declan's jaw is as hard as granite, and the bodyguards at the other tables look like they're about to jump out of their skins.

"What's wrong?" I ask, sliding into my seat.

Sloane says, "Declan got a call. We need to go."

"Now? We didn't eat yet!"

Sloane's look could melt off my face. I hold up my hands in surrender. "Sorry."

We all get up and head toward the restaurant's entrance. Everyone is so uptight, they don't notice I'm wearing Spider's suit jacket. Probably a good thing.

As we walk, Spider asks Declan in a low voice, "What's happened?"

"They found Diego."

"What do you mean? His head?"

"No. Whoever that body belonged to that the cops found in the landfill, it wasn't him. They misidentified it. Not sure yet if that was an accident or not."

"Bloody hell!"

"Aye," says Declan darkly. "But it gets much more interesting than that, mate."

"What do you mean?"

"Diego's still alive."

Spider's shock is palpable. He almost trips over his own feet when he hears that piece of news.

Whoever this Diego is, he's obviously someone important.

NINE

RILEY

The trip back to the house is weird. Everyone is tense and silent. Spider drives like he's trying to qualify for the Indy 500. Sloane keeps glancing nervously at Declan, who grinds his jaw so hard and frequently, I worry for his molars.

When we're finally home, the men all disappear into the kitchen, and Sloane brings me back to my room.

As soon as she closes the door behind us, I turn to her and demand, "Okay, spill. Who's this Diego and why is everyone so freaked out?"

Sloane sits carefully on the edge of the bed and takes a breath. "Diego was Declan's boss. Until he was captured by MS-13 and murdered. Only now it seems he wasn't murdered, but that someone deliberately made it look like he was."

She looks at me rummaging through my carry-on. "What are you doing?"

"Getting snacks. This sounds juicy. Keep talking."

She waits to continue until I'm sitting across from her in a chair, tearing into the plastic wrapper on the Twizzlers box with my teeth.

"There was a fire in a warehouse—"

"Where? Here?"

"New York."

"Which part?"

Sloane says tartly, "Would you like me to draw you a map?"

"Sorry. Just trying to get a good visual of the action. Go on." I chow down on two Twizzlers at once. For a moment, Sloane watches me chew with a constipated look on her face, then starts talking again.

"Diego was found at the warehouse when the fire department arrived to put out the flames. They've taken him to the hospital."

"So, he's injured?"

She nods. "We don't know how badly yet."

"Why would someone try to make it look like he was murdered but keep him alive?"

"We don't know that yet, either."

I chew thoughtfully. "I bet he was tortured for information by a rival syndicate."

Sloane's voice comes out faint. "That's a likely scenario, yes."

"Were you close with him, this Diego?"

"No. I never met him."

"Then why are you so upset?"

Taking a moment to gather her thoughts, she passes a hand over her face and exhales.

"Diego . . . had a lot of information. About a lot of people. Secret information. Things that could be devastating if they ever came out. Many people could be affected."

Her tone makes me understand that by "affected," she means killed.

"Holy shit."

"Exactly."

We sit in silence while I devour another piece of candy. Then I'm stopped by a horrible thought. "Is Declan in danger?"

"He's always in danger," she says softly. Then she closes her eyes, pinches the bridge of her nose between two fingers, and whispers, "Fuck."

I'm about to go over to the bed and attempt to comfort her, when a knock comes on the door.

"Come in."

Declan enters, his eyes hunting for Sloane. He spots her sitting on the bed and strides forward. "I've got to leave."

She stands, looking alarmed. "Leave? When?"

"Now."

He takes her by the shoulders and stares into her eyes with ferocious intensity. "I'll be back as soon as I can. In the meantime—"

"No way, gangster," she interrupts loudly, her face turning red. "No fucking way are you going anywhere without me."

He glowers at her. "Sloane."

"I'm coming with you. It's not a negotiation."

Her voice is flat, but her expression is murderous. Declan looks to me for help.

I hold my hands in the air. "If you think I can change her mind, I'm flattered. But once that horse is out of the barn, there's no putting a saddle on it."

Sloane scowls at me. "Where are you getting these stupid metaphors?"

"It was in the last manuscript I edited. I thought it was a good one."

"It's not." She turns her attention back to Declan. "Here's the deal. If you try to leave me behind, I'll book a commercial flight and follow you."

He growls, "I'll order the men to keep you on the property."

She lifts her brows. Regal as a queen, she says, "Do you really think they'll listen to you over me?"

Declan's face turns red. A vein pulses in his neck. His jaw is as hard as stone, and he's grinding his molars again.

I think his head is in danger of exploding.

"Goddammit, woman—"

"End of discussion. Let's get going."

She wrenches herself free of his grip and heads to the door.

He turns, glaring at her back.

I eat another Twizzler, anxious to see what will happen next.

Apparently, Declan realizes he's lost the battle. He drags his hands through his thick black hair. Muttering a curse, he stalks off after her.

"Hey!"

Halfway out the door, they turn and look at me.

"What am *I* doing? Are you gonna fly me home now?"

At the same time, the two of them pronounce, "You'll stay here."

"Here?" I look around the enormous bedroom in horror. "By *myself*?"

Sloane says, "You like being by yourself, remember?"

"Yeah, in my own place with all my own stuff. Not in the Bermuda Triangle Colosseum."

Declan says sternly, "This is the safest place for you at the moment, lass. Nobody on earth knows about this location."

The underlying message is that majorly bad guys would do majorly bad things to Declan and whoever's in his vicinity if they knew where he was.

For the first time, I understand how dangerous Sloane's situation is. She's literally risking her life to be near him.

She's risking her life for love.

I stare at her in disbelief. In a history full of reckless decisions, this one takes the cake.

She snaps, "You're not leaving, Smalls."

"But—"

"You brought your laptop so you could work from here. Right?"

I'm starting to get panicky. I do *not* want to stay here alone in this castle with only echoes for company. I'm a city girl. My apartment at home is smaller than nine hundred square feet. This much open space creeps me out.

"Yeah, but I thought I'd be staying only a few days. How long will you guys be gone?"

Declan says, "I don't know." He points a finger at the floor, as if about to make a final, irrevocable declaration. "But until this situation is settled, you're staying right here."

Then they turn around and walk out, slamming the door behind them.

The bastards!

I look around the room in dread. "Oh my god! I'm a captive!"

I leap to my feet and run to the door. Then I trip because I still have the stupid heels on. Cursing, I kick them off, throw Spider's coat on top of them, and run out the door and down the hallway in my bare feet.

I catch up to Declan and Sloane in the sitting room, where it looks like a gangster convention.

Dozens of burly men in black suits mill around, muttering to each other in what I suppose is Gaelic and throwing dark glances at the windows. Spider's there, too.

I say, "You guys, wait! This might be important!"

I can tell by her exasperated expression that Sloane thinks I'm about to argue with her again, but I've got something else on my mind. This Diego situation has rearranged a few things in my head.

I'm not sure if everyone else should hear what I have to say, though, so I wait until I'm standing right in front of them and keep my voice low.

"There was this guy, when I went to the ladies' room at the restaurant. He thought I was a sex worker."

Sloane snaps, "We don't have time for this right now!"

She thinks I'm talking about our bet. "No, listen. He was *in* the restroom when I came out of the stall. He was really big, and sort of, I don't know. Weird. You know, like dangerous weird."

Declan does the exact same bristling thing that Spider did at the restaurant. He literally gets bigger, badder, and a thousand times more intense. His blue eyes flash with cold fire.

"What happened?" he growls, stepping closer. "What did he look like? What did he say? Did he hurt you?"

I'm a little put out that he waited until the last question to ask if I'm hurt, but whatever.

"I'm fine. He didn't lay a finger on me, he just freaked me out. He said that I didn't have to sell myself, and it wasn't too late for me, and he could tell I still had hope left . . ."

I trail off, trying to remember more about the big beast.

Mostly what I remember is how gentle he was when he brushed his knuckles across my cheek, and how soft his voice was when he said my eyes were pretty.

And how gorgeous he was.

My god, that face. That mouth. Those pale, piercing green eyes. Paired against his brute masculinity, the fineness of his features was even more stunning.

He makes Declan look like Justin Bieber.

Infuriated, Sloane turns to Declan. "There was no guy. This is about a bet we made before we left for the restaurant."

"No, Sloane, it's not."

She folds her arms over her chest. "Okay, so where did this weird, dangerous guy go after he propositioned you?"

I'm starting to get exasperated. My voice rises. "He *didn't* proposition me. You're not listening—"

"Spider!"

At the sound of Sloane's sharp call, he snaps to attention and runs over. "Aye?"

Sloane gestures at me. "My sister claims a man accosted her in the ladies' room at the restaurant. Would you like to tell us what you saw?"

He looks at me, frowning. "A man? In the ladies' room?"

"You were with her, correct?"

He looks confused, and now I'm getting desperate.

"Aye. I was with her the entire time, standing right outside the door."

"Did you see a man enter or leave?"

"No. No one went in or out except her."

"When she came out, did she say anything about a man being inside?"

Spider glances at me. His expression is apologetic. "No."

Sloane turns back to me, nostrils flared and lips flattened. "Jesus, Riley. For a singing bird box? If you needed money so badly, all you had to do was ask."

"This isn't about the bet, Sloane!"

"Game's over. Spider, take her back to her room." Everyone in the room is now staring at me.

Me, in my stupid slutty dress, with my stupid bleached hair and my white-hot mortification at being called a liar.

By my own sister, the asshole who wanted me to come here in the first place.

Without waiting for Spider to humiliate me further by grabbing my wrist and dragging me away, I turn and walk out, keeping my head held high despite the rock in my throat and the water welling in my eyes.

So help me god, this is the last time I'll ever speak to her again.

TEN

MAL

*W*hen I return to my perch in the belfry, Declan's house is dark.

The only lights that remain burning are the landscape flood-lights and in lamps in three rooms on the first floor.

One of those rooms is a bedroom.

I can't see much from this angle, but I can see French doors with curtains drawn over. There's a small, private patio off the room, dec-orated with pots of blooming flowers.

An armed guard passes by the patio, rifle at the ready. They're crawling all over the property, these guards. As if it makes a differ-ence.

I don't know if Declan and his entourage have already gone to bed or if they went somewhere else after I left the restaurant, be-cause I didn't come straight here. I drove around the island, think-ing. Trying to clear my head.

Of her. The waif.

I'm angry with myself that I frightened her.

I'm even more angry that I care that I frightened her.

I never care about scaring anyone. No matter their gender.

I've been the recipient of people's fear for so long, it no longer means anything to me.

But hers did. I hate that.

When I close my eyes to draw a breath, an image of her terrified face pops up against my eyelids. I allow myself to sit with it for a moment, taking pleasure in the details.

Everything about this girl is in the details.

She's not tall, like Declan's woman. She's not flashy, or curvy, or sexy, or anything obvious that would catch a man's eye.

She's like a little bird that looks plain at first glance. Only when you focus your attention can you see the incredible intricacy of her feathers.

The ring of gold around her pupils.

The flecks of it all through her sweet brown eyes. The fine arch of her brows.

The perfect bow of her upper lip.

The way the small bump on the bridge of her nose makes her glasses sit slightly askew.

The way light reflects off her poreless skin, making it glow.

The way she looked at my mouth and made me feel like a wild animal.

I open my eyes, and she disappears. I exhale, breathing easier.

Until she reappears again, this time on the patio of the bedroom on the first floor.

She's still with him. She didn't take the money and leave.

My heart starts to pound so hard, I have to grip the rifle with both hands to steady myself. I stare through the sights at her magnified image and watch as she walks slowly to the edge of the patio.

She picks up one of the flowerpots and hurls it over the balustrade.

The pot lands intact on the grass on the other side and rolls a few feet before stopping.

She picks up another pot. This time, she hurls it against the patio itself, jumping back to avoid the jagged shards of clay as the pot smashes against the stone and disintegrates.

Then she starts to pace.

It appears she's talking to herself. Angrily.

Anger rises in me, too, as burning hot as the midday sun on this hideous island. Not because of the money I gave her. Money means nothing to me.

Because the longer she stays with him, the more danger she's in from his sick appetites.

And what the fuck has he done to her?

That she's enraged is obvious. Is she also hurt? Has he beaten her? Raped her? Savaged her in some way only a man like him could?

I might be a killer with a reputation to match the level of my skill, but a man like Declan O'Donnell is a worse thing even than me.

Every person who's felt my rifle's bite has earned it. They had blood on their hands. They were more vicious than rabid wolves, to a one.

They weren't innocent.

Though she sells herself, this girl is still an innocent. She's a doe, not a wolf. I saw it in her eyes.

She's a little bird caught in a lion's trap.

And if I don't do something, if I don't try something else, she'll be devoured.

She isn't your problem, Malek. She isn't why you're here. You already tried to help her. Forget the waif. Focus.

No. I can't focus until I know she's safe. What the fuck is wrong with you?

I don't know.

Something, though. This isn't like you. You've never done this before. What's wrong with your head?

It's filled with her.

Abandoning the argument with myself, I stand and make my way down the belfry stairs, sighing heavily.

It's time to do something stupid and dangerous again.

ELEVEN

RILEY

*S*mashing flowerpots isn't nearly as cathartic as I'd hoped it would be.

I go back inside the bedroom, closing and locking the patio doors and drawing the curtains over them again. I'm starving, having only had a dinner roll and some candy for supper, but I'll be damned if I'll call down on the stupid house phone for food.

I don't want to speak to another Irishman for the rest of my life. The whole lot of them are arrogant bastards!

Okay, fine, they're all really nice. The truth is that I'm too embarrassed.

It seems more reasonable to starve to death than to have to face the disappointed, condescending looks of Declan's staff when they bring food up to Sloane's lying little sister.

I have no doubt whatsoever that they've all been gossiping about me since I left the room earlier in such disgrace.

The judgmental sons of bitches.

I decide to take a hot bath to try to scrub my humiliation away. It doesn't work, but at least I'm clean and a shade less weepy.

I polish off another box of candy, spend a millisecond worrying about tooth decay, then brush and floss my teeth, turn out the lights, and climb into bed.

I must fall asleep, because I find myself sometime later staring up into the darkness with my heart pounding wildly from the terrifying sense that someone else is in the room with me.

There's no sound. No movement. Not a single breath disturbs the air.

But there's the distinct scent of the woods and a big fucking *presence.*

I sit bolt upright in terror, clutching the sheets to my chest and hoping one of Declan's guards will hear my scream before my body is hacked into a million pieces.

Shaking all over, I suck in a deep breath—

"Don't scream, *malyutka*. I won't hurt you. I give you my word."

The voice is deep, rich, and hypnotic, and one I instantly recognize.

Oh my fucking god, it's him! It's him, it's him, it's him! He's in my bedroom, and it's him!

I start to hyperventilate so badly, I'm in immediate danger of passing out.

"Thank you."

He's thanking me for not screaming. What he doesn't know is that I'm trying to, but my throat muscles are unwilling to cooperate. They're frozen stiff with terror, like the rest of me.

Hearing a small rustle to my right, I jerk my head in that direction. Unfortunately, I'm not wearing my glasses. So even if the room were lit, I'd still see nothing but the watery blur I'm seeing now.

I knew I should've gotten LASIK when my optometrist suggested it.

"Why didn't you leave when I gave you the money?"

"I was too busy being brain-fucked."

That's what I wanted to say, but what I actually produce is something along the lines of the sound an elephant might make giving birth. It includes a lot of awkward grunts and trumpeting.

"Breathe, *malyutka*. You're in no danger from me."

Except for the danger of my ovaries exploding at the same time my head does, you mean.

I don't understand how the husky timbre of his voice can be both arousing and frightening, but I suppose I've always been good at multitasking.

I sit in bed with the sheets clutched in my fists, breathing like I'm in labor, until finally I regain enough control of my larynx and vocal cords to speak. "What's that word you keep calling me?"

I know it's not the most pressing question, but I'm under extreme duress, so I'm giving myself some slack on this one.

"*Malyutka.*"

He draws it out, enunciating the syllables. Whatever language he's speaking, it's masculine, rough, and sexual.

I hate myself for loving it. "What does it mean?"

"Roughly . . . little one. Baby."

I stop being terrified long enough to marvel at that. I have a nickname?

Giant Hot Dangerous Stranger is calling me *baby*?

I clear my throat, desperate to understand what the hell is happening. "Um . . . uh . . ."

"Is the Irishman keeping you prisoner here?"

"Ha! How did you guess?"

Okay, that actually came out in normal words. And with my normal amount of blatant sarcasm. So I must not be as scared as I think I am.

Only I am. Holy shit, I'm scared. I'd make a run for it if I didn't already know my damn legs were paralyzed by fear.

I'd take one step out of bed and fall flat onto my face and probably knock myself unconscious in the process.

"I can help you." His voice lowers. "I want to help you."

There was a slight emphasis on the word "want" that makes my skin break out into goose bumps. I go cold, then hot, then start hyperventilating again.

"I . . . I . . ." Frustrated with myself, I clear my throat and start again. "Whoever you are, you should leave. There are like a million armed guards around here."

"I know. I've seen them."

His tone is tranquil. He couldn't care less about the armed guards. Interesting.

We sit in silence until I run through the entire list of intelligent, clearheaded questions a person should ask in this kind of situation. Then I say brightly, "My name's Riley. What's yours?"

Someone please shoot me. Just shoot me now and put me out of my misery. I'm the dumbest victim of an impending violent crime who ever lived.

Out of the watery darkness comes a sound that sends a cascade of shivers down my spine.

It's a chuckle, sexy and masculine, rich and deep.

I'd like him to make that sound against the side of my neck. Or maybe the inside of my thigh.

Or maybe I should go ahead and throw myself onto the nearest sharp object and spare the world another second of my incurable stupidity.

I'm not surprised when he doesn't answer my question, so I offer more remarkable proof of my total lack of intelligence by saying, "Your money's on the dresser."

Somehow, I made it sound like I'm offering payment to the gigolo who just serviced me sexually.

My cheeks flame with heat. "I mean, I assume that's why you're here. To get it back."

When he doesn't respond, I add meekly, "Right?"

"I'm not here for the money."

Breathe. Don't pass out. Lungs, if you fail me now, I'll start smoking ten packs of cigarettes a day to get back at you.

"It's a lot of money, though."

"Not to me. But the amount doesn't matter."

We sit in another space of nerve-racking silence while my heartbeat crashes in my ears and the entire bed trembles underneath me until I gather enough courage to venture, "So if you're not here to get back your money, and you're not"—gulp—"going to hurt me . . . why are you here?"

He takes his time responding to that. I feel him thinking about it, mulling it over in his head.

Finally, he says, "I don't know."

He sounds bewildered. Not like he's playing a game, but like he honestly has no idea why he suddenly found himself in my bedroom in the middle of the night.

His confusion makes me relax.

I mean, serial killers usually know why they broke into your bedroom, right?

I decide I'd like to see his expression and reach over to the nightstand for my glasses. But my sudden movement causes him to react. It happens so quickly, I don't even have time to blink.

He grasps my wrist in his big hand and growls, "Don't try to shoot me. A bullet in my gut will only make me mad."

He towers over me, a force field of heat and tension beside the bed. He's so close, his warm breath brushes my ear.

"I was reaching for my glasses!" I blurt, panicking. "I don't have a gun!"

After a beat, his grip on my wrist softens. Then he releases me and steps away, standing close enough to the bed that I can still see his form.

I scramble for the glasses, shove them onto my face, and stare up at him in cold fear.

His height makes him even more terrifying. From this angle, I feel like I'm craning my neck to gaze up at a skyscraper. Only it's so tall, I can't see the top. His face is wreathed in darkness.

Then he bends his long legs and kneels beside the bed, bringing his face into view.

Even through the shadows, I see the intensity in those pale green eyes.

I see how they search. How they burn.

I make a bleating sound like a scared lamb. It's involuntary, and I hate myself for being such a wuss. His reaction seems involuntary, too.

He shushes me softly. He reaches out and caresses my cheek, cooing a stream of gently spoken words.

"*Ty v bezovasnoshti so mnoy, malyutka. Ya ne prichinu tebe vreda.*"

Russian. It's Russian he's speaking.

I recognize it without knowing how and almost fall out of bed.

Recap: a huge, beautiful Russian man broke into my bedroom. Ten feet away from a row of toilets, he gave me one hundred thousand dollars and told me I had pretty eyes. He can appear and disappear like smoke, smells like an ancient forest, and has a voice, a body, and a face that make me want him to do bad things to me.

He thinks I'm a prisoner. And a prostitute.

He's confused about pretty much everything else.

Also, he's still caressing my face. I hope he'll keep doing that forever.

My voice shaking, I say, "I feel like you should tell me your name now. I need to know what to call you."

Kneeling with one tattooed hand spread open over his massive thigh and the other on my jaw, he stares so hard at me, he can probably see my bones.

"You can make one up if you want. Or I'll make one up for you, if you prefer. It's just that I can't keep calling you Giant Hot

Dangerous Stranger in my head too much longer. It's a mouthful, you know?"

His thumb sweeps back and forth over my cheekbone so slowly and gently, I'm getting hypnotized.

"Riley."

Ignoring my request for his name, he tests my name on his tongue instead. He says it again, even more softly than the first time. He blinks, frowning, and shakes his head slightly. I can tell he doesn't understand what's happening.

Me, neither.

"Riley Rose," I say breathlessly, feeling electrocuted. Feeling every beat of my heart and every hot pulse of blood roaring through my veins.

Why am I not screaming for the guards? As soon as I ask myself that question, I know the answer: I don't want the guards to come.

Gazing at me like he's witnessing his first sunrise, he lightly sweeps his thumb over my top lip. He whispers gruffly, "You're made of fine materials, Riley Rose."

Jesus fucking yellow penguins, this man is unreal.

Sensing he'd tell me anything I wanted to know right now, I insist, "What's your name?"

When he moistens his lips, I think I'll pass out. "Malek."

Malek. Like Alek, only way fucking hotter.

"Why are you in my bedroom, Malek? What do you want from me?"

"Nothing," he replies instantly. His eyes tell a very different story.

Our gazes lock. My skin ignites. My heart, head, and loins explode with fire.

A voice comes through the door. "Lass, you all right in there? I thought I heard voices."

It's Spider.

Fuck! It's Spider!

I turn my head to the door and call out, "I'm fine, thanks. Good night!"

When I turn back to look at Malek, he's gone. The curtains in front of the closed French doors billow slightly, then settle back into tranquility and hang still.

I sit watching them, stunned.

He's a ghost. Or a vampire. Or an alien who can walk through solid objects.

Or a figment of my overactive imagination, which would make way more sense.

With an edge in his voice that suggests he might force his way in if I don't comply, Spider says, "Open up, lass."

I take a moment to compose myself, then throw off the covers and pad barefoot over the carpet to the door. I unlock it, open it, and lean my shoulder on the edge, squinting against the bright hallway light.

Tense and suspicious, he peers past me into the dark room. "Who were you talking to?"

Instead of answering that, I deflect. "Why were you listening at my door? Are you spying on me?"

The tactic works. His cheeks turn ruddy, and he glances away. Sounding flustered, he says, "No, lass. I just . . . uh . . . wanted to check on you. Make sure you were safe."

"Why wouldn't I be? Has something happened?"

He glances back at me and shakes his head, but I sense a hesitation.

"Spit it out. What's up?"

He passes a hand over his hair, looks at the floor, runs a finger under his shirt collar. "What happened earlier."

When I tried to tell Sloane about seeing Malek in the ladies' room at the restaurant, he means. When she humiliated me in front of everyone by calling me a liar.

Heat rising up my neck, I say stiffly, "I don't want to talk about it, thanks."

He peers at me with an odd expression. His voice comes out muted. "You said 'he.'"

"Excuse me?"

"When you opened the door to the ladies' room and asked me if I saw someone come out. You first referred to that person as 'he.' And you seemed disoriented."

My heart picks up its pace. "What's your point?"

He stares at me, a muscle in his jaw flexing. "Was there a man in the bathroom with you, lass?"

"Would you believe me if I said there was?"

He considers that for a silent beat, then nods.

I don't know why, but it makes me want to cry. My chest tight, I look away, blinking. "Thank you. But it doesn't really matter now."

Spider says softly, "Aye, lass. It does." After a moment, he prompts, "Look at me."

"I can't. I'm too busy trying to pretend I'm not upset so you won't think I'm crazy."

"I don't think you're crazy. But I do think you're proud enough not to trust me from now on because I had to tell your sister the truth about what I saw."

"No, I understand. You were just doing your job."

He seems dissatisfied by that, shifting his weight from foot to foot and passing a hand over his hair again. He exhales and squeezes the back of his neck. Then he shakes his head as if he's made some kind of decision.

After a rough throat clearing, he says, "I'll let you get back to bed. Sorry for the disturbance."

Then he turns and stalks off down the hallway, muttering to himself in Gaelic.

I go back to bed and lie awake for a long time. I finally fall into a fitful, dreamless sleep, waking every so often to the scent of cedar sap and pine needles, of fog clinging to ancient tree trunks in a dark, moonlit woods.

When I get up in the morning, a single long-stemmed white rose rests on the pillow beside my head.

TWELVE

RILEY

*F*or the next two days, nothing happens. I have no mysterious midnight visitors; no more formerly dead, headless Mob
bosses are discovered alive and intact after a warehouse fire; and
nobody gifts me an envelope full of Benjamins in a restroom to try
to get me to abandon the hoe life and make a fresh start.

I stay locked in my bedroom trying to work and trying not to
think about Malek.

I succeed at the first thing far better than the second.

On day three, I ask Spider if he'll drive me into town so I can
work at a coffee shop. I can't take a single minute more of swimming around in the huge, empty fishbowl of the guest bedroom,
gulping air and longing for another heady sniff of pine needles.

Spider's immediate response is a flat "No."

He caught me in the kitchen, where I've taken to sneaking at
odd hours to pilfer food from the fridge in hopes I won't have to
encounter any of the staff and endure their withering derision.

In my head, I've created an entire ten-season Netflix saga of what all the Irish bodyguards have been saying about me behind my back since Sloane and Declan left.

It's ugly. Even if only 2 percent of it is true, I can't face them ever again.

I'm not anxious by nature, but I am easily mortified. Even a minor mistake makes me want to die of shame if it's committed in public.

"Please?" I say, trying to appear winsome and irresistible. "I have to get out of this place. It's too quiet. I'm going nuts. I need some noise and chattering people around me so I can concentrate."

Spider gazes at me sternly. "Orders are you stay here, lass."

"Orders. Right." I pause to purse my lips and examine his steely exterior for cracks.

He says emphatically, "No."

"What? You don't even know what I was going to say."

"Whatever it was, it involves me doing something I'm not supposed to do at your request."

"I'd never ask you to do something that would get you in trouble."

When he only stands there, staring down his nose at me with his arms folded over his chest, I tell the truth.

"Okay, I probably would, but if you did get in trouble, I promise I'd feel bad about it. How about if we just go for a drive around the block with the radio on? I'm sure we're allowed to do that."

He chuckles, shaking his head. "You're so much like your sister."

"Say that again, and I'll give you a smack on that big skull of yours."

He pretends to be offended. "My skull isn't big!"

I laugh at that. "Yes, it is. It's as enormous as the rest of you."

He stares at me, slowly lifting his brows.

My face decides it's time to turn a nice bright shade of tomato red. "I didn't mean it like that."

"No? So the rest of me is small?"

He's teasing me, the jerk. Time to change the subject.

"How about the library? I'm sure Declan would agree I'd be safe at a library, right?"

"We're not going anywhere."

"Fine. If you won't help me, I'll run away. I'm sure that won't get you into any trouble."

I don't really mean it. I'm just being dramatic because I'm not getting my way. I turn around and flounce off with the plate of chicken wings I found in the fridge.

Ten minutes later, Spider knocks on my bedroom door.

"Yes?"

He sticks his head through. "All right, lass. Let's go."

Sitting cross-legged on the floor, I perk up. "Really?"

"Aye, really."

I munch on a wing for a minute, debating, then shake my head. "That's sweet, but I was only joking about running away. And I really don't want to get you in trouble."

He chuckles. "You won't be. I got permission to take you out for that joyride."

"From Declan?"

"Aye." His grin is so big, it's nearly blinding. "If anyone knows firsthand how a Keller woman can pester a man to death when she wants something, it's him."

Abandoning the plate of wings, I mutter, "Yeah, I bet he does," and jump up to gather my things.

Ten minutes later, we're pulling out through the big iron gates, and I'm in full interrogation mode. Apparently, freedom makes me chatty.

"So how long have you worked for Declan?"

"A long time."

"Is it a hard job?"

"Depends on what you mean by hard."

"Do you have to kill people?"

He sends me a sideways look that means *Of course.*

"Oh. Wow."

I think for a moment about what a bummer it must be to have that in your job description, then let it go because there's nothing I can do about it.

I'm not one to dwell on things that can't be fixed.

"Is a mobster what you wanted to be when you were growing up? And don't give me some oblique answer. I want specifics this time."

I can tell he's trying not to laugh. "Oblique?"

"It means indirect."

"I know what it means, lass. I'm just amused by your choice of words sometimes."

Offended, I say snippily, "So I'm a word geek. Sue me."

"Aw, don't be sore. What's your favorite word?"

That stumps me. I mull it over for a while as we drive, passing more gigantic estates set back behind locked gates and tall hedges. Bermuda seems to be entirely populated by paranoid rich people.

"Serendipity."

"Serendipity?"

"Yeah, because of the way it sounds, and also because I like its meaning."

Spider nods. "Happy accident."

And here I thought he was just another pretty face.

"Yes, exactly. I also like the word 'mellifluous' because when you use it in a sentence, people think you're super smart. And it's pretty. Mel-li-flu-ous. It sounds like you're chanting a spell. That's what I wanted to be when I was growing up, by the way. A witch. God, it would be so badass to be able to put curses on people, don't you think? And fly. Except I wouldn't want to fly around on a broom. A broomstick stuck up your cooch would be crazy uncomfortable."

Spider has his fist over his mouth. He's trying to stifle his laughter.

"Hey! I'm being open and honest here! You could at least have the manners to keep a straight face."

"Witches are supposed to ride their brooms sidesaddle, lass, not with the bloody thing clamped between their thighs."

I roll my eyes. "Excuse me for not knowing the proper way to mount a broomstick. I missed that day at Hogwarts."

Spider laughs and laughs, clearly enjoying himself. I wonder when the last time was that he had a good laugh. His job probably doesn't afford many occasions.

Staring at his grinning profile, I say suddenly, "Are they going to be okay?"

He knows who I mean. His voice gentle, he says, "Declan's a wicked smart man, lass. And wicked powerful. He'll not let your sister come to any harm."

"But what about him? I bet there are lots of guys who want to do him harm, right?"

"Aye. But he's been around this game a long, long time. He knows every trick in the book, even the ones that haven't yet been written. More than twenty years he's had in the life, and he's still standing. He'll stand for another twenty easy, mark my words."

Spider is obviously very proud of his boss. His confidence in Declan sounds unshakable. It makes me breathe a little easier, but I also know that nobody's invincible.

No matter how smart you are, there's always someone smarter. Even the highest and most secure castle walls can be breached.

Case in point: Malek.

He came in and out without being seen by any of Declan's guards. I locked the patio door, and he somehow unlocked it from outside. I haven't heard a peep about triggered security alarms or violated perimeters, but he snuck onto the premises without raising any red flags, appearing noiselessly in my bedroom, where he could have quite easily murdered me.

But didn't.

He called me baby and left me a white rose instead.

I haven't decided what I'm going to do if he shows up again.

I'm not naïve. I know he's dangerous. He wears violence like cologne. Trusting men like him is what gets women like me killed.

But there's something both powerful and undeniable that draws me to him. An irresistible natural force, like gravity. He knelt next to my bed and took my face in his big rough hand, and my heart opened like a flower.

Clearly, I have the same brains god gave a flea.

"Did Declan tell you anything about the situation with his old boss when you talked to him about taking me out for a drive?"

"It was a text message."

"Oh."

"But I did talk to him last night."

I can tell from his voice that he's got information. Sitting up straighter in my seat, I look at him eagerly. "And? What did he say?"

"Long story short, without getting into all the gory details, Diego's got amnesia. Can't remember a bloody thing that happened to him."

I gasp. "No way!"

"Aye. They saw him in the hospital. The poor sot doesn't even recognize Declan. Doesn't know his own name. Has no bloody idea who or where he is."

"That's awful!"

Spider makes a noise of agreement. "It's quite a mess all around."

I examine his face. "Sounds like there's more to it than amnesia."

Looking serious, he glances in my direction. "When Declan thought Diego had been killed . . . let's just say he didn't take it sitting down."

"Oh, boy. That sounds murdery."

"Aye. Retaliation in kind when a boss is killed is normal business. But with Diego alive, certain actions Declan took have been proven unnecessary. And with Diego not being able to recall who kidnapped him and locked him up, the whole thing's one giant clusterfuck."

I get that there's going to be blowback on Declan for whatever murdery stuff he did to avenge Diego, and I don't think it's fair.

"But Declan has an excuse. He really thought Diego was dead. There was a body and everything!"

Spider chuckles darkly. "Tell that to the rest of the families."

"Wow. I'm glad you can be so nonchalant about it. I think I'd be having a heart attack."

He shrugs. "It's the life. Never a dull moment. Dodging death keeps a man young." He pauses. "What's that screwy face for?"

"What you just said is probably the most macho thing I've ever heard."

"Thank you."

"I'm not sure it was a compliment. Oh, look, a bookstore! Can we go in there?"

I point at an adorable little shop we're passing by. The façade is painted bright blue. Potted red geraniums line the big bay window in front. A few bicycles are parked outside beside a row of small café tables. People sip coffees and chat in the morning sun.

"Your wish is my command," says Spider, smiling. He makes a right turn, taking us around the block.

"In that case, I wish for season tickets to the 49ers."

Spider makes a retching noise. "Ugh. American football."

"What's wrong with it?"

"You Yanks wear too many bloody safety pads. Wankers. And the helmets!" He scoffs. "To cover your dainty eejit brains."

"Ah. I see where this is going. You're about to extol the manly virtues of rugby, right?"

He glances at me, grinning, before pulling into a parking spot. "Extol?"

I say mildly, "Oh, shut up."

As soon as Spider turns off the SUV's engine, I open the door and hop out, collecting my laptop. When I turn around, he's standing right in front of me.

Scowling.

Taken aback, I say, "What?"

He says crossly, "You're supposed to let me open the door and help you out, lass."

"Why? Do I look like I normally have trouble exiting vehicles?"

"No, because I'm a man and you're a woman."

When I only stand there staring at him with my face scrunched up, he adds, "Also, I'm working. It's my job."

"You should've started with that."

"Why?"

"Because then I wouldn't suspect that you have old-fashioned, inflexible ideas about gender roles."

He chuckles. "I *do* have old-fashioned, inflexible ideas about gender roles. But trust me when I say that they're all to your benefit. Now, will you let me open the door to the bloody bookshop for you, or will your wee feminist ego insist we arm wrestle over it?"

I lift my nose in the air and sniff. "I wouldn't arm wrestle you."

I was trying to be snooty and dismissive, but he seizes the opportunity of my refusal to make a point.

"Of course you wouldn't. *You'd lose.* Would you like to know why?"

Knowing where he's going with this, I exhale a heavy breath and roll my eyes. "Because you're stronger than me."

"Aye. And that's because . . . ?"

"Because you're a man and I'm a woman."

"Correct."

"God, you're a pain in the ass."

"You're not the first woman to tell me that."

"Shocker."

He grins. Then he closes the passenger door and guides me into the shop with his hand on the small of my back.

Conversation at the café tables stops dead as we pass. One woman stares at Spider with her mouth hanging open so wide, I have to suppress a giggle.

Inside, we look around at the charming space. There's a little coffee counter on one side of the store at the front, along with a few more small tables. The register is on the other side. Behind both, rows and rows of crammed bookshelves stretch all the way to the back of the building.

Heaven.

"Can I buy you a coffee, lass?"

"Sure. Thank you. Americano, no sugar or cream."

He crinkles his nose. On such a muscular, macho guy, it's adorable. "So basically hot bean water. Did you spend much time in prison?"

"Ha. And thank you for judging my choice in caffeinated beverages. Is it okay if I browse the shelves a bit before we sit down?"

"Of course. I'll catch up with you." His look sharpens. "Don't wander too far."

He stands in line behind an old man leaning heavily on a cane, and I stroll down the main aisle until I hit the travel section.

I turn down the aisle on a whim.

It's surprisingly large, with a selection of everything from walking guides through Kyoto to spelunking guides for the underwater caves of New Zealand.

The books on Russia are at the end of the aisle.

I flip through several of them, not knowing what I'm looking for. Then a large, colorful volume on a top shelf catches my eye. It's sticking out a few inches from the rest.

Deciding I'd like to look at that one, I set my laptop on the floor and grab a rolling shelf ladder someone left in the middle of the aisle. I roll it over, climb up a few steps, and reach for the book.

I'm about to pull it out when another hand reaches up and settles over mine.

It's big, male, and covered in tattoos.

The arm it's attached to is encased in a black wool coat sleeve.

The sharp breath I drag into my lungs is infused with the scent of pine needles.

Malek.

THIRTEEN

RILEY

I spend several frozen moments staring wide-eyed at his hand covering mine and attempting not to topple off the ladder from shock. Then I whisper, "Did you follow me here?"

His reply is low and instant. "Yes."

"Have you been watching me?"

"Yes."

Holy shitsicles. He's been watching me. How? From where?

I swallow hard. He's standing so close behind me, I feel his body heat. He's radiating it. The man is burning up. He's his own five-alarm fire.

I want to ask him why the hell he's wearing a black wool over-coat when it's eighty degrees outside, but get distracted when he leans closer and puts his mouth beside my ear.

"Come with me now," he says urgently. "I can get you away from the guard. I'll take you anywhere in the world you want to go. You can start a new life."

Cue the sound of screeching brakes.

Shit. I forgot. He thinks I'm Declan's captive prostitute.

Turning my head to look over my shoulder, I meet his eyes.

His pale green, blazingly intense, burn-the-barn-down eyes.

Wow, this is gonna be super awkward. "Um . . . I'm not what you think I am."

His grip on my hand tightens. After a beat, he says gruffly, "I'm not trying to fuck you. I'm trying to save you."

Hearing him say "fuck" makes my cheeks burn.

But I don't know how to feel about the rest of it. Should I be offended or complimented that he thinks I'm a hooker, just not one he'd pay to have sex with?

Deciding this conversation is awkward enough already without him having to make his case for a swift escape to my profile, I turn around on the ladder and face him. Because I'm up two steps, we're at the same height. We're standing eye to eye, and he's even more stunning up close in broad daylight.

After a moment, I manage to get my tongue to work. "No, I meant that I'm not a prostitute."

He draws a slow breath. Somehow, he makes it look sexy. His tone gentle, he says, "I'm not judging you, *malyutka*."

Okay, I really like it when he calls me that. I like it an unreasonable amount. It's not healthy. But I can't get distracted from what I need to say.

"I'm not a sex worker. And I'm not saying that because I'm afraid of you judging me. I'm saying it because it's true."

A furrow appears between his dark brows.

That he apparently doesn't believe me is irritating. "Making the jump from me wearing a revealing dress to me selling myself is a big stretch."

"It wasn't only the dress," he says, frowning.

"What else was it? The heels?"

Ignoring that, he steps even closer and demands, "Who are you, then? Why are you staying with him? Why did you say he was keeping you prisoner?"

"No, you go first. Why are you watching me? And what are you doing in Bermuda?"

"I'm watching you because I like to. And maybe I live here."

Bypassing all the internal screaming his "because I like to" comment evoked, I say, "Nobody who lives in Bermuda owns a knee-length black wool overcoat."

"I could be on holiday."

"I think a man who spends his time spying on people, dispensing cash like an ATM, and appearing out of thin air in locked rooms is up to something other than vacationing."

"Then maybe you should stop thinking."

"So you're telling me you're a good guy?"

After a pause, he says darkly, "No. I'm not good. In fact, Riley Rose, I'm the worst man you'll ever meet."

He stares at me with the truth of it burning in his eyes.

I'm sweating. My heart is pounding. My knees knock together so loudly, he can probably hear them.

Despite all that, I'm not scared.

Jacked up on adrenaline, yes. But deep down, not really scared.

But we've already established that I'm a moron, so this shouldn't be news.

I say breathlessly, "But you're not a danger to me."

"Not to you, no."

The way he says "you" confirms my suspicions.

Malek isn't a danger to me, but he *is* a danger to other people.

People, for instance, like my future brother-in-law, the head of the Irish Mob.

I close my eyes and moisten my lips. When I open my eyes, Malek is staring with intense focus at my mouth.

I whisper, "Declan."

His lashes lift. His fierce gaze drills into mine. He says nothing.

"That's why you're here, isn't it? You came for Declan. But then you saw me and got distracted from killing him by trying to help me."

The expression on his face is indescribable, but it does tell me one thing for certain: I'm right.

I put together the trail of crumbs, made a stretch even bigger than the one he made about me being a prostitute, and I'm right.

Starting to shake, I say, "Please don't kill him."

He replies vehemently, "You don't know what you're asking. And why do you care if he lives or dies? *Who are you?*"

"His future sister-in-law."

Malek's reaction is so stunned, I might as well have slapped him across the face.

His nostrils flare. His pupils dilate. He jerks back abruptly, like you'd recoil from a snake, and stares at me with eyes filled with revulsion.

A man calls out, "Riley?" It's Spider.

From the sound of his voice, I know he's close. He'll walk around the corner of the aisle any second. And when he does, one of two things will happen.

He'll shoot Malek, or Malek will shoot him. The thought of it makes me lose my senses.

I jump off the ladder, grab my laptop from the floor, and turn back to Malek. "I'm begging you. Please don't hurt Declan. I believe you could, and if you did, it would kill my sister. I could never live with myself if that happened."

I turn and run down the aisle, rounding the corner just as Spider's walking up.

He stops. Holding a cup of coffee in each hand, he peers at me suspiciously. "Why such a hurry?"

"We need to go. Now."

I brush past him, walking fast, not looking back. Within seconds, Spider's right by my side.

Like I knew he would be. "What is it, lass?" he demands.

"I'll tell you in the car."

I burst through the front door of the bookstore and make a

beeline for the SUV, clutching my laptop to my chest like a shield. Following on my heels, Spider tosses the coffee cups to the sidewalk and jogs ahead of me, opening my door. I hop in, he slams the door behind me, then runs around to get into the driver's seat.

We pull out of the parking lot, tires squealing.

As we're taking a corner at warp speed, Spider commands, "Talk to me."

"A man followed me into the bookstore. The same man who followed me into the ladies' room at the restaurant the other night. He's here to kill Declan."

Spider takes all that in stride. He simply drives faster, glancing into the rearview mirror. It isn't until I add, "He's Russian. His name is Malek," that he almost drives off the road and up onto the curb.

Narrowly missing driving head-on into a streetlight, he shouts, "Jesus, Mary, and Joseph! *Malek?*"

I take it they're acquainted.

"Bloody hell, Riley! Did he hurt you?"

"No. Please tell me you're not going to turn around and try to kill him."

"As if I could! The bastard's a bloody ghost! He'd have my head on a spike before I knew what hit me!" He stops hollering and looks at me. "Why don't you want me to kill him?"

A very good question, indeed. I rack my brain for a reasonable answer.

"I don't want to be around when anybody kills anybody else, okay?"

It must have sounded sensible enough, because Spider turns his attention back to the road. Tense and glowering, he snaps, "Tell me everything he said to you. At the restaurant and just now. Don't leave out a word. It's important."

I do my best to tell him everything I remember. When I'm finished, he's horrified.

"Christ. *He came into the house?*"

"Yes."

"He could've killed you, lass. He could've strangled you in your sleep!"

I say drily, "Thanks for that. But he didn't hurt me. And I believed him when he said he wouldn't."

"That's daft!"

His outrage makes me feel defensive. "Daft or not, he was actually quite sweet."

Spider almost drives off the road again. He thunders, "*Sweet?* The man's a bloody assassin! He's the most ruthless bastard there is!"

I decide this isn't the time to point out that he's sweet, too, and he also has murder in his job description. "So you've met him before?"

Raking a hand through his hair, Spider huffs in frustration. "No one's met him before. He's like the bogeyman: a nightmare who exists solely by reputation. He's the right hand of the Moscow Bratva king, and the main reason the man rose to power. Malek's extremely talented at removing obstacles."

And by obstacles, he means enemies.

The man who tried to rescue me from a life of prostitution and gently cupped my face in his hand like it was made of porcelain is a Russian assassin of such terrifying reputation, he makes "regular" killers like Spider quake in their boots.

I bury my face in my hands and moan. It makes Spider freak out.

He shouts, "What is it?"

Oh, nothing. I just realized I'm attracted to a killer who walks through locked doors and makes the Terminator look like Britney Spears. This sort of thing happens to me every day. Nothing to see here. No big deal.

"Lass!"

"Please stop shouting at me. I'm having a minor breakdown is all. Last week, I was living my nice quiet life in my nice quiet apartment in San Francisco. Since then, I've discovered that my sister is getting married to the head of the Irish Mob, and that I caught the eye of a notorious Russian assassin whose hobbies include stalking, appearing out of thin air, making wildly incorrect assumptions about people based on their wardrobes, and handing out large quantities of cash to strangers in restrooms. He's also on a mission to kill my future brother-in-law. It's been an eventful few days."

Spider blows out a hard breath. He mutters a series of colorful curses. Then he takes a sharp turn off the two-lane road we're speeding down onto a larger highway.

He's not headed back to the house. "Where are we going?"

"The airport."

"Why?"

He glances at me. His jaw is as hard as his eyes. "When the Hangman discovers where you live, you disappear before he can pay you a visit." With an oath, he corrects himself. "*Another* visit."

He stomps his foot onto the accelerator. We rocket down the highway. He picks up his cell and makes a series of calls, speaking tersely in Gaelic through each one.

While I sit slumped in the passenger seat, replaying everything in my head.

Especially Malek's nickname: the Hangman.

I try hard not to imagine how he got it.

FOURTEEN

MAL

They arrive at the airport burning rubber and screech to a stop outside a hangar.

The blond guard with the spiderweb neck tattoo pulls Riley out of the SUV and drags her across the tarmac by the hand.

They disappear inside the hangar.

Ten minutes later, the hangar doors open. A large white private jet sits inside. The jet's engines roar to life.

It doesn't surprise me they found a pilot on such short notice.

The head of the Irish Mob is a powerful man.

Not that his power will be able to protect him. Nothing on earth can protect him now.

Grinding my teeth, I watch from a distance as the jet pulls out onto the tarmac, turning to head down the main runway and wait for clearance to take off.

I watch it lift into the sky, glinting under the sun as it rises.

I watch it shrink until it's nothing more than a tiny white dot against a vast sea of blue.

All the while, I force myself to breathe deeply to control the raging wildfire of fury burning inside my chest.

The last time I was this enraged was when I learned of Mikhail's death.

This is almost worse. This shock comes with a deep sense of betrayal.

The waif I wanted to help is Declan's sister-in-law. Not a prostitute.

Not his victim. His sister-in-law. *Family.*

Thinking of what I'm going to do next, I feel better.

I suppose it could be called poetic justice. Or serendipity, a word I've always liked. Whatever the name, the result will be identical.

Declan O'Donnell took something from me. It's my turn to take something from him.

By the time the jet starts to taxi down the runway, I've already memorized the tail number and turned away.

FIFTEEN

RILEY

When we arrive in Boston, it's pouring rain. The weather is so bad, the jet has to circle the airport for an hour before we get clearance to land. When we do finally land, it's with a violent jolt that makes me bite my lip so hard, it bleeds.

I try not to take that as a bad omen.

But suddenly, everything feels like a bad omen. From the moment we lifted off in Bermuda, I've had an unshakable feeling of doom.

The brutal turbulence during the flight didn't help. Neither did the flock of geese we murdered on our descent into Boston. I looked out the window and saw a blizzard of feathers and bloody bird parts flying past, and white-knuckled the arms of my seat until we landed.

Now we're here, and Spider's hustling me down the aisle toward the opening cockpit door with such impatience, it would probably be easier if he picked me up and carried me instead.

"Hurry, lass," he urges from behind me, propelling me forward with a hand between my shoulder blades.

"I can't hurry any faster than I already am."

He gives me a gentle shove. "Try."

That he's so nervous makes *me* more nervous. He's the one with the gun!

Outside, another black SUV awaits on the tarmac, engine running. Spider throws his suit jacket over my head to shield me from the downpour, then follows me down the airstairs, right on my heels.

He whisks me into the car, climbs in behind me, and slams shut the door, all with the speed of a tornado.

"Kieran. Good to see you, mate." He nods at the big brute in the driver's seat, wearing a black suit identical to his own.

The brute sends him a chin lift in return. "Spider. Bout ye?"

"Minus craic. You up to date?"

"Aye." He shakes his head. "Declan had a quare gunk when he got yer call."

Spider mutters, "And no wonder. It's bloody ogeous handlin'."

"Desperate altogether."

In the rearview mirror, Kieran glances at me pulling the jacket off my head and around my shoulders, shivering from the cold.

He says, "Hullo, lass."

"Hi, Kieran. I'm Riley. I have no idea what you guys are saying, but it sounds bad."

"'Tis," he replies, nodding. "But don't ye worry. Things'll perk up now that yer not spendin' all yer time with this bleedin' melter."

He jerks his chin again in Spider's direction. Spider says something in Gaelic that sounds unflattering.

They share a wry grin, then we're off, speeding away from the airport like we're being chased by an army of demons.

We drive in silence for about ten minutes until Kieran makes a turn off the road. We're in an industrial area not far from the airport. Huge warehouses line both sides of the street. We pass dozens of them, then slow for a chain-link fence topped with barbed wire that crosses the end of the road.

Kieran punches a code into a small black box on a metal stand beside the roadway. In a moment, the gate rolls to one side, allowing us to pass.

Directly ahead of us is a four-story square redbrick building. It has no windows on the first floor. The windows on the upper floors have iron bars and dark tinting. Smoke billows from three cement stacks on the roof.

It looks creepy, like a crematorium. "What is this place?" I ask Spider.

"A safe house."

He offers nothing more, which I also find creepy. Shouldn't he be reassuring me we'll be safe in the safe house?

Or does he have doubts?

We drive around back, stopping in front of a huge roll-up metal door. Kieran enters a code into another small black box. Mounted on either side of the door near the top are cameras, their red eyes burning.

I notice a curious opening in the center of the wall above the door. It's about three feet long and maybe six inches high. "What's that hole in the wall for?"

Kieran says, "The machine guns. They're remote-controlled. Fifty rounds a second. Press of a button, and there'll be a bloody grand hole in the ground where a trespasser used to be."

When he sees my expression, he chuckles. "Did ye think we'd be tossin' water balloons at our enemies?"

"No, I suppose not." Then I smile. "Though it might be kind of fun to throw them afterward. Go up to the roof and see who can get the most balloons inside the bloody grand hole."

Spider gives me a strange look.

"What?"

"Not much scares you, does it?"

Kieran snorts. "The wee lass takes after her sister, then."

The next person who says I'm like my sister is in danger of losing a testicle.

The door opens, revealing the space inside. The walls are raw brick. The floor is unpolished cement. A single bare bulb hangs from the ceiling.

The entire first floor of the building is empty.

We pull inside and stop in the middle of the space. Kieran puts the truck in park. The metal door we entered through rolls back down, slamming against the concrete with a boom that echoes off the walls. Nothing else happens.

When I look over at Spider, he says, "Wait."

I'm about to ask *for what?* when the ground moves beneath us. With a jolt, the SUV starts to sink. Within seconds, the entire vehicle has sunk below floor level. We're surrounded on all sides by cement block walls.

We're on a hydraulic lift, descending underground.

"Whoa," I say, deeply impressed. "This is some Batman shit right here."

"The living areas are all underground," says Spider.

"What's on the top floors?"

Kieran chuckles. "Lots and lots of ammo."

I exhale and press my fingertips against my closed eyelids.

In a low voice, Spider says, "You don't have to worry. Nothing and no one can get inside this building unless they're invited in."

I bet that's what he thought about the castle in Bermuda, too. "Are Declan and Sloane here?"

"No. They're in New York. They think it's safest if you're not to-gether for the moment."

I drop my hands from my face and look at him. "Safest for me or for them?"

"You, lass. Declan's the one with the target on his back."

Then I hope wherever they're staying in New York is as secure as

Fort Knox. From what Spider told me about Malek, Declan won't be safe anywhere else.

Watching me think, Spider says gently, "Sloane feels awful."

"That she didn't believe me about a man being in the bathroom at the restaurant, you mean."

"Aye. Declan says she's inconsolable. Blames herself for not taking you at your word, how she spoke to you in front of the lads, everything." He pauses. "I'm probably not supposed to tell you that."

I mutter darkly, "Don't worry. I won't ever be speaking to my sister again, so I couldn't repeat it, anyway."

He smiles at me, shaking his head.

"What?"

"The two of you are so much alike."

"Say that again, and I'll make sure you'll never be able to have children."

Kieran snorts. "Yer just provin' his point, lass."

"Oh, no. Don't tell me you're as much of a pain in the ass as he is."

Spider pretends to be hurt. "Oy! I'm sitting right here!"

"Calm down. I called you that already. To your face."

"Aye, but you were joking before."

I say acidly, "Was I?"

Trying not to laugh, Spider pulls his lips between his teeth.

Our descent ends with another jolt. Kieran drives off the pneumatic lift and parks the SUV against a wall, then hops out of the driver's seat. Spider exits, too, coming around my side to open my door. When I step out of the car I see that we're in a small garage area, with parking for maybe a dozen vehicles.

Ours is the only one here.

"This way," says Kieran, holding open a door.

The three of us enter a short, lighted passageway. At the end of it is another door. Kieran enters a code into the keypad on the wall, and the door unlocks.

"Ladies first," says Kieran, gesturing for Spider to proceed ahead of us.

"A pox on your mother, you spanner."

"Shut up about my ma, ya feckin' gobshite, or I'll burst ya."

Their friendly, incomprehensible insults end when I push past both of them through the door. They protest loudly, like I've broken some ancient, ironclad, macho rule.

"We have to clear the place, lass!" says Kieran, all in a huff. "Ye can't just waltz in like the bloody queen!"

"Wait, *what*? You have to clear a safe house?"

"Aye!"

"Then by definition, it's not safe!"

Spider is doing that lip-biting thing again. I know he's thinking that's exactly something my sister would say and send him a look that conveys in no uncertain terms that the wee rabid badger is about to give him a smack.

He holds up his hands in surrender. "I didn't say a word."

"Smart man."

"Wait here a moment, lass. We'll be right back."

"Can you bring me a sandwich when you come back? I'm dying of hunger. I haven't had a proper meal since we met. I've been living on the candy I brought with me."

Kieran is scandalized by that nugget of information. He turns to Spider, aghast. "Are ye tryin' to starve the poor *cailín*?"

"Yeah, Spider. Are you trying to starve me?"

He ignores us both and heads inside, shaking his head.

Kieran watches him go, tutting. "Don't worry, lass. I'll get ye fixed up as soon as we're done sweepin' the place."

"Thank you, Kieran. I knew I liked you from the get-go."

He puffs out his big chest and proudly lifts his chin. "I've been told I'm very likable."

Then he struts off after Spider, leaving me wondering if it was Sloane who told him that.

With the way my luck is running lately, it's probable.

Spider returns in about five minutes, just as I'm about to sit down on the floor. "All clear. In you go."

"Will you give me a tour?"

He looks surprised. "Aye, if you like."

"It's just that I've never been inside a mafia safe house before. Hey, is there cash hidden inside the walls? Gold bars? Drugs?"

He snorts. "No."

I'm oddly disappointed by that.

I follow him inside the place, looking around in curiosity. It's like a regular home inside, only with a lot more bedrooms and no windows.

One other thing I don't see is an exit. "Is that garage the only way in?"

Showing me around the bedroom that will be mine, he says, "There's a tunnel we can use in an emergency. It runs underneath this block and ends on the other side of the industrial park." He turns to look at me. "Why? You gonna threaten to run away again?"

"I'm not running anywhere. I just feel a little claustrophobic not being able to see outside."

"You get used to it after a few weeks."

Hearing that, I start to panic. "*Weeks?* Hold on a minute—are you telling me I'll be stuck in this underground bunker for that long?"

He says gently, "It's not up to me how long you'll be here, lass."

"That's not what I asked!"

"The priority is your safety, whether it takes a few days or a few weeks."

"It?"

His expression darkens. "Dealing with Malek."

From Spider's tone, I get that "dealing" with him won't be pleasant. Or easy.

I remember the look of revulsion in Malek's eyes when I told him who I was, and a shiver of fear goes through me.

Maybe when he said I was in no danger from him, it's because he thought I was a prostitute.

Maybe being Declan's almost sister-in-law changes the game for the worse.

And maybe I should've kept my big fat mouth shut, because maybe the notorious Russian assassin would like to wipe Declan's entire family off the face of the earth.

"Oh, shit," I say, wide-eyed.

Spider frowns. "What is it?"

"Is Malek after Declan for anything in particular?"

When that muscle in Spider's jaw flexes, I know it's going to be bad. But I never could've guessed exactly how bad it would be.

"Aye. Declan killed Malek's brother."

And I'm going to kill my sister for dragging me into all this.

When I only stand there staring at Spider in horror, he takes my shoulders in his hands and says firmly, "You're safe here. Nothing ties this place to Declan. No one knows it exists. You're safe, lass. I promise."

He's convinced what he's saying is true, but there's a worried voice inside my head reminding me that promises are made to be broken.

And in only a few hours, I'll be proven right.

Because I wake up with Malek's huge hand clamped over my mouth and his furious green eyes glaring down into mine.

SIXTEEN

RILEY

*H*ello again, little bird. Make a noise, and I'll break your neck."

The words are spoken in a deadly soft tone that leaves no doubt he won't be giving me another white rose anytime soon.

My heart starts to pound. Cold flashes over me. My entire body detonates with panic.

I lie perfectly still, staring up at him in pure terror, convinced I'm about to die.

Or something less pleasant.

Malek slides his hand down to my throat. When I gasp, he squeezes.

"Go ahead," he whispers, eyes glittering. "Scream. I'll enjoy silencing it."

For whatever reason, instead of scaring me more, that comment royally pisses me off. The icy cold that first gripped me now turns to blistering heat.

"This is where I remind you that you gave me your word you wouldn't hurt me."

My tone is so scathing, it makes him blink. But he recovers quickly, leaning closer until our noses are almost touching.

"I lied."

That makes me even angrier. Seething, I glare at him. "Then you're a piss-poor excuse for a human being. Liars are the worst. You know why? Because they're cowards. Go ahead and kill me, but be prepared for my ghost to haunt you forever. And when I say forever, I mean it literally. I hold grudges like new mothers hold their infants."

His eyes flare. So do his nostrils. He can't believe my nerve.

Neither can I. But apparently, imminent death brings out my inner ninja, who wants to bitch slap everyone in sight.

We breathe angrily at each other until he growls, "You've got a big mouth for such a little thing."

"And you've got a little brain for such a big thing. Even if you do kill me, do you really think you'll get out of this place alive?"

He snaps, "Your bodyguards don't even know I'm here."

"That's what you think. I already hit the panic button next to the bed. You have ten seconds to leave before they charge through the door, guns blazing."

Through gritted teeth, he says, "There's no panic button."

"Guess we'll find out, won't we?"

He makes another growling sound. This one comes from deep within his chest. It's low, rumbling, and dangerous, like the warning of a bear.

He's infuriated by my attitude. But he also isn't strangling me, so I think the sass might be a good distraction.

"How'd you get in here anyway? This place is a fortress."

"Do you always talk this much when you're about to die?"

"Yes. I find pre-death conversation relaxing. Answer the question."

His hand tightening around my throat, he snarls, "You're not in charge here, little bird."

I really wish he didn't smell so good. Or look so good. His attractiveness is unnerving. I gaze up into his blazing green eyes, wondering how it's possible my sister and I have such terrible taste in men.

It's a good thing we never met Ted Bundy. Charismatic, violent killers are apparently our thing.

"I realize I'm not in charge, but I'm curious. You seem to be able to walk through walls."

"Hence the nickname."

"What does the name Hangman have to do with walking through walls?"

He frowns down at me. "My nickname's Ghost."

"That's not what I heard."

He pauses to think. His hand is still wrapped around my throat, but its grip has slackened slightly. "Hangman?"

"Yeah. I figured you must be good with a noose."

"No. I have no idea how to tie that kind of knot."

"Oh."

"But I did once strangle a man with his own intestines."

Feeling queasy, I say, "How creative."

"Thank you. I thought so."

We stare at each other. I become acutely aware of his bulk hovering over me, of the heat of his skin burning through his clothing, of the feel of his rough hand on my neck.

"Ten seconds are up. Where are your bodyguards?"

When I don't respond, he leans close to my ear and says, "Who's the liar now?"

His voice is low and husky, and his wild, woodsy scent is in my nose. An involuntary shudder runs through me. I close my eyes and moisten my lips, desperate to pull myself together.

"You're right. There's no panic button. But I'll still haunt you forever if you kill me."

"People don't come back from the grave."

"You have no idea how stubborn I am."

He turns his head, and his beard tickles my cheek. Looking into my eyes, he presses his thumb against the throbbing pulse in my throat, then doesn't do anything for several seconds.

I think he's counting my heartbeats.

He could also be deciding where to bury my body.

"Why aren't you afraid of me?"

"I am afraid of you."

He examines my expression. "Not very much."

"Does that insult your ego?"

He makes a motion with his head that's not a *yes* or a *no,* but more like a *maybe.*

"If it will keep you from killing me, I'll act very scared. I'll cry and everything."

He's starting to look frustrated. "That's exactly what I'm talking about."

"I can't help it. I really did believe you when you said I wasn't in danger from you." I think for a beat. "I mean, mostly. You are pretty scary. And very large. And Spider almost shit himself when I told him I saw you in the bookstore."

"Spider's the blond bodyguard who was with you?"

"Yeah. Oh—can I ask you a favor? Will you please not hurt him? Kieran, either. He's the other bodyguard. The bigger one. They're both really nice."

Malek stares at me in disbelief.

"Sorry. Is that asking too much? It's just that I'd never get over it if they got hurt because of me. They're only trying to do their jobs."

After a moment, he says angrily, "You know who I am. You know what I do. Correct?"

"Yes. I've been filled in on the particulars."

"And you're lying there with my hand around your neck asking me not to hurt your bodyguards."

He says it like my sanity is in question. "I know it's maybe a little unorthodox."

"No," he says flatly.

"Please?"

He growls, "What the fuck is wrong with you?"

"There's no need to get testy."

"Testy?"

"I'm just saying. You don't have to get all mad about it."

Furious again, he glares at me, grinding his jaw and probably calculating how much pressure it will take to snap the brittle bird bones in my neck.

Before he does, I say, "I also want to thank you for the rose you left me. That was really nice. I've never had a man bring me flowers before. I know it was only the one, and also you thought I was a captive prostitute at the time, but still. It was thoughtful. So thank you."

He stares at me with an expression somewhere between confusion and amazement, with a healthy dose of disgust on the side.

"Now is probably a good time to remind you that I'm still the same person you left the rose for. So if you did kill me, you'd be killing her, too. Just a thought."

"Are you on drugs?"

"Not at the moment, no. Why, do you have any?"

"There's something wrong with you. Mentally. Right?"

That makes me laugh. "Oh, totally. I've got more than a few screws loose. At least that's what my dad tells me. But he's super uptight, zero imagination, so his opinion doesn't really count. Not that he's wrong, because he isn't, but normies shouldn't judge creatives. They just have no idea how we're wired. Why are you looking at me like that?"

"I've never had a conversation with an insane person before."

"Very funny."

"It wasn't a joke."

"Ouch."

We stare at each other in silence. His hostile, mine hopeful.

He still hasn't murdered me, so things are looking up.

"Malek?"

"What." He says it flatly. With dread.

"Thank you for not killing me."

He says emphatically, "Don't thank me yet."

"You're still deciding?"

"If only to get you to shut up, yes."

"In that case . . ." I make a zipper motion across my lips.

He watches with outrage, astonishment, and absolute disbelief.

"Actually, before I shut up, I also want to say that it was really sweet that you tried to save me from being a sex worker. I mean, what a gentleman! A gentleman killer who gives strangers big wads of cash in restrooms. You're quite the puzzle, Mr. Ghost. Or is it just Ghost? I'm never sure how the nickname thing works, except between me and my sister, but that doesn't count because my whole family is a little weird. I'll just call you Malek, if that's all right. Or Mal for short, since we're such buds now, what with you breaking into my various bedrooms for midnight visits and all. Okay, I'm shutting up now. Here I go."

I press my lips together and gaze up at him, watching him struggle with dueling urges to cut off my air supply or break something over my head.

Maybe he's right about me being insane, because rather than terrifying, I find his indecision understandable.

He's not the first man I've driven to the brink of murder.

He's just the most capable of actually going through with it.

"Oh, one more thing—"

"I know a way to keep that mouth quiet," he snaps. Then he kisses me.

SEVENTEEN

MAL

She sucks in a shocked breath through her nose. Her entire body stiffens. She's frozen for a split second.

Until the freeze thaws, and the claws come out. She bites my lip. Hard.

Cursing, I jerk away. She glares up at me, pushing against my chest with all her might, trying to shove me off.

I don't budge. Instead, I clamp a hand around her jaw and kiss her again.

She writhes beneath me, making angry sounds, fighting. Not giving in or opening her mouth.

I'm surprised at the resistance. She doesn't look strong enough to stand upright in a brisk breeze.

I'm even more surprised when she yanks at my hair, scratching my scalp with her nails. Underneath all this anger is attraction, however, which is the real turn-on.

I pull away, chuckling. "My little bird has claws."

"Call me a bird one more time, and I'll—"

"What?" I demand, pressing my chest to hers so I feel her heart pounding right through my shirt. "You'll do what? Shoot me? Stab me? Drown me in a sea of words?"

"Fuck you."

"Is that an invitation?"

"You wish, you arrogant prick!" She's so mad, she's almost spitting.

I like this side of her. This feisty, angry side. It's so rare that someone challenges me.

"Careful," I whisper, brushing my lips against hers. "Combat makes my dick hard."

She stops fighting me instantly. But not a single ounce of her anger fades. She lies beneath me, breathing raggedly, glaring murder into my face. Her lips are pressed together so tightly, they're white.

It's disarmingly cute. Like a furious kitten, all puffy tail and tiny hisses.

No—we're enemies. I can't let myself get distracted. I'm already distracted. Fuck.

So improvise. You're good at that. Kill two birds with one stone.

Gazing deep into her eyes so she can see I'm serious, I say, "Open your mouth for me, or I'll shoot both your bodyguards."

She snaps, "I thought you wanted me to keep my mouth shut."

"Let's try this again, smartass. Let me kiss you, or two men die. Choose. Now."

"That's blackmail."

"Yes. I told you I'm a bad person. Choose."

She's so furious, she's trembling. If she had lasers in her eyes, my head would explode.

My dick and I are both really enjoying this.

"How do I know you won't shoot them anyway?"

"You don't. One more question, though, and I will."

She's getting desperate. I see her struggling to find a way out of this, to find an escape, and almost laugh out loud when I finally see her give in.

She licks her lips, then says defiantly, "Fine. Kiss me. But I won't like it."

Challenge accepted.

Instead of pressing my lips to hers, I turn her head and run the tip of my nose along her jaw. Beneath her ear, I inhale. Then I kiss her there, my mouth barely brushing her skin.

I have to suppress a chuckle when she shivers.

I think I might've been going about this revenge business all wrong.

"One more thing. You have to kiss me back. Lie there like a cold fish, and your friend Spider eats a bullet."

"I take back what I said about you being a gentleman."

"I'll burst into tears over that right after you *give me your fucking mouth.*"

She inhales, closing her eyes and swallowing. When she opens her eyes again, I know it's war.

I've seen hardened killers look less psychotic. My smile makes her gnash her teeth. "Ready?"

"Go to hell."

"Can't. The devil has a restraining order against me."

"That's not even original! I saw it on a T-shirt once!"

"You want original?" I put my mouth close to her ear and growl, "I want to impale you on my cock. I also want to wring your neck. I'll settle for a kiss, instead."

She mutters, "I can't believe I didn't let Spider shoot you when I had the chance."

Ignoring that, I press my lips to hers.

It's gentle, not hard like the first time. A warm, lingering touch, mouth closed. I do it again, brushing our lips together lightly.

She wasn't expecting gentleness. I can tell because she stares up at me, startled.

"Close your eyes. Unclench your hands from my hair. And get your knee out of my ribs."

"How many more rules will there be for this one kiss?"

"Do it. Now."

She does everything I asked. Grudgingly. Then, when I only stay still, staring at her sweet mouth, she whispers, "Hurry up and get it over with."

Her voice trembles.

I know it's not from fear.

I also know the way to deal with her isn't with brute force.

She won't respond to that. It'll only make her fight harder.

This girl needs to be teased open. Unfurled slowly, one petal at a time.

I gently kiss one corner of her mouth. Then the other. Then I softly kiss her nose and chin.

"What the hell are you doing?"

"Kissing you. Shut up."

She makes an aggravated noise, which I ignore. Trailing my lips down the side of her neck, I pause to press another gentle kiss to the pulse throbbing there. I stroke the tip of my tongue along it.

A fine tremor runs through her chest. She says my name breathlessly.

I ignore that as well.

Nuzzling my nose into the curve where her neck meets her shoulder makes her shudder. I inhale deeply against her skin. She smells so sweet, I want to bite her.

So I do.

"Malek!"

"The sooner you stay quiet, the sooner this will be over. Keep interrupting me, and I'll make this kiss last all night long."

Which, now that I think of it, might not be a bad idea.

She's breathing hard now. Tense and trembling beneath me. I know exactly why she wants me to stop. It's the same reason I won't.

She likes the feel of my mouth on her skin. And I like how much she hates that she likes it.

I kiss a soft trail along her clavicle to her shoulder, nosing the neckline of her white cotton T-shirt aside to get there. I kiss my way back and dip my tongue into the dent at the base of her throat.

"Please. Stop. Stop this."

Her voice is hoarse. Her whole body trembles. I feel like someone just lit me on fire.

"You want Spider to die?"

"I just want this to be over."

"It will be."

"When?"

"Soon enough."

When she opens her mouth to protest, I slide my thumb inside it and growl, "Suck on that, or I'll give you something to choke on."

Her teeth press down hard against my finger. I fist my other hand into her hair.

"Draw blood, and I'll make Spider's death last a few weeks."

She makes an angry noise, staring up at me in fury.

"You want this to be over? Close your eyes. And suck."

Our eyes clash. She doesn't obey me immediately, so I wait to see what she'll decide.

I know full well that the bite of an adult human can cause massive destruction to a finger. Possibly even sever it. She'd do damage to her teeth and jaw, but I doubt she'd care.

I don't care, either. It would be worth losing a finger just for this look on her face.

Finally, she closes her eyes. She exhales a short, angry breath through her nose.

When she starts to suck on my thumb, my already-hard dick throbs in response.

I lower my head and kiss her throat, licking and nipping at it.

She moans around my thumb.

That sound shoots an arrow of heat straight through my body, right down to my balls. I've never heard anything sexier.

She's your enemy. Enemy! Remember?

My brain keeps trying to tell me that, but my dick has other ideas about our relationship.

Other, very strong ideas.

I remove my thumb from her mouth and replace it with my tongue.

She forgets she hates me kissing her and arches into me with a sigh, opening her mouth to kiss me back passionately.

She's all heat and shivering nerves, pounding pulse and hunger. If her earlier angry resistance surprised me, the way she responds when she's aroused surprises me even more.

She's needy. Greedy. Almost as much as I am.

The kiss grows deeper and hotter. We're both breathing hard. I'm starting to sweat. I love the way her mouth feels. The sweet, soft heat. Her warm lips. I love the way she clings to me with her body curved and both hands dug into my hair.

I love the feel of her hard nipples against my chest.

I want to feel them against my bare skin, not through my shirt. I want to suck on them, bite them, pinch them until she begs me to fuck her.

And I do want to fuck her.

I want to fuck her hard and deep. I want to make her claw my back and come for me. I want to make her scream my name until she's hoarse. I want—

SHE'S YOUR ENEMY!

I jerk away and stare down at her, trying to catch my breath. Trying to clear my head of the searing images of her naked and moaning underneath me, her breasts bouncing against my chest, her slender legs wound around my waist as I thrust deep inside her body.

Her eyes drift open.

She gazes up at me with a soft, hazy look, blinking slowly like she has no idea where she is. Her face is flushed. Her lips are wet. She whispers my name.

Whispers it so sweetly, it makes me want to break something. Declan O'Donnell murdered my brother.

One of her family killed one of mine.

I should be anywhere else on earth but in this room with this woman.

My voice comes out thick. "Tell anyone I was here, and they die."

I rise from the bed and leave.

EIGHTEEN

RILEY

From one second to the next, he disappears, leaving me alone in the room.

Alone and shaking badly.

I sit up in bed and reach for my glasses on the nightstand. When I get them on, I look around the room in disbelief. It's exactly the same as it was when I went to sleep.

Except now it smells like big, rugged male and unresolved sexual tension.

I rip off the glasses, turn over, bury my face into the pillow, and scream.

It doesn't help. I still want him.

Him, the assassin who's going to kill Declan. Him, the asshole who threatened to kill me.

Him, the killer, stalker, walk-through-solid-walls son of a bitch who touches me like I'm made of glass and kisses like he's starving.

Man, I thought I had a messed-up romantic life before, but this is some next-level shit right here.

Rolling back over, I shove my glasses on again and rise from bed. Heart hammering, I open the door and peek out into the hallway. It's dark and silent. All is still.

Oh, god—what if it's so still because Spider and Kieran are already dead?

With a strangled sound of horror, I tear down the hallway into the main living area. It's dark in here, too, but there's a blue glow from a cable box near the TV that lets me see where I'm going. I run into the kitchen and hit the lights, expecting to see a trail of blood on the floor or bloody handprints or brain matter decorating the walls.

When I find neither, I stop to drag in a breath. I lean against the counter, bracing myself to go search the rest of the bedrooms. Preparing myself mentally to deal with whatever carnage I might find.

"What's the craic, lass?"

I jump, scream, and whirl around.

Spider stands in the doorway of the kitchen, blinking sleepily.

His white dress shirt is rolled up his forearms and open at the throat. His jaw is shadowed with stubble. His hair is mussed.

There are no visible bullet holes in him.

I'm so relieved, I nearly slide to the floor. Instead, I press a hand over my thundering heart and start laughing weakly.

He frowns.

"Sorry. God, I'm so sorry, I just . . . I thought . . ."

"Tell anyone I was here, and they die."

Recalling Malek's warning, I swallow nervously and avert my eyes. "Um. I was hungry."

"Hungry," he repeats suspiciously, looking me up and down.

I make my voice firm, stand straighter, and manage to look him in the eye. "Yep. Starving, in fact."

"You had a big meal not three hours ago."

Shit. He would have to remember what time it was when I scarfed down my dinner.

"Don't shame me for having a hearty appetite, Spider. I like to eat." I saunter over to the fridge, pull open the door, and stare inside.

This is when I realize that all I'm wearing is the short T-shirt and white cotton undies I went to bed in.

White cotton undies that are probably soaked right through.

I shut the fridge door, turn around, fold my hands in front of my crotch, and force a smile. "On second thought, I think I'll go back to bed. It's never a good idea to go to sleep on a full stomach. See you in the morning."

I walk back to my room as casually as I can, feeling Spider's gaze on me the whole time.

I can't go back to sleep. I lie there for hours in the dark, staring at the ceiling, starting at every little noise, expecting Malek to appear out of thin air at any moment.

Appear and kill me. Or kiss me again. It's a coin toss at this point.

In the morning, I'm dragging ass. I shower and dress in the same clothes I wore yesterday, because they're the only ones I have with me. There are things in the closet, clothes left over from whoever might have stayed here before, but they're all too big and smell like cigarettes.

I don't know if I can face Spider's too-knowing eyes again, so I stay in my room most of the day. Kieran knocks on the door in the afternoon, bringing a tray of food. When he asks how I'm doing, I don't lie.

"I feel like I've been run over by a truck."

His smile is warm and understanding. "It'll be all right, lass. Try not to worry. If ye like, I'll be happy to bring ye a wee nip of whiskey. That always helps set my head straight."

He's so nice. Him and Spider both.

I really hope Malek doesn't kill them.

"Thanks, Kieran. But I think I'd rather keep my head sharp, if you know what I mean. This situation is constantly evolving."

He nods. "Aye. Is there anything else you need?"

"Clothes. My computer. A frontal lobotomy."

Chuckling, he says, "I can help with the first two, lass. Yer on yer own with the third."

"You can get my laptop? I left it in Bermuda."

"The lads have cleared out the house and vehicles. They'll make a stop here tonight on their way to Declan."

"Have you heard from him? Is he okay?"

If my tone is too tight with worry, Kieran doesn't notice. His shrug is nonchalant.

"He's right as rain. Musterin' the troops, makin' plans. You know. Boss business."

I hope that "boss business" includes wearing full-body armor and a bulletproof helmet at all times, but I don't say that out loud.

Kieran leaves. I eat the food he brought me. I pace. I struggle with the idea of telling him and Spider that Malek broke in, but can't decide if that bastard assassin would know if I blabbed.

What if he bugged my room?

Or the whole safe house, for that matter? What if he installed secret cameras? What if he can transport himself telepathically and overhear everything that's going on in here?

I can't discount the possibility. He seems capable of anything.

Ultimately, I decide not to say a word. I refuse to be responsible for anyone getting hurt. Malek might hurt them anyway, but I don't have control over that. I don't want it to be because he told me not to do something, and I didn't listen.

He seems like the kind of man disobedience greatly displeases.

Around nine o'clock, Spider knocks on my door.

"Hey," I say when I open up. "How are you?"

He gazes at me for a silent beat before saying, "Grand. You?"

"Same."

"Got your bag. Laptop, too." He lifts my duffel. "Where should I put it?"

"Oh, great! On the desk is fine, thanks."

I open the door wide and let him in. He's dressed in his immaculate suit and tie, not a hair out of place, and his angular jaw is clean-shaven. I guess Declan has a dress code for these guys, because black Armani is all they ever wear.

He sets the duffel bag on the desk and turns back to me. Then he just stands there silently, looking uncomfortable. "What's up?"

"I think I owe you an apology."

That catches me completely off guard. I look at him with my eyebrows lifted. "Me? Why?"

He shifts his weight from foot to foot, clears his throat, then glances at the door. "For catching you last night in the kitchen in your kex. You seemed awful embarrassed."

I get that "kex" must mean underwear and feel relieved.

Unless it means "soaking wet underwear," in which case I'm fucking mortified.

My laugh is small and nervous "It's, um . . . no biggie."

He glances back at me. The tips of his ears turn red. "I didn't see anything, if that's what you're worried about." After a short pause, he corrects himself. "I mean, I didn't see much."

I slap a hand over my eyes. "Jesus. Could you make this any more painful?"

"I'm sorry."

"Apology accepted. Now please go, so I can die of shame by myself."

"You've got nothing to be ashamed of, lass."

His voice has gained a husky, unfamiliar edge. I think he's trying to compliment me.

And now my ears are red, too.

I slide my hand from my eyes down to my mouth. I stare at him in silence. Then I drop my hand to my side and sigh. "Well. Thank you. I think. Can we please never talk about this again?"

He runs a hand over his hair. "Aye." He turns to leave, but turns back at the door. "Your sister wants to speak with you. She asked me to have you call her."

"Tell my sister that I'd rather eat a shit sandwich than talk to her."

He presses his lips together to keep from laughing and nods. "Will do."

"And stop thinking that we're alike. We're nothing alike."

He holds my gaze, looking like he's arguing with himself over something. Finally, he says, "No, you're not. Except for that lion's blood that runs in the family."

I say quietly, "Thank you for that. But I'm not a lion. Compared to her, I'm . . . a cub."

"A baby lion is still a lion."

After a moment of awkward silence, he turns and walks out.

I become more determined than ever that if it's within my power, I won't let Malek hurt him.

Spider will make someone a very good partner one day. He doesn't deserve to get shot on babysitting duty for his boss's fiancée's dorky younger sister.

I work on my laptop for a few hours until I get sleepy. I dig the final box of Twizzlers from my bag and eat the whole thing. Then I take a shower, standing under the hot spray for a long time, thinking about everything that's happened since I left San Francisco. Thinking about what I'll say to Malek when I see him next time.

Because I know there will be a next time. I know it in my bones.

Whatever's happening between us is unresolved. I know he

wants to hate me, and maybe part of him does. But there's another part of him that doesn't.

Judging by last night, that part of him is in his pants.

And I don't know what to do about any of it. This entire situation is so far out of my league, I can hardly think straight.

I'm just an introvert who loves books, candy, and arguing with strangers on the internet. My idea of excitement is starting a new Netflix series. I live in one of the most exciting cities in the world, yes, but everyone I hang out with is about as thrilling as stale bread.

They're computer geeks. Video game addicts. Coffee shop philosophers with man buns, degrees in the arts, and maybe an extra set of genitals.

Okay, that part's exciting, but you get my point. There are no gangsters in my world.

There are no guns, violence, safe houses, or private jets. Most importantly, there are no large, terrifying, beautiful Russian assassins with vengeance on their minds breaking into my bedroom at all hours of the night to overpower me with testosterone and kiss me to within an inch of my life.

I don't know what to do.

If I called one of my friends and told them the story of the past week, they'd ask me why I was hoarding my Molly and demand I send them some.

No one would believe it.

I don't believe it. What I need is a plan.

Though I hate to even think like this, that's what Sloane would do. She'd assess the situation and make a plan. A plan that would crush the competition and leave a smoking path of destruction in her wake.

The only smoking path of destruction I've managed to create so far has been in my underpants when Malek was kissing me.

By the time I step out of the shower, I'm a prune. I still don't have a strategy. I towel dry my hair and body, then wrap the towel around myself and brush my teeth.

Then I wipe a clear circle in the steam on the mirror over the sink and almost die of a heart attack.

Malek towers behind me, pale eyes burning under lowered brows.

NINETEEN

RILEY

*M*y reaction is pure instinct.

I whirl around and slap him across the face.

It doesn't budge him. He simply stands there and smolders. "It's good to see you, too, Riley Rose."

The husky tone of his voice suggests he's seen quite a lot of me, most likely as I was coming out of the shower.

Heat pulses in my cheeks. Furious, I slap him again, this time with all my strength.

He licks his lips and says hotly, "What did I tell you about combat making my dick hard?"

He yanks me against his chest, fists a hand into my wet hair, and kisses me.

This is no sweet soft kiss, like last night. This is ravaging. Demanding. *Owning.* As much a claim as anything else, a cocksure declaration that he can come and go as he pleases and there's not a damn thing anyone—including me—can do about it.

I've never been so angry in my life.

"You smug son of a bitch!" I hiss, breaking away from his mouth.
"Get out!"

"If that's what you want."

"It is!"

"All right. But I'll be taking a few dead bodies with me."

"You know what? Go ahead and kill me! At least then I won't
have to deal with you anymore."

"I wasn't talking about you, little bird. I'll keep you alive so you
can watch me toss all your bodyguards' corpses into a big pile and
light it on fire."

Breathing hard and shaking, I glare at him, my hands flattened
over his massive chest. I try to shove him away, but it's like trying
to move a house.

"You're a monster."

"Yes."

"Let me go."

Gazing down at me with half-lidded eyes, he licks his lips.

His voice turns husky. "If I let you go, the towel goes, too."

"I hate you!"

"Understandable."

"You're an asshole!"

"Guilty."

All this agreeing with me he's doing is driving me mad. "Yesterday, you threatened to kill me."

"I decided there are other things I'd like to do to you first." The
tone of his voice leaves no question about his meaning.

"That's just . . . argh! You're a sick, twisted—"

"Blah, blah, blah, yes. Whatever other bad names you're about
to call me, yes, you're right." His voice drops. "Now give me that
fucking mouth again. It's all I've been able to think about for the
last twenty-four hours."

He lowers his head so our faces are an inch apart. His blazing
gaze burns into mine.

"And kiss me like you mean it or the body count starts."

After that, he does nothing. He simply remains still, staring into my eyes with one hand fisted in my hair at the scruff of my neck and his strong arm wound around my back, pinning me against him.

He's waiting for me to kiss him, the bastard!

My whisper is vehement. "I don't want to kiss you."

"If I put my hand between your legs right now, I could prove you a liar."

NASA must be able to hear me grinding my teeth in anger all the way into outer space.

I mean, he's right, but I'd rather die than admit it. I bypass his comment instead.

"Fine. I'll kiss you. After that, you'll leave?"

"No. I just won't kill anyone. Tonight."

I blow out a hard breath and close my eyes. "How do I know you won't change your mind?"

"I give you my word."

"You gave me your word you wouldn't hurt me, too. Since then, you've threatened to kill me several times."

"That was before I knew who you were."

I open my eyes and look at him. "I'm the exact same person."

"Not to me."

I take a moment to examine his expression, then say, "This isn't a plea for my life. I know you wouldn't care about that. But let's be clear about this: I just met Declan. I haven't seen my sister in three years. I have nothing to do with the Irish Mob. I had nothing to do with what happened to your brother."

"Maybe not. But if anything happens to you, your sister will blame herself. Then she'll blame Declan. Then his life will be miserable. I want him to be miserable for a while before I kill him. I want him to be so fucking miserable, he wishes he were never born."

I think for a moment, then admit reluctantly, "Your logic doesn't suck."

"Thank you."

"But you really expect me to kiss you still? With my own death hanging over my head?"

"You seemed very capable of it last night."

His eyes burn so hotly, I have to look away. He grasps my jaw and turns my face back to his. "Convince me not to kill you. Kiss me like your life is on the line. Because it is."

"Are you *trying* to make me hate you? Spoiler alert: it's working."

His eyes flash. He growls, "My patience is wearing thin."

My heart beats like a hammer. My face is flushed. My stomach is clenched and my chest is tight, and if I had a gun in my hand right now, I'd shove it under his chin and pull the trigger.

Staring up into his eyes, I say very deliberately, "I'm only doing this for Kieran and Spider. And don't forget what I said about my ghost coming back to haunt you. If you don't like this kiss, and I die because of it, I'll haunt your arrogant ass until the end of time."

Then I go up on my toes and kiss him.

He opens his mouth with a moan and kisses me back with a vengeance.

I guess vengeance is like his whole thing.

Though I initiated the kiss, he takes over within seconds. Curling his hand around my throat, he tilts my head back with his other hand and drinks deep from my mouth, holding my head in place as I cling to him, desperate not to make the small noises of pleasure building in my chest.

I have to remind myself as he sweeps his tongue against mine that this is for Spider. It's for Kieran. It's for me, too, but I'm pretty much already dead, anyway.

Second by second, this kiss is killing me. Whenever he decides to end it, I'll slide to the floor and expire at his feet.

Maybe that's been his plan all along. This is how he'll murder me.

Death by estrogen overload.

"You taste so fucking sweet," he rasps, breaking away. He's breathing as hard as I am.

I say faintly, "It's the Twizzlers. Are we done?"

"Not a goddamn chance."

He kisses me again, fitting his mouth to mine, letting go of my neck to dig both his big hands into my hair. He presses against me and takes my mouth so ravenously, I'm bent back over the sink. I have to wind my arms up around his shoulders for balance.

We stand like that, mouths fused, pressed together from crotch to chest, kissing and kissing and kissing until I'm dizzy and my knees are shaking and I'm about to pass out.

Then he sweeps me up into his arms and carries me out of the bathroom.

I panic as he approaches the bed. "What are you doing?"

"Anything I want."

The only light in the room is from the bathroom, but it's enough for me to see the intense expression of hunger on his face.

Holy shit. I'm about to be devoured.

The worst part is, I know the only thing I could do to stop it—namely, screaming for Spider and Kieran—is also what would end their lives.

On the verge of hysteria, I say, "Please don't hurt me. I'd rather you killed me, instead."

He knows exactly what I mean.

"If I were going to fuck you, little bird, I wouldn't have to force myself on you. I'd make you beg for it. And you would."

I go from horror to fury in two seconds flat. "You're insane!"

"We've already established that you're the crazy one. I'm the monster, remember?"

He drops me onto the bed. I gasp and clutch the towel closer to my chest, then scramble sideways, trying not to flash my vadge at him in the process.

Malek sits on the edge of the bed and drags me back to him.

He leans over me and plants his hands on either side of my head, pinning me in place.

Wide-eyed and hyperventilating, I shrink into the mattress.

We stay like that for a while, until I realize he's waiting for me to calm down. I take a few deep breaths, watching him warily, wondering what he'll do next.

"Better?" he says.

"No."

"Yes, you are. You want me to tell you to kiss me again."

"I can't believe you have the nerve to call *me* crazy."

Ignoring that, he says, "You also want me to tell you to spread your legs."

My face goes hot. "You're disgusting."

"So I can put my face between your thighs and relieve that ache with my tongue."

A vivid picture of him doing just that appears in my mind, affecting my entire nervous system. My heartbeat goes haywire. My mouth goes dry. I suck in a sharp breath, trembling.

He sees the effect his words have on me and leans close to my ear. His tone is low and gravelly.

"Say please, and I will."

I can't speak. I can only shake my head and pray that he gets bored of this game. Gets bored and disappears, this time forever.

He presses the softest of kisses to my throat, then whispers, "Say please. Let me taste you."

Giving me a little preview of his skill, he takes my earlobe between his warm soft lips, and sucks on it.

Blistering heat flashes over my body. A faint moan slips from my mouth. My nipples harden, and my brain starts screaming *Please!* repetitively. I bite my lip so it doesn't come out.

Then Kieran bursts through the bedroom door and everything goes to hell in a handbasket.

TWENTY

MAL

As always in a gunfight, things happen fast.

The bodyguard makes his first tactical mistake by not hitting the lights. If he did, it would've temporarily blinded me. But my eyes are adjusted to the dark, and his aren't.

Also, he's standing in the middle of the doorway, outlined in light from the hall.

He couldn't have made himself a better target if he'd tried. I get off the first shot.

He drops to a knee and fires back.

He misses. The slug embeds itself into the drywall over my shoulder.

I'm aware of Riley screaming, but block it out, concentrating on the bodyguard. I plug him with two more rounds before he's down, coughing up blood.

The blond bodyguard with the spiderweb neck tattoo appears in the doorway. He's crouched low, weapon at the ready, finger on the trigger. I expect to feel a bullet rip through me somewhere, but movement from my right distracts me.

It's Riley.

Jumping in front of me. Screaming, "No!"

There's a split second of confusion where I don't understand what's happening. *What is she doing? Why isn't she staying on the bed?*

Then a shot rings out. Her body jerks. She slams back against me with a cry, then drops to the floor at my feet and lies there, unmoving.

The bodyguard crouched in the doorway stares at her in blank, white-faced horror.

The moment of confusion clears, and I understand what happened.

She just took the bullet meant for me.

Deliberately.

Howling rage burns through my soul. A roar of fury rips from my chest. I step over Riley, gun pointed at the guard's head, but stop short when she groans.

"No, Mal. Please. Don't hurt him."

The guard is frozen in place. He can't look away from Riley. He's still holding his gun out, but his eyes are wide and unblinking, focused on her.

I've seen this before, this type of disbelief. It's a kind of denial so powerful, it can shut down a man's entire nervous system.

His brain is refusing to acknowledge what he's done. His whole being has become nonoperational. I could empty an entire magazine into his chest and he wouldn't even blink.

"Mal. Please."

It's weak. The barest of whispers.

But hearing it, hearing the way she says my name, takes just enough edge off my murderous impulse to rip the guard to pieces with my bare hands.

I bludgeon him with my gun, instead.

He topples sideways with a grunt, blood pouring from his temple.

I turn around, pick Riley up, and cradle her motionless body against my chest as I walk out the door.

TWENTY-ONE

DECLAN

When I answer the phone, Spider is in such a state of distress, I can't understand a word he's saying.

All I hear is a garbled mess of English and Gaelic, shouted at high speed.

"Calm down, mate. You're not making any sense. What's happened?"

He drags in great gulps of air, then produces a single word that raises all the hair on the back of my neck.

"Malek."

Bloody hell.

From where I'm sitting in the leather chair in the living room of the safe house in Manhattan, I can see Sloane making herself a drink. Standing in the dining room pouring whiskey into a crystal highball glass, she looks preoccupied. Worried.

Knowing that overhearing this conversation will make that look worsen, I rise and walk quickly into the bedroom.

As soon as I'm out of earshot, I demand, "Tell me."

After listening for less than thirty seconds, I'm so angry, I could crush the phone in my fist.

Through clenched teeth, I say, *"How the fuck did he get in?"*

"I don't know. We were locked down. None of the alarms went off. He's a bloody ghost, that one."

"Kieran?"

"Down. Shot three times. Still breathing, but it doesn't look good." He pauses to gulp more air. "There's more. It's bad."

I brace myself for the worst, which is exactly what I get. "Before that Russian bastard ran off with Riley . . . I . . ." His voice breaks. "I accidentally shot her. It was meant for him, but she got in the way."

Breath rushes out of my lungs in an audible whoosh. My life flashes in front of my eyes.

When Sloane finds out about this, we're all dead. Kieran, Spider, the entire crew.

Me included.

I manage to ask, "Is she alive?"

"I don't know. It was dark. Fuck, boss, I'm so sorry. I'm killing myself over it."

I can hear the truth of that in the absolute misery in his voice, but his guilt will have to wait for later. There are far more important matters to deal with first. I blow out a hard breath and snap into command mode.

"Get Kieran to the hospital. When he's set, review the cameras. See if you can find out how that son of a bitch got in. Then clear out and burn it. Understood?"

"Aye."

"I'll call you in two hours. Don't speak to anyone else until then."

I disconnect just as Sloane is walking in. She takes one look at my face and says, "Oh, fuck."

It's both a blessing and a curse that she can read me so easily.

Slipping my cell into my pocket, I walk toward her slowly, holding her worried gaze. "What I'm going to tell you will be upsetting. You should sit down."

She shoots the whiskey instead. "Fuck sitting, gangster. I think better on my feet."

I reach for her, but she puts a hand up to stop me. "Just give it to me straight. What is it?"

I draw a slow breath, longing to take her in my arms and tell her a pretty lie, but knowing it would only make her angry.

Keeping my voice even, I say, "Malek found the safe house in Boston. He broke in. Gunfire was exchanged. He got away . . . and took Riley with him."

Sloane's face drains of blood. She stands unmoving, the pulse throbbing wildly in the side of her neck. She says slowly, "Took. Her."

Fuck, it's so hard not to pull her into my arms. "Aye."

"Where?"

"We don't know yet. But we'll find her." I pause to let that sink in, then say gently, "She's been injured, love. Shot."

Sloane drops the empty glass and covers her mouth with both hands.

I can't help it now. I have to touch her. I grab her and hold her tight, wrapping my arms around her back and lowering my head so I can speak urgently into her ear.

"I don't know how bad it is, but we'll find her. I promise you. We'll do whatever it takes."

She trembles in my arms, breathing erratically. I think she might be going into shock.

Until she pulls away abruptly and pins me with a death glare. "You also promised me she'd be safe in that safe house! So no more promises, okay? What's the game plan? How are we going to find her? How are we going to get her back? What specifically are we going to *do*?"

This is one of the many reasons I love this woman. This clear-headedness. This grace under pressure. This absolute, no bullshit, fearless badassery.

I almost feel sorry for Malek.

If my queen ever gets her hands on him, he'll wish he were never born.

"I'll put the word out. Offer money. A lot of it. If anyone's seen or heard anything, I'll know fast. The major transportation hubs will be monitored. If he tries to take her through an airport or a bus terminal, he'll be stopped. And I'll call Grayson as soon as we're done talking."

Grayson is my handler in the FBI. If anyone's going to be able to discover where a notorious Russian assassin is circulating in the U.S., it's him.

Sloane swallows. She nods slowly. She moistens her lips.

Then she says something that enrages me.

"I'll call Stavros to see if he knows anything."

"Absofuckinglutely not!"

When she only stands there looking at me with watering eyes, I feel like an arsehole and lower my voice. "He's attempted to kill me twice in the last month."

"He hasn't succeeded. And you know he won't, no matter how many times he tries. The man has only ever shot at fish. He's never hit any of those, either. He's completely incompetent at murder."

"He's also obsessed with you."

"Exactly. He's our best bet."

"I'll call Kazimir. He'll know more than your gobshite ex–boy toy."

"Kage is your enemy. He hates the Irish. He won't tell you shit."

She's probably right about that, but the bastard still owes me a favor. I had his FBI file erased, for fuck's sake.

She adds, "Unless I call Nat first."

"I don't think it's necessary to get her involved."

Ignoring my comment, she thinks for a moment, then nods, as if she's made a decision. "She's known Riley since she was a baby. She'll want to help. And if anybody can make Kage talk to you, it's her."

Without waiting for me to answer, she whips her cell out of the pocket of her jeans and dials her girlfriend.

I watch her, shaking my head.

Whoever said it's a man's world was bloody fucking deluded.

TWENTY-TWO

KAGE

*L*ying naked in bed beside Nat, I've got a full belly, a full heart, and an empty set of balls.

My baby's gonna be sore in the morning.

"You good?" I murmur, my lips moving against her hair.

Her laugh is soft and satisfied. Head resting on my chest, she snuggles closer to me, pressing the length of her nude body against mine. "You know I am. People could probably hear me screaming in Seattle."

I tilt her head up and kiss her gently on the lips. In the dim light of the room, I see how soft her eyes are, how full of devotion, and am amazed all over again that I get to love her.

Men as bad as I am don't deserve this kind of luck.

"Dinner was great."

"Thank you. I'm glad you liked it."

"Liked it? I had four servings of that lasagna. I almost licked the plate."

She whispers, "But you licked me, instead."

Thinking of how hard she came for me makes my dick stiffen. I growl, "You're goddamn straight I did. And you were *loud*."

Her laugh is so sweet, it makes my dick even harder. I roll her onto her back, press my chest against hers, and kiss her again, this time hungrily.

When we come up for air, she's still laughing.

"Honey! Give me a minute to catch my breath, will you? I've already had three orgasms in the past hour!"

"Only three?" I say, outraged. It makes her laugh harder.

She stops when the phone on the nightstand beside her side of the bed starts ringing.

"Woman," I say sternly. "What did I tell you about keeping your cell next to the bed?"

"Something bossy that I ignored."

"Turn it off."

"Let me just check and see who it is real quick. It could be Sloane."

"That's what I'm afraid of."

She pushes at my chest. I don't move. The phone keeps ringing.

"What if I make you a deal that this is the last time I'll keep the phone in the bedroom?"

"We already made that deal. You conveniently forgot."

"Oh. Right." She gazes up at me, biting her lip, silently pleading with her big doe eyes.

"*No*, baby. Don't give me that look."

"Please?"

Ah, fuck.

She knows I can't resist that sweet, soft tone, and those sweet, soft eyes. I don't know why I ever bother trying.

I roll off her with a heavy sigh and lie on my back, staring at the ceiling.

"Thank you, honey." She leans over and gives me a peck on the cheek before grabbing the phone and answering it.

"Hello?"

There's a long silence as she listens. Then she blurts, "Oh my god! No! Sloane, I'm so sorry!"

It's Sloane. Of fucking course it is. And I can already tell that whatever it is she's telling Nat is some giant clusterfuck I'll have to get involved in.

I should've thrown that goddamn phone out the window when I had the chance.

Nat listens for a few moments longer, then says urgently, "Absolutely! Put him on right now! I'll put Kage on, too."

She rolls over, thrusts the phone at me, and demands, "You need to talk to Declan."

I turn my head on the pillow and look at her. My voice flat, I say, "Natalie."

"Don't take that tone with me, Kage! This is important! Sloane's little sister was kidnapped by some Russian assassin named Malek, and she got shot in the process. We have to help find her!"

That son of a bitch.

I sit up and grab the phone from her hand. Into it, I bark, "Start talking, asshole."

"Fuck you, too, you worthless piece of shite. Did you have anything to do with this?"

"I don't even know what *this* is."

"No? You have lots of rogue players on your team? Because I was under the impression you were the big Bratva boss. And if you are, you should know exactly what the fuck is happening on your turf. Or have I overestimated your power?"

That last part is said with so much contempt, my vision goes red.

It's his blood I'm seeing. And his dead body right in the middle of a big pool of it.

"Just get to the fucking point, Irish."

"Malek Antonov. You familiar with the name?"

"Yes. He's not under my jurisdiction."

Declan shouts, "This whole bloody country is your bloody jurisdiction, you bloody twat!"

I close my eyes and breathe slowly through my nose. I count to ten. When I open my eyes, Natalie is pacing naked back and forth at the end of the bed, chewing on her thumbnail.

That she's so worried is the only reason I don't hang up. Keeping my tone tightly controlled, I say, "He's out of Moscow. You know as well as I do that the old country has their own chain of command."

"Not with us, it doesn't."

"We were around long before the Mob was even conceived. Russia is more than two hundred times bigger than Ireland. Things are more complicated."

"Bollocks."

"Okay. Good talk. Fuck off into the sea, Irish." Glowering, I hold the phone out to Nat. "Take this away from me before I break it."

She glowers right back at me, squaring off to fold her arms over her chest. "Finish the conversation, Kazimir."

Fuck. She's calling me by my real name.

The only time she ever calls me by my real name is if I'm in trouble with her.

Seething, I put the phone back to my ear. "What do you want?"

"I want you to tell me where I can find him."

"No idea."

"You're a bloody liar."

"Yes. But not about this."

A blistering Gaelic oath comes over the line. It makes me happy.

Hiding my smile because Nat is watching me, I say, "Perhaps if you hadn't gone on that killing spree and murdered his brother, you wouldn't be in this predicament. Just a thought."

"I didn't know he was his brother! They lived in different countries! And do you know how many of you bloody Russians have the same last name?"

"Some free advice? Next time you want to kill someone in the Bratva, don't."

He roars a filthy string of curses so long and scathing, I have to hold the phone away from my ear so I don't go deaf.

When silence finally falls, I put the phone back to my ear. "Let me be clear. I don't know where he is. I don't have any control over him. I didn't give him permission to touch Sloane's sister."

A brief silence follows. "But you knew he was here. You spoke to him. I can tell by your voice."

So maybe this asshole is smarter than I give him credit for. Maybe.

"I had nothing to do with this kidnapping. I give you my word on that."

He scoffs. "Your bloody word."

I lower my voice. "Yes. The same way I give you my word I haven't told any of your Irish Mob friends or the other families who and what you really are. Or who you're working with. Because if I had, we both know what would've already happened."

In his pause, I sense the wheels turning a million miles per hour inside his head. But he remains silent.

"Thank you for not insulting my intelligence with a denial."

"You're welcome. And I'll thank you not to insult my intelligence with a denial, too."

"Like it or not, I'm telling you the truth."

"I'm not talking about Malek now."

Christ, he's exasperating. He talks in fucking circles. "Then what the hell are you talking about?"

"Your involvement with Maxim Mogdonovich's death."

He says it with such utter conviction, I know he's got intel that he shouldn't have. He's not guessing.

He knows.

Fuck.

When I don't speak for a moment, purely from surprise, Declan says, "You remember Max, aye? Your old boss? Died in a prison riot, conveniently elevating your ruthless arse to the number one spot? Funny how that happened. I wonder what your Bratva boys would have to say if they found out you arranged the whole thing?"

"You're an ignorant slug."

"And you're a can of piss. My point is that we both know things about the other that we shouldn't. Let's focus on the important issue here. Tell me where I can find this bastard Malek. Where does he live? How does he travel?"

"I'm telling you, I don't know."

"You do realize you still owe me for getting your FBI file erased?"

"Incorrect. I let Sloane stay with us while you were out taking care of your business. Your *dangerous* business that's now blowing back in your face. I didn't have to do that."

His voice rises. "Listen to me, you—"

"I gave your woman shelter. My debt is paid. The end."

There follows a silence so long, I think he might have hung up. Then he says, "If you help me, I'll grant you a favor. One favor. Anything you ask. No conditions."

"Okay. Shoot yourself in the head."

"Anything other than that, you bloody great wanker."

When I don't reply, he prompts, "You know what I'm offering is valuable. All you have to do is give me something to go on. Give me somewhere to look. Give me fucking anything that will help us find her, and I'll owe you a marker. No questions asked."

I consider it.

A dozen different extremely useful things I could ask him for run through my head. Though I hate to admit it, Declan O'Donnell is a powerful man.

You never know when having a man like that in your debt will come in handy.

And I did specifically tell Malek not to hurt any women while he was getting his revenge. I was very clear on that. Now, a girl has been shot in the process of a kidnapping that wasn't supposed to happen.

Not just any girl.

One who Natalie cares about. One she wants me to help find. Decision made.

"All right, Irish. You've got yourself a deal. Let me make a few calls. I'll get back to you when I have something."

I hang up before I have to hear his annoying accent again. Then, with Nat watching nervously, I start dialing.

TWENTY-THREE

RILEY

The pain is everywhere.

It's mostly in my stomach, but it's also all over me, everywhere at once. Every breath is agony. The smallest movement is torture. Even the air brushing my skin makes it hurt.

It hurts so bad, I wish I were dead.

My eyes are closed and my mind is sluggish, dulled by the blunt force of the pain, but I'm still vaguely aware of my surroundings.

I smell antiseptic.

I hear words spoken low in a foreign language.

I feel a cold pinch of metal as a needle is inserted into my arm, then a faint burning in the vein.

The sharpest edge of the pain dulls within seconds. My moan of gratitude is a reflex.

A cell phone rings.

Heavy footsteps move away.

A voice I recognize says in English, "I'm within my rights. It's not for you to question."

It's Malek. He sounds furious.

More silence. Then he speaks in rapid-fire sentences, biting the words off his tongue.

"I took her as repayment for Mikhail. What I do from here is none of your business. This is all the explanation you'll get, Kazimir. She's mine now. Don't contact me again."

The heavy footsteps move closer. Malek speaks again, this time in Russian.

Also in Russian, the answer comes from my right.

It's a man's voice. He sounds nervous. I sense there are others nearby, watching silently, just as nervous as him.

When Malek responds, I understand it, so it must be in English. But my brain is as fuzzy as a cotton ball. Whatever's getting pumped into my arm is dragging me quickly toward unconsciousness.

"Do it," he growls. "If she dies, so do all of you."

The words slip-slide out of my grasp even as they're spoken, rising up on lazy drafts of air to echo against the ceiling until they fade away.

A wave of darkness crashes down and swallows me whole.

Like a tide, the darkness slowly recedes.

Dappled light filters through my closed eyelids. I smell him somewhere close by, that heady scent of a dense nighttime woods. My pulse surges. A steady mechanical beeping accelerates to match it. I must be hooked up to a monitor.

"Live, little bird," Mal says, close to my ear, his voice low and urgent. "Fly back to me."

I drag my eyelids open long enough to glimpse him there, hovering over me like the angel of death, beautiful and otherworldly, his pale eyes burning bright.

I understand that he believes I'm going to die.

He takes my cold hand and squeezes it. Hard. He commands gruffly, *"Live."*

The tide of darkness rolls in to claim me once again.

I'm lifted in strong arms. The pain is excruciating, but I can't cry out. I have no power over any part of my body, including my vocal cords. I'm limp, my limbs dangling lifelessly like a doll's. I don't have enough energy to even open my eyes.

I'm also cold. Freezing cold.

I've been entombed inside an iceberg.

Then there's movement. Disorienting movement. I can't tell what direction is up or down. The arms that were carrying me have disappeared. I'm stretched out on a comfortable surface.

I must have been placed flat, but can't remember it. I also still can't open my eyes.

Something soft and heavy covers my body. A low hum of noise soothes my screaming nerves. A rocking motion lulls me into a trance. I'm cradled in warmth and security, and though the pain in my body is intense, I feel strangely calm. Calm and detached from myself, as if I'm floating weightlessly in the air several feet away, observing.

Maybe I'm dead already.

I thought the afterlife would be less painful than this.

The rocking slows, then stops. I inhale a breath that smells like snow.

"Good evening, sir. May I see your passport, please?" The voice is male, friendly, and unfamiliar.

After a pause, the friendly man speaks again. "How long do you plan to stay in Canada, sir?"

"A few days."

"Are you here for business or pleasure?"

"Pleasure. I've always wanted to see Niagara Falls from the other side."

"Do you have anything to declare?"

"No."

There's another pause, then the friendly man wishes Mal a safe journey.

The humming noise starts up again. The rocking motion lulls me back into a trance.

I tumble back into darkness.

When I open my eyes one minute or one hundred years later, I'm lying on my back in a strange bed.

The room is cool, bright, and quiet, a comfortable blur. Without my glasses, I can't see the details of my surroundings, but it doesn't feel like a hospital. Doesn't smell like one, either.

The air smells distinctly of campfire and pine needles. Of dense rain clouds and wet undergrowth. Of thick green moss climbing ancient tree trunks shrouded in fog at the tops.

Of the kind of wild outdoors where no people are.

It reminds me of a camping trip near Muir Woods my family took together when I was a kid. Gathering kindling for the fire, cold nights spent tucked into cozy sleeping bags, the sky overhead a glittering blanket of stars. Sloane and I whispering and giggling late into the night in our tent after our parents had fallen asleep in theirs.

It's one of the last good memories I have of the two of us before our mother died.

I lie still for a moment, just breathing. Trying to stitch my ragged patchwork memory back together. Only bits and pieces of things surface, brief moments of awareness between long stretches of black. Even the things I can recall are blurry and full of static.

I have no idea how much time has passed. "Hello? Is anyone here?"

My voice is a frog's croak. My mouth tastes like ashes.

Heavy footsteps draw closer, stopping beside me. I know it's him even before he speaks. I'd know his step and his scent anywhere. That dark presence, as powerful as gravity.

"You're awake."

Surprise softens the naturally rough timbre of his voice.

Surprise and something else.

Relief?

Disappointment, more likely.

I moisten my lips, swallow, cough. When my stomach muscles contract, it feels like someone rammed a white-hot poker straight through my gut. I cry out in agony.

He murmurs something in Russian, soothing nonsensical words, then supports my head with one hand and presses a glass to my lips.

Water. Ice cold and clear. It's the most delicious thing I've ever tasted.

I drink deeply until there's nothing left. He takes the glass away and runs his thumb along my bottom lip, catching a dribble.

I whisper, "Where am I? What happened? Is Kieran okay?"

The mattress dips with his weight. He leans over me, setting his hand beside my pillow, bringing his face into focus. He gazes down into my eyes and answers my questions as succinctly as I asked them.

"You're at my home. You were shot by your bodyguard. The blond one. I don't know if the other one's alive. I'll find out if you want me to."

"Yes, please."

He nods. We stare at each other in silence. Somewhere outside, a crow caws three times.

It seems like a bad omen, like the flock of geese murdered by the plane as we descended into Boston.

"I . . . I don't remember being shot."

He nods again, but doesn't respond to that.

"Will I be okay?"

"You lost a kidney. And your spleen. And a lot of blood."

"Is that a yes or a no?"

"It's a maybe. How do you feel?"

I think about it, searching for the perfect word to describe the sensation of extreme weakness, overwhelming exhaustion, and throbbing, bone-deep pain.

"Shitty."

He gazes at me in unsmiling, laser-focused silence, then says suddenly, "Soup?"

I blink in confusion, not knowing if I heard him correctly because my brain is cottage cheese. "Excuse me?"

"Do you think you can eat something?"

Now I get it. "What kind of soup is it?"

He frowns. "The kind I made. Do you want it or not?"

We're talking about soup. This is crazy. Focus, Riley. Find out what's going on. I close my eyes and exhale slowly. "Why am I here?"

He pauses. Then his voice comes very low. "Because I want you to be."

I'm afraid to open my eyes, but I do it anyway. He stares down at me with a million unspoken things burning in his gaze, all of them frightening.

I try to make my voice strong. "How long will I be here?"

"As long as it takes."

I don't have the nerve to ask him what that means or the energy to handle whatever the answer might be. I just bite my lip and nod, as if any of this makes any sense whatsoever.

He rises and leaves.

I hear sounds from another room. Pots clatter on a stove. A door opens and closes. Water runs into a sink.

Then he's back, sitting on the edge of the bed again, a plain white ceramic bowl cradled in his hands. He sets the bowl on the small wood table beside the bed.

"I'm going to lift you. It will hurt."

Before I can protest that I'm hurting enough already, he drags me up by my armpits to a sitting position.

He wasn't exaggerating: it hurts. It hurts like a bitch. A thousand knives stab into my stomach and slash it apart. The pain leaves me breathless and gasping.

Steadying me with one hand, he props the pillow against the headboard with the other. Then he helps me lie back against it, shushing me gently when I groan.

He sits next to me again, picks up the bowl, ladles the spoon into it, then holds the spoon to my lips. He waits patiently until I've controlled my ragged breathing and open my mouth, then he slides the spoon between my lips.

The soup is hot, creamy, and delicious. I swallow greedily, licking my lips.

He grunts in satisfaction and feeds me another spoonful.

It isn't until I'm halfway through the bowl that I speak again. "How long have I been here?"

"Since last night. You spent six days in the hospital before that."

I've been unconscious for a week? Impossible.

He sees my shock and says, "You were in a trauma unit until you were stable enough to be moved."

"Trauma unit," I repeat, struggling to find the memory. There's nothing. It's a dead end. A blank wall.

"A place we use, off the books. You had surgery. You've been given analgesics, antibiotics, and hydration through IV. Blood transfusions, too." He pauses. "You shouldn't be alive."

My voice faint, I say, "I told you I was stubborn."

"Yes. You did."

He gazes at me with such searing intent, I grow self-conscious.

The self-consciousness vanishes when my fried brain synapses decide to start firing again, and I remember something Spider told me when we were fleeing from Malek at the bookstore.

"He's the right hand of the Moscow Bratva king."

The important part being "Moscow."

My heartbeat surges into a thundering gallop. My voice turns hoarse. "When you said I'm at your home . . . where are we, exactly?"

Holding my gaze, he says a word. It's not in English.

My instincts suggest it's the name of a town, but it can't be what I'm thinking. I refuse to believe it's true.

I whisper, "Where have you taken me? Where is this place?"

He remains silent. His eyes are full of darkness. Such deep, impenetrable darkness, it's like looking into an abyss.

"You already know where you are. And this is where you'll be staying."

Then he stands and leaves the room, closing the door behind him.

TWENTY-FOUR

DECLAN

I have something."

The sound of Kazimir's voice on the other end of the phone is both a relief and an instant aggravation. "It's been over a week!"

"You're lucky I found anything at all." He pauses meaningfully. "Your FBI contact come through for you?"

"You bloody well know he didn't," I say through gritted teeth.

"Yes. And I had to kill three men to get this information. So a little appreciation is in order."

"Just get to the fucking point already!"

"Since you asked me so nicely, I will."

His voice oozes sarcasm and self-congratulations. I mutter to myself, "This bloody minger will be the death of me."

"With any luck. Do you want to hear this or not?"

He seems satisfied that my silent seething is a yes and continues. I immediately wish he hadn't.

"She's in Russia."

After I regroup from that shock, I say, "How? We had eyes on the whole country. Airports, bus terminals, ports, everything."

"He's a slippery motherfucker, that's how. And the Canadian border is notoriously porous."

Canada. He went north. Fuck. "Go on."

"He stole a truck, changed the plates, and smuggled her though the border near Niagara Falls. Smart move, considering the amount of daily tourist traffic they get. The truck was found abandoned near a small airfield in Hamilton, Ontario. They flew out from there."

"The final destination?"

"Malek's hometown. Moscow."

Moscow. One of the largest cities in the world, with over twelve million people. And not a single one of them willing to help us find Riley.

"So she was alive when they left the States."

"Yes. Though from what I'm told, barely."

This just keeps getting better and better. "And now?"

"No idea. His trail is dark. Nobody knows exactly where he lives, and nobody in Moscow was willing to talk to me."

I snap, "You should've offered them money!"

He chuckles. "Oligarchs aren't interested in bribes."

"What are they interested in, then? What can we offer them to get them to help us?"

After a pause, Kazimir says, "I agreed to help you in return for a valuable favor. A personal favor. That doesn't extend to the rest of the Bratva. If you want to make a deal with Moscow, contact them yourself."

This smug prick. Infuriated, I snap, "I'll tell them about Maxim Mogdonovich."

"And I'll tell the Mob about your extracurricular activities as a spy. Checkmate."

"It's not checkmate, you dryshite. It's stalemate at best."

"Agree to disagree. The point is, I got you the information you were looking for. Now you owe me a marker. You'll hear from me when I need to cash it in."

He disconnects, leaving me shaking in rage. Riley's in Moscow. How the bloody hell am I supposed to tell that to Sloane?

"Where did he take her?"

I turn at the sound of Spider's voice. He stands on the other side of the desk in the office in the safe house, staring at me with haunted, feverish eyes.

He arrived in New York from Boston two days ago. Since then, he hasn't slept, showered, or eaten, as far as I can tell. He merely paces the length of whatever room he's in, then turns back and paces the other way, grinding his teeth the entire time.

He looks like seven shades of shite. The two inches of stitches crawling down his temple from where Malek bludgeoned him don't help.

I tuck the cell phone back into my shirt pocket, fold my arms over my chest, and look him up and down. "You need to get some rest."

He insists, "Where did he take her?"

I've known him long enough to know that he'll keep badgering me with that question until he gets an answer. So I give him one, though I'm not confident his reaction will make me glad I did.

"Moscow."

He stands stock-still for a moment, processing it, then says gruffly, "How is she?"

"Barely alive, from what Kazimir said."

He swallows hard, looks at the floor, then glances back up at me and says vehemently, "What time do I fly out?"

"You don't."

He steps forward, eyes flashing, a muscle jumping in his jaw. "I'm going. Like it or not, I'm going to Moscow. It's my fault. This is my responsibility. I'm going to find her."

Keeping my voice even, I say, "You'll go where I tell you to go. Right now, we need you here."

He shakes his head in frustration. "I'm useless here, and you know it. I can't focus. I can't sleep. I can barely fucking think!"

"Lower your voice. Take a breath. Pull yourself together."

He closes his eyes, drags his hands through his hair, and exhales heavily. "I'm sorry. Fuck." He drops his hands to his sides and looks out the window. His voice lowers an octave. "I have to find her. I have to. I'm going bloody mad."

Something in his tone makes me look at him sharply.

I know he's drowning in guilt over what happened. He blames himself more than Sloane or I do. His misery is palpable. He walks around under a black cloud of suffering so thick, it has its own atmosphere.

Maybe there's a reason for that beyond the obvious.

Watching him carefully, I say, "I'll need you to look after Sloane while I'm gone. I'll get a crew together, keep you informed of our progress once we get there."

"I'm going!" he roars, pounding a fist on my desk. "I'm not asking permission!"

I don't react. I simply stand and gaze at him until he realizes he's given himself away.

He would never speak to me with such disrespect unless his heart was involved.

He sinks into the chair beside him, drops his head into his hands, and groans.

After a moment, I say quietly, "She doesn't seem like your type."

He exhales. "I've never met a woman who could make me blush before."

Jesus Christ. Anger makes my tone harder than it should be. "Do I know everything I need to know about this situation?"

He jerks his head up and stares at me beseechingly. "I never laid a finger on her. I swear on my mother's grave. Nothing happened. She doesn't even know."

"You're saying it's one-sided?"

"Aye."

I know he's telling the truth. Spider doesn't have the kind of face that can hide lies.

I turn to the window and look out, thinking. *What a bloody mess.*

From behind me, Spider speaks in a low, urgent voice. "Malek will be expecting you to come. He'll be waiting. Watching. Nobody will expect me."

"He's seen your face. He knows you."

"He knows you better. Everyone does. You walk down a street in Moscow, and within an hour, every Bratva in the country will know you're there."

He pauses to let that sink in. "And you know you can't go and leave Sloane here. Even if you tried, she wouldn't let you. Do you really want her following you to Russia? Because we both know she would. One way or another, she would."

I say crossly, "I'm aware."

"So send me. I can fly under the radar in a way you can't."

Sighing, I turn from the window and sit across from him.

"Moscow is huge. It could take you ten years to search. We don't even have a starting point. It would be like looking for a single grain of sand on a beach."

"Aye," says Spider, nodding. "So the sooner we start, the better."

I don't like the look in his eyes. There's an uncharacteristic defiance there. A hint of mutiny.

I hold his rebellious gaze and say firmly, "The answer is no. I'm not sending you. It would be a death sentence. I'll arrange something else."

Breathing shallowly, Spider stares at me. I can tell he's struggling to control his emotions and carefully choose words that will change my mind.

Finally, he gives up. He stands and walks to the door.

Before walking out, he turns back to me. Holding my gaze, he says softly, "I'll not stand idly by while that Russian son of a bitch does whatever he likes to the lass, Declan. I'll not stand idly by."

He leaves, closing the door softly behind him. Two hours later, he texts me from LaGuardia.

My flight is about to take off. I'll call you when I have her.

"You barmy son of a bitch," I say aloud to the empty room, astonished. "You'll get yourself murdered."

Then I pick up the phone and call the only person in the world who can help me now. A man who knows everyone and everything, even though he died more than a year ago.

Killian Black.

TWENTY-FIVE

RILEY

I lie still for a long time, staring at the wall. My vision's blurred without my glasses, but I can tell the wall is made of logs.

I'm bedridden with a gunshot wound in an assassin's log cabin in Russia. I've been unconscious for a week, and parts of me have been removed.

I'd laugh if I didn't already feel like crying.

I need to use the toilet, so I gingerly swing one leg over the edge of the mattress. Minutes later, when my breathing has returned to normal, I swing the other leg over and sit up.

The pain is so intense, my eyes water. I think I might puke. Malek appears in front of me and takes me by the shoulders.

I get the sense he wants to shake me in anger, but he doesn't. He growls at me instead.

Panting, I say to his feet, "I have to use the bathroom."

"You need to stay in bed."

"I need. To use. The toilet. You can help me stand up, or you can get the hell out of my way, but I'm not peeing in this bed."

Silence. A dissatisfied grunt. Then he gently lifts me up by my armpits and stands there holding me as I groan and sway and struggle to get my balance.

"Fuck. *Fuck!*"

"Focus on your breath, not the pain."

I grip his corded forearms and drag in deep breaths until the worst of it has passed.

I read somewhere once that a gunshot wound is more painful than childbirth, and I remember laughing at that. Like how can pushing a human through your cooch hurt less than getting hit by a bullet?

This is how. This right here.

Childbirth only rips your vagina apart. A bullet rips up your whole body.

"Did I lose part of my intestines, too? It feels like my guts were torn out and replaced with razor blades."

"Gunshots to the abdomen are among the most painful of all injuries."

"You say that like you have personal experience on the matter."

"I do. Are you steady?"

"As much as I'm going to be." Which isn't much, but I'll be damned if I'll admit that I'm probably going to fall flat on my face as soon as he releases me.

I might be an invalid, but I still have my pride.

"The bathroom is over there." He gestures to something.

"That would be helpful if I could see where you pointed."

"Your vision is that bad?"

"I'm legally blind without my glasses."

"I'll get you another pair."

"They're prescription."

"Let me worry about that."

He takes one step back, keeping his hands underneath my armpits. I shuffle forward. He takes another step back. We go halfway across the room like that until he loses his patience.

"This will take forever. I'm picking you up."

"I need to walk. It helps with blood flow and healing. Lying in bed too long after surgery puts you at risk for blood clots and lung problems like pneumonia."

I sense surprise in his pause. "How did you know that?"

Because that's what the doctors told my mother after the surgery she had to remove her cancerous ovaries, but I'm not in the mood to share painful personal anecdotes.

I say crossly, "I've got a big brain."

His answer is mild. "Your head is uncommonly large for such a small person. Have you ever been approached by the circus and offered a job?"

"That's not even a little bit funny."

"Then why are your lips turning up?"

"That's the face I make before projectile vomiting."

He picks me up and carries me the rest of the way to the restroom, as if we didn't already go over this. When he sets me down in front of the toilet and stands there with his arms folded over his chest, staring at me, I blanch.

"You're not standing right there while I pee."

"You could fall."

"Yes, I could. That would be an appropriate time for you to appear and assist me. Not now."

He doesn't budge. Which, of course, makes me mad.

"Why go to all this trouble for someone you were threatening to kill? You could've just let me die back there and been done with me."

As if he thinks he's making perfect sense, he says calmly, "You took a bullet for me. I'm responsible for you now."

"I'm not lucid enough to unravel that logic."

Ignoring that, he turns to go. "I'll be right outside the door if you need me."

I lean on the edge of the sink, staring in confusion at the closed door, until I decide I'd better sit down before I topple over. Moving carefully, I creep to the toilet.

"Are you all right?" Through the door, his voice sounds sharp.

"Until you hear a loud thump, assume I'm fine."

"I thought I did hear a loud thump."

"That was just the sound of all the hope leaving my body."

It's not until I finish using the toilet and look at myself in the mirror above the sink that I realize the underwear and long black sleep shirt I'm wearing aren't mine.

All the ramifications of what that means are pushed aside by the sheer horror of seeing my reflection in the mirror.

Even without my glasses, I can see that I look like Death. Like the literal, physical embodiment of Death.

I'm pale as chalk. My eyes are red and sunken. My lips are chapped, and my hair is a nest of snarls where rodents have obviously been fighting.

I've lost weight, too. Maybe ten pounds. My clavicle bones stick out like a skeleton's.

In disbelief, I touch my cheek, then my hair.

Then, overwhelmed by the reality of my situation, I start crying. I crumple against the sink and break into sobs so loud, I don't hear it when Mal bursts through the door.

Without a word, he takes me in his arms and holds me against his chest as I weep.

No, that sounds too delicate for what I'm doing. This is a breakdown. A full-body event complete with blubbering and bawling, howling and wailing, shaking and quaking and lots of snot.

Mal remains silent during it all. He simply holds me. It's the only reason I don't fall to my knees.

When the loudest wails have tapered and I'm a hiccupping, red-faced mess, he releases me long enough to turn to the counter and grab a tissue. He holds it against my face and tells me to blow, like I'm a five-year-old with a head cold.

It's surprisingly soothing.

I blow into the tissue. He wipes my nose, tosses that tissue into the trash, gets another one, and wipes the tears from my cheeks. He picks me up in his arms and heads back to the bedroom.

My head resting against his chest and my eyes closed, I whisper, "I don't understand what's happening."

"You don't have to. All you have to do is heal, *malyutka*. And that will take time."

Hearing his nickname for me makes me teary again, but I sniffle and squeeze my eyes shut so the tears don't come out.

I grimace in pain when he lowers me to the bed but don't make a sound. He adjusts the pillow behind my head.

"I need to check your sutures. I'm going to pull your night-gown up."

I don't bother protesting. I know he won't listen to a word I say. Besides, I don't have the energy. Mal as my caregiver is just one more mindfuck my poor brain has to wrestle with. All my energy is going into not having a mental break with reality.

With gentle hands, he pulls up the sleep shirt and lightly probes around my belly while I wince and grit my teeth.

"There's no sign of infection around the sutures," he says quietly. "And your abdomen isn't hard, which is good. I'll change the dressing, then get you your meds."

"Meds?"

"Pain medicine. Antibiotics."

"Oh."

"I need you to tell me right away if you develop pain or swelling in one of your arms or legs, if you have shortness of breath or feel dizzy, or if you have blood in your urine."

I close my eyes and say weakly, "Oh, god."

"Don't despair yet. It gets worse. Even if you heal perfectly, you may experience PTSD. It's a common side effect of a gunshot wound. Nightmares, anxiety, jumpiness—"

"Got it," I interrupt. "Even if I don't end up being a mess, I'll still probably be a mess."

He stops his inspection of my stomach and looks at me. "You're young and strong. Your chances are good."

Something in the way he says those words makes me nervous. I inspect his face closely for any clues, but his expression is neutral.

Suspiciously neutral.

"Wait. I could still die, couldn't I?"

"Yes. Sepsis isn't uncommon for this type of wound. You could also develop blood clots, airway collapse, fistula formation, peritonitis, abscesses, and other life-threatening complications."

At least he doesn't sugarcoat it. I have to give him credit for that.

I say faintly, "You're just a ray of sunshine, aren't you?"

"Also, with only one kidney, you can never drink alcohol again."

I close my eyes and groan. "I think I'd rather be dead."

"Look on the bright side."

"There is no bright side!"

"Think of all the money you'll save. And you'll never have another hangover."

He makes it sound so rational, I have to laugh. That causes more pain to rip through me, and the laughter quickly turns to groans.

Mal squeezes my hand. He murmurs, "Breathe through it. It'll pass."

I suck in deep, desperate breaths through my nose, squeezing his hand so hard, I'm probably crushing bones.

I don't care. It's his fault I'm in this predicament in the first place.

My eyes closed, I say, "My sister. Sloane. Does she know what's happened to me?"

There's a pause before he answers. "Yes."

I sense miles of twisted story behind that, but he offers no further explanation.

"So she knows I'm alive? And with you?"

"Yes."

I open my eyes and look at him. He's kneeling beside the bed, leaning over me. My hand is still in his. "Aren't you worried they'll try to come get me?"

"If Declan O'Donnell sets foot in this country, it's the last step he'll ever take."

He says it with such conviction, I understand not only that he's already made arrangements for that to happen, but also that he won't necessarily have to pull the trigger himself.

"You've got people watching him."

He simply nods.

My voice comes out small. "Please don't kill him."

He shakes his head in frustration. "You keep asking me not to kill other people, but you've never asked me not to kill *you*."

I think for a moment. "I'm pretty sure I have."

"No. You haven't. You just threatened to return from the dead to haunt me if I did."

"I was like ninety percent certain all along that you weren't going to kill me. Why are you glaring at me now?"

He says flatly, "I *was* going to kill you."

"No, you weren't."

"Yes, I was."

"You *wanted* to, but you were never going to. That's totally different."

Heaving a sigh, he releases my hand, stands, and leaves the room. I holler after him, "You never would have kissed me so much if you really planned to kill me!"

"Tell that to my late ex-wife."

That leaves me breathless, and not just because my stomach hurts from the effort of shouting. I lie there with my heart beating like mad, thinking of all the ways he might have murdered his poor ex, until Mal sticks his head back through the door.

"I don't have an ex-wife. I've never been married. I only said that to scare you."

"It worked."

"I told you I was a bad person."

That makes me smile. "Yeah, but if you were *really* bad, you wouldn't have admitted it."

He closes his eyes for a moment, shaking his head. "I have to go out for a while. I'll try to be back before dark."

I start to panic all over again. "You're leaving me here alone? What if I die while you're gone?"

"Then I suppose I'll have some digging to do when I get back."

My mouth drops open. "Okay, that was just mean."

I can tell he's trying not to smile. "Would you prefer cremation? I can arrange a funeral pyre for you, if you like."

"That is *so* not funny."

"It's a little bit funny."

"No. It's not."

"Your lips are twitching."

"That's because I'm in a lot of pain!"

His head disappears. He returns in a moment holding a white paper bag.

"What's in that?"

He sits on the edge of the bed and starts removing pill bottles of various sizes and colors from the bag. Some of them have labels, others don't. The ones that do are written in gobbledygook that must be Russian.

When he shakes a few pills from different bottles into the palm of his hand and holds it out to me, I look at the pills with trepidation.

"How do I know what these are?"

"Because I told you what they are."

"Yeah, but you also just told me you were going to kill me all along. I can't trust you now."

With exaggerated patience, he says, "Take the fucking pills."

I grudgingly hold out my hand. He dumps the pills into it and pours water from a carafe on the nightstand into the glass next to it. Then he holds it out to me with a look like I'll be in trouble if I say another word.

So of course I have to.

"Okay, but if I wake up dead, I swear I'll come back to haunt you."

"I'm really starting to regret that I saved your life."

Smiling at his glower, I pop the pills into my mouth and accept the glass of water he holds out to me. I swallow all the pills in one big gulp. "Ugh. I think that big white one got stuck in my throat."

"That's the cyanide. You won't be worried about your throat in a second because you'll be dead."

"See, you can't do that now. I don't know whether or not you're joking!"

"Look at my face. This is my joking face." His expression is absolutely serious.

"Oh my god. I just realized something."

"What?"

"You're a jerk."

One corner of his mouth lifts. "Not too quick on the draw, are you?"

"At least I'm not a jerk."

He stares at me silently, his eyes warm. I think he wants to smile, but I'm not sure he knows how to.

Then he stands and leaves me alone, telling me before he goes that he'll be back as soon as he can.

When he returns that evening, he's covered in blood.

TWENTY-SIX

RILEY

I don't notice it at first because it's dark outside, there are no lights on inside, and I can't see more than a few feet in front of my face without my specs. But when he comes into the bedroom and starts lighting the candles that are all over the place, then sits down on the bed beside me, I notice his hands.

"What is that?"

He looks at the dark, rust-colored smear on the back of one hand and tries to wipe it on his coat sleeve. When it doesn't work, he chooses to simply ignore my question.

"Here. This should be enough to find a match." He sets a bulky pillowcase on my lap.

"What's in this?"

"You'd know if you looked."

I pull it open and peer inside, surprised by what I find. "There's like four hundred pairs of eyeglasses in here."

"You have a flair for exaggeration. Has anyone ever told you that?"

"Yes. My creative writing teacher in college described my ag-grandizement of language as incredible."

"I'm sure it wasn't a compliment."

"I got an A in that class."

"Because he knew if he failed you, you'd have to take the class again. He couldn't bear to live through that twice. Try the glasses on. I'll get you something to eat."

He rises from the bed and goes around the cabin lighting can-dles while I try on pair after pair, looking for one strong enough. I call out, "Why don't you have electricity?"

"I do have electricity," he answers from the next room. "I just don't like fluorescent lights."

"So get LED."

"Don't like those, either."

I guess I should count myself lucky that he likes indoor plumbing.

"Oh! I found a pair that works!"

With clear vision, I look around the room in awe.

The walls and floor are made entirely of knotty polished wood the color of honey. Heavy beams run the width of the ceiling. The doors are wood, too, and so is the bed I'm lying in, which looks hand carved. There are several colorful wool blankets on the bed, and a large dark brown fur that I suspect is from a real animal.

A real *big* animal. Maybe a bear.

The furnishings are simple, rustic, and also have that hand-carved feel. There is no computer, television, or clock in the room, but there is a bookcase and a fireplace.

There's also an enormous stuffed moose head on the wall oppo-site me, gazing down at me with black glass eyes.

It's terrifying.

Mal returns to the room, and my terror increases. "Oh my god," I whisper, seeing him.

His face is covered with the same rust-colored splatter and

smears that are on his hands. It's dried now, but I can tell from the way it dripped and ran down his jaw that it was once liquid.

Once-bright-red liquid that has turned dark from exposure to air.

"What?"

"You have blood all over you."

He reacts to that horrible piece of news as if I've just told him my zodiac sign: with total indifference.

He sets a tray on my bedside table, shucks off his heavy wool coat, throws it on a chair, then pulls his black Henley off and tosses that on top of the coat. Then he's standing there naked from the waist up, and I'm sitting in bed with my mouth hanging open, wondering if maybe I'm suffering from a severe brain injury as well as a gunshot wound.

It's not possible for a human to be that beautiful.

I blink to clear my vision, but all I see swimming before my eyes are acres of muscular flesh decorated by a constellation of tattoos. His bulk is surpassed only by his height, which is surpassed only by the gut punch of that *V* thing leading from his washboard abs downward, like a pair of muscle arrows pointing to the goodies in his crotch.

He's tatted, ripped, and altogether masculine. Devastated, I look away.

I've been blinded. He's seared my eyeballs. I'll never be able to see again.

He sits on the edge of the bed and picks up a bowl of steaming liquid from the tray, as if all this is completely natural. As if he walks around half-naked with blood on his hands and face every day.

Which, considering his line of work, is a possibility.

"Take a few deep breaths," he says calmly, stirring a spoon around in the bowl. He knows my brain is malfunctioning.

"I wonder how many times you'll have to tell me that by the end of this week," I say weakly, wanting to fan my burning face.

He holds the spoon to my lips and waits for me to piece myself back together. When I finally do, I manage to swallow a delicious spoonful of soup.

My assassin kidnapper's homemade soup that he's feeding to me like a baby.

I've lost my mind. That's the only explanation.

"Were you able to rest while I was gone?"

"Some."

He feeds me another spoonful of soup. "How's your pain level?"

"Splendiferous."

"Try again without the sarcasm."

"On a scale of one to ten, it's a forty-seven."

"Without exaggeration, too. If you can manage it."

I accept another spoonful, trying to look anywhere but at his chest.

Dear god, his chest. His breasts are beautiful. Pecs, I mean. Is that what they're called?

I've lost half my vocabulary in the past sixty seconds.

"Riley. Your pain. How is it?"

"Right, sorry. Um . . . painful."

He gives me a stern look, but I'm too distracted to find it scary.

"Why do you have blood on you?"

"Work. How's your pain?"

"A little better. Or at least not worse."

He seems satisfied by that, nodding and holding out another spoonful of soup. We're both quiet as I finish the bowl, staring alternately at the blankets, the wall, the ceiling, and the terrifying moose, anywhere but at him and his devastating beauty.

Then he sets the spoon and bowl aside and announces he's going to take a shower.

He stands and heads to the bathroom, leaving me flattened on the bed, drained of energy by the sight of his body and the single word he used to explain the blood.

Work.

He was working today. Doing assassin stuff.

Killing people.

My brain refuses to get a handle on it. I simply can't reconcile the idea of Mal the gentle, attentive caretaker who cleans my wounds and feeds me soup with Mal the guy who blows people away for a living. Who came to Bermuda to kill Declan.

Who may or may not have wanted to kill me.

I'm thousands of miles from home, injured, in horrible pain, in a foreign country I was brought to while unconscious, where I might die of complications from the gunshot my bodyguard gave me or the bootleg surgery I underwent to repair it.

This is just too fucking much.

I start to cry again, hating myself with every tear that falls.

Sloane wouldn't cry in this situation. She'd already have made an escape vehicle from the moose head and burned the cabin down.

When Mal returns to the bedroom, I'm lying with my arms flung over my face, dragging in big, shuddering gulps of air.

He pulls my arms away from my face and stares down into my watering eyes. Then he says something that sounds gentle and soothing, but I can't understand a word of it because it's in Russian.

"You know I don't know what that means."

"Yes. Which is why I didn't say it in English."

"That's not nice."

"You wouldn't think that if you knew what I said."

Biting my lip, I stare up at him. His wet hair is slicked back off his face. The white terry cloth towel wrapped around his waist is the only thing he's wearing. He smells like clean skin and healthy male in his prime, and holy Ghost of Christmas Past, I can't look at him for one second longer.

I close my eyes, turn my head, and whisper, "Why did you bring me here?"

He gently folds my arms over my chest and sits beside me. I can feel him looking at me, but refuse to open my eyes. After a moment, he asks his own question, ignoring mine.

"Why did you take a bullet for me?"

"I don't know."

"Yes, you do. Tell me the truth."

His voice is low and urgent. I imagine those beautiful green eyes gazing down at me with their usual penetrating intensity and wish with all my heart that I didn't currently look like I've been sleeping under a bridge.

I take a deep breath, let it out, and tell him the ridiculous truth in a voice so small, he probably can't even hear it.

"Because I didn't want you to die."

His silence is long and intense. He exhales. Then he lifts my hand to his lips and kisses it, brushing his mouth softly across my knuckles, turning my hand over and pressing his lips against my open palm.

He rises from the bed without another word.

I hear him moving around the room, opening and closing drawers. His footsteps recede. When they return, I open my eyes to find him fully dressed, boots and all. He lowers himself into the big brown leather chair in the corner.

He folds his hands over his stomach, tilts his head back, and closes his eyes.

"What are you doing?"

"Going to sleep. So should you."

"You're gonna sleep in that chair?"

"What did I just tell you?"

"How can you sleep sitting upright? Isn't there a sofa in the other room that you can lie down on?"

He lifts his head and looks at me. "Stop worrying about me."

"But—"

"Stop."

When he can tell I'm about to start pestering him again, he says gruffly, "Yes, there's a sofa. No, I'm not going to sleep on it. I need to be in this room. I need to hear if you cry out. I have to know if you're in pain or you need anything. Don't ask me why, because I won't tell you. Now go to fucking sleep."

His eyes blaze at me for a few moments longer until he closes them again and I'm released from their burning power.

TWENTY-SEVEN

RILEY

The dream is horrifically violent.

It starts with gunfire and gets worse, with blood and body parts flying everywhere. I hear screaming and smell smoke. The building I'm in is on fire. I'm trying to run, but my legs are powerless. The walls catch fire, then so do my clothing and hair. My skin turns black and curls off my body like burning paper.

I jerk awake with a strangled scream, my heart pounding.

"It's okay. You're safe. I'm here."

Mal pulls me up and against his chest. He rocks me and murmurs soothing words in Russian as I shake and gasp for air. Clinging to him as the dream fades, I bury my face in his chest.

He says gently, "Next time you have a nightmare, remind yourself that you're dreaming. It's not real. Then tell yourself to wake up."

"That makes no sense. How can I tell myself anything if I'm asleep?"

"Your subconscious will remember I told you. From now on,

you'll be able to wake yourself up from a bad dream. It won't stop you from having them, but it will help."

I ponder that, wondering if he has bad dreams, until he says, "I'm going to run a bath."

"Didn't you just take a shower?"

"It's not for me. It's for you." He pulls away and smooths a hand over my hair. "You stink."

I say drily, "That is so not helpful."

"Helpful or not, it's the truth. Drink some water."

He leans over to the nightstand and hands me the glass he retrieves from it. He watches in silence until I've gone through half the water, then rises and goes into the bathroom.

I feel around on the nightstand for my glasses. When I get them on, I realize the terrifying moose head is gone.

I find that very, very disturbing. Did I imagine it?

When Mal returns to the room, I point at the blank spot on the wall where the hideous thing used to reside. "Wasn't there a moose there?"

"No." Before I can freak out that this is definitive evidence I've lost my shit, he adds, "It was an elk."

"Oh, for fuck's sake."

"I took it down."

I consider that for several seconds. "You took the elk head off the wall after I went to sleep?"

"Yes."

"Why?"

"Because you didn't like it."

That makes me blink in surprise. "So in addition to being able to walk through walls, you can read minds."

"No, but I can read faces. Yours is unusually expressive."

Oh, that's *wonderful*. What the hell must my face have been telling him when he was strutting around with his damn shirt off? I hope it wasn't the same thing my ovaries were saying, because those horny little egg producers have only one thing on their minds.

My cheeks heating, I glance down at my hands. Mal approaches the bed, flips the covers off my legs, and picks me up. As he carries me to the bathroom, I say, "I'm supposed to be walking."

"You will be. Let's get you clean first."

I don't have much time to worry about the "let's" part, because he makes his intentions clear when he sets me on my feet in front of the tub and starts pulling at my sleep shirt.

"Whoa! What're you doing?"

I jerk away from him so hard, I lose my balance. With his hand gripped around my upper arm, he steadies me so I don't fall.

He says calmly, "You're feeling shy. There's no need to be. I've already seen all of you there is to see, inside and out."

I gape at him in horror, mentally recoiling from all the possibilities of that statement, until he provides me with a detailed explanation that leaves no room for doubt.

"I stood at the head of your bed when they opened your stomach to get the bullet and your damaged organs out. I gave you sponge baths while you were drugged. I changed your clothes, changed your bedsheets, and helped the nurse change your catheter when it got plugged. There isn't an inch of your body I'm not already familiar with."

I squeeze my eyes shut and chant, "Wake up. Wake up. Wake up."

"You're not dreaming."

"This has to be a dream. There's no universe in which this can possibly be real."

He exhales in impatience. "Don't be dramatic. Bodies are just meat."

I open my eyes and glare at him in outrage. "Excuse me for not being deadened to all sense of humanity, Mr. International Assassin, but *my* body is not meat to *me*."

He examines my expression for a moment. "Are you angry because you think I might've touched you inappropriately?"

"Jesus!"

"Because I didn't. I would never take advantage like that. I'm a psychopath, not a pervert. I believe strongly in consent."

"Well, that's tremendous news! I feel so much better now!"

Ignoring my scathing tone and blistering hostility, he adds in a husky voice, "And there are many things I'd like to get your specific consent for, Riley Rose, but touching you while you're unconscious isn't one of them."

I thought he'd mindfucked me before, I really did. But that leaves my brain twisted into such a knot, I lose the power of speech.

He turns to the bathtub and tests the water with his hand. Satisfied it's the right temperature, he shuts off the faucet and straightens. "You can't get your sutures wet, so the water will only cover your legs. I'll wash your hair first."

At the opposite end of the bathtub from the faucet is a small wood stool, a clear plastic pitcher, and a large, oblong metal bucket. Gesturing toward the bucket, he says, "Tip your head over the edge of the tub."

Then he tugs at my sleep shirt again.

"Mal, I can't. I can't get naked in front of you. If this wound doesn't kill me, the embarrassment will."

"Embarrassment over what?"

"You seeing me naked!"

"I've already seen you naked. I just explained that."

"You haven't seen me naked while I'm awake!"

"So you want to smell like a pigpen, is that it?"

"No!"

"Then let me give you a bath."

"You say that like *I'm* the unreasonable one!"

"The faster you get over your useless modesty, the faster this will be done."

"Mal—"

"I promise I won't look at anything. How's that?"

"Right. You won't look at anything while you're washing my hair and all my naked parts. I'm sure that will be very easy for you."

"Easier than living with your stench."

"You know what? I just decided I hate you."

"Hate me all you want in the bathtub."

We stand in silence after that. Him waiting patiently, me glaring daggers at his head. I get the sense he'd wait until the end of time before speaking again, so I go first.

"Can't you understand what this must be like for me?"

"Yes, I can. And I'm sorry. I don't want to make you uncomfortable. But you're not steady enough to get in and out of the tub by yourself or lift the pitcher to rinse your hair. I doubt you even have the strength to lift a bar of soap."

He seems sincere, but I narrow my eyes at him anyway.

This is a man who kills people for a living. I'm sure he's quite the accomplished liar.

"I won't force you," he says softly. "It's your choice. I just want to help you feel better. I think a bath will do that."

"So I could ask you to take me back to bed, and you will?"

"Yes."

He didn't hesitate, which makes a dent in my hostility. I glance at the water longingly, imagining what it would be like to sink into it. To wash the ripe smells of sickness and stale sweat off my skin.

"Fuck it," I mutter. Then I turn and give him a hard look. "But don't make it weird!"

He's smart enough not to respond to that.

When he turns his back, it confuses me. "What are you doing?"

"Would you prefer I stare at you while you take off your night-gown?"

Look who's decided to be a gentleman.

Sighing, I remove my glasses and set them on the sink. This will be easier if I can't see anything. Then I grab the neckline of the sleep shirt and try to pull it over my head. It's a struggle and leaves me breathless, but I manage it.

When I'm standing there in my underwear, I cross my arms over my chest and whisper, "Okay."

He turns, picks me up in his arms, and lowers me slowly into the water, kneeling down beside the tub until I'm all the way in, sitting up with my legs sticking out in front of me.

Covering my breasts with my arms, I bow my head.

He murmurs, "I'm going to help you lie back."

I nod. I feel burning and tingling in my cheeks and know they're scarlet.

Supporting my shoulders with an arm around them, he lowers my upper body until I'm resting against the back of the tub. I know I look ridiculous in panties that are now wet, but at least they're black, so he can't see right through them.

He cradles my head in his hand and asks if I want a towel to support my neck.

"Yes, please." I've never spoken two more difficult words. My self-consciousness is searing.

He places a rolled-up hand towel under my neck. Then he dips the pitcher into the bathwater and tips it over my head, massaging my scalp as the warm water runs through my hair.

It feels so good, I almost groan aloud in pleasure. But that's nothing compared to the bliss I experience when he works shampoo through my hair with both his hands.

His fingers are strong and gentle. He takes his time, making circles with his thumbs at my temples, stroking under the back of my head and neck, lightly squeezing the muscles at the base of my skull as he lathers my hair.

I spend a brief moment worried I might be drooling, but quickly surrender to the loveliness of it, the overwhelming luxury of the sensation. After less than a full minute, I feel drunk. Exhaling, I drop my arms from my chest and let my hands float by my hips in the water.

Mal starts to talk to me.

The pace unhurried and the tone low, he speaks in Russian. It sounds like he's telling a story or explaining something important. I know it's on purpose, that he's deliberately not speaking English so I won't understand, but somehow it doesn't bother me.

He continues to speak as he rinses my hair. The water splashing into the metal tub sounds like rain on a rooftop. He speaks as he dips a bar of soap and a washcloth into the water. Speaks as he gently washes my arms, armpits, chest, and neck.

By the time he's washing my feet, kneading my soles with those strong fingers, I'm in a stupor. My head lolls sideways. My eyes are closed. My breaths are slow and deep.

And still, he's talking.

I don't ask what he's saying. I don't want to break the spell.

He has to prop me up to wash my back. I sag against his arm, my chin hanging over his bent elbow. I feel boneless. Gelatinous. Like he could bend me into a pretzel, and it wouldn't hurt.

When he's finished washing and rinsing my body, he runs the washcloth over my face and behind my ears.

"Open your eyes, little bird," he murmurs in English.

My lids drift open. His face is inches away. His expression is tortured.

My voice faint because it's coming from outer space, I say, "Are you okay?"

He shakes his head, but doesn't explain. "I'm going to lift you out of the water. Do you think you can stand up?"

I consider it, then nod. "Not for long, though."

He lifts me from the tub and sets me on my feet on the bath mat, keeping a steadying hand on my hip as he reaches for a towel. Working fast, he dries me off with gentle, clinical efficiency, then wraps the towel around my body and picks me up again.

I rest my head against his shoulder and close my eyes as he brings me back to bed.

When he's got me arranged comfortably on the mattress, he opens the towel enough to change the dressing on my wound, leaving my breasts and panties covered.

I watch him work, wondering why he's doing any of this. "Mal?"

"Hmm?"

"Thank you."

That stops him cold. He glances up at me, his eyes dark, his brows drawn together. Storm clouds gather over his head.

"Don't thank me."

"Why not?"

"You were shot because of me."

"I'm alive because of you."

His lips thin. He closes his eyes, exhales a short, aggravated breath through his nostrils, then opens his eyes again and glares at me.

"No. *I'm* alive because of *you*. Because you took a bullet meant for me. Don't get it confused in your head. And don't thank me." Glowering, he goes back to work.

"Am I allowed to thank you for taking away the big scary moose?"

When he glances up at me, eyes flashing, I say, "I mean elk."

"Be. Quiet."

I whisper, "Because I really hated that thing."

He mutters something in Russian that doesn't sound nice, then finishes changing the bandage on my belly. He uses medical tape to make it stick. Rising, he goes to the closet and returns with a black Henley identical to the one he's wearing.

He helps me sit upright and gets me into the shirt.

It's huge, comfy, and smells like him. I might never take it off.

"Lie back."

I do as he commands, watching his face as he pulls the shirt down over my hips, then removes the towel from around me, pulling it out from under my body. When that's done, he says, "Panties on or off?"

Instead of answering, I lift my hips.

He pulls the wet panties off, reaching under the shirt to get to them, then sliding them down my legs. Along with the towel, he takes them into the bathroom.

When he returns, I'm yawning. He pulls the bedcovers over me and tucks me in.

He bends and kisses me on the forehead. Then he returns to the leather chair in the corner and sits down, folding his hands over his stomach and closing his eyes.

"Mal?"

"What?"

"Were you really going to kill me?"

He doesn't answer. I take his silence as a yes. I yawn again, nestling down against the pillow, snug and clean and exhausted.

I fall asleep with my silent assassin caretaker watching over me, keeping me safe.

This time when I dream of gunfire, he's there to protect me with a shield and a flaming sword.

TWENTY-EIGHT

RILEY

For the next few days, Mal is strangely silent. He doesn't leave me alone again. Whenever I wake up, he's in the room, sitting in the leather chair, watching me.

He helps me take short walks around the cabin, letting me lean on his arm as I wince and shuffle.

He takes my temperature, cooks my meals and feeds them to me, gives me water and medicine, and helps me in and out of bed when I have to use the bathroom.

When I ask him why he doesn't own a television, he shakes his head. When I ask how anyone can live without a computer, he sighs. He rebuffs almost all my attempts at conversation, especially if it has anything to do with his lifestyle or something personal about him.

On day four of the silent treatment, he asks out of the blue if I'd like to take another bath.

"Yes," I say, relieved he's finally back from wherever he went inside his head. "I'd like that very much."

Looking pensive, he nods.

He's sitting on the edge of the bed with his elbows on his knees and his hands hanging down, staring at the rug. It's dark outside. All the candles in the cabin are lit, giving it a warm, homey glow.

When he doesn't move or say anything else, I ask tentatively, "Did you mean now?"

As an answer, he rises, goes into the bathroom, and turns on the bathtub faucet. He comes back and picks me up in his arms.

I don't argue that I should be walking. He's not in the mood for my sass, that much I can tell. I just let him carry me into the bathroom and undress me, feeling hideously self-conscious again but trusting now that he won't make it more awkward for me than it already is.

When I'm lying in the water and his hands are in my hair, he starts to speak to me again in Russian, like he did the last time he gave me a bath.

He talks and talks, his voice low, the cadence of the foreign words hypnotizing.

There's emotion in his tone, but it's not anger. If anything, it seems like the opposite. Like he's trying to get me to understand something of vital importance to him.

I want to ask him what, but I don't. I know he won't answer.

When he's rinsed me, dried me off, and put another of his huge clean shirts over my head, he announces it's time for my stitches to come out.

"Oh. Okay. Do I have to go to a hospital for that?"

The look he gives me is insulted. He picks me up and brings me back to bed.

He fluffs the pillow under my head, pulls the sheets up to cover my crotch, lifts the shirt up to just under my breasts, and peels off the bandage. From a drawer in the nightstand, he removes large tweezers and a pair of surgical scissors, both wrapped in plastic.

Anxiety blooms over my skin like a rash. "Is this going to hurt?"

"No. You'll feel a tug or two, but that's all."

I nod, knowing that he'd tell me if it was going to be painful.

He opens the tools, cleans them with a gauze pad and a sharp-smelling liquid from a brown bottle, then leans over me and goes to work.

After a moment, he says, "You've healed well. This scar won't be bad."

I've resisted looking at the wound until now, so that's a relief to hear. When I lift my head and peek down at my uncovered stomach, however, the relief evaporates, replaced instantly by disgust.

"Not bad? It's hideous!"

"You're exaggerating again."

"I'm Frankenstein! Look at that gash! It's a foot long! And why the hell is it shaped like a lightning bolt? Had the surgeon been drinking?"

"He had to go around your belly button."

"Couldn't he have made a crescent moon? I look like Harry fucking Potter times ten!"

"Stop shouting."

Groaning, I let my head fall back to the pillow. "So much for wearing bikinis."

"You could get a tattoo to cover it up. Add to your collection."

His voice remains even when he says that, but there's an echo of warmth in it that gives me pause.

"I'm sensing you have something you'd like to say about my tattoos, Mal."

Snipping and tugging at the ugly black stitches, he quirks his lips. "Just curious."

I sigh and roll my eyes. "Where do you want me to start?"

"With the one on the inside of your left wrist."

The speed with which he answers makes it obvious he's been thinking about that one for a while. It's a single line of cursive black writing and consists of four words:

Remember Rule Number One.

"Well, if you must know, that one's my favorite."

"What's rule number one?"

"Fuck what they think."

He stops mid-snip and looks up at me. "Who's 'they'?"

"Everyone. Anyone else but me. It's a reminder that other people's opinions don't matter. To live my life how I want, regardless of outside pressure. To be unapologetically me."

After a moment, he nods slowly, satisfied. He goes back to work, teasing out a severed stitch and placing it to one side on the old bandage. "And the words 'you can' on your right ankle?"

"I used to say 'I can't' to my mom a lot when I was little. It was just an excuse for something I didn't want to do, or something I thought was too hard, but she wouldn't let me get away with it. She'd just stay calm and say, 'You can.' And then I would, because I didn't want to disappoint her. The tattoo reminds me to keep going when I want to give up."

I'm quiet for a moment, lost in memory. "My mom was the best friend I've ever had."

Mal glances up at me, his eyes piercing. "Was?"

I nod. "She died when I was a kid. Ovarian cancer." My voice drops. "It's not a good way to go."

"There aren't any good ways to go. Some are just faster than others."

"My great-grandma died in her sleep at ninety-nine. That seems pretty good."

"Sure, if you didn't have to live to be ninety-nine to get there."

"What's wrong with getting old?"

"Don't know many elderly people, do you?"

"Not really. Why?"

He says cryptically, "Old age isn't for the faint of heart."

The little pile of snipped black stitches is growing. And he was right: I've barely felt a tug. He's good at this.

From what I can tell, he's good at everything.

"What about the dragon on the nape of your neck?"

I grimace. "Big yikes."

"Translate."

"I got that during my *Game of Thrones* phase. I was obsessed with Khaleesi. A little boss bitch who owned three dragons and kicked butt all over the men? Yes, please. Wait. Is that . . . is that a *smile* I'm seeing?"

"No," he replies instantly. "That's just the face I make before projectile vomiting."

"Ha."

"And the pattern on the back of your right arm?"

"I thought it was pretty. What about that big scary hooded skeleton on your back?"

He gives me a look that says *Think about it.*

"Oh. Right." My laugh is small and embarrassed. "How about that line of text going up your ribs? What language is that?"

"Cyrillic."

"What does it say?"

"No past, no future."

"Wow. That's dark."

"There's not much humor to be found in my line of work. Except if it's black."

"Makes sense. What about that big red *V* on your left shoulder? That one looks fresh. Is it someone's initial?"

"No."

"Is it a Roman numeral?"

"No."

"Then what does it stand for?"

Finished with removing the stitches, he sets the scissors and tweezers aside, balls up the bandage with the cut-up pieces of thread, puts it on the dresser, then looks at me.

"Vengeance."

I open my mouth, then close it again.

"Well, well, well," he murmurs, his gaze intense. "Look who finally got quiet."

I bite my lower lip. His gaze briefly drops to my mouth, then he looks back into my eyes.

Honestly, I can't think of a single thing to say. There is nothing to say. There are no words for this situation.

After a tense few moments pass, he says, "You haven't asked me to take you home."

There's a question in there. The question is *Why not?*

To avoid his penetrating gaze, I glance down at my stomach. Then I slowly pull the shirt down, covering my scar. "Okay."

"That's not an answer."

I don't have an answer, at least not one that makes sense. I feel him staring at me with blistering intensity, and my cheeks start to burn.

He's about to say something when a sharp noise makes me jump. It comes from the window on the other side of the room and sounds like a person is standing outside in the dark, rapping their knuckles on the glass.

My voice turns high with panic. "What's that sound? The wind? A bear? A serial killer?"

Cool as a cucumber, he says, "It's Poe."

"What's a Poe?"

Rising from the bed, Mal crosses the room and slides up the windowpane. Cold night air rushes in. Onto the sill hops an enormous black crow, fluttering its wings.

The thing probably weighs twenty pounds. It has glittering black eyes, a razor-sharp beak, and a frightening air of intelligence.

It looks at me, squawking like Satan sent it for my soul. "Oh, god!"

"No, Poe." Mal holds out his arm. The creature hops onto his forearm, looks up at him, and makes a chattering birdy noise of affection.

"You're shitting me. You have a pet crow?"

"Don't talk about him like he's not in the room. You'll hurt his feelings."

I can't tell if that's a joke or not, because his face is serious. Like it always is.

"Do you want to feed him?"

I look at the bird with trepidation. Unimpressed, it stares back at me. "What does it eat?"

Mal deadpans, "Human eyeballs."

I say drily, "Great, you're a comedian now."

He sits at the foot of the bed and holds his arm out toward me. The bird hops down to his wrist, head bobbing. I let out a small sound of fear.

"Amuse him for a minute while I go get his food."

The crow flutters down from Mal's arm and lands on my thigh. It feels like someone dropped a toddler on me. The sound of fear I make this time is louder.

Mal rises. Before he turns to leave the room, I could swear I spot a smirk on his face.

Poe stands defiantly on my leg, adjusting his wings and glaring at me.

Trying to sink as far back into the pillow as I can, I say faintly, "Hi, Poe. Um. Nice to meet you. I hope you're not a carrier of the plague."

Squawk!

"Was that insulting? You'll have to excuse my manners. I don't often have conversations with winged creatures."

Squawk!

I get the distinct sense this fucking bird wants a better apology than the one he just got, so I add lamely, "I'm sorry for saying that thing about the plague. It was rude. Um . . . you have very pretty feathers."

I know the glint of satisfaction in its eyes isn't my imagination, because it emits a softer squawk and starts grooming its feathers.

Mal returns to the room holding a small dish. When Poe sees him, he caws in excitement, hopping up and down on my leg and probably causing bruises. Mal hands the dish to me. I peer over the edge and see that it's filled with small brown pellets.

"What is this?"

"Cat food. Crows love it."

As if to prove his point, Poe flaps his wings, lands on my chest, pokes his head into the bowl I'm holding, and starts eating.

"Mal?"

"Yes, Riley?"

"There's a giant crow on my chest."

"I can see that."

"Is it dangerous?"

Poe stops gobbling cat food pellets for a moment to turn his head and glare at me.

With faint laughter in his voice, Mal says, "Only to people who refer to him as 'it.'"

Poe stands on my chest, waiting.

Feeling like an absolute idiot, I apologize to the bird again. "Sorry, Poe. I've only ever had goldfish. They don't have nearly as much personality as you."

Poe produces a quiet, rambling series of clicks and grating rattles to show his displeasure with me, then he starts eating again.

I've been dismissed.

The three of us are silent until Poe finishes off the cat food.

Then he flies back to the open window, making me jump as he takes off from my chest.

With a final farewell squawk, he flies off into the night. Mal closes the window behind him and turns back to me, leaning against the wall and crossing his arms over his chest.

"Do you have any other animal friends I should expect for a visit?"

"There's a family of raccoons who comes over from time to time."

"Any bears?"

"Not friendly ones. Time for you to go to sleep."

"Are you this bossy with all your patients?"

"Are you this mouthy with all your doctors?"

"Only the ones I like."

There's a pause where he simply stands and stares at me, his eyes warm. Then a miracle occurs: he smiles.

It's beautiful.

He murmurs, "Go to sleep, Riley Rose."

"How can I sleep with you standing there staring at me?"

"You've been doing well with it so far. Now close your eyes."

I heave a sigh, flop my arms dramatically at my sides, then obey him and shut my eyes.

I must fall asleep almost immediately, because I remember nothing after that.

When I wake up in the morning, Mal is sleeping on his side next to me in bed, his arm under my neck, a leg thrown over both of mine, his big warm hand splayed over my belly.

Right over my scar.

TWENTY-NINE

RILEY

*J*ust breathe," he murmurs, his mouth close to my ear.

Okay, so he's not asleep. And he obviously felt all the muscles in my body clench when I realized he was lying beside me.

I inhale a deep breath, but it isn't calming. How could it be? It draws his heady masculine scent through my nose and deep down into my lungs, where it settles, making me dizzy.

My ovaries wake up from a dead sleep and start shrieking like zoo monkeys.

A million things I could say run through my mind, but what comes out of my mouth is a strangled "Oh. Hi. This is new."

He chuckles. "Don't panic."

"Who, me? Psh. I'm not panicking. I'm totally cool. I'm the coolest."

He slides his hand from my belly to my wrist. He presses his thumb against the pulse point there. I know he can feel it throbbing wildly, because that's what my heart is doing, too.

After a moment, he chuckles again.

"Don't gloat. It makes me want to stab you."

He doesn't respond to that. He does hold on to my wrist, however, wrapping his big hand around it and folding my arm across my chest so I'm cocooned in a hug, safe in the delicious weight and warmth of him.

I close my eyes and try hard not to tremble.

"You twitch in your sleep like a puppy."

His voice is low and warm. My ovaries have stopped shrieking, but now they're busy running around lighting everything in my lower body on fire.

I don't know what to say, so I don't say anything.

"I have to go to work today." He pauses. "I'll be back late."

I suspect there's more he wants to say. The pause felt significant. I wait, my heartbeat going even faster.

After a while, he speaks again. This time, his tone has changed. It's grown dark. "Don't try to run away."

I whisper, "I won't."

"You should."

"Why?"

"You know why."

Oh, god, the sex in his voice. The raw, hot, dirty sex he put into those words has me hyperventilating. I can't help it now: I start to tremble.

It does something to him. Brings out a feral animal he's been keeping under tight control, leashed behind his tense silences and watchful eyes.

He drags me onto my side and back against his chest, pinning me there with his arms and legs, his heat and bulk all around me. Into my ear, he says gruffly, "You know exactly what I want from you, don't you? Or you think you know. But if you really did, you'd run as fast and as far away from me as you could, *malyutka*. You'd run away screaming."

I blurt, "I know you're not going to hurt me."

"I want to."

"No, you don't."

His voice turns into a wolf's growl. "Oh, yes, I do. I want to hold you down and bite you and fuck you until you're sobbing. I want to come deep inside your pussy, your mouth, and that perfect little ass. I want to see my teeth marks on your tits and my fingerprints on your thighs and the tears in your eyes when I put you on your knees and make you gag on my cock. Don't get it wrong, sweet girl. *I want to fucking devour you.*"

Breathing erratically behind me, he seems out on the far edge of his control, as if he might snap at any moment and tear me to pieces.

Long and rock-hard, his erection digs into my bottom.

I lie there wide-eyed and shaking, aroused and breathless, expecting at any moment to feel his teeth sink into my neck and his hands rip off my clothing.

What happens instead is that he grips my jaw in his hand, turns my head, and kisses me.

It's deep and searching. Raw and ravenous. Passionate and scorching hot. Everything he wants from me is in it, as if he's allowing himself this one moment of release to show me the depths of his desire.

The moment is over as quickly as it came.

He releases me, springs from the bed, and strides out of the room, slamming the door behind him.

A few seconds later, another door slams, and he's gone.

I spend the day in a daze, shuffling from room to room like a zombie. I can't concentrate. Without a television or computer, I feel like time is standing still. I'm confused, restless, and emotional, unsure what I'm supposed to do about what happened, nervous about what will happen when he comes back.

By the time Mal comes home late that night, I'm a mess.

I needn't have worried, though, because he's returned to pensive caretaker mode.

The animal is back in its cage.

"You're still awake," he says, standing in the doorway of the bedroom.

I'm sitting in the big leather chair, thumbing through a book I can't read because it's in Russian. I set it aside and look at him. "I couldn't sleep."

He's holding several large white paper bags with handles, like the ones from a department store. He sets them on the floor and removes his coat, throwing it onto the desk chair.

"I brought you some clothes. Shoes. Other things, too."

He gestures to the bags. Hopefully, my sanity is in there somewhere.

"Thank you."

I'm stiff and uncomfortable, unsure what to say.

He stands still for a moment, watching me, then unexpectedly kneels in front of my chair. Grasping my wrists in his hands, he pulls me toward him.

When my face is inches from his, he searches my eyes. Then he murmurs, "Now you're afraid of me. Good."

"Why do you want me to be afraid of you?"

His answer is gentle. "Because you should be. Because it will keep you alive."

"These whiplash mood changes of yours are all very exhausting. By the way, I've been thinking."

"Now *I* should be afraid."

"That's not funny. I asked you how long you were going to keep me here. Your answer was 'As long as it takes.' As long as *what* takes?"

A small shake of his head is my only answer. His refusal makes me angry.

"I deserve an explanation."

A muscle in his jaw slides. His green eyes flash. "I'll decide what you deserve. And when you get it."

Oh, the innuendo there is hair-raising. I don't let it distract me. "Why did you bring me here? Why did you save me? Why have you bothered doing anything you've done since we met? What's the *plan,* Mal?"

"The plan is none of your business."

"This is my life we're talking about!"

In his wolfish growl, he says, "Your life was forfeited when Declan killed my brother. Your life belongs to me now."

Our gazes are locked, unblinking, and furious. Electricity crackles through the air.

Refusing to be intimidated by him, I keep my voice cool and even. "So I'm your slave. You own me. Is that what you're telling me?"

His eyes grow hot. He licks his lips. He likes the idea.

"I'm not telling you anything one way or another except this: you'll stay here with me as long as I want you to."

He stands abruptly, looking down at me with hot, half-lidded eyes. "As for the question of ownership, you might want to ask yourself why you still haven't begged me to take you home."

He turns on his heel and leaves the room.

I shout after him, "I've been kidnapped! It's implied that I want to go home!"

That low, satisfied chuckle I hear from the other room tells me he doesn't believe me, either.

I don't speak to him for two days. I can't. I'm too angry.

I'm not sure which one of us I'm more angry with, however, him or me.

He's right: I should have begged him to take me home by now. I should've done it the first time I opened my eyes. But I haven't, and that means something.

Something disturbing I haven't quite figured out.

Or maybe I don't want to figure it out. The implications aren't good.

Or maybe I don't want to know what he'd do if I asked him to take me home.

Maybe he would, and I don't want him to.

And maybe my brain just needs a vacation from all the maybes, because not a single thing makes sense anymore. I hardly know which way is up.

On the third day, he takes me outside for the first time. Bundled in a heavy wool blanket and a sweater and sweatpants he brought me, my feet snug in a pair of nubby cotton socks, I stand blinking on the porch in the bright light, leaning a hip against the wood railing and holding a hand up to shield my eyes from the sun. My breath steams out in front of my face in billowing white clouds.

It's icy cold. The air is still. The sky is a clear, brilliant blue. All around the cabin, for as far as the eye can see, a pristine alpine meadow glitters under a dusting of snow. The tall fir trees surrounding the meadow are dusted, too, their powdered-sugar branches arching gracefully.

Other than the occasional chirp of a bird, it's utterly silent.

I feel like we're the only people in the world. In a make-believe, fairy-tale world of our own design, where no one exists but the two of us.

Standing beside me, looking out at the endless view, Mal says quietly, "Mikhail and I grew up here. The Antonovs have lived in this house for four generations." He pauses. "Well, not this house. The original cabin my great-grandfather built burned down. Hit by lightning. Mik and I rebuilt it from the ground up."

I look at his profile, so handsome and hard.

He belongs here, in this silent wilderness. Belongs the same as the wolves, the elk, and his friend, the arrogant crow. He's as untamed as all the wild creatures who inhabit this place, and he lives the same kind of life as theirs.

Savage.

"I grew up in a cabin, too."

When he glances at me, his eyes are so piercing, I have to look away.

"In Lake Tahoe. It was smaller than this place. My great-grandfather didn't build it. But it reminds me of there. The smell. The pines. The wildness around everything, how being so close to nature reminds you that you're part of it, too. In my apartment in the city, I always felt separate from things. Like real life was somewhere else, out there. It couldn't get to me. But in the woods, I feel more . . ."

I stop, searching for a word until Malek provides it. "Alive."

I nod. "And unsafe."

"Which is why I like it."

"It suits you."

After a short pause, he says, "I have a place in the city, too. Moscow. I stay there when work requires it. But this is where I'd rather be."

"How far is it to Moscow from here?"

"An hour by car to the nearest town, then a two-hour flight."

That startles me. "Oh."

"What?"

"You can take care of your business in a one-day round trip that includes six hours of travel?"

He says quietly, "I'm very good at what I do."

I breathe in the clean, cold air, letting it clear my head and calm me. "Killing people."

He spends a while staring at my profile, then says, "It's interesting to me that you don't seem bothered by it."

"Of course I'm bothered by it." I think for a moment. "Though, to be honest, I'd be a lot more bothered if you were killing kittens. People in general are overrated. And you're probably just offing other bad guys, mafia guys and whatnot, so part of me thinks you're doing something beneficial for society. And yes, I'm aware that's ridiculous, and I have no way of knowing if you're out raping nuns and burning down orphanages and blowing up kindergarten classes, but there's just this dumb little voice inside my head that tells me that for a bad guy, you're actually pretty good."

My sigh is heavy. "But I'm not in my right mind, so take all that with a grain of salt."

Minutes of silence pass. Then he says in a low voice, "Of all the people I've met who know what I do, you're the only one who's ever treated me like I'm human."

We stand in silence, looking out at the meadow and the trees.

There's an ache inside my chest that's growing rapidly. "Mal?"

"Yes?"

"I'm sorry about your brother."

He stiffens.

"I'm not saying that because I don't want you to kill Declan. I mean, I don't want you to kill Declan, but that's a separate thing. I just . . . I'm sorry for your loss. Even though we're not that close, if my sister died, part of me would, too."

After a moment of thought, I admit reluctantly, "Maybe the best part."

I glance at him. He inhales slowly, his nostrils flared and his lips flattened.

I turn my attention back to the view, unsure what else to say. We stand side by side for a long time, listening to the silence, until he exhales.

"Your bodyguard. Kieran."

My breath catches. "Did you find out something?"

"He's alive. Spent a while in ICU, but he'll make it."

Pressing a hand over my pounding heart, I exhale a shaky breath. "Thank god."

"The other one. The blond."

The tone of his voice makes me nervous. "Spider? Is he okay?"

He nods, then says thoughtfully, "I have to give it to your Irishmen, they're a persistent bunch. Dumb, but persistent."

"What do you mean?"

He turns his head and gazes down at me with emotionless eyes. "Spider's in Moscow. He came to search for you."

That leaves me breathless. With shock, but also with fear, because I know what Mal will do next.

And it isn't bringing Spider a welcome basket.

Panicking, I turn to him and grab his arm. "Please don't—"

"Save your breath," he interrupts. "I won't kill him."

I collapse against the porch railing, closing my eyes and inhaling a deep breath. "Thank you."

"You seem particularly fond of that one."

His tone is even, but there's an undercurrent there. An edge.

When I look at him, he's gazing at me with half-lidded eyes.

It's a smoldering look. An intense one. And obviously possessive.

My mouth goes dry. I moisten my lips before I speak. "I am. He's my friend."

"Friend."

He draws the word out, repeating it like it tastes bad in his mouth.

"Yes. A friend. I'm sure you're familiar with the concept." His jaw tightens. He stares down his nose at me, all swaggering machismo and snorting bull.

"I don't have friends."

"Yes, you do."

"No, I don't."

"Yes, you do, you stubborn ass."

"Name one."

"Me."

He looks at me like I'm certifiably insane and should be locked away forever for the safety of humanity.

I sigh heavily. "Oh, shut up. I know it doesn't make any sense. It's still true."

His hands clench. A vein stands out in the side of his neck.

He steps closer to me, eyes blazing.

Before he can shout insults into my face, I say loudly, "I don't care if you don't like it."

"I kidnapped you!"

"You saved me from dying of a gunshot wound."

"A shot that was meant for me!"

"Yes, and since then, you've been pampering me and worrying yourself sick over my every little cough and sparing people you'd normally kill because I asked you to. Unless that thing about Spider was a lie, but I don't think it was, because I know you don't like to disappoint me."

When he does his growling-bristling-macho-man routine, I wave my hand at him dismissively. I'm not done talking.

"Also, you've kept your hands to yourself and your dick in your pants, though we both know you don't want to, and there's not a thing I could do to make you stop if you decided to have your way with me."

Through gritted teeth, the cords in his neck standing out, he says incredulously, "Have my way with you?"

"You know what I mean. The point I'm making is that people who aren't family and aren't sleeping together but who look out for each other and take care of each other and make sacrifices for each other they wouldn't normally make are called friends. Deal with it."

He glares at me. Judging by the way his eyes bulge, his head will explode any second.

Instead, he stalks off the porch and into the trees. I don't see him again until the next morning.

THIRTY

MAL

I never would have taken her if I'd known she'd be this much trouble.

She's upended everything. My entire life has been turned upside down by a tiny demon waif with a mouth as big as her balls.

She isn't afraid of me. She thinks I'm her friend.

She thanks me for everything, when she should be screaming at me in rage or terror.

I don't understand any of it.

I stare down at her sleeping form. She's curled up in bed on her side with her hands folded under her cheek, looking deceptively angelic.

I know that's a ruse. That sweet, innocent exterior hides a six-hundred-pound gorilla with an iron will.

With the exception of my snub nose Beretta, I've never known anything so small that was also so fierce.

I walk silently out of the bedroom and close the door, resisting the urge to leave a note for her telling her when I'll be back.

Three hours later, I'm at the Lenin Hotel in Moscow, watching Spider at the bar.

He's staring down into his drink, ignoring the buxom woman to his left who keeps trying to get his attention. Several other women at nearby tables keep glancing in his direction as well, but he seems oblivious to them all.

He's preoccupied. Swirling his whiskey. Lost in thought. I know what he's thinking about.

Rather, who.

The demon waif has an annoying way of holding a man's attention hostage.

I take the stool to his right. He glances at me, does a double take, then jolts to his feet, snarling.

"Pull the trigger, and you'll never find her," I say calmly to the gun he thrusts in my face.

The woman to his left screams and stumbles off her barstool. The other patrons follow her as she runs out. Then it's only me, Spider, and the bartender, who pours me a double vodka.

He sets it in front of me and shakes his head at the two security guards who are just coming in, alerted to trouble by the swift exodus of the crowd.

They take one look at me and turn around and walk back out.

Sometimes it's good to be a gangster.

"Have a seat, Spider."

Livid, he shouts, "Where the fuck is she?"

"Someplace safe. Have a seat."

I see the instant he decides to shoot me in the leg instead of the face. Before he can, I'm on my feet with the barrel of my gun shoved under his chin.

Unfortunately, his reflexes are good. He doesn't drop his weapon, stumble back, or make any other tactical error.

He simply responds in kind, shoving the muzzle of his Glock under my jaw.

We stand like that, elbows locked, weapons loaded, ready to blow each other's heads off, until he says through gritted teeth, "She's alive?"

"Yes. No thanks to you."

"Where are you keeping her?"

"Don't waste my time with stupid questions."

"I should fucking kill you!"

"Probably. But if you do, she'll starve to death. Alone. Is that really what you want?"

He curses violently in Gaelic. It's obviously taking every ounce of his self-control not to pull the trigger.

"She likes you, you know."

Taken off guard by that, Spider blinks. "What?"

"It's the only reason you're not dead right now. She asked me not to kill you. Even after you put a bullet in her gut, she still said you were her friend. It's really something else, when you think about it. Personally, if I'd lost a kidney, a spleen, and two liters of blood, my mood would be a little less forgiving."

He licks his lips and adjusts his weight from foot to foot. His voice gruff, he says, "Let me take her home."

"She is home. She's mine."

His eyes flare with rage at all the terrible things he's imagining I've done to her. "You sick fuck!"

"Come on, now. You'll hurt my feelings."

"She doesn't deserve this! She's innocent!"

"You think I don't know that?"

"Then let her go!"

I stare into his eyes, already knowing the answer before I ask the question. "Would you let her go if you had her?"

He clenches his jaw. His face turns red. He curses at me again, this time in English, using creatively colorful language.

"That's what I thought. Tell me, did your boss send you, or was this little rescue mission your idea? I can't imagine Declan embarking on such a desperate, destined-to-fail endeavor."

"Where. The fuck. *Is she?*"

"This is getting tedious. Is there anything you want me to tell her before I go?"

He digs the muzzle of his gun deeper into my neck and snaps, "You're not going anywhere."

Stubborn as a bloodstain, this Irishman. Despite my inclination to hate him, I find myself admiring his resolve.

"Last chance. No apology you want me to pass along?"

"Give her to me. She's nothing to you!"

"No sincere words about how sorry you are that you almost killed her?"

"It was an accident! It should've been you!"

"But it wasn't. You shot her. Now she's mine. I can see you're having a hard time with both those things, which is good. You deserve to suffer. And I applaud your tenacity, but if you don't leave Moscow within twelve hours, you'll be buried here."

I allow myself a small, humorless smile. "My promise that I'd spare you doesn't extend to the rest of the Bratva."

He's about to override his good sense and pull the trigger to end me, when his eyes go hazy. He blinks and shakes his head, trying to focus, but his pupils won't cooperate.

When he sways on his feet, I grab his gun from him and shove it under my belt.

He staggers against the bar, gripping it for balance, blinking as he tries to clear his vision.

"What have you done to me?" he rasps.

"Nothing permanent. You'll have a nasty headache when you wake up. Get something for it at the airport. And you really shouldn't accept a drink from strangers in a foreign country. You never know what might be in it. Or who paid them to put it there."

He's still cursing me as he goes down.

I watch him for a moment, out cold on his back on the floor.

Then I hand the bartender a folded wad of cash, down my vodka, and head back home.

THIRTY-ONE

RILEY

*B*efore I even open my eyes in the morning, I'm aware that Mal is lying beside me.

If his heat wasn't a dead giveaway, the giant erection poking into my hip is.

"Don't worry," he murmurs, his mouth near my ear. "I'm not going to fuck you."

It's probably my imagination, but I could swear that sentence was followed by an unspoken *Yet*.

Commence hyperventilating and swallowing convulsively.

When I've managed to pull myself together, I whisper, "I thought you were mad at me."

"I was. I'm over it."

"Where have you been?"

"Why? Were you worried?"

"No. I just didn't know what to tell Poe when he showed up looking for you."

After a moment, he chuckles. "Liar."

I open my eyes and immediately wish I hadn't. Not only is he lying beside me, he's under the covers with me. He's naked from the waist up.

And his big hand is splayed possessively over my belly again. Underneath my shirt, pressed against my bare skin, his palm is fire. His touch burns straight down to my soul.

Jesus, take the wheel. I'm drunk driving.

Mal inhales against my hair. His voice turns husky. "You have no fucking idea what it does to me when you tremble like that."

"Please stop saying the *F* word."

"I'm enjoying your response to it too much to stop."

"Why are you in bed with me if you're not, um . . . you know."

He says deliberately into my ear, "Going to fuck you?"

I squeeze my eyes shut. My toes curl involuntarily.

His laugh is low and pleased. "I'm in bed with you because it's comfortable. Because I like lying next to you. Because I want to be here."

Damn, he smells good. And he feels good, so warm and strong. And he's hard. Everywhere.

He runs his thumb gently along my scar. "How's your pain today?"

"Not as stabby. More like a dull ache."

"Did you take your meds last night before you went to sleep?"

"Yes."

"Good girl." After a pause, he says in a throaty voice, "Are you doing that deliberately?"

I blurt, "I can't help it if I'm shaking!"

"It's more like quivering. Shivering, all over."

"If you'd stop using that tone, I'd be fine!"

"What tone?"

"That sex tone!"

He says something in Russian that sounds filthy, then chuckles when my shivering grows worse.

I try to get up, but he throws his leg over mine and drags me back against him, rolling me over so my stomach is pressed to his. I tuck my head under his chin and hide my face in his chest as he laughs at me.

Stroking his hand up and down my spine, he gives me time to calm down before pressing a kiss to my neck and making me hyperventilate all over again.

He murmurs, "Why are you so skittish? I said I wasn't going to fuck you."

"It's your beard."

"What?"

"Your beard."

He sounds confused. "What about it?"

"It tickles."

He goes from confused to blistering-hot sex god in half a second, saying gruffly, "And you'd like to feel that tickle between your thighs, wouldn't you?"

"No."

"Then why are you squeezing your legs together?"

"I'm not."

His laugh is slightly breathless, but extremely pleased. "Oh, yes, you are, baby."

"I really hate it when you're smug."

Shaking with silent laughter, he presses his lips to my shoulder, nosing aside the neckline of my shirt to do it, making sure to drag his beard lightly across my skin. He reaches down, takes a handful of my ass, and squeezes.

Then he makes the most purely masculine sound I've ever heard, a chest-deep groan of pleasure.

I'm sweating. My heart is palpitating. My nipples are hard, and the throbbing between my legs is intense.

And the *shivering*. You'd think I was lying naked on a bed of ice!

He rolls me to my back, grips my head in his hands, looks deep into my eyes, and makes a long and passionate speech, entirely in Russian.

At the end of it, he kisses me. Deeply.

Hungrily. Thoroughly.

Then he rolls off me, stands, and goes into the bathroom, slamming the door behind him.

He turns on the shower.

He's in there for a long, long time.

For a full week after that, he hardly looks at me.

He sleeps sitting up in the leather chair in the corner of the bedroom every night.

He chops firewood with an axe like he's executing condemned royalty.

He goes hunting in the woods, disappearing for hours. He returns with elk, venison, and rabbit, which he expertly skins and butchers while I watch, fascinated and grossed out.

He cooks our meals, makes the coffee, washes the dishes, tends the fires in the fireplaces, repairs a leaking sink, mops the floors, cleans his weapons, hammers a loose board on the roof, takes inventory of supplies, drives into town to restock canned goods and sundries, shovels snow off the porch, shaves under his jaw with a straight razor, fixes a sagging windowsill, and completes a dozen other tasks with such utter competence, I feel like I'm getting a master class in the art of manliness.

And every night, he bathes me.

What began as an exercise in humiliation, born out of necessity because we couldn't get my sutures wet, changes slowly into something else.

Something intimate.

It becomes a ritual we never exchange a word about. After dinner in the evenings, when he's cleared the dishes and I've brushed my teeth, he fills the tub, removes my glasses, then undresses me.

I lie naked in the warm water with my eyes closed, feeling his hands move over my body and listening to him talk.

Always, always in Russian.

The touching is sensual and deeply relaxing, but never sexual. It's like he's memorizing my body with his hands, mapping all my curves and angles with his fingertips, committing me to memory.

Groggy with pleasure, I lie passively in the tub as his soapy fingers slide over my skin.

Later, in bed alone, I burn.

I can't deny my physical response to him, the way he makes me ache and tremble. And I know he wants me, too. The evidence of it is all over him. From his smoldering glances over breakfast to his clenched jaw when I stand too near to the bulge behind the fly of his jeans when he dries my body after the baths, his desire is obvious.

But he keeps it under lock and chains and throws away the key.

He doesn't get into bed with me again. He doesn't say the *F* word again.

He especially doesn't kiss me.

With the exception of the bath ritual, he treats me like I'm his patient. He takes a keen interest in how I'm healing, asking me every day about my pain level and making sure I'm eating enough and taking my meds, but other than that, he's distant.

Clinical. Cold.

I think a lot about how he said he was responsible for me since I took a bullet for him. I think about how hard he tries to keep an emotional wall between us, how he only reveals himself in a language I can't understand.

Most of all, I think about the battle he so obviously wages with himself every time he looks at me.

He can't reconcile what Declan did to his brother with what I did for him.

He doesn't understand how someone he thinks should be his enemy can call him a friend.

And he's incredibly conflicted about his desire.

He wants me, but he doesn't want to. It's obvious in a thousand different ways.

And slowly, I begin to understand that when he answered *as long as it takes* when I asked how long he would keep me here, he meant as long as it would take for him to work it all out in his head.

I think the biggest monkey wrench in his progress is my continued refusal to beg him to let me go.

"Refusal" isn't the right word. It's more like disinterest.

To my profound surprise, I've discovered that I like it here.

I like the clean air and the quiet. I like seeing a million stars at night. I like the simple rituals of meals, baths, and bedtime, of Poe knocking on the window with his beak every few days for treats.

I don't even mind it when Mal has to leave me for hours or sometimes days to go into the city, because I've discovered that I like to walk alone in the woods with the sun on my face, the cold air biting my cheeks, and the satisfying crunch of frozen pine needles underfoot to keep me company.

I like the cabin that he and his dead brother built with their hands.

Most of all, I like the time I have to think.

I never did much of it before, not really. I studied and worked and spent any free time in front of a screen, distracting myself. Deadening my feelings.

Some people eat when they're depressed. Some people drink, or do drugs, or have sex with strangers. The way I dealt with emotional pain was by feeding myself a steady diet of social media and video games and pretending it wasn't there.

It seems so obvious now. I was lonely.

In a city of nearly a million people, I always felt alone.

But here, in the middle of nowhere with only a crow and a killer for company, I don't feel alone.

I feel safe.

I feel content.

I feel, some days, like that bullet was the best thing to ever happen to me.

"I'll be gone overnight."

I look up from my scrambled eggs. Mal sits across the table from me, looking at his plate, pushing food around on it with his fork.

"Overnight?"

He nods. "I'm leaving right after breakfast."

"Okay."

He glances up at me. In the morning light, he's breathtaking. His pale eyes are the color of fine jade.

"How's your pain?"

I smile. He asks me the same thing every morning. "Pretty much gone, unless I try to lift something."

His dark brows draw together into a frown. "Why would you try to lift something? You should ask me."

That makes me smile wider. "It's good for me to push myself."

His frown deepens to a scowl. "No, it's not. You could get hurt."

I hold his gaze for a beat, then say softly, "Bending over to pick something up isn't nearly as dangerous as what you do."

"I'm a professional. You're injured. They're two completely different things."

His tone is tight. I inspect his face for a moment. It's tight, too, as are his shoulders.

"What's wrong?"

"Nothing."

"Since when do you lie to me?"

He snaps, "Since I'm your kidnapper."

He's in a foul mood, but I don't know what set him off. I put my fork down, lean back in my chair, and take him in.

"Stop staring at me." He shovels a forkful of eggs into his mouth.

"Why are you upset, Mal?"

"I'm not."

He chews angrily. I can practically hear him crushing his molars together.

"Okay. Except you are. Did I do something?"

He swallows, looking at me with blazing eyes and a set jaw. "Why haven't you asked me to take you home?"

This again. As if I have a logical answer. "Would you if I did?"

That seems to make him even angrier. "That wasn't my question."

"I know. It was mine."

He stares at me, breathing audibly. Looking as if he's only controlling himself through a great deal of willpower, he says, "Spider is still in Moscow."

Startled by the news, I remain silent.

"I saw him. I drugged him. I threatened to kill him if he didn't leave. He stayed anyway. Do you know what that means?"

My heart jumps into my throat. I put my hand over my chest and stare at him in horror. "You *drugged* him? Why?"

Mal shakes his head in frustration and ignores my question. "It means he won't leave without you, even though he's risking his life. He *doesn't care* that he's risking his life, understand?"

He's trying to make a point, but I don't know what it is. "That's his job. He risks his life all the time, on Declan's orders."

"I don't think this was Declan's doing. I think it was his own decision. And I think there's a lot more than guilt motivating him."

"My head is spinning. What are you saying?"

"I'm saying why the fuck are you not begging me to take you to Spider right now and let him take you home? He's your friend, according to you. I suspect he wants to be much more than that.

He's from your world. He's part of your family. He cares for you. Yet here you sit, with me. Why?"

I look at his beautiful face. I look at his beautiful eyes. I think of all the ways this killer has proven himself to be so much more than that. All the ways he's denied himself what he wants, including—so far—revenge for the murder of his brother.

And the truth just comes out.

"Because there's nowhere else I'd rather be."

His lips part. His pupils dilate. He stares at me, motionless.

Then he looks away and swallows hard. He exhales and says gruffly, "If you don't go back with him, he dies. I'll kill him."

"You're not going to hurt him."

"Yes, I will."

"No, you won't."

He looks at me again, and his eyes burn with anger. "Goddammit! You're not listening to me!"

"Yes, I am, but you're lying. Because you know that if you hurt Spider, I'll never forgive you. And no matter how much you try to tell yourself that shouldn't make a difference, it does."

Infuriated, he stares at me in crackling silence.

Feeling daring, I add softly, "And we both know why."

He jolts to his feet, flattens his hands on the table, and leans over it, glaring at me. "If you think I care about you, you're wrong."

"Okay."

"I mean it. You're only here because I'm punishing Declan."

"Okay."

His voice rises. "You're nothing but a means to an end. You're part of my plan. This"—he waves a hand between us—"isn't anything. It's nothing. You mean *zero* to me."

I look down at my hands, then back up at him. I say quietly, "Okay."

His temper snaps. He shouts, "Why do you keep agreeing with me?"

"Because we both know you're full of shit, so arguing would be pointless."

He stares at me. A vein throbs in his temple. Then he straightens abruptly and stalks out of the kitchen.

I sit in my chair, listening to him storm around the cabin, stomping from room to room. After several minutes, the front door slams.

Now I'm alone, wondering if I've just signed Spider's death warrant.

You never know what a trained assassin will do when he loses his temper.

I jump up and run out to the front porch. Mal is nowhere in sight in the meadow, so I run around the side of the cabin, stumbling in my haste. I've never seen where he parks his car—there's no barn or detached garage within sight—but it must be nearby, hidden somewhere in the trees.

When I regain my footing and look up, ready to sprint into the woods, my heart drops. I suck in a terrified breath and freeze.

A bear stands motionless ten feet away, its attention focused on me.

It's an adult. I can tell by the sheer size of the thing. It must weigh eight hundred pounds.

Its head is a massive wedge shape. Its fur is a glossy dark brown. If it stood up on its hind legs, it would tower several feet over me.

It makes a terrifying chuffing sound, a low grunt of aggression. It lowers its head, clacks its teeth, and pounds a huge paw against the ground.

Shaking in fear and badly hyperventilating, I take one careful step backward.

The bear watches with hostile black eyes as I take another step.

Then it lunges.

THIRTY-TWO

RILEY

*I*t happens so fast, I don't even have time to scream.

I whirl around and run. I haven't gone five steps when I'm knocked off my feet by a powerful blow to my back. I land flat on my face in the snow, the wind knocked out of me. I scramble to my knees, heart thudding, but get knocked down again, this time from the side.

I roll over several times. The sky and earth fly by like I'm on a merry-go-round. When I stop, I'm lying on my back, panting and disoriented. My glasses have fallen off, so I can't see much.

I struggle to rise, not knowing where the bear is or even if it's still tracking me, but then I hear a terrifying snarl and smell wet fur and realize the thing is almost right on top of me.

With a slight turn of my head, it comes into view.

Black nose and beady eyes, sharp canines dripping with saliva. It's so close, all I can see is the head.

The bear snaps its jaws at my face. Then it's on me.

At the same time I scream, crushing weight descends on my

chest. The sun is blocked out. There's fur in my mouth and the overpowering smell of animal in my nose, suffocating me.

I endure a split second of remorse that I'll never see Mal's face again. I'm going to die without ever again seeing those beautiful eyes, and the knowledge is agony.

But then there's a deafening roar. Something warm and wet splatters over my face.

And I'm dragged out from under the motionless bear by my arm.

Mal drops his shotgun, falls to his knees on the ground beside me, and starts ripping at my clothing.

"Where are you hurt?" he shouts, clawing at my shirt with shaking hands. "Riley! Talk to me! Where are you hurt, baby?"

I've never seen him like this. His eyes are wild. His face is white. He looks completely unhinged. Like a totally different person.

A terrified person.

Not at all like a man who thinks I'm nothing to him but a means to an end.

When I'm unresponsive, purely from shock, Mal picks me up in his arms and runs back to the cabin. He kicks open the front door. He drops to his knees in the living room, lays me on my back on the rug in front of the fireplace, and starts pulling at my clothing again, desperately trying to find where the bear mauled me.

"Riley, baby, oh god, oh fuck."

He's panting in panic. Groaning between breaths. His hands move so fast to find my injuries, they're a blur.

The feeling is coming back into my stunned body. My head starts to clear, and I realize the blood on my shirt isn't mine. Aside from an aching shoulder and not being able to draw a full breath, I haven't been harmed.

Because he was there.

Because, once again, Mal saved my life. I reach up and touch his face.

He freezes, staring down at me. Breathing hard, his eyes frenzied, he looks at me like he can never look away.

My voice is faint but surprisingly calm. "I'm not hurt. I'm okay, Mal. I'm okay."

So distraught he can't speak, he simply stares at me, his chest heaving.

What I see in his eyes lights my soul on fire.

Emotion rushes at me, lightning and thunder and starlight, a crash of adrenaline roaring in my ears like the sea. I ache with it, splitting at the seams, unraveling under its power.

I sit up, take his face in my hands, and kiss him.

He hesitates. He fights himself for a split second, accustomed to not giving in. Then a small moan slips past his lips, and he surrenders.

He crushes me against his chest, buries a hand in my hair, and takes my mouth like he's been starving for it since the day he met me.

I'm pretty sure that's because he has.

The kiss is the most passionate and all-consuming I've ever experienced. It's as if floodgates have opened wide. Like a dam has broken. He puts his whole body into it, wrapping around me and holding me painfully tight, his hands shaking, his breathing harsh. He makes desperate sounds into my mouth as he ravages it, groans of pleasure and sweet, longed-for relief.

Then he's cradling my head in his hands and kissing me desperately all over my face as I laugh breathlessly, staggered by the force of his emotion.

That wasn't just a kiss.

It was an opened door into his soul.

"Say it again," he demands. "Tell me again, baby. Tell me."

"I'm okay. I'm not hurt. I'm right here, and I'm okay."

He falls on top of me, pressing me back against the floor and our bodies together, and kisses me again. I sink my hands into his hair and close my eyes, dizzy from his taste and how savagely my heart is pounding.

He kisses my jaw, my cheek, my neck, speaking in Russian as his lips move over my skin. Words pour out of him and onto me, baptizing me with fire.

I wrap my legs around his waist and find him hard, like I knew he would be. I grind against his erection, letting him know exactly what I want.

"You're still healing," he rasps, breaking away to gaze down at me with fevered eyes. "The gunshot wound. We can't—"

The words die in his mouth when I pull my shirt over my head and fling it away.

I'm not wearing anything underneath it. His gaze on my bare breasts is as devouring as his kisses.

Breathing hard and staring up into his eyes, I whisper, "We can. We are. Right now."

There's no hesitation this time. He's pure heat, speed, and physical force, a bull smashing through the starting gate.

He rises to his knees, yanks off my shoes, sweats, and panties, rips open the fly of his jeans so his hard cock springs out into his hand, then falls between my spread thighs and shoves it deep inside me.

I arch and gasp, clutching his shoulders.

He's huge, hot, and invading, sinking all the way in with a single thrust. He covers my mouth with his, swallowing my moan of pleasure, then fucks me hard and ravenously, one hand gripping my ass, the other fisted in my hair.

He's still completely clothed.

I'm naked and delirious beneath him. I've never been so naked in my life.

He breaks away from my mouth to kiss my breasts. His hot, wet mouth is heaven on my rigid nipples. The tickle of his beard raises goose bumps on my skin. He sucks hard on a nipple, then nips at it with his teeth, making me gasp again. My fingers twist in his hair.

He rises to an elbow and grips my throat. Staring deep into my eyes, he fucks me until I'm writhing and moaning his name.

"*Malyutka*. My little bird. My sweet angel. What have you done to me?"

His voice is raw, choked with emotion. His eyes are filled with anguish.

I climax with his hand around my throat, cutting off a scream.

He drops his head and hides his face in my neck. Shuddering, he fucks me straight through my orgasm. Then the motion of his hips falters. He releases a guttural moan.

With one final, forceful thrust, he comes inside me.

THIRTY-THREE

RILEY

*M*y back smarting from rug burn, I lie panting and shaking with my arms and legs wrapped around him, his body buried inside mine.

When his breathing finally slows, he lifts his head and gazes into my eyes.

He lets me see everything.

The darkness. The wreckage. The longing. The need. The loneliness that matches mine exactly.

The confusion that we are what we are, but what we should be is enemies.

I whisper, "I know. We don't have to figure it all out right now."

His lids flutter closed. He exhales heavily. Then he kisses me again, this time tenderly.

He withdraws from me, presses a soft kiss to each of my breasts, then picks me up in his arms and carries me into the bathroom.

Setting me on my feet, he makes sure I'm steady before he turns on the shower. Then he undresses, takes my hand, and leads me under the warm spray.

He cleans my face with soap and a washcloth. He rinses bear blood from my hair. He washes my body with such care and attention, it seems like someone paid him a great deal of money to do it.

He washes himself as an afterthought, turns off the water and dries us both with the same towel, then carries me to bed.

"I'll forget how to walk," I murmur, my head resting against his strong shoulder.

"If you don't want to, you'll never have to walk anywhere again."

My chest expands. My insides turn squishy.

He means I wouldn't have to walk because he'd gladly carry me.

He settles me on my back in bed, crawls in beside me, and pulls the covers over us. He slides his arm beneath my neck and flattens a hand over my belly in the same spot he always does, directly over my scar.

Then he puts his nose into my damp hair and inhales.

When he exhales, it sounds like decades of misery have been relieved, like maybe he was just released from prison.

We lie like that for a long time, holding each other, just breathing.

I know I'll remember this moment for the rest of my life.

When he finally speaks, his voice is soft and drowsy. "When I first saw you, I thought you were homeless."

Too blissed out to be offended, I laugh instead. "Such a sweet talker."

"You were so unkempt. Small, gray, and rumpled, like a tissue someone had kept in their pocket too long."

My eyes widen. "Good god. You might want to consider shutting the hell up, lover boy, or you'll never get lucky again."

He squeezes my hip, snuggling me closer. "You made me want to rescue you. To take care of you. I had no idea you were a dragon in disguise, like that tattoo hidden under your hair on the nape of your neck."

I say grumpily, "Keep talking. You have a lot to make up for."

His voice drops to a murmur. "A tiny fire-breathing dragon,

who can cut a man down to size with only a few words from her beautiful mouth."

I ponder that, unsure if it was an insult or a compliment.

"What did you think when you first saw me?"

"That I was about to be featured on an episode of *Law & Order: Special Victims Unit*."

After a short pause, he starts to laugh. It's a purely masculine sound, belly deep and genuine.

I love it.

"I'm surprised you know that reference, considering your hatred of TVs."

"I never said I hated television. I just don't have one here."

"Do you have one at your place in Moscow?"

"Yes."

"Oh. Why not here?"

He slides his hand from my belly to my breast, cupping it gently and thumbing over my nipple until it hardens. His voice drops.

"Because this is my sanctuary. The only things I keep here are ones I can't be without."

I close my eyes, turn my face to his neck, and wait until my heart has resumed beating to say, "So you watch American crime shows, huh?"

"They're very entertaining. Your criminals are the stupidest in the world."

"They're not *my* criminals."

He cups my jaw and kisses my forehead. "No. You only have one of those."

I roll onto my side and cuddle up against him. He gives me a big squeeze. A few minutes of comfortable silence pass, then I whisper, "I almost got eaten by a bear, Mal."

"Bears don't eat people. They just slash them to pieces."

"That's great," I say drily. "Thank you."

"Do you want me to put its stuffed head on the wall where the elk's used to be?"

"So I can be retraumatized every time I look at it? Pass."

"You don't seem traumatized."

I smile into his chest. "Maybe an orgasm is the cure for PTSD."

"Or maybe the little boss bitch Khaleesi's got nothing on my waif."

"Waif?"

"That's what I call you in my head sometimes. The demon waif." After a beat, he says, "Is that bad?"

"Let me overthink it for a minute."

"Because I don't want you to be offended."

"Oh, sure. Who would be offended by being described as a skinny stray from hell?"

"It's interesting how you made that sound like a death threat."

"I'm multitalented. Wait until you see me juggle chain saws while aiming a flamethrower at your head."

He laughs again. Because I'm pressed against his chest, I feel the rumble of it beneath my cheek and can't help but smile.

He cups my jaw in his hand, turns my face up to his, and tenderly kisses me.

"Tell me I didn't hurt you. I'll never forgive myself if I did."

I know he isn't talking about his hideous nickname for me. I gaze into his beautiful eyes, smiling. "Only in the best way."

When he cocks a brow, I clarify. "I'll probably be sore. A lot sore. You're not exactly . . . let's just say your dragon isn't tiny like me."

He rolls to his back, taking me with him, and laughs and laughs as I lie on his chest and gaze down at him, amazed.

Who is this happy assassin? Where did my growling, scowling Malek go?

"You're very giggly all of a sudden."

He stops laughing and looks at me. "Giggly?" he repeats, insulted.

"Sorry. You're right, manly men like you don't giggle."

"Exactly."

He tries to scowl, but fails miserably. His lips curve up into a smile instead.

I reach up and trace the outline of his mouth, finding it impossible not to smile back at him. "I'm curious. How does someone born and raised in Russia speak English without an accent?"

He passes his hand through my hair, watching with heavy-lidded eyes as the strands flow through his fingers.

"Because when that someone travels the world using different passports and identities, it's helpful not to sound Russian. My size makes me stand out enough as it is. I practiced for a long time to sound like I came from nowhere in particular."

The man with no past and no future who comes from nowhere and lights a girl's heart on fire with only the force of his pale green eyes.

What a fascinating mystery he is.

I fold my hands over his chest and prop my chin on top.

When I stare at him for too long, he says, "What?"

"How old are you?"

That amuses him. His smile deepens, and his eyes dance with laughter. "Why do I get the feeling this is just the beginning of a long and arduous interrogation?"

"It's called conversation. I ask questions, and you answer them."

"No, that's interrogation. In a conversation, the questions go back and forth."

"You'll get your chance. I'm going first."

"That's what I was afraid of."

I reach up and touch his beard. It's soft and springy under my fingertips, delightfully crisp. If he ever shaves it off, I'll kill him.

"Why are you smiling?"

"Never mind. Back to my question about your age."

"I'm thirty-three." After a pause, he adds, "Your eyes just got big."

"You're nine years older than me."

"Really? You look younger than that by years."

"It's all the preservatives in the candy. What's your favorite color?"

"Black."

"Shoulda guessed. What do you do in your free time besides watch American crime dramas?"

"Come here as often as I can. Hunt. Read. Hike. Watch the stars. When I'm in the city, I don't do much except handle work."

"Work."

He nods. I get that he won't describe the nitty-gritty. "And how did you get into your line of work?"

He inhales deeply and looks at the ceiling. After he exhales, he's quiet for a while. "By accident."

"Meaning?"

He closes his eyes. A muscle slides in his jaw. "I killed a man in a bar fight when I was seventeen."

He's silent again. Lost in memory. I can tell whatever he's remembering is painful for him and wait quietly for him to continue as I stroke his beard.

"He was harassing my brother. Mikhail wasn't a big guy. And he was quiet. Smart and quiet. The kind of kid bullies gravitate to. We were on a family trip with our parents, visiting our aunt in Moscow. Mik and I went to a bar after our parents went to bed. I came out of the restroom and found this asshole talking shit to Mik. I told him to fuck off. He didn't like that. Threw a punch that missed. I threw one back that connected. Next thing I know, he's on the floor, face covered in blood, not moving. He never got up."

Drawing a slow breath, he opens his eyes and looks at me. "He was Bratva. First cousin of Pakhan, just my fucking luck."

"Pakhan?"

"It's an honorific title. Means the big boss. King. Everyone in the bar knew the guy I hit was connected. Before the police could get there, Pakhan rolled up with a dozen of his soldiers. Said me and my whole family could eat bullets to pay my debt, or Mik and I could go to work for him. Obviously, he didn't like his cousin much, or we would've been dead on the spot.

"Pakhan put Mik in a street crew working as a lookout on jobs. It's the lowest position in the Bratva, but within a year, he was leading his own crew. Like I said, he was smart. Knew how to navigate tricky situations. Made himself valuable. Kept moving up."

"And you?"

"I made myself valuable, too. Only there was no upward mobility in my position. I stayed right where I started out, because nobody could do for Pakhan what I could."

His voice drops. "I proved to be extremely talented at making his enemies vanish."

He's silent for a long while, lost somewhere in his head.

Then he draws a slow breath and continues.

"Pakhan liked Mik. Trusted him. Knew the death of his cousin was really my fault, not Mik's, so when Mik eventually asked permission to go to America, he got it."

"Why did he want to go to America?"

"Same reason everybody does: opportunity. Pakhan knew Mik was ambitious. Knew he'd eventually outgrow his position here. Knew that a lot of his soldiers would defect if Mik made a move to take over. And I think he genuinely liked Mik. He didn't want to have to kill him if it came to that, so he sent him off with his blessing. Told him his debt was paid.

"Mine, however, would never be paid. I was the one who took his cousin's life. My debt wouldn't be paid until I drew my last breath, one way or the other."

I rest my cheek on his chest. He cradles my head in one hand and rubs the other slowly up and down my spine.

"Our parents were dead by the time Mik went to America.

Killed in an avalanche, if you can fucking believe that. The aunt we stayed with in Moscow died of cancer. Her husband had a heart attack. That was our entire family, so Mik and I were the only Antonovs left."

He swallows. "Then Mik was killed."

His voice is rough with emotion. Under my ear, his heart beats strong and fast.

I close my eyes and squeeze him. For the first time since all this started, I'm furious with Declan.

But this is their life, Declan's and Malek's both. Kill or be killed. There's no other option.

It's a terrible catch-22, because revenge starts the cycle all over again. You killed my cousin, now your life and the lives of everyone you love belong to me. You killed my brother, now I have to kill you.

And maybe also take a family member hostage for good measure.

And because you did that, now I have to retaliate, and on and on and on.

There's no end to it. It's probably been going on like this for centuries. War, blood, death, vengeance, start from the beginning and do it all over again.

I whisper, "What if there was another way?"

"Another way for what?"

"To get closure. What if you could do it without violence?"

His hand falls still on my back. When he speaks, his voice is surprisingly hard.

"Closure is an American idea. A fantasy. There's no such thing. When someone you love is murdered, that scar never heals."

I lift my head and gaze into his eyes. "So then revenge doesn't really help."

"It's not about help. It's about restitution. Balancing the scales."

"So you believe that if you kill Declan in retaliation for Mikhail, the scales will be balanced?"

"Yes."

My reply is as soft as his is forceful. "Except you're wrong. The scales won't be balanced. Because you'll have hurt my sister."

"I don't care about your sister."

"But you care about me. And I care about her. You can't drop a stone in the water without causing ripples. Everything you do has an effect on something else. Some*one* else."

Angry, he glares at me. I know I'm stepping out onto dangerously thin ice, but this needs to be said.

"What do you think will happen the day I find out you killed Declan? Do you think we'll be lying here like this after that? Do you think nothing between us will change?"

He says flatly, "Now you're blackmailing me."

"I'm asking you to consider if there isn't some other way."

"Of course there's no other way!"

"Yes, there is."

"Like what?"

"Forgiveness."

He stares at me with blazing eyes and a jaw turned to stone, his entire demeanor enraged. But he keeps his voice controlled when he says, "Don't be naïve."

"Don't be condescending."

"Riley."

The way he says my name feels like a slap. My cheeks burn with heat, but I don't back down.

"You said you wanted him to suffer. I can tell you for sure that he is, because I was shot. Because you kidnapped me. Because my sister, despite her shortcomings, will blame herself for all this, which in turn will make Declan miserable. Way more miserable than if you shot him dead, because then he'd be released from his guilt and her pain."

He sits with that silently, staring at me for so long, I think I might have made a dent.

But then the assassin takes deadly aim and pulls the trigger. "Except there's nowhere else on earth you'd rather be than here, remember? Which means my kidnapping you hasn't been punishment for anyone."

"They don't know that."

"But I do."

Is he deliberately trying to humiliate me? My throat gets tight. My eyes fill with water. I whisper, "Mal."

Ignoring my distress, he says, "I know that if Declan O'Donnell could see you now, he wouldn't be worried. Neither would your sister. They wouldn't like the situation, obviously, because of who I am. But they'd know you were safe. They'd know you were happy, wouldn't they, Riley?"

His tone drips acid. He wants it to burn, and holy hell, it does.

Leave it to a man to take something beautiful and crush it in his fist.

I roll off his chest, muttering, "Fuck you."

Before I can rise from bed, he captures me and presses me down against the mattress, flattening me with his weight, pinning my arms over my head. He stares down into my eyes, all fire and fury, his tone as sharp as the edge of a knife.

"You can keep your fantasies and your forgiveness. I live in the real world. A world where actions have consequences. And don't forget that I'm not the one who started this."

"You could be the one who ends it."

"He murdered my brother!"

"And I took a bullet for you. I could've died."

"You didn't."

"No, because you saved me. Do you know why?"

He growls, "Don't fucking say it."

"Because you're good. Deep down inside, you're a good man."

He's got that wild look in his eyes again, the unhinged one I saw earlier. Only this time, it's less panic and more rage.

It doesn't deter me.

"Glare at me all you want, I know it's the truth. You stuck up for your brother when he was getting harassed. You didn't mean to kill that guy in the bar. It was an accident. Since then, you've been working off a debt that will never be paid, just so your family would be safe. You've been doing what you've been doing all this time *for other people*."

Through gritted teeth, he says, "Stop. Talking."

"You didn't kill Spider. You didn't kill me. I'm starting to think you don't really want to kill anyone, you're just used to following orders."

"You don't know what the fuck you're talking about."

"You could walk away now, couldn't you, Mal? Now that everyone you love is gone, you don't have a reason to keep doing what you do for Pakhan anymore."

He shouts, "No, I don't—*but I want to!*"

We lie nose to nose, breathing hard and staring at each other, until he gets his temper under control. Then his voice comes low and hard.

"This is my life. This is who I am. Don't go making up pretty lies to tell yourself. To make yourself feel better that you fucked a killer."

"I hate you right now."

"You should hate me. *I'm not good.* I'll never be good. I told you once that I'm the worst man you'll ever meet, and that was the truth, *malyutka*. Like it or not, it was the truth."

He releases me, rising from the bed to stalk naked into the closet. He disappears inside it, reemerging quickly, fully dressed. He's holding a black bag in one hand and carrying his overcoat.

Without another word or a glance in my direction, he's gone.

THIRTY-FOUR

KAGE

*L*ying in the hospital bed with tubes bristling from his nose and both his arms and bandages plastered over almost all his visible skin, including his face, the kid looks like shit.

I had to come see it for myself. I can't believe this stubborn little fucker is still alive.

"Hello, Diego."

He gazes at me. His dark eyes are surprisingly focused. From what I'd heard, he was pretty much brain-dead.

I suppose having a burning wood beam fall on your head will do that to you.

I take a seat beside his bed and set my gun on the nightstand. Except for the mechanical beeping of his heart monitor, it's quiet in the room. Quiet and dark. The night-shift nurses are on now. So are his night-shift bodyguards, stationed outside the door.

Diego watched me silently as I dropped in from the HVAC duct in the ceiling after I removed the grate. Though his expression is obscured by all the bandages, he doesn't seem surprised to see me. He hasn't moved a muscle or made a sound.

It doesn't look like he can.

Keeping my voice low, I say, "I hear you don't remember a thing. Not even your own name. Is that right?"

No answer. Not a surprise.

"If it makes you feel any better, I'm not happy about this." I make a gesture to indicate his overall fuckedness. "You're my enemy, but I'm not a complete savage. This is no way for men like us to go."

His gaze never strays from my face. I can't tell if he's listening or if he's as aware of his surroundings as a baked potato would be.

His memory loss has saved me a lot of trouble. Trouble of the worst kind.

It's strange I don't feel happier about it.

"For what it's worth, I didn't torture you. I kept you locked in a cage for a few weeks, sure, but it was only with the expectation that you'd break and start talking. You never did, though. Gotta say, I admire that. A man's nothing without his honor."

I sigh heavily, dragging a hand through my hair. "Funny thing is, Diego, I've lost my taste for the hard stuff. I think Malek might've been right when he said women make you soft. A while ago, I'd have hung you on the wall and played target practice on your torso to get the information I wanted. Now, seeing you like this . . ."

I sigh again. "It only makes me depressed."

Diego lies in his bed, unblinking.

Poor bastard. I'd rather die a million times over than live like a zucchini.

Weirdly, his silence makes me want to keep talking.

"You might be interested to know that I made it look like it was MS-13 who captured you. I heard their leader made a comment about my girl, and obviously, that couldn't stand. Nobody talks shit about my baby. He lost his head for that." I chuckle. "One thing I'll say for that prick Declan, he doesn't pull any punches when he's out for revenge.

"I know it doesn't make sense that I pulled you out of the warehouse fire. Doesn't make much sense to me, either. It would've been smarter if I'd let you burn. That building's owned by an offshore corporation that can't be traced to me. I should've just dusted off my hands and been done with you. But when I got the call from Sergey, it didn't feel right to leave you there.

"Investigators still don't know what caused it, by the way. They know it wasn't electrical, and it wasn't a device like an IED. Maybe it was spontaneous combustion. You ever heard of that phenomenon? People just going up in flames for no reason?"

I shake my head. "The world's a strange fucking place."

"It wasn't spontaneous combustion. It was me."

I'm so startled he's talking, I almost grab the gun and shoot him. Instead, I stare.

He stares back with a very non-zucchini-like sparkle in his eye. "I lit the fire. Not sure if you caught that. Thought I'd repeat it since you look a little distracted."

His voice is different. Raspy and rough, maybe from smoke inhalation. Added to the bandages and his sudden reanimation, the overall effect is eerie.

I say slowly, "You don't have amnesia."

"Congratulations. You're a genius."

I'm impressed that someone who looks like a bag of smashed assholes still has a sense of humor. Plus, I'm still trying to grasp what the hell is going on. It must be why I don't clock him and ask a question instead.

"How did you light the fire?"

"With the Bic in my pocket. I couldn't take sitting in that cage any longer. I figured if I died in a fire, at least I wouldn't have to listen to you talk anymore. You have a tendency to drone on and on. I think it's because you enjoy the sound of your own voice. I'm not sure if anyone's ever told you this, man, but you've really got an ego on you."

After a pause, I say, "Don't get ahead of yourself, Diego. I could still kill you."

"You're not gonna kill me. I just heard your confession. You'd feel too bad."

"I'd get over it."

He ignores that. "Besides, I have an offer for you."

I look at him in disbelief, lying burned, bruised, and bandaged in his hospital bed, this asshole I kidnapped, caged, and pulled out of a fire. "You. You have an offer for me."

"Yes."

"You see there's a gun right next to me on this table, right?"

"I see it. Use it, and in five seconds you'll be dead, too. My bodyguards are great shots."

"So am I."

"So then we'd all be in hell together. For all eternity. Doesn't that sound fun?"

After a solid sixty-second stare down, I say, "I didn't think it was possible for someone to be as annoying as Declan, but you've got him beat by a mile."

"Here's the offer: I'll continue to pretend I have amnesia, and you'll continue to pretend you have no knowledge of what happened to me."

When he doesn't go on, I frown in confusion. "How is that an offer? It's exactly what's been happening until now."

"Exactly. We'll keep the status quo."

"To what end? What do you want out of it?"

"I just want out."

"You're gonna have to translate that for me. I don't speak dumbass."

He moves his head restlessly on the pillow, like he wants to shake it but can't quite pull it off. "Look. I thought being the boss would be great. Money, power, pussy, all that. Right?"

"Right."

"Except it sucked donkey balls."

I squint at him. Maybe he did get some brain damage after all.

"After only a few months on the job, I knew it wasn't for me. All you pinche pendejos fighting like a bunch of little bitches all the time. Wah! You took my drugs! Wah! You stole my cargo! Wah! You moved in on my turf! It's fucking exhausting. My little sister has more smarts than all of you put together."

I'm not sure if I should laugh or shoot him.

"I just want to retire. Let Declan deal with you. He lives for that shit."

"Your boy Declan does a helluva lot more than deal with me, Diego. He's got his fingers in a lot of pies."

"Yeah, I know. He thinks he's saving the world. I mean, I know it's admirable, but as far as I can tell, it's a total waste of fucking time. You kill this bad vato over here, another bad vato pops up over there. Your whole life's *Groundhog Day*. What a headache."

I study what I can see of his face. "So you know he's a spy."

"Tch. I don't know anything. I'm just a thug who grew up on the streets. All this shit is over my head."

"Somehow I doubt that."

"If you're thinking *I'm* a spy, think again. Who wants to work for the fucking government? Fuck those guys. Bureaucrats are the worst. I'm just a homie who got promoted to a C-suite position who's better suited to the mail room. I felt like I was being suffocated. There were too many expectations, too many eyeballs on me all the time. It's very simple: I need my freedom. I want out."

I think for a while, then admit, "I don't really know what to say here, Diego. This is just about the strangest and stupidest thing I've ever heard."

If I insulted him, he doesn't show it. He simply sighs. "Honestly, man, you did me a favor. So I'm gonna do you a favor and keep my mouth shut. I know if everybody found out it was you who faked my death and started all this shit in the first place, you'd have mad problems on your hands. Am I right?"

"You're not wrong."

"Exactly. Mad problems. You're welcome."

"I could kill you right now if I wanted to ensure your silence."

"Yeah, you could."

He doesn't sound like he cares one way or the other.

Strangely enough, I believe this idiot. He really does just want out.

"Tell you what. I'll think about it."

Through the bandages comes a dry chuckle. "You do that. If I don't wake up, I'll see you in hell, *pendejo*."

"It'll take a while for me to get there."

"I'll wait."

He closes his eyes. When it becomes obvious he's either fallen asleep or is too exhausted to continue, I rise from the chair.

Before I can climb back up into the HVAC duct, Diego stops me cold by saying, "One more thing. Your comrade Stavros. You can't trust him."

I turn and look down at him. His eyes are still closed. "Why not?"

"Let's just say he's not as loyal to you as he should be."

The hair on the back of my neck prickles. When I don't say anything, Diego opens his eyes and looks at me.

"Snitches are bitches who end up in ditches."

"What the fuck does that gibberish mean?"

"It means put the screws to that little bitch and find out."

I snort. "You'll have to do better than that."

He pauses, then says, "This place has turned into a confessional booth. People think you've got amnesia, all kinds of strange shit comes out of their mouths. Everybody wants to tell you a story. Just like you, when you dropped in."

I get it instantly, and my blood starts to boil. "Stavros made a deal with Declan."

"Just so you know, it wasn't Declan's idea. Your boy offered. Threw you right under the bus without batting an eyelash. Cold as a snake."

"What was the deal?"

"Don't worry, it didn't pan out. I'll let Stavros tell you the details, but the point is, don't leave that *puto* alone with your silverware. He'll be tinkling like a wind chime on his way out the door."

"Why would you tell me this? Even if it's true, what's in it for you?"

"Eh, you treated me pretty good when I was in that cage. Gave me a little vacation. A little time to think about my future. Plus, bottom line, you saved my life. Like you said, it woulda been smarter for you to let me burn, but you didn't."

I narrow my eyes at him. It dawns on me that he's brighter than he seems.

"You knew I'd come, didn't you? When you started that fire, you knew I'd show up to try to get you out."

His smile is faint. His eyes drift close.

"Don't take this personally, but whoever your friend Malek is that you mentioned, he was right when he said women make a man soft. I've seen it too many times now, with homies even harder than you. A man starts getting really good pussy, like *life-changing pussy*, he can't remember what he used to be so mad about all the time. Sound familiar?"

I don't answer.

Diego doesn't speak again.

I really hate it when other people are right.

THIRTY-FIVE

MAL

*I*t's pissing rain when I get back to the cabin a few hours before dawn.

I stand outside the front door in the dark with my hands braced
on either side of the frame and my head hanging down, taking a
moment to try to cool off.

Every mile closer I drove, the harder it was not to jam my foot
onto the accelerator.

She's the most powerful magnet, pulling me home.

From the moment I left, I've thought of nothing else. Through
car rides and plane flights and meetings, while driving an ice pick
through a man's skull. Her face was in front of my eyes the whole
time. Hovering there. Haunting me.

That's what I feel like. Haunted.

She's a ghost who's moved inside my head and won't leave.

A sweet, mouthy, maddening little ghost. Who challenges me at
every turn and sees the best in me, even when I'm shouting at her
that she shouldn't.

Especially then.

I've never met a woman I wanted to strangle, protect, scream at, cherish, fight with, and fuck, all at the same time.

It's insane.

It's frustrating.

Worst of all, it's addicting.

I'm in the grip of a powerful addiction that I can't shake, no matter what I try. No amount of denial, rage, or bargaining is going to get me out of this.

There's no rehab for this obsession of mine. There's no withdrawal, either.

It's simply a fact: without my fix of her, I'll lose my fucking mind.

I draw a breath, pick up the bag from where I dropped it by my feet, and open the door.

Except for the guttering fire, it's dark inside the cabin. Dark and warm, quiet and still. I stand there for a moment, breathing air scented of her.

Even her scent is arousing.

I've heard the natural smell of a woman's skin described as sweet or floral, or something outdoorsy like sunshine or rain. But Riley smells different. There's no food, flowers, or candy on earth that could describe it.

I can't describe it, either, except to say that she smells like home.

And it's already a disaster. I know it is. The whole thing. Her, me, what we're doing together. If I didn't already know, this short time apart from her proved it.

This time, because I'd already tasted her, being away from her drove me mad.

We're the musicians on the deck of the *Titanic,* blissfully unaware as we play our violins that there's a giant fucking iceberg right around the corner.

One of us is unaware, anyway. But she'll make it onto a lifeboat. I'll get her onto one, no matter what.

I'll still be playing that violin when the ship goes down.

What started as revenge has turned into something far more dangerous. Something that will probably end me.

The worst part is, I don't even care.

She came into my life at the moment when I thought I had nothing left, and filled every dark, empty space with sunshine.

Stupid, bright, horrible sunshine, which I fucking hate. Except I don't anymore.

Now all I want to do is lie down naked in the sun and bask in the healing glow of its rays.

Fuck. I can hardly stand to listen to myself. I'm goddamn pathetic.

I walk slowly through the cabin to the bedroom, my steps silent on the floor. Outside the bedroom door, I pause again to gather myself.

It's so fucking hard not to kick it down and crash inside. It's almost impossible.

"Mal?"

My heart. Jesus, my heart. That voice of hers. So soft and sweet. So hopeful.

She's in there, awake in my bed, waiting for me. She felt me, felt my energy like I can always feel hers. It's nonsensical that we can feel each other through a closed door, but we do.

God, we fucking do. My chest aches with it.

I turn the knob and push open the door, and there she is. Sitting up in bed. Covers pulled up to her chin.

Staring at me like I'm her reason for everything.

I drop the bag, cross the room, fall to my knees next to the bed, and pull her into my arms. I bury my face in her neck and groan.

She hugs me back hard, trembling.

We stay like that as the rain grows louder, peppering the windows, drumming a plaintive song against the roof.

"I missed you."

It's barely a whisper, but it makes my soul burn. "I know."

"Please don't leave me alone again."

"I won't."

"You'll take me with you when you need to go to the city?"

"Yes. I can't stand it, either."

She burrows against me, trembling harder. "I'm sorry I made you angry."

I groan again, pulling away to show her with a kiss that she never has to apologize to me, not for anything. She kisses me back with passion, making desperate little noises in the back of her throat.

Then I'm desperate. Desperate with longing. Desperate for her. I know there's a clock ticking down the days until this thing between us will end, because men like me don't get the fairy tale.

And women like her deserve a white knight, not a monster. Not the dragon the knight is sworn to slay.

"What? White knights and dragons? What are you saying?"

Fuck. I'm delirious. I'm talking out loud.

"Nothing," I murmur, taking her face in my hands. "Only that you're mine. Don't ever forget that. No matter what happens, you're mine."

She gazes into my eyes with her heart shining through hers, her lips wet with my kisses.

"You're different," she whispers. "What's happened?"

I don't bother hiding or denying this time. I let it all go and tell her the truth.

"I decided to give in to the addiction."

"What addiction?"

"You, baby. You."

She bites her lip. Moisture wells in her eyes.

If I wasn't already a goner, those emotional gold-flecked eyes of hers would push me right over the edge.

Same as they've been doing since the beginning.

When our lips meet again, it's with a new urgency. A new understanding drives our need. I push her down against the mattress and kiss her hard, my hands tangled in her hair, her chest pressed to mine. We kiss until it feels like we've fallen through a hole in the earth, into darkness and heat, tumbling over and around, losing all sense of direction.

Then she's tugging at my belt. Yanking down my zipper. A warm, soft hand curls around my hard cock.

I push up her nightgown and suck on a rigid nipple as she strokes my shaft, panting and rolling her hips. When she slides her thumb over the slit in the crown of my cock, I groan into her flesh, shuddering.

"Let me—I want to—"

She's pushing at my chest, trying to move me. I lift my head and gaze down at her, not understanding what she wants.

Until she wriggles out from under me, slides down, and takes my cock down her throat.

My moan of pleasure is loud and broken.

She flattens her hands on my hips and pushes again. I roll to my back on the mattress and bury my hands in her hair. Kneeling beside me, she opens her throat and takes me in, her head bobbing as she sucks me. She curls both hands around the length of my shaft and licks the crown.

When she slides her tongue along the slit and fondles my balls, I have to force myself not to hold her head still and fuck her mouth like an animal.

"Ah, fuck. *Malyutka.* Christ. Your *mouth.*"

Panting, I slide a hand up her thigh and over her ass, squeezing it briefly, then slipping my fingers under her panties from behind.

Her pussy is soaking wet.

I slide two fingers inside her tight, slick heat. She moans around my cock, canting her hips so her ass tilts farther into the air. I find the swollen bud of her clit and stroke it, spreading her wetness all around.

Then I put my fingers in my mouth and suck the sweet taste of her off them.

When I slide my fingers back inside her, she moans again.

She sucks faster, her hands working in time with her mouth.

It feels fucking incredible, but I need more than this.

I drag her on top of me so her knees are on either side of my shoulders and her belly is resting against my chest. Then I position my face between her spread thighs, pull aside her panties, and bury my face in her wet pussy.

When I suck on her clit, she jerks. My dick pops out of her mouth. She lets out a long, low moan.

I slap her ass, and she jerks again.

"Suck that cock, baby," I growl. "Take every inch down your throat."

She obeys me instantly, fitting her mouth around me and opening wide.

I go back to sucking her clit, flicking my tongue over it and lapping at it greedily. I finger fuck her while I do it, listening to her muffled cries of pleasure grow louder.

When I reach down with my free hand and fondle her breast, she trembles. I pinch a nipple, and she starts to ride my face, wantonly moaning around my cock, rocking her hips against my mouth.

I need to come so bad, and I haven't even taken off my clothes yet.

My baby goes first, though.

Still with her tight nipple caught between the fingers of one hand, I pull my other fingers out of her slick heat and slide them up between her ass cheeks. Then I shove my tongue inside her pussy at the same time as I breach the tight little knot of muscle in her ass.

I sink my finger in past the knuckle. She sobs around my cock.

Then she comes, bucking against my face as I tongue fuck her pussy and finger fuck her ass.

She moans and shudders and makes desperate noises, all with my hard cock still down her throat.

By the time her shuddering eases and I feel her body relax, I'm seconds away from coming in her mouth. I pull her head back by her hair.

"Easy, baby. Not yet."

I can barely get the words out, I'm panting so hard.

I roll her to her back. Sitting up, I get her out of her nightgown and panties, then tear off my clothes. All of it gets impatiently thrown to the floor.

I take her in my arms again and take us back down to the mattress, positioning myself between her legs.

Lying on her back, she looks up at me with melting eyes and a sweet, soft smile that nearly breaks me in two.

As I slide inside her, she breathes, "Hi there."

"Hi there, yourself."

"That was very dirty."

"You loved it."

"I did," she agrees, nodding. Then, softer, "I love everything we do together."

She wraps her legs around my back and her arms around my shoulders and kisses me.

It's like falling off a cliff all over again.

All the adrenaline, all the dizziness, all the tumbling down into lakes of burning flame. I thrust into her silken wet heat, loving the way her breasts bounce against my chest, swallowing her small cries of pleasure as she feeds them to me.

When she breaks the kiss and I look down at her, my breath catches.

Time slows to a crawl.

I feel every throb of my heart, every bead of sweat on my skin, every hot pulse of blood coursing through my veins. I'm aware of the ache in my chest, the smell of her hair, the sounds our bodies make as they move together.

The room has shrunk to the space of us, only us on this bed.

The power we're generating is enough to light the whole world on fire.

This is why some men don't like missionary.

It's too intense. Too vulnerable. Too intimate, all the emotion and energy getting exchanged right up close.

Watching her face go through a dozen different expressions at once is overwhelming.

It's overwhelming for her, too. She stares right back at me, gazing deeply into my eyes as our bodies move together. As we share all those things that can't be put into words.

Those sacred things that can only be spoken by two hearts beating in tune.

The silent, holy language that souls speak.

Eyelids fluttering, she whispers my name. Then she arches and moans.

Hard, rhythmic contractions milk the length of my cock.

She comes with her eyes closed and her head thrown back as I watch her, thrusting deep, feeling her pussy throb and her taut nipples slide back and forth across my chest.

With a sudden, violent jerk, I'm over the edge, too.

I drop my head to her shoulder, close my eyes, and shudder as my climax slams hard into me.

It's so intense, I lose my breath. I can't make a sound. I just ride it out, pulsing deep inside her as she rocks her hips, her thighs quivering around my waist.

The loud, rumbling bass of thunder masks the moan of despair that slips past my lips.

Even as we come together in the windswept dark and hold each other, trembling, I hear a clock ticking in the background.

Maybe she was right when she said I'm not really bad.

If I were, I wouldn't care that I'm being selfish by keeping her here, chained up in the dragon's lair.

If it weren't for that damn white knight, I'd keep her chained to me forever.

THIRTY-SIX

RILEY

When the rain tapers off and the sun comes out, I'm lying spent in Mal's arms, drunk with afterglow.

Beneath my ear, his heart thuds a strong, steady beat. My arm is flung over his chest. One of my legs is twined between his. I'm tucked snugly into his side, shimmering with happiness.

My head rises as he inhales deeply. Stirring, he presses a kiss to my hair.

"How's your pain today?"

I laugh softly. "You would've made a good grandmother."

"I'll pretend you never said that. How's your pain?"

"Right now, I can honestly say I'm pain free."

He grumbles in discontent. "And the rest of the time?"

I turn my nose to his chest and inhale. My exhalation is a soft, satisfied sigh. "Only the occasional twinge."

He insists, "Like when for instance?"

So bossy. "I sat up in bed too fast last night, and that hurt a little."

"When I came in?"

"No. Before that. I had a nightmare."

He kisses my head again, stroking his open palm up my back. "Was it bad?"

It was horrible, but I'm not about to admit it and ruin the mood. "I used your trick to wake myself up. I told myself it was only a dream, and it worked. I couldn't believe it."

"It's called lucid dreaming. If you want, now you can make a sword appear that you can use to chop off the head of your enemy."

"Or, murder boy, I could snap my fingers and turn my enemy into a bunny rabbit so I don't have to do any chopping."

"Hmpf. What if the bunny was ten feet tall and rabid?"

"Then I'd snap my fingers again and make him fall in love with me."

"Yes, you have a gift for that." After a moment, he murmurs, "You just started shivering."

"Shut up."

"Are you cold?"

"Will you shut up, please? You know I'm not cold."

He rolls me to my back, props himself up onto an elbow, and smiles down into my face.

The morning light worships him, highlighting the angle of his cheekbones, burnishing his dark hair richest bronze, glinting copper off the curving tips of his lashes.

And those eyes! For fuck's sake, they might as well be priceless emeralds!

I whisper, "God, you're beautiful. It's sick."

He throws back his head and laughs.

"I'm glad you find me so hilarious."

Still chuckling, he kisses the tip of my nose. "I'm supposed to be the one paying the compliments."

"You know what? You're right. Go ahead. I'm waiting."

Framing my face in his hands, he looks into my eyes and says softly, "There's not a compliment in the world that could do you justice."

I make the sound of a buzzer. "Wrong answer. Try again."

Pressing his lips together to stifle his laughter, he drops his head and hides his face in my neck.

"Oh my god. You suck at this!"

"I'm not used to giving compliments on demand."

"Well, get used to it! I need a compliment, Mal. Like, now!"

He rolls to his back, drags me on top of his body, holds my hair back from my face, and looks into my eyes.

"All right," he says, voice gruff. "Here it is. You make me wish I'd lived a different life. You make me wish I could go back in time and start over again. You make me think the world isn't a shitty place after all, that goodness exists and happiness isn't make-believe and true love is possible. You make me believe in miracles, Riley Rose. When I'm with you, I feel like my life hasn't been such a waste."

After a long, silent moment, I burst into tears. "Oh, fuck," he says, appalled. "It was that bad?"

I pound a fist on his shoulder and drop my face to his chest, sobbing.

"Sweetheart. Sweetheart, stop crying." He wraps his arms around me and holds me tight.

"I never cried before I met you! I swear to god, I never cried once! And now look at me! I'm a wreck!"

"You're not a wreck."

"I'm wailing like a banshee!"

He chuckles, making his chest shake. "It's good to see the exaggeration didn't disappear in my absence."

"Stop laughing at me, you jerk!"

He exhales, murmuring, "Ah, my little bird."

Then he simply holds me while I cry it out until only the occasional sniffle is left.

Embarrassed by the outburst, I decide to pretend like nothing happened. I wipe my face and change the subject. "Is there still a dead bear outside?"

"I don't know. Did you move it?"

"Ha. No, I didn't move it."

"Then there's still a dead bear outside. I'll take care of it today."

"I lost my glasses when it attacked me, but I found another pair in that giant sack you brought."

"That's good."

"Where did you get that, anyway?"

"I robbed an optometrist."

I lift my head and look at him. "Is that a joke?"

"No."

"You robbed an optometrist?"

"A store, not a person. No one was there at the time."

"Oh. Okay."

He smiles at my befuddlement. "You're so fucking adorable. Why does that make you crinkle your nose?"

"Because people only use the word 'adorable' when they're talking about small animals. Do I look like a small animal to you?"

He narrows his eyes and considers me. "A little like a chevrotain."

"What the fuckety-fuck is a chevrotain?"

"It looks like a woodland creature from a fairy tale. It's about the size of a rabbit, but resembles a deer. They have big ears, skinny legs, and cute little noses. Instead of antlers, the males have tiny fang-like tusks. Some people call it the mouse deer."

I glare at him. "Do you have a death wish?"

"They're adorable!"

"Say that word one more time. I dare you."

"I think if you could see the tiny fang-like tusks, you'd have a change of heart."

"Yeah, the tusks and the big fucking ears sound super charming!"

He dissolves into laughter, lying with his eyes closed, his head canted back on the pillow, and his arms squeezing me tightly. He laughs so hard, it shakes us both and the bed.

I grumble, "Laugh it up, jerk. Get it all out of your system.

Because as soon as I get my hands on a machete, you won't be laughing anymore."

He rolls me to my back and plants a big kiss on my mouth. Grinning from ear to ear, he says, "You're not going to chop me up."

"Oh, yeah? Give me one good reason!"

His eyes soften. So does his voice when he says, "You like me too much."

The look on his face makes my heart skip a beat and my stomach clench. I glance away so he can't see me melt. "You're okay. I guess."

He peppers soft kisses all along my neck and collarbone. "I guess you're okay, too," he whispers into my ear.

Only we both know what he's really saying.

He rolls back onto his side, tucking me into his shoulder and twining his legs through mine. I wrap my toes around his muscular calf and sigh in contentment.

"I have something to say now."

His chuckle stirs the hair near my ear. "Really? I can't imagine."

"A couple of things, actually."

"Hold on. I need to prepare myself mentally. Okay, go ahead."

"It's a good thing you're so pretty. That personality of yours is a deal breaker. As I was saying . . . Spider."

All the warmth goes out of him like he's been thrown into a vat of ice water. His body stiffens, and his voice turns hard.

"I don't ever want to hear you speak another man's name in my bed again."

I know it's all kinds of wrong that I find it hot when he's possessive. Wrong, wrong, wrong, and yet so very fucking right.

And here I thought I was liberated.

"Fine. I'll refer to him as the Arachnid from now on. Satisfied?"

He growls, "I've taken it easy on you so far, baby, because you're not completely healed. But I'll remember all this mouthiness when you are. Then you'll be sorry."

Or maybe I won't. Judging by the heat in his voice, I'll be getting plenty of pleasure from whatever punishment he has planned.

Bypassing his sexy threat, I say, "You told me you drugged him. Is he okay?"

"Yes."

It's terse. Angry. Basically a three-letter fuck-you.

I tilt up my head and kiss his jaw. "I'm sorry. I'm not trying to make you mad."

"You're doing a crap job of it."

"Are you jealous of Spi—the Arachnid? Because there's no need to be."

"Anyone who wants what's mine is on my shit list."

What's mine.

I close my eyes for a moment, letting that sink through me. "There's nothing between us. There never was."

"Maybe not for you."

I'm curious what makes him so certain, but don't dare ask. I mean, I'm brave, but that's definitely not the hill I want to die on.

He snaps, "Next fucking subject."

"Okay. Um . . ."

He lifts his head and glowers at me. "What?"

"Oh, pipe down, Hulk. It doesn't have to do with another man."

He doesn't look like he believes me. He still hasn't blinked. Sighing, I say, "I thought you might like to know that I'm on Depo-Provera."

"Is that a medication?"

Before I can answer, he lifts to an elbow and stares down at me, saying loudly, "Are you on a prescription I don't know about? Why didn't you tell me? I could've gotten it for you! You could've been taking it this whole time!"

"Mal—"

"Christ, Riley, you have to tell me what you need, or I can't give it to you. Despite what you think, I'm not a mind reader!"

I reach up and stroke his beard, smiling. "You're a psychopath."

"Don't try to flirt your way out of this."

That makes me smile wider. "Only you would think a woman calling you a psychopath is flirting."

He scowls at me with flattened lips and flared nostrils, waiting for an explanation.

I say softly, "It's birth control. A shot. I'm just telling you that so you don't have to worry about getting me pregnant."

The anger disappears. What it's replaced by, I couldn't say, because I've never seen this particular expression before.

After a moment, he only says, "Oh."

"Okay, the way you just said that? It makes me think maybe you have genetically engineered super sperm who laugh at birth control as they fly past it on their way to inseminate eggs."

"No. I mean, yes, my sperm are obviously super, but no to the rest of it."

After a moment of examining his expression, I say, "Because your sperm don't laugh is what you're saying. Your sperm have resting bitch face, like you."

His brows shoot up. "Excuse me?"

"Don't get all in a kerfuffle."

"Kerfuffle?"

"If you'd like a definition, it's exactly what you're doing now."

"I'm not in a fucking kerfuffle!"

"Sure. Let me just wait a sec while my ruptured eardrums heal and we can continue this discussion."

His face goes through a few expressions—fury, amusement, disbelief—then he flips me onto my belly and spanks my bare ass five times in quick succession.

It's shocking.

Hard, stinging, and shocking, primarily because of how much it turns me on.

Heat blooms over my skin. My bottom feels like it's on fire.

Then the rest of me does, too, because Mal is looking at my wide-eyed face with hunger in his eyes.

"You liked that."

His voice has gone low and gravelly. He watches me, licking his lips like a predator before a juicy meal.

My heart thrumming, I say breathlessly, "I'll have to break my answer into two parts, because first, no, I didn't like it. My brain is judging us both very harshly. My Women's Studies professor from college is, too. But secondly, *holy fuck, that was hot.*"

"You've never been spanked before?"

I give him an incredulous look. "Who would dare spank the mouse deer with the tiny fang-like tusks?"

The smile that spreads over his face is utterly debauched. He drawls, "What else have you never done?"

"None of your business, Romeo."

He smooths his palm over my burning backside and kisses me gently on the shoulder. Turning his mouth to my ear, he murmurs, "You liked it when I had my hand around your throat, yes?"

I think of when we had sex on the living room floor. I attributed the intensity of that experience to the bear attack, but maybe having him squeeze my neck had something to do with it, too.

I came so hard, I saw stars.

He also did that when he broke into the safe house in Boston. Put his big rough hand around my throat and squeezed, threatening to choke me.

Right about then was when I stopped being scared and started acting feisty.

Holy shit.

Are Twizzlers not my only kink?

Biting my lower lip, I look at him and nod.

He lowers his head to brush his lips against mine. "Okay. That's a good starting place."

Do I die now, or wait until later when we're doing whatever kinky fuckery I suspect he's got planned?

I don't have time to ponder it, because he rises from bed, picks me up, carries me into the bathroom, and fucks me again in the shower. He holds me up against the wall as he drives into me, biting my neck.

Maybe being adorable isn't so bad after all.

Days go by. Mal doesn't leave for the city again.

Our nightly bath ritual continues, only now Mal speaks in English instead of Russian as he washes me. He tells me about his childhood. His family. His friends. His pets.

His brother, Mikhail.

He tells me how he saw a Clint Eastwood movie when he was little and decided he'd be a cowboy when he grew up. Then, later, he got into boxing and thought he might have a chance to do it professionally.

Until that night at the bar. Until that fateful punch. Until he met Pakhan, and all his dreams were crushed.

He paints a picture of a man living wholly alone in both mind and body, existing only to carry out orders handed down from above. He never had children or married because it wasn't allowed.

His life wasn't his own. Bratva first and forever. Duty or death.

Sometimes I go cold as I listen to his stories. Sometimes I want to cry. But always I wonder what he might have been had his life taken a different path.

But I'm perversely glad things went the way they did, because if his life had taken a different path, we never would have met.

I feel guilty about it, and I know it's wrong, but it's the truth. I'm glad for all his dark, twisted roads, because they led him to me.

It's a secret I guard carefully.

One day as we're finishing breakfast, he asks me out of the blue if I'd like to learn how to shoot a gun.

It frightens me. His answer doesn't reassure. "Why would I need to know how to shoot a gun?"

"Better to know how and not need to than need to and not know how."

It sounds like sage advice, but it also sounds like a warning. Like at any moment, our little slice of heaven in the wilderness could be torn in two.

So I learn how to shoot a pistol. Then I learn how to shoot a rifle.

When we discover that not only am I very good at hitting stationary targets, I actually enjoy it, too, Mal suggests I go hunting with him and try to hit something that moves.

"I could never shoot an animal," is my immediate response.

"If you had my shotgun in your hands when that bear charged at you, would you have pulled the trigger?"

"Self-defense isn't the same thing as going out and looking for something to kill."

Mal gazes at me in silence for a moment. His eyes are endless and dark.

"Killing is killing, no matter the intent behind it. Moralizing doesn't change the fact that you made something alive be unalive."

He leaves it at that.

Since he's an expert on the subject, I'm wise enough not to argue with him.

Then, late one evening, he gets a call that changes everything.

We're in bed, lying back to front, his legs drawn up behind mine. I'm drifting off to sleep when a buzzing noise jerks me back into consciousness.

It's his cell phone, ringing in the pocket of his coat. "Are you going to answer that?"

"I should." He doesn't move.

"It's okay if you have to. I don't mind."

He squeezes me, murmuring, "You should."

But then he sighs, rolls out of bed, and retrieves the phone.

He holds it to his ear and says curtly, *"Da."*

He's silent for several moments, listening. Then he lowers his head and says "Da" again, only this time it sounds resigned.

When he turns to look at me, his eyes have shuttered like blinds drawn over windows.

"What is it? Is everything okay?"

"You need to pack a bag. Right now."

My heartbeat picking up pace, I sit up. "Why?"

"We're going to the city."

THIRTY-SEVEN

RILEY

*I*t's a ten-minute walk through the woods to where Mal keeps his truck, concealed in a low brick structure built into the side of a hill. From there, it's an hour on a rutted dirt road into town, a charming alpine village with an airstrip for small planes on one end. The flight to the city lasts just under two hours.

Like everything else he does, Mal pilots the Cessna with ease and confidence.

We land in Moscow without ever having spoken a word since we left.

I don't know why.

I don't know why I'm afraid, either.

But I sense instinctively that this is a big deal, him taking me into the city. More than simply being the place where he works, it's also the place where his boss is. Where Spider is. Where danger waits for both of us.

In the forest, we could pretend he lived a different life. His absences were short interruptions in an otherwise peaceful little bubble. We were a snow globe on a shelf.

But the snow globe shatters the moment we touch down at Sheremetyevo airport, and I'm exposed to the other side of Mal's life.

The darker side.

Where all his monsters live.

A black Phantom waits for us on the tarmac. The driver takes our bags and loads them into the trunk without looking at me, not even to acknowledge my existence.

It feels purposeful. Like he knows something terrible will happen if he glances my way, and he won't dare risk it.

Mal says something to him in Russian. Then the driver bows—*he bows*—and opens the back door.

Mal climbs in behind me, then we're off.

And I can't stop looking out the windows. Moscow at night is a glittering fairy tale of lights, people, and movement. It seems larger than San Francisco by a factor of ten.

Mal takes my hand and squeezes it. "What are you thinking?"

"There's no snow."

"We're not in the mountains anymore." After a beat, he says, "What else?"

How well he can read me. When I look down at my hands, he wraps an arm around my shoulders and pulls me against his side, lowering his head to murmur, "What else, *malyutka*?"

I lean my head against his shoulder and close my eyes. "Everything else."

He kisses my forehead gently. I'm glad when he doesn't say more.

The drive to his home from the airport lasts under thirty minutes, but by the time we get there, I'm a nervous wreck. Even the incredibly beautiful views of the city passing by the windows can't distract from my panic.

I feel frazzled and strung out, like I've had way too much caffeine. After the tranquility of the woods, everything is too loud, too close, too bright. My heart is palpitating.

We pull into the parking garage of a glass tower and stop in front of a bank of elevators. Four hulking men in black suits step forward. One of them opens my door, another one rounds the back of the car and opens Mal's.

He doesn't need to instruct me to stay put. My intuition tells me there are rules here, new rules I'm not aware of. The primary one being to follow his lead.

Mal exits the Phantom, walks around to my side, and holds out his hand.

The men in suits step back to form a line in front of the elevators. Hands clasped behind their backs, faces impassive, they look off into the distance.

I take Mal's hand and step out, feeling shaky. He curls his big hand around mine to steady me.

One of the men in black presses a call button for the elevator, then goes back to pretending to be a statue.

When the doors slide open and Mal and I walk past the men, all of them bow in unison.

I wait until the doors slide shut and the elevator starts moving before I say, "What the heck was that?"

He says simply, "Respect."

"Are those your bodyguards?"

"I don't have bodyguards."

"Why not?"

He slants me a look.

"Oh. Right. You're the guy other people need bodyguards for."

He looks at me for a moment, his eyes half-lidded, then takes me by the arm and pulls me against his chest. He cradles my head in his hands and kisses me.

It's a firm kiss, but not a passionate one.

It's a kiss that tells me to calm down. That he's in control, and I have nothing to worry about.

That he won't let anything bad happen to me.

I drop my forehead to his chest and heave a sigh. "Thank you."

"You needed that."

"Yes."

"I know."

Despite my jangling nerves, I smile. "So what happens now?"

"Now we get you settled, then I go to work."

Work. So much violence contained in so few letters.

The elevator slows to a stop. The doors slide open. Mal takes my hands and leads me into the foyer of a dark apartment. The view of the city through the floor-to-ceiling windows lights up the space in a ghostly glow.

"Holy shit."

"You like it?"

I don't know if I like it exactly, but it is beautiful, so I stick to the positive. "It's incredible."

He leads me through a living room, empty except for a giant black sectional sitting in front of a big-screen TV on the wall. We pass an open space that seems like it's supposed to be a dining room, but it's also empty. Then we're in a kitchen, a vast echoing space of white marble and glass, as sterile as an operating room.

Mal flicks on a light, illuminating the kitchen. It's so bright, my eyes water. He walks to the stainless steel fridge and opens the freezer door. Inside, dozens of identical boxes of frozen dinners nest side by side. He removes two and tosses them onto the counter.

"Are you hungry?"

Without waiting for an answer, he tears open a box, removes the plastic tray from inside, turns to the microwave above the sink, and pops it open. He sets the timer and closes the door.

When he turns back to me and sees me standing there, looking lost, he abandons the other box he was about to open and comes to me.

Murmuring something in Russian, he wraps his strong arms around me and squeezes.

I whisper, "I'm okay."

"You're not."

"I will be."

"What do you need?"

"I don't know."

"Think about it."

I do, for several long minutes while he holds me, stroking a hand over my hair, his lips pressed to my temple.

I exhale and close my eyes. With my cheek resting against his chest, I say, "It's just . . . weird."

"Keep going."

"This place. Those frozen dinners. It's beautiful, but everything is very cold here."

"I'll keep you warm."

He takes my jaw in his hand, tilts my head up, and kisses me. This is a different kiss than in the elevator. It's deeper, more emotional, and ten times as hot. I cling to him, trembling, as his tongue sweeps against mine and his mouth turns my body to liquid fire.

When the knock comes on the front door, I jump, gasping. "Easy, baby," Mal murmurs against my lips. "It's just Dom with the bags."

"Dom?"

"The driver."

"Oh. Okay."

But when Mal opens the door, it isn't the driver. It's a beautiful young brunette, carrying a large black box tied with white ribbon in her arms.

She bows like the men at the elevators did, then says something I can't hear and holds out the box.

Mal accepts the box without a word and closes the door. He stands with his back turned for several long moments, his shoulders stiff. When he turns to face me, I go cold.

His jaw is set. His eyes are black. His expression is stony. Whatever's in that box, it isn't good.

He walks slowly across the apartment until he's standing in front of me again. Just standing there, holding the box, looking at me like it's the end of the world.

"What is that?"

"It's for you."

The hollowness of his voice terrifies me. I look at the black box with its pretty white ribbon and take an involuntary step back.

Mal sets it on the big marble island and lays his hand on top. "It's a dress."

Now I'm confused. "A dress? For me?"

"Yes."

"Oh. Then why are you being so strange?"

"Because I didn't buy it."

My stomach twists into a knot. Something unpleasant crawls down my spine, a feeling like a centipede is slithering along my skin, its tiny insect legs cold and prickly.

"Who bought it?"

"Pakhan."

The only sound that breaks the following silence is the whirr of the microwave. We stare at each other until the timer bell rings, then Mal says, "He's invited us to dinner. We leave in ten minutes."

"Now? It's got to be one o'clock in the morning."

"The time is immaterial."

I'm sensing all kinds of weirdness coming off him. It makes my already frazzled nerves fray even more. "This isn't good, is it?"

He hesitates. "It's unexpected."

He's hedging his answers. There's something he doesn't want me to know, and it freaks me out. "Did you tell him about me?"

"No."

"How did he find out?"

He hesitates again. "Any one of a million ways. He's the most powerful man in Russia."

My breath shallow, my heartbeat zooming, and my palms starting to sweat, I look at the box as if it's full of snakes. "But . . . but if he sent that dress, he knew about me before we got here."

"Yes."

Oh, god. Has he been watching us? And if he has been . . . why?

I can think of a few reasons off the top of my head, none of them good. Adrenaline floods my system, leaving me shaking.

Mal walks over to me and takes my face in his hands. "You're not in danger."

"Are you sure? Because it sounds like you're only saying that to convince yourself."

"This is a chess move. A power play. He wants me to know he knows about you, that's all. I never would've brought you to the city if I thought you wouldn't be safe."

I lick my lips and try to swallow. My mouth is as dry as a desert. Fear has leached all the moisture from my body. I close my eyes and inhale a shaky breath.

"Look at me, *malyutka*."

When I gaze up into his eyes, he says vehemently, "Any man who even looks at you wrong will die. Any man, including him. If I sense any hint of a threat, if anything whatsoever happens that displeases me, I will make him unalive. Do you understand me?"

Trembling, I say, "Not really."

"But do you trust me?"

His eyes are fierce. His intensity is breathtaking. And the truth of his words is obvious in every taut line of his body, in every muscle and pore.

This man will kill to protect me. Even his own boss, the most powerful man in Russia, isn't exempt from the Hangman's noose.

Gun. Knife. Whatever he uses. The fact remains: my assassin has my back.

Fortified by that thought, I stand straighter, taking a breath. "Yes."

He pulls me against his chest, hugging me hard and exhaling into my hair.

"Good. Now let's get dressed. The sooner this is over with, the better."

With that cryptic statement hanging over my head, Mal picks up the box and leads me into the bedroom.

THIRTY-EIGHT

RILEY

*E*xcept for a king-size bed, the master bedroom is as empty as the rest of the apartment.

The walls are painted stark white. The floor is glossy white marble. The bed itself is a masculine affair of black duvet and angular pillows. There are no rugs or drapes to muffle the echo of our footsteps.

Whoever decorated this place didn't want it to be comfortable. It's about as homey as a mausoleum.

Mal shows me around, then leaves me in the bathroom with a kiss on my head and a reminder that I have five minutes before we have to leave. I stand in the middle of the enormous space, feeling like I've crash-landed on Mars and hostile aliens are swarming over the horizon.

When I set the box on the sink and open it, the feeling of doom intensifies.

It's not the dress, which is lovely. It's sleeveless sapphire velvet with a long, slim skirt and cinched waist. It's not even the shoes, a pair of low strappy heels in an elegant champagne color that are mysteriously my size.

It's the contact lenses.

The small rectangular box of contacts has my name printed on a label on the outside, along with my prescription.

My precise prescription, including power, curve, cylinder value, axis, and brand. Everything needed to correct my astigmatism perfectly.

In short, somebody had a nice little convo with my optometrist about my eyeballs.

This isn't some shit you grab off a shelf. These are custom lenses. It normally takes weeks for them to arrive when I order them, and they're expensive. They're also delicate and tear easily, which is why I switched back to glasses.

But tonight, my glasses will be staying home.

I don't dare insult the most powerful man in Russia before I've even met him.

I take off the clothes I'm wearing and leave them folded on the sink. I put on the dress, which fits perfectly. The shoes do, too, and so do the lenses.

Then I stand and stare at myself in the mirror, wondering if maybe I'm still in the hospital and this is all a strange dream.

At least I've put back on the weight I'd lost, thanks to Mal's cooking. And the color and fit of the dress are very flattering. Whoever this Pakhan is, he's got better taste than Sloane.

Nobody will mistake me for a sex worker tonight.

It's small comfort, but I'm taking what I can get. I turn my back on the mirror and head into the bedroom, where I stop short and suck in a breath.

Mal stands waiting for me near the foot of the bed.

He's in a beautiful fitted black suit with a crisp white dress shirt open at the throat, no tie. His black leather shoes are polished to a mirror shine. His wavy dark hair has been brushed back against his scalp and glossed with some kind of pomade. The unruly ends curl against his collar.

He's breathtaking. Gangster chic, a dangerous beast disguised in a gentleman's clothing.

He takes me in with one greedy look, licks his lips, then growls something hotly in Russian.

My blood thrumming in my veins, I whisper, "You look nice, too."

"Come here."

The hand he holds out is a magnet. So is that hungry look in his eyes, drawing me in. I cross the room with butterflies flitting madly around in my stomach and step into his arms.

He kisses me deeply, one arm wrapped around my waist and a hand gripped firmly around the back of my neck. When I'm certain I'm about to combust, he breaks the kiss and says gruffly, "You're fucking delicious."

The Big Bad Wolf couldn't sound nearly as ravenous. I shiver, pressing closer to the hard expanse of his chest and tightening my arms around his shoulders. "Thank you."

"I want to tear you out of this dress with my teeth."

"I don't think we have time for that."

Gazing at me with hot eyes, he licks his lips again. He debates for a moment, then shakes his head impatiently. "You're right. Later. Where are your glasses?"

"On the bathroom counter. There was a pair of prescription contact lenses in the box with the dress. My exact prescription, as a matter of fact."

He says drily, "And I'm sure the dress and shoes are your exact size, as well."

"I'm trying hard not to be freaked out, because I trust you, but this seems like a very deliberate message your boss is sending."

"Yes, it does."

"You agreeing with me doesn't make me feel better."

He gazes at me for a moment, his face pensive. Then he brushes a strand of hair off my forehead and tucks it behind my ear.

"I'm going to tell you something. It's important."

"Oh, shit."

"Just listen to me carefully and remember this. If Pakhan asks you a question, no matter what it is, tell him the truth. The entire, unvarnished truth. Don't try to dress it up or make it sound pretty."

His voice lowers. "And especially don't try to lie. He can smell a lie like a shark can smell a drop of blood in the water."

Feeling sick, I say faintly, "That image is great, thanks."

He gives me a squeeze and a firm kiss on the lips. "You'll be fine. Are you ready?"

"No."

"Yes, you are. We're going. Remember what I said."

With that final warning echoing in my ears, he takes my hand and leads me out the door.

The restaurant is a ten-minute drive through traffic from the apartment. We seem to be in the city center. Skyscrapers tower all around us for miles. Pedestrians are everywhere, though the hour is so late. There's a bustling, cosmopolitan, 24-7 vibe that once again reminds me of San Francisco, but much bigger and without the steep hills.

I wait for homesickness to hit me, but it never comes. Sitting beside me in the back of the Phantom, Mal is silent.

I can't tell if he's tense. His body is relaxed, but there's a watchfulness in his eyes. A certain way of slicing his gaze from one point to another that reminds me of a big cat lying in wait in tall grass for a gazelle to pass.

When we pull up to a valet stand outside a glass building with opulent gold and blue spires on top and I swallow nervously, Mal says, "Stay right beside me at all times. Don't go to the restroom. Don't let go of my hand. If anything happens, get under the table and stay there until I tell you to. Say yes so I know you understand."

"Yes."

There. That sounded like a person in control of herself who isn't about to soil her undies in fright.

The driver opens the door for Mal, who then opens the door for me. We walk into the restaurant with our hands tightly clasped, Mal a step in front. I'm wishing for a paper bag to hyperventilate into as the most beautiful woman I've ever seen floats over to us from behind the hostess stand.

She's who the word "statuesque" was coined for. A few other choice words, too, including "stunning," "bombshell," and "boner inducing." Everything about her is lush, golden, and perfect, and I suddenly feel like a pet rodent someone dressed up for Halloween.

"*Privet*, Malek," she says in a liquid purr, then something else I don't pay attention to because I'm too busy being blinded by her cleavage. The sparkly gold minidress she's wearing does a death-defying plunge from her shoulders straight down to her navel. I have no idea how her boobs haven't already popped out into Mal's face.

"Masha," he replies coolly, looking past her into the restaurant. "He's here?"

A momentary flicker of annoyance mars her perfect features.

I don't know if it's because Mal's not gobbling up all the tasty bait she's laying or because he spoke in English, but she decides the problem is me and sends me a look that could wither crops.

I smile at her, feeling better already.

"*Da*. Follow me, please."

The golden goddess slinks off into the dining room, hips swaying.

"Friend of yours?" I say acidly.

"I haven't fucked her, if that's what you're asking."

"Not for lack of trying on her part."

He sends me a glance, arching a brow. "Are you jealous, little bird?"

"Who, me? Of Miss Universe? Nah. She probably doesn't own a single pair of sweats."

His lips curve up at the edges.

Then we're walking into the restaurant, hand in hand. It's by far the most ostentatious space I've ever seen.

Like Masha the hostess, everything is gold and sparkling. The wallpaper, the chandeliers, the table linens, the chairs. The carpeting underfoot is plush, with a bold, gold-and-plum swirly pattern that would outdo any Vegas casino. The ceiling, far overhead, reflects the room from a thousand mirrored panels. Ferns and stands of potted palms adorn the nooks and crevices of the room, and a subtle, expensive scent perfumes the air.

All the elegant dining tables sit empty, with the exception of the three we're walking toward.

The two large round tables are occupied by men in expensive dark suits. All of them are large, bearded, and middle-aged, though not the kind of soft middle age you see in suburban dads.

These are Vikings. Warriors. The sort of men who know exactly how to wield an axe to sever a head.

Seated behind them in a curved leather booth against the wall is their king.

He's larger than all the rest of them, hale and broad. His russet beard is shot through with gray. A black wool overcoat with a thick silver fur collar is draped over his shoulders. Tattoos decorate each knuckle of his left hand: stars, flowers, initials, a knife plunged through a skull. His lionlike head is wreathed in smoke from the cigar he's smoking.

He was handsome once, I can tell. But his face is now craggy and his eyes are as hard as flint, no doubt from all the violence he's committed.

I must make a meep of fear, because Mal squeezes my hand and murmurs, "Steady."

When we pass between the first two tables, all the men rise from their chairs. They incline their heads to Mal, who ignores them.

Then we're standing in front of Pakhan.

He looks at me first, for a long, silent moment. His gaze is powerful and ice-cold. I stand stock-still, trying not to shit my pants.

When his gaze shifts to Mal, I feel like a bunny released from a steel trap. It's all I can do not to topple sideways, gasping. "Malek," Pakhan says in a rumbling, accented voice. "You've been a busy boy."

It's said in English, no doubt so I can understand. But the tone is as neutral as his expression, so I can't tell if he's angry or amused.

Sounding undisturbed, Mal replies in Russian. It seems like a greeting, because afterward he inclines his head slightly.

Pakhan looks briefly at our clasped hands, then back at me.

He gestures with his cigar.

"Come sit next to me, Miss Keller. I want to have a look at you."

Oh, no, the king of the Russian mafia knows my name. This is so not good.

When I find myself unable to move, Mal gently prods me forward, helping me into the booth. I scoot around the curved tabletop, closer to Pakhan, looking everywhere but at him. Mal settles himself beside me and takes my hand under the tablecloth.

As soon as we're seated, all the Vikings take their seats as well. Half a dozen beautiful young women in skimpy gold outfits appear from nowhere with trays of drinks. They serve Pakhan first, then me and Mal, then the Vikings, who start talking amongst themselves in Russian as if this is just another boys' night at the club.

I grab the whiskey one of the girls set in front of me. Before I can chug it, Mal places his hand on my wrist to stop me.

Shit. I forgot I can't drink! This is the worst possible time to be missing a kidney.

Silence reigns for a moment after I set the glass back down.

Then Pakhan says, "You're nervous."

I exhale a hard breath. "No, I'm terrified. Thank you for the outfit. It's lovely. For the contacts as well."

He smokes his cigar, considering my profile. On my other side,

Mal is quiet and still. A dark lake with deep waters hiding vicious monsters beneath.

"What are you afraid of, child?"

It's probably the grandfatherly way he addresses me that makes me feel a sliver more comfortable, but I find myself able to glance at him without fainting.

"Well . . . you."

"Me?" Pakhan looks to Mal with raised brows.

I blurt, "It's not his fault!"

Now both of them are frowning at me. I'm looking at Pakhan, but I can feel Mal's glower without seeing it. It makes me panic all over again. I bite my lip to keep from making another sound.

"What exactly isn't his fault?"

"Me being afraid of you. He didn't say anything bad, you're just . . . sort of . . . scary."

When he simply stares at me, I cringe. "Sorry. I'm not trying to insult you. I'm just telling you the truth."

"The truth. Hmm."

He smokes thoughtfully. Mal still hasn't said a word.

"Tell me, Miss Keller, how are you?"

That catches me completely off guard. I blink. When Mal squeezes my hand, I take a breath and hope he meant it when he said to tell the truth, because here goes.

"Right now? Totally freaked out. In general? Better than I've been in maybe ever."

"Better than ever? Most women who've been shot, kidnapped, and held captive might find a different way to describe their predicament."

He says it to me, but he's looking past me to Mal. He doesn't look happy.

How the hell does he know all this stuff? And why would he care if Mal kidnapped me?

Doesn't matter. Focus.

"He saved my life. Twice. And yes, technically he did kidnap me, but I haven't asked him to take me home. I think if I did, he would, but I don't want to ask him to. I actually, um . . . sort of . . . have feelings for him."

I've seen the expression Pakhan is wearing before. Mal has looked at me exactly like this a hundred times, when I've said something he thinks is even more insane than what I'm usually saying.

"Did he tell you to say that?"

"No."

Pakhan's eyes are bloodhounds, lie detectors, and CIA agents interrogating prisoners at Guantanamo. If they could waterboard me, they would.

I let him look. Nuts or not, I'm not lying.

After what feels like eons, he says, "Are you sleeping with him?"

What the actual fuck? I take a breath and try to keep my face and tone calm. "Yes."

"So he's forcing you."

Irritation jolts through me. Indignant on Mal's behalf, I speak more sharply than I should.

"*No.* He would never force himself on me, even if he wanted to. I know that because he *did* want to. As a matter of fact, *I'm* the one who made the first move in that direction."

Pakhan makes a dismissive gesture with his hand. He doesn't seem impressed.

"Women often lie to themselves in these situations. It helps them deal with the trauma if they feel like they're not a victim. That they had a choice."

He's telling me Mal has taken advantage of me, but I'm not smart enough to know.

He's telling me I've been raped, but I don't realize it. He's telling me I'm a silly little girl.

Heat crawls up my neck. My heart starts pounding. I stare at him, wanting to yank his cigar out of his hand and snuff it out on his forehead. The room and everything in it disappears.

I don't care if this is the most powerful man in Russia. He's got it coming, and I'm gonna let him have it.

Looking him straight in the eye, I say, "I don't know what kind of women you've been involved with, but if this man had harmed me in any way, he'd be missing his dick. I would never sit here and defend him, not even if he threatened to kill me if I didn't. He would've had to drag me kicking and screaming into this room by my hair.

"Yes, he kidnapped me. I know it's not an ideal way to start a relationship, but it'll be a great story when someone asks how we met. But he also got me emergency surgery that saved my life after my own bodyguard shot me, changed my bandages and made sure I took my medicine, spoon-fed me like a baby with meals he cooked himself, took an elk head off a wall because I hated it, robbed an optometrist so I could see, killed the bear that was trying to eat me, taught me how to shoot in case I needed to defend myself, and a bunch of other stuff I can't remember right now because I'm so mad.

"Mal is the most generous, competent, intelligent, self-disciplined, wonderful man I've ever met. He kills people for a living, but nobody's perfect. And before you ask, yes, he told me how he came to be in your employ. He also told me he's not going to stop working for you, even though his whole family is now dead and he doesn't have anybody to protect anymore. So he's also loyal to a fault. So please don't insinuate that I don't know what the hell I'm talking about when I say I have feelings for him, because I do. Because he's worth it!"

In the wake of that speech, there's total silence. With horror, I realize that I raised my voice to such a level that the two other tables of men heard me, too.

Everyone in the room is now staring at me.

I swallow and moisten my lips. I exhale a slow, shaky breath. In a more muted tone, I say, "I apologize if that was disrespectful. It wasn't meant to be. I was just—"

"Defending Malek," interrupts Pakhan.

His tone is soft. His eyes are hard. I can't tell if he's going to pat my hand or kill me.

I whisper, "Yes."

He doesn't do anything for a moment except look at me. The tension in the room is palpable, as if everyone is holding their breath, waiting to see what he'll do.

Mal's hand in mine is cool, dry, and steady.

Then Pakhan takes a puff of his cigar, blows out a cloud of smoke, and smiles.

Everyone in the room relaxes.

The men resume their conversations, the girls arrive with platters of food, and my heart remembers how to beat.

Chuckling, Pakhan says something in Russian to Mal.

"You should see her when she's really angry," he replies, and takes a sip of his whiskey.

Everything after that is a blur.

I know we eat, but I couldn't say what. I know there's conversation, but it's in Russian, so I don't understand a thing. At one point, Mal says the name Kazimir in a questioning tone, to which Pakhan shakes his head. Then dinner's over, and we're standing to leave.

"Miss Keller," says Pakhan, still sitting. He holds out a ringed hand.

When I look at it, uncertain if I'm supposed to kiss it or what, he says gently, "I don't bite, child."

I doubt that but grasp his hand anyway. Then I watch in shock as he lifts my hand to his lips and kisses my knuckles.

"Thank you for an interesting evening. It was a pleasure to meet you."

His powerful, piercing gaze makes me feel shy. My cheeks faintly burn, and I find it hard to meet his eyes. "You're welcome. It was nice to meet you, too. And thank you for not being upset with my bad manners."

His smile is small and mysterious. "Those bad manners will serve you well in the future. Empires aren't run by the meek."

It sounds eerily like a prophecy.

Like he knows something about me that I don't.

But there's no time to dwell on it, because Mal is pulling me away, dragging me out of the restaurant and into the waiting car.

He pushes me into the back seat, slams the door behind him, and lunges at me.

THIRTY-NINE

RILEY

*T*he kiss is rough, dominant, and demanding. It's also totally unexpected and takes my breath away.

With his hands gripping both sides of my head, Mal ravages my mouth until I'm mewing and shaking all over, clutching the lapels of his suit. Breathing hard, he breaks away and stares at me with eyes like fire.

He says gruffly, "You told the king of the Bratva that you have feelings for me."

I'm too dizzy to know if that's praise or a rebuke, so I shake my head wordlessly.

"Yes, you fucking did. Said it to his face, in front of all his captains. Said it in a fuck-you tone that would've gotten anyone else killed."

He kisses me again, devouring my mouth.

When he breaks away this time, my heart is racing, and I'm gasping.

He drags me onto his lap, pulling me over so my legs are spread open around his hips and my dress is bunched up around my thighs. He sinks his fingers into the tender flesh of my ass and yanks me against his crotch so I'm sitting astride his erection.

Fisting a hand in my hair, he pulls my head down and rasps, "You said I was generous. Wonderful. Loyal."

He crushes his mouth to mine and drinks deep from it until I'm whimpering.

Then he turns his mouth to my ear and growls, *"You fucking defended me."*

I say breathlessly, "I can't tell if you're mad or happy about that."

He flexes his hips, grinding his erection against me. His answer comes through gritted teeth.

"Oh, baby, I'm gonna show you exactly how I feel about it."

He takes the neckline of my dress in both hands. With one hard yank, he rips it wide open, tearing the fabric apart. Then he latches onto one of my exposed nipples and sucks on it, hard.

When I gasp, he grips both my breasts in his hands and goes back and forth between them, sucking and licking, teasing my rigid nipples with his thumbs, tongue, and teeth. Shivering, I sink my hands into his hair.

Between my spread legs, his erection is rock-hard. "Mal," I whisper. "The driver."

"Dom!" he barks over my shoulder. He says something else in Russian.

I hear a low hum and glance back. A tinted privacy partition rises between the driver's seat and the passenger section of the car, separating them.

Then Mal's greedy fingers are between my legs, pulling aside my panties and sliding inside me.

"Always so ready for me," he growls. "This sweet pussy is always so plump and slippery, ready for my dick."

He goes back to sucking my nipples, finger fucking me as I rock back and forth on his hand. When he presses his thumb against my engorged clit, I groan, dropping my head back and closing my eyes.

My heart beats like mad. My skin burns like fire. My nipples ache, and my breathing is rough.

I want him to fuck me, right here on the back seat of this car.

He knows. Of course he knows. With an animal's snarl, he pulls his fingers out of me, unbuckles his belt and unbuttons his trousers, and rips open his fly. His big, stiff cock springs out into his hand.

Rubbing it against my soaked folds, he whispers harshly, "Mouth."

I kiss him. He kisses me back like I'm a life preserver and he's drowning. He flexes his hips, nudging the crown of his cock at my entrance. With a thrust, he slides in.

He's thick, hard, and throbbing. He grips my hips and starts to pump into me, grunting in pleasure, then leans in and takes a mouthful of my breast.

He bites it, sinking his teeth into the flesh beneath my nipple. I love the way it feels, pain and pleasure wound up in a hot little concentrated ball. The feeling makes my pussy throb and my chest ache. I start to grind against his pelvis, rubbing my clit against him as his fat cock spreads me open wide.

He slides a hand around from my hip to my ass and fondles the sensitive bundle of nerves between my ass cheeks, teasing his fingers back and forth over it.

"I want to fuck this little rosebud," he whispers hotly, panting. "Have you let a man fuck you here before?"

Shuddering, I moan his name.

"No, I know you haven't. But you're gonna let me. You're gonna let me be the first and last. But before that, you're gonna come on my cock, baby." His voice drops. "And I want you to come *hard*."

He presses with his finger. It slides into my ass. I cry out, trembling and starting to buck against him helplessly. I cling to his shoulders and ride him, listening to him murmur every filthy thing I never knew I needed to hear a man say.

When my moans grow louder and more broken and I'm clawing at his shoulders, my entire body tensed, Mal pulls my head down with a hand in my hair and puts his mouth next to my ear.

His voice dark and rough, he commands, "Come for me, baby. Give it to Daddy."

He shoves his finger deep inside my ass and bites my throat like a savage.

I climax, sobbing.

My pussy clenches rhythmically around his cock, violent contractions that shake my whole body. My clit throbs and pulses. My thighs shake. I shoot into outer space at a million miles per hour, impaled on his cock, his mouth hot and voracious on my skin.

It goes on and on for what seems like forever. Pleasure crashes over me in waves. I feel surrounded by him, devoured by him, consumed.

I never want it to end.

Then he's kissing me, thrusting his tongue into my mouth as he pumps his hips faster, moaning and pulling my hair, fucking me in a frenzy. He drops his head to my shoulder and releases my hair, wrapping an arm around my back and pulling me tightly against his chest.

With one final, violent thrust, he orgasms. He groans against my neck.

It goes all the way through me.

I feel him pulse and throb and listen to his beautiful husky groans of pleasure, and something unlocks inside the center of my chest.

The moment feels powerfully significant. I have to fight the sudden urge to cry.

We stay like that, locked together, panting and shaking, until

Mal rubs his beard gently against my neck. He exhales, squeezing me tight.

He murmurs something in Russian. It's achingly soft. I don't ask what it is.

I'm overwhelmed enough already.

When the car pulls into the parking garage at Mal's building, I'm snuggled in his lap with the jacket of his suit over my shoulders and his arms wrapped around me. I feel boneless, like Jell-O, and high.

My torn dress covered by his jacket, he carries me to the elevator as I rest my head against his chest. Even with my eyes closed, I know the men in suits are bowing as we pass.

He doesn't speak on the ride up. He stays silent as he carries me into the bedroom. When he lays me down on the bed and undresses me, he still doesn't utter a word.

He kneels next to the bed, throws my legs over his shoulders, and puts his face between my thighs. Running his hands up and down my naked body, he lavishes my clit with his tongue. I arch and moan, shivering in pleasure.

I get the feeling I'm being rewarded.

When my cries are loud and I'm nearing climax, he turns his head and bites my thigh.

He whispers, "You said 'relationship.'"

Delirious, panting, I say, "What?"

He glances up at me. In the shadows, his eyes glitter with intensity. "You said kidnapping wasn't a good way to start a relationship, but it would make a great story."

Holding my gaze, he lowers his head and sucks gently on my clit.

My uterus contracts. My nipples tingle. The room feels like it's on fire.

"Oh, god—Mal—*oh*—"

He whispers, "Is that what you think we have? A relationship? Because it feels more like an obsession to me. A compulsion. A knot too tangled to be unwound."

He goes back to sucking, adding a finger and pumping it slowly in and out.

When I moan loudly, he drags me to the edge of the bed so my ass is hanging off. He supports my bottom with both hands as he eats me, going back and forth between licking my clit and thrusting his tongue inside me the way he likes to do, fucking me with it.

I dig both hands into his hair and rock my hips against his face, not caring about the sounds I'm making or the way my heart feels like it's cracking in two.

I can honestly say I don't care about anything anymore. Except him.

Us.

This dark and powerful thing we have together that feels as final as death.

When I climax, it's with his name on my lips.

He hums his approval into my flesh as I buck and thrash against the bed. I scratch his scalp and pull his hair, totally out of control from the pleasure he's giving.

When I come back to myself and am lying there quivering and spent, he's chuckling.

He rises and unbuttons his shirt. Gazing down at me with a lazy smile, he says in a husky voice, "Good girl."

Whimpering, I roll to my side and bury my face in the duvet.

He chuckles again, only this time, it sounds dangerous. "You think you can hide from me? You can't hide. I see you, little bird. I see everything."

He grips my wrists and pulls me to a sitting position at the edge of the bed. Gazing down at me, he takes my face in his hand and slides his thumb into my mouth. With his other hand, he pulls down his zipper. The engorged head of his cock juts out above his briefs.

"I'm gonna fuck your mouth, sweet girl," he growls. "Then I'm gonna put you on your hands and knees and choke you while I fuck your pussy. If you want that, say yes."

He slides his thumb out of my mouth and cups the back of my neck, gripping it firmly and waiting, dominant even in his patient silence.

"Yes."

Though it's the truth, a single-syllable word has never been more difficult to pronounce in the history of humanity. I eke it out, breathless and trembling, watching his lethal smile grow wider.

I reach up, pull his briefs down, and wrap my hands around his erection. Holding his gaze, I open my mouth and take him in.

The crown is thick and tastes like me. I swirl my tongue around it. A thrill goes through my body when his stomach muscles clench and he exhales a faint, involuntary moan.

"Fuck yes," he whispers, watching my mouth with avid eyes. "Now suck."

I obey him, sucking the crown only, my hands still wrapped around his shaft.

"More. Deeper."

I take one hand off his shaft and cup it under his balls, then take him farther into my mouth. The vein on the underside of his cock throbs against my tongue. I start to stroke his shaft in time with the movement of my head, doing it more enthusiastically when he moans again, this time louder.

"My sweet, perfect girl. Suck that cock. Show me how much you love it."

His voice is ragged. His chest heaves. He stares down at me with hot eyes and a clenched jaw, so fucking sexy and masculine, I'm shamelessly eager to do anything he demands.

Maybe he was right when he said this is a compulsion, because I no longer feel like I'm in control.

The thing between us is driving me now, and I'm happily letting it.

I suck, lick, and stroke until his hands are shaking against my head as he thrusts into my mouth. With an oath, he pulls out, flips me onto my belly, drags me up onto my knees, and spanks my ass.

I yelp, jerking.

He bends down and kisses the sting away, then puts his hand between my shoulder blades and pushes me down so my face is against the mattress and my ass is in the air. Kneeling behind me, he leans over and cups my breasts, thumbing over my hard nipples. Then he slides his hands down my rib cage and over my waist, squeezing my hips.

"Riley Rose," he says gruffly, stroking the head of his cock back and forth through my wet folds. "My beautiful obsession. This monster belongs to you, sweet girl. I'm tied up in chains at your feet."

His hard thrust sinks him all the way inside me.

When I moan, he puts his big, rough hand around my throat and gently squeezes.

He fucks me hard, driving into me over and over, his balls slapping against my pussy, his husky moans ringing in my ears.

I feel everything in exquisite amplification. The blood rushing through my veins. The sheets rubbing against my cheek. The wetness on my thighs, and his fingers digging into my hips.

Into my neck.

Crying out and clawing the sheets, fireworks exploding in my vision, I climax.

Falling back onto his heels, he drags me against his chest and holds me there as I jerk and gasp, clenching around him helplessly. Putting a hand between my legs to squeeze my throbbing flesh, he repeats something over and over, murmured into my ear.

"*Ty moya. Ty moya. Ty moya, dorogoya.*"

Cradled in his arms and spread open around his cock, I orgasm so hard, I'm overcome with emotion. I start to weep.

"I know," he whispers. "Oh, fuck, baby, I fucking know."

When he throws back his head, shouts at the ceiling, and comes with me, I realize that any thoughts I may have had about protecting myself from him are now useless.

No matter how crazy or wrong this might be, I'm all in.

All I can do now is hold on and ride this roller coaster until the end, wherever it might take us.

FORTY

RILEY

*M*al and I lie entangled in bed in the dark for a long time before he finally speaks.

"Are you all right?" He sounds somber. Like he's worried he did something wrong.

"You didn't hurt me, if that's what you're asking."

"Your throat . . . ?"

"You could've squeezed twice as hard and I wouldn't have felt it."

He exhales in relief. "Breath play can be dangerous. We should've talked about it first. Had a safe word."

Dear god, hearing him say "breath play" and "safe word" makes my imagination run wild with every kinky scenario people can engage in, in pairs, trios, or groups.

I picture him in the middle of a writhing pile of naked bodies at a sex club, godlike and glistening as he fucks every random hole in sight, and feel as if I might faint.

"Here's a safe word for you: I have zero interest in hearing about your past sexual experiences. The thought of you doing what we just did with another woman makes me want to bury a hatchet in your chest and set you on fire."

After a moment, he says, "That's too long for a safe word. Hard to remember in the heat of the moment." I hear laughter in his tone, the bastard.

"You know what I mean."

"Yes, I do," he murmurs, squeezing me. "You're jealous."

"Pfft."

"Deny it all you want, but I didn't mention anything about my past. I simply suggested we needed to communicate about what we do together, then suddenly you were threatening me with death."

Embarrassed because he's right, I hide my face in the crook of his neck. When he softly kisses my throat, I whisper, "I'm sorry."

"Don't be sorry. I know exactly how you feel."

"You do?"

"Why don't you bring up your blond bodyguard again and see how I take it?"

That dials down my aggravation to a manageable degree. I burrow closer to him, closing my eyes. "No, thanks. But can we talk about what happened at dinner?"

He peppers soft kisses down my throat and along my collarbone. "What happened is that you sassed the king of the Bratva, and he loved you for it."

"You're sure he won't change his mind later?"

"I'm sure. The man hasn't had anyone dare to even raise their voice to him for twenty years. He found your angry little speech very entertaining."

"I can't figure out why he was so mad at you, though."

He pauses kissing me to say thoughtfully, "Me neither."

"Are you not allowed to kidnap people?"

He chuckles. I take that as a no.

"What were you guys talking about in Russian?"

"Mostly business."

"Did he tell you how he found out about me?"

"No. I asked if it was the man he sent me to in New York to help me find Declan, but he said it wasn't. Said it was a dead man, an old friend of his who knew everyone and everything."

"A *dead* man? Does he spend a lot of time on a Ouija board talking to spirits?"

"I didn't understand it, either, but Pakhan said he wanted to introduce me to him." His voice drops. "Now that he'd met you."

"Me? What do I have to do with anything?"

"I don't know."

"This is all very strange."

"Yes. Especially the part where he told me to take a vacation."

I lift my head and look at him. "A vacation?"

"A month off," he replies, nodding.

"Has he ever given you time off before?"

"Never."

"Don't you think that's odd?"

"I do."

"So what are you going to do about it?"

He smiles. "Take a month off."

A dangerous thrill goes through me, like I'm standing at the edge of a perilously high cliff, looking down. Aiming for nonchalant, I say, "Where will you go?"

His smile is indulgent. "Look at you, trying to act innocent. You know exactly where I'll go." He presses the softest of kisses to my lips. "And with who."

"To the cabin," I whisper, kissing him back. "With me."

Rolling on top of me, he takes my mouth in a deep, hot kiss, curling his hand around my throat as he does it. "Yes, with you," he says, voice husky. "My mouthy little captive."

I wrap my arms around his back, shivering in delight at the feel of his big, strong body against mine. "Your wrinkled gray tissue someone left in their pocket too long."

"My stubborn fighter."

"Your homeless deer mouse with the tiny fang-like tusks."

"My world."

It's said in a murmur as he gazes deep into my eyes with a look of adoration.

I swallow, my heart beating faster. "Can I say something now?"

"No."

"It's super complimentary, though. You'll like it."

"I already know, baby. I can see it in your eyes."

"Oh. Okay. So the feeling's mutual?"

"Fucking hell, woman. Shut up."

He kisses me again, giving me a very good reason to.

In the morning, we return to the cabin in the woods.

On the drive from the airport down the rutted dirt road, I gather my courage and ask Mal about Spider. I'm hoping since we're not in bed, he won't get so mad.

I'm wrong.

As soon as I mention his name, he goes stiff. "He's alive."

"Is he going to stay that way?"

"Not if you keep asking me about him."

"I'm only asking because you haven't told me anything. The last I heard, you'd drugged him and told him to leave the country, but he hadn't."

He's silent for a long time. I'm not sure he'll ever answer me, but then he does, his jaw tight, looking straight out the windshield as he drives.

"He's still in Moscow. Sniffing around like a dog."

"What are you planning on doing about him?"

"Nothing."

I examine his profile, but can't get a clue to what he's thinking. It's like looking at a brick wall.

If the brick wall wanted to smash something, that is.

"I'm sorry that this conversation is pissing you off, but I have to know that he's going to be okay."

With slow, precise enunciation, he replies, "Why is that so important to you?"

"Mal, look at me."

He clenches his jaw instead.

"Come on. Just for a sec."

He draws an exaggerated breath, exhales, then glances in my direction.

As soon as our eyes meet, I say softly, "I don't have feelings for him. I never did. I promise you. But I liked him, and he was really nice to me. I don't want anything bad to happen to him. Okay?"

He holds my gaze for a moment longer, then looks back out the windshield.

We drive for a while in silence. I let him work it over in his head without pestering him, and am finally rewarded when he says grudgingly, "I've already put the word out that he's off-limits. No one's to touch him. If anything bad happens to him, it won't be our doing."

Relieved, I scoot across the seat and duck under his arm. Cuddling up to him, I kiss his cheek and whisper, "Thank you, sweetie."

He says vehemently, "I hate that Irish fucker."

"I know."

"So should you. He shot you!"

"It was an accident. I'm sure he feels awful."

His reply is a disgruntled growl. I kiss his cheek again, and he squeezes me closer into his side.

I decide to leave my questions about Declan's future for later.

In my heart of hearts, I already know the answers, anyway. If Mal were going to kill Declan, he already would have.

We arrive at the cabin just as Poe is landing on the wood railing on the porch, squawking at us impatiently for treats.

The next few weeks are a blissful dream.

The snow starts to melt in the meadow. A riot of wildflowers springs up from the thawing ground. I perfect my target shooting skills and learn how to shoot a bow and arrow, though only at trees. I even start work on a book, a project I always dreamed of but never had time for.

When Mal asks me what the story is, I tell him it's about a girl who doesn't know she's dead.

"Like that movie," he says. "'I see dead people.'"

I smile at him. "No, this is a love story."

"A love story with *ghosts*?"

"Keep making that face, and I'll never let you read it." He chuckles, kisses me, and leaves it at that.

We go to bed early and sleep late, sometimes staying in bed all day. We make love on every surface in the cabin, including up against all the walls. I've never been happier.

I promise myself that when Mal has to go back to work, I'll call my sister. I'll deal with "real" life, but not yet.

For the first time, I'm happy, whole, and completely at peace. I feel like I was wandering lost in a wilderness, but now I've been found. I want to live in the cabin in the woods forever.

Until the day Mal goes into town to restock supplies and everything falls to pieces.

I should've known something so beautiful was too good to last.

FORTY-ONE

MAL

I spot him the instant I step into the grocer's, because nobody from here looks like that.

Nobody from anywhere looks like that.

Leaning against the wall by the restrooms near the back, his arms folded over his sizeable chest and a toothpick stuck between his movie star teeth, he's the picture of effortless cool.

He's tall, muscular, and has full sleeves of tats down both arms. His dark hair waves down to his shoulders. He's got the angular jaw of a superhero and the proud bearing of a bullfighter. In a tight white short-sleeved T-shirt, faded jeans, cowboy boots, and mirrored aviators, he looks like the love child of James Bond and Elvis Presley, with a dash of the pirate Blackbeard sprinkled on top.

I hate him on sight.

I also know instinctively that he's not here by accident. He's here for me.

The odd thing is, he's not trying to hide it. He wants me to see him. That's obvious. Judging by the way he's lounging against the wall, arrogant as the devil, he wants everyone to see him.

He removes his sunglasses and looks me up and down. I'm gratified to see him purse his lips in dissatisfaction.

"*Dobroye utro,* Malek," says the old woman behind the counter to my left.

"Good morning, Alina," I reply in Russian, turning to her. I walk casually to the counter, making sure the movie star sees my relaxed smile. "How are you today? How's the knee?"

"Perfect! I can't believe how good. Years of hobbling everywhere are over like that." She snaps her fingers. "God favored me when I was moved to the head of the line for that replacement."

It wasn't God who moved her forward in the Ministry of Health's long waiting list, but I don't mention that.

"I'm glad to hear it. Do you have my order ready?"

"Vanya is putting it together. Only a few minutes more. Sit and have a drink while you wait."

She gestures to a self-serve coffee bar on the opposite side of the store. Behind it is a wall of glass with a view to the street beyond.

"I'll do that. Thank you."

Without looking at the movie star, who's still lounging against the wall near the restrooms, watching me, I walk to the bar, select a paper cup from a bin, and pour myself a large coffee.

I never take it with cream or sugar, but today I do.

I make an elaborate show of choosing an artificial sweetener, riffling through the colored paper packets in their little metal container as if I'm hoping to find a gold bar. Whistling, I stir the sweetener into the coffee. Then I take a thoughtful sip, shake my head, set the cup onto the wood counter, and add a generous dollop of fresh cream.

I sip again. When I produce a loud, satisfied, "Ah!" a voice from beside me says, "Jesus, Mary, and Joseph, you're in the wrong line of work. You should've gone into acting, mate. That deserved a bloody Oscar."

His tone is dry. His accent is Irish. I want to plunge a knife into his chest.

He slides onto a metal stool beside me and sets his sunglasses on the counter. That's when I notice the tattoos on the knuckles of his left hand: stars, flowers, initials, a skull with a dagger through it. A black square that looks like it's covering something else.

My body falls still.

I know those tats. I've seen them before. In that specific order on each finger.

I've been staring at them for the past sixteen years.

In Russian, he says quietly, "Pakhan sends his regards."

This Irishman speaks Russian. He knows Pakhan. He wears the same ink on his skin. He knew where to find me and exactly the time I'd be at this store.

I set my coffee down slowly, taking a moment to center myself.

When I turn and look at him, he's watching me with an alert expression, possibly a respectful one, but no trace of fear.

"Who are you?"

"A friend. Or an enemy. It all depends on you."

I recall something Pakhan said to me over dinner, and a light-bulb goes on over my head. "The dead man who knows everything."

He makes a face. Switching back to English he says, "Ach, is that what they're calling me now? I sound like a B movie."

After a moment where I only gaze at him, he gestures to the stool next to me. "Have a seat, mate. I don't like to crane my neck. You're a bloody skyscraper."

I sit on the stool and stare at him. He grins like he's being interviewed on TV. There's a dimple in his cheek I'd like to stab a fork into.

"So? Where should I start?"

"Your name."

"Killian."

"Last name?"

"You get a last name if we decide we're not going to kill each other."

"If I wanted you dead, you already would be."

He smiles. "That's my line. I like you already."

"What is this about?"

"In a nutshell, the future of nations."

He says it with a straight face, as if I'm supposed to have any fucking clue what that means.

"Uh-huh. Sounds important."

"There's no need for sarcasm."

"Are you one of those annoying people who can never get to the point?"

"And now you're insulting me." He shakes his head. "When Pakhan said you were short on charm, he wasn't kidding."

Fighting the urge to take his skull between my hands and crush it, I say slowly, "Get. To. The fucking. Point."

His tone dry, he says, "Since you asked so nicely." He reaches over, picks up my cup of coffee, and takes a sip. "Hmm. That's quite good."

I'm about to smash a fist into his nose, when he says, "Pakhan has cancer. Pancreatic. He's got a few months left, if that."

It sets me back onto my heels. I sit with that piece of information for a moment, digesting it in silence.

Killian watches me with eyes as sharp as a hawk's.

"Why isn't he telling me this?"

"He will. I mean, if you're still alive by the time that conversation occurs."

"Threaten me again and see what happens."

He casually lifts a shoulder. "It's not a threat. It's a fact. If this meeting goes sideways, you're a dead man."

I chuckle. "You might be the stupidest person I've ever met."

"I wouldn't expect you to be afraid, but I'm telling you the truth. I'm very good at what I do."

"Not as good as I am."

He smiles at me like you'd smile at a baby. "Okay. Moving on. Are you still planning to try to kill Declan O'Donnell?"

"Try?" I repeat through gritted teeth.

"That wasn't an insult. I just need to know where your head's at."

I growl, "You have exactly ten seconds before I lose my patience and send you to meet your maker."

It could be my imagination, but I think this son of a bitch wants to roll his eyes.

"Pakhan recommended you as his replacement."

I almost fall off the stool.

"Oh, look," Killian says, amused. "Godzilla is surprised."

I manage to repeat, *"Replacement?"*

"Aye, but here's the rub, Malek. Pakhan isn't doing what you think he's doing. That job he's got? Big boss of the Bratva? That's for show. What he's really doing is far more important. Stop squinting at me. It won't help you understand anything better."

After a moment, I say, "If this is a fucking joke, I'm not finding it funny."

I get the condescending smile again. "You do seem to be lacking in the sense of humor department, but no, it's not a joke."

We stare at each other. While I decide what to say next, he drinks more of my coffee.

"So you're the one who told Pakhan about Riley."

His voice warms. "Ah, yes. Riley. I'd like to meet her. I think she and my wife would really get along. They have a lot in common. Juliet's the daughter of a man who tried to kill me several times. One of my worst enemies. Oh—you might've heard of him. Antonio Moretti? Does that ring any bells? He used to be the head of the Cosa Nostra in New York, but he's dead now."

He chuckles. "Dead like I am, I mean."

The longer this conversation continues, the more liable I am to burst a brain vessel.

"Pakhan was very concerned that he'd misjudged you when he heard you'd kidnapped Riley. He didn't take you for a rapist. Thought it was out of character. Needless to say, he was relieved to discover the wee lass was not only unmolested, she'd taken quite a shine to you."

"Unmolested?" I say, astonished. *"Shine?"*

He waves a hand dismissively.

I've seen Riley make the exact same gesture when she thinks I'm being a pain in the ass.

"You saved her life. Your brother's murderer's soon-to-be sister-in-law. A man you'd vowed to kill for revenge. It's all very Shake-spearean, don't you think? Like me and Juliet."

He smiles again, a thing he seems overly fond of doing. "Don't you love a good romantic drama?"

Glowering at him, I say, "I love a good murder."

"Ach. You're no fun."

"How do I know any of this is true?"

"Call Pakhan. He'll fill you in."

"Why would he want me as his successor? I killed his cousin."

"The kid was an asshole. Everybody thought so. And you've been incredibly loyal and efficient. Plus, you have that do-gooding side. He thinks you're up for the job."

"Do-gooding side?"

"Sticking up for your little brother who was getting bullied. Trying to save prostitutes with generous donations of cash. Alina's knee. Only a few of numerous examples."

"How the fuck do you know about any of that?"

His smile is smug. "They don't call me the man who knows everything for no reason."

With the exception of Declan O'Donnell, I've never known anyone I'd like to kill more. "Why didn't Pakhan just tell me all this himself?"

"I had to vet you."

"*Vet* me?"

"Stop repeating everything I say."

"If you'd make any sense, I wouldn't have to."

Killian exhales a short, annoyed breath. "Look. I'm the leader of a multinational organization. A clandestine group of thirteen men who specialize in espionage, geopolitics, guerrilla warfare, and advanced spycraft to thwart global terrorism. We're the real power behind the thrones. Don't make that face at me, you bloody grand gobshite."

"It's just that this is a fascinating yarn you're spinning. Please, continue."

He mutters something in Gaelic. "As I was saying. We're all working undercover in some capacity, masquerading as Mob kings, corrupt politicians, shady business tycoons, you name it."

"Uh-huh. And the point of all this masquerading?"

"Saving the world."

Unbelievably, he says that with no trace of self-consciousness or awareness of how ridiculous he sounds. His hubris is staggering.

I decide to play along with his insanity. "What do you call yourselves? The Avengers?"

"The Thirteen."

I snort. "Sounds like a boy band."

"Fuck you."

"Let me guess—you came up with that winner?"

He glares at me, and now I find myself having fun. "And I suppose you're Number One, right?"

"You know, I liked you better when you were only making a Broadway production out of pouring yourself a bloody coffee."

"Who's Number Two? Because that's all sorts of awkward. Does everybody giggle during meetings when his name is called?"

I can tell he's debating whether or not he should go ahead and kill me, and I can't help but smile.

From across the store, Alina calls my name. "Your order's ready!"

"That's my cue, Number One. You realize you've nicknamed yourself piss, right? You're the head urinator."

"They only say that in the U.S."

"No, everybody knows it."

"No, they don't."

"Yes, they do."

He grinds his teeth for a while, then stands. He shoves his sunglasses back onto his face and props his hands on his hips.

"Obviously, we're not interested in you for your personality, because it's shite. You've got skills we can use. Weaponry, technology, languages, disguises, critical thinking. It took me a long time to find you, which never happens, so you're an expert at covering your tracks. You can pilot a plane. You can operate drones. You're proficient with ingress and egress of locked spaces."

"You could just say getting in and out. You don't have to be so pretentious about it."

The breath he exhales is slow and controlled. I'm making him mad.

My grin could be described as shit-eating.

He decides the pleasantries are finished and pronounces, "If you refuse to join us, you die."

I lift my brows. "Not exactly a rousing recruiting slogan, is it?"

"That's not an idle threat."

"Yes, I can see you're very serious. Your dimple is winking at me."

After a pause, he says sourly, "You're an arrogant prick."

"I'd say it takes one to know one, but I'm so frightened that you'll lose your temper and murder me."

When I flatten my lips together to keep from smiling, he shakes his head in disgust.

"I'll be in touch again in a few days. In the meantime, talk to Pakhan."

"Great to meet you, Number One. Have fun back at the asylum."

Muttering in Gaelic, he walks toward the exit.

I call after him, "Say hi to Number Two for me!"

The door slams behind him, and he's gone.

I load the groceries into the truck, then start the drive back to the cabin. On the way, I call Pakhan. We talk for the entire hour it takes me to get home.

By the time I arrive, Pakhan has confirmed everything Killian told me.

He's dying of cancer.

He wants me to be his successor.

He and the cocky Irishman with the Jesus complex have been working undercover together for years to infiltrate and eliminate the biggest rats in the nest, as it were, along with the other members of the Thirteen, who are definitely not a boy band.

Last but not least, my options are limited: accept the role I'm being offered, or spend the rest of my life dodging bullets from this irritating fucking Killian person and his crew of twelve murderous, highly trained, and well-funded do-gooding disciples.

The bottom line being that no matter what happens next, I can't keep my little bird caged any longer.

I'll either be a dead man or the king of the Bratva with a thousand new targets on his back and more secrets than any man should have.

There's only one way I can protect her now.

Open her cage door, and let her fly away.

A mile from the cabin, I pull off to the side of the road and hop out of the truck. Cursing furiously, I unload the magazine of my gun into the nearest tree. I reload and empty another one. Then I get the axe I keep in the toolbox in the bed of the truck and hack up several other trees until I'm sweating and panting and my hands are raw.

None of it helps. There's nothing that will ever help me get this pain out of my system.

I knew this day would come, one way or the other. I'm still not prepared for it. But the fact remains, a girl like Riley doesn't belong with a man like me. A man with my life and all the horror that comes with it.

Everyone knows the dragon doesn't get the princess in the end.

The dragon doesn't save the day. That's what white knights are for.

I throw the axe to the ground and blow out a hard breath. I tilt my head back, close my eyes, and stand motionless, just breathing, until I know my voice will sound steady.

Then I fish my cell from my pocket and dial the Lenin Hotel in Moscow. When a woman at the front desk picks up, I tell her to connect me to room number 427.

Then I wait, heartbroken and sick to my stomach, for Spider to answer the phone.

FORTY-TWO

RILEY

I can tell something's amiss the moment Mal walks through the door.

Carrying brown paper bags of groceries, he's tense. His energy is weird. He won't look at me.

Sitting at the kitchen table with my yellow legal pad, I watch him drop the bags onto the counter and turn back to go out again.

"Mal?"

He stops midstride. He doesn't turn around.

"I'm going to ask you what's wrong, and you're going to tell me the truth. Are you ready?"

He doesn't respond.

"What's wrong?"

I watch his shoulders rise as he inhales. When he speaks, his voice is low and gruff.

"I talked to Pakhan."

My stomach drops. If he's talking to Pakhan, that must mean it's time for him to go back to work. His vacation is over.

Our perfect little bubble has popped.

I stand, cross to him, and curl my hands into the front of his shirt. Looking up into his face, I say, "Are you okay?"

He closes his eyes and exhales in a gust. Sounding miserable, he says, "You worrying about me above everything else makes it all so much worse."

"I can't help it. I like you."

He opens his eyes and stares down at me with a tortured look.

"Okay, wow. That face is scaring me."

He frames my face in his hands and kisses me. The kiss is achingly tender and freaks me the fuck out.

My heart starting to pound, I say, "Is this about you having to go back to the city?"

When he nods, I'm weak with relief. The way he was acting, I thought it was something unexpected. "Well, if it will put your mind at ease, I can stay here while you have to go to work if you want."

He just stares at me silently. It seems like he's waiting for more of an explanation.

"I mean, I'm all healed now. I know how to shoot every type of gun in case another bear decides to visit. And, to be completely honest, the thought of staying in that crypt of an apartment of yours while you're out working doesn't exactly light me on fire. I don't want to be away from you, but I'm also hoping never to see Masha the Golden Goddess ever again or live on frozen dinners."

I smile at him. "And you only ever leave for a day or two at a time, so I think you'll be able to survive without me that long."

His voice thick, he says, "I'll have to stay a while this time."

I tease, "Such dedication. Pakhan must be so proud."

He swallows, his Adam's apple bobbing.

I go up on my toes, wind my arms around his neck, and kiss him. "I know," I whisper against his mouth. "I didn't want it to end, either. But maybe Pakhan will give you another vacation soon. Since he likes me so much and all."

With a faint groan, he takes my mouth in a desperate kiss, bending me back at the waist and devouring me. When we come up for air, I'm laughing.

"I should send you to the grocery store more often!"

He stares at me with those tortured eyes again, then releases me abruptly and stalks out.

Staring after him, I debate if I should follow, but decide to give him his space. I put the groceries away and go back to writing.

That night, he fucks me with such intensity, it frightens me.

We lie in the dark afterward, silent and sweaty, limbs entangled. His heart pounds underneath my cheek. I want to say something, but I don't know what, so I keep quiet and let him hold me in his strong arms.

Near dawn, he rises from bed and stands naked at the window, staring out. His hands clench and unclench, as if he needs to hit something.

"Sweetie? Come back to bed."

Without turning, he murmurs, "Let me ask you a question, *malyutka*. If you had a choice between keeping something precious to you safe, but safety would mean letting it go forever, or keeping it in constant danger, but having it close to you, which would you choose?"

"Hypothetically?"

"Yes."

"Like if it was you?"

He braces an arm against the wall, bows his head, and nods. His demeanor scares me. I know this isn't a simple hypothetical question. He's weighing a choice, and it has to do with me.

I say firmly, "I'd keep it in constant danger."

His laugh is low and mirthless. "No, you wouldn't. You're not that selfish."

"Yes, I am. I *am*."

He turns to look at me. In the lifting gray light, he's as beautiful as he always is. His eyes are burning. "You've never lied to me before."

"I've never felt like it was necessary. What's going on?"

He doesn't answer. Avoiding my eyes, he goes into the closet, emerging quickly, fully dressed. When he disappears into the kitchen, I fly out of bed and get dressed, too, then follow him, trying not to panic.

I find him standing at the kitchen sink, staring down into it, unmoving.

"Mal. Malek."

He doesn't respond. It royally pisses me off.

"I'm going to stand here repeating your name until you tell me what the hell is going on."

Sounding resigned, he says, "I have to go back into town again. I left something at the grocer yesterday."

"I'm coming with you."

He turns his head and peers at me. His expression is unreadable.

"I'm coming," I insist. "If you think you're leaving me here after dropping that bomb about letting something precious to you go forever, you're nuts."

A smidgen of my panic is relieved when he smiles. He says softly, "All right, *malyutka*. You'll come with me." He holds out an arm.

I cross to him and hug him, wrapping my arms around his back and burying my face in his chest. My words are muffled by his shirt. "When we get back, will you promise to talk to me?"

He draws a deep, slow breath. When he exhales, he whispers, "I promise."

I don't understand why it sounds so anguished.

The drive into town is spent in silence so loud, it's deafening. I sit right beside Mal, gripping his hand, shooting an occasional worried glance at his profile.

It's as hard as granite. He's unreachable, retreating somewhere inside his head where he obviously doesn't want me to follow.

I know this new distance has to do with his call with Pakhan. Maybe Mal's in trouble. Or maybe there's something exceptionally dangerous he's been tasked to do. The specifics don't matter to me as much as why he won't talk to me about it.

His silence is the terrifying part. He's up in his head, playing with his monsters, and he won't let me in.

We arrive at the grocer as they're unlocking the doors. Mal parks the truck in front, shuts off the engine, and says, "I'll be right back. Stay here."

"The hell I will," I mutter, opening the passenger door. I jump out, slam the door behind me, and stand there waiting for him with my arms folded over my chest, scowling.

He stares at me through the windshield for a moment, then shakes his head and gets out.

Taking my arm, he leads me into the grocery store.

It's small and charming, with a mom-and-pop feel. There's a coffee bar on one side, across from the cash register, and a big display of veggies in round baskets up front. Other than us and the old lady turning the sign in the front window, the store is empty.

Mal greets the woman with a few words in Russian. She nods, smiling, and shuffles off toward the back of the store.

"I need to use the restroom. Stay out of trouble."

He kisses me on the temple, inhaling against my skin for a moment and giving me a squeeze before pulling away abruptly and heading to the back of the store.

I watch him enter the men's room and close the door, then I turn to the display of vegetables.

After a moment, an uncomfortable sensation raises all the hair on the back of my neck. Frowning, I look up and around, then suck in a shocked breath.

Dressed in black combat gear from head to toe, including the boots and bulletproof vest, Spider stands motionless beside the cash register, staring at me.

He looks terrible. Thinner, strung out, and wild-eyed as a junkie. A ragged pink scar snakes two inches down his temple.

With a flash of horror so cold, it leaves me frozen, I realize what Mal's done.

I breathe, *"No."*

Spider jolts into motion at the same time I do. I don't even make it out the door before he's got me.

"Mal!" I scream, thrashing in Spider's arms. "Mal! No! No! Don't do this!"

Spider is saying something to me, speaking rapidly in a low voice as he drags me out the door, but I can't pay attention to it because I'm too busy screaming and trying to get away.

It's useless. Thinner or not, Spider's still far stronger than me. His arms are iron bars. I kick and twist, but he manages to wrestle me into the black van that's idling at the curb, its side sliding door open. He pushes me in and slams the door closed.

I fall on it, panting and yanking, but it won't open. It's locked.

On my hands and knees over the bare metal floor of the van, I scramble to the pair of swinging doors at the back. They're locked, too.

Spider guns the engine. The van peels out, slamming me against the back window.

Mal steps out of the store.

He stands motionless, staring at me with anguished eyes as I scream his name over and over and pound my fists on the windows.

I'm still screaming long after he's out of sight.

FORTY-THREE

DECLAN

*B*reathing easier, I disconnect with Spider and turn to look at Sloane.

She stands still as a statue, her eyes searching my face. From the moment we got the call yesterday that Spider had located Riley and was going to get her, she hasn't eaten, slept, or spoken a word. The only thing she's done is wring her hands and pace.

I say softly, "He has her."

She sinks to her knees on the carpet, covers her face in her hands, and breaks into tears.

I kneel beside her and hold her, rocking her silently in my arms.

When the worst of it is over and she's sniffling, I murmur, "They're in the air now. They'll be here in about nine hours."

"How is she? Did he say anything? Is she hurt?"

"She didn't appear to be hurt." I hesitate, not wanting to fan the flames. "But he did say she was hysterical."

Sloane lifts her head and stares at me with watery red eyes. "Well, no wonder! After what she must've been through, she's hysterical with relief, the poor baby! She's dying to come home!"

That wasn't exactly the way Spider put it, but I'll hold off on that. I need to set eyes on Riley myself to judge her condition.

"Why don't you try to get some sleep?"

She says irritably, "I'll sleep when she's here. If I were to lie down now, I'd just stare at the ceiling." She groans and covers her face with her hands again. "Oh, god. She hates me. She has to. It's my fault all this happened in the first place."

"Let's focus on the positive, love. We got her. She's coming home. Come on, let's get you to the sofa. I'll make you a drink."

I help her stand and settle her onto the couch. Then I kiss her forehead and go into the kitchen to pour us a healthy measure of whiskey.

I have a feeling we're going to need it.

Ten hours later, I'm proven right when Riley bursts through the door ahead of Spider, channeling the energies of Katniss Everdeen from *The Hunger Games* and the samurai sword–wielding assassin lass from *Kill Bill*.

If they were both high on methamphetamines and had been living in a tree in the woods.

"Send me back!" she shouts as a greeting. "Send me back right this fucking minute!"

Then she stands in the middle of the living room with her legs spread open and her hands clenched to fists, breathing hard and growling.

Sloane is frozen in shock beside me. Her lips are parted and her eyes are wide. She can't believe what she's seeing.

Understandable, because her little sister obviously isn't her little sister anymore.

She's transformed into some kind of punk pixie version of Rambo.

Her bleached hair shows three inches of darker roots. She stands taller because of the military-style boots she's wearing. Her trousers are the tactical kind hunters wear—with lots of Velcro pockets for gear—and her tight black T-shirt shows off her surprisingly well-developed biceps muscles.

And those eyes. Christ.

They were always hidden behind thick glasses before, but now the glasses are gone and her eyes are flashing golden-bronze fury all over the room.

Sloane says tentatively, "Riley?"

Riley's furious gaze slashes to her. She looks her up and down, then says curtly, "Hi, Hollywood. Tell your man to get my ass back onto a plane to Russia within the hour, or I'll burn this house down."

Spider walks slowly into the room behind Riley. Horrified, Sloane looks to him for help.

He shakes his head. "She's been like this since I picked her up."

"Abducted me," Riley corrects.

Sloane cries, "He *rescued* you."

"Really? Did he ask me if I wanted to leave? Because if he did, I sure didn't hear it. I was too busy kicking and screaming."

"Of course you wanted to leave! You were in *Russia*!"

"Yeah. Guess what? That's where I live now."

Sloane puts a hand to her throat and pauses for a beat to gather herself. "Let's take a step back for a minute. Declan, will you please get us all a drink?"

Riley says, "I can't drink alcohol anymore."

"Why not?"

"I'm missing a kidney."

It wasn't meant for him, but Spider stiffens anyway. He snaps, "You know it was Malek who told me where to find you, right? He called me. *Himself.*"

The look Riley sends him could melt steel. "Of course I know it was him. Nobody else is that selfless."

Spider's face turns red. He steps forward, bristling. "Selfless? The murderer who broke into your bedroom and ran off with you in the middle of the night is *selfless*?"

Riley looks at him for a long moment, then says quietly, "You're a good man. And I know you wanted to help me by going to Russia, so thank you for that. But you and your boss here have both killed people, so don't sling the word 'murderer' around like you're on some kind of moral high ground. Malek Antonov is the best man I've ever met."

Spider looks like he just took a kick to the gut.

Riley turns back to me and pins me in a death glare so forceful, I almost step back.

"And *you*."

"Me? What did *I* do?"

She shakes her head like she's deeply disappointed in me. "This job you have. This thing you do for a living. Mr. Bigshot Mob Boss. You chose this life, didn't you?"

I feel like this is a trick question, so I fold my arms over my chest and stare her down.

She doesn't look intimidated.

"That's what I thought. Nobody forced you into it. Nobody put a gun to your whole family's heads, did they? Nobody said, 'Become my personal hitman or everyone you love dies.' But that's exactly what happened to Mal. Everything he's ever done has been in service to other people, including what he just did for me."

"Let's not paint too rosy a picture, lass. He went to the Bahamas to kill me, remember? Who was that in service to, if not himself?"

Her eyes glitter. Her voice drops. "You killed his brother. His last living relative. A person he loved and protected his entire life. So yes, he came here to get revenge, but he didn't. Can you guess why?"

When nobody says anything, her voice rises.

"The reason is standing right in front of you. I asked him not to kill you, you and Spider both, and he didn't, *because he didn't want to fucking disappoint me.* So you're welcome for saving your lives. Now get me on a plane back to Russia!"

After a long, silent moment, Sloane turns and looks at me. "How fun," she says drily. "Stockholm syndrome runs in the family."

FORTY-FOUR

RILEY

*I*t's funny, being in love. You can't see it up close. It's too massive.

It isn't until you're on a plane headed five thousand miles away that the big picture emerges, and you realize that the person you're leaving behind is someone you can't live without.

You realize that because, mile by mile, your heart feels like it's getting crushed and your stomach is twisted into knots and all the cells in your body scream his name at the top of their little cellular lungs.

The pain of separation is overwhelming. You feel as if you're going to die.

You *want* to die if it means you can never see him again.

And the anger. Oh, god! The anger that he's the one who forced the separation in the first place. Him with his stupid principles and his overdeveloped penchant for self-sacrifice.

If he only knew that he'd be killing me with this separation, not saving me, maybe he'd have thought twice.

As soon as I see him again, I'm going to kick his big bearded ass.

A tentative knock on the door pulls me out of my head.

I'm in one of the bedrooms in this new place of Sloane and Declan's, wearing a groove in the wood floor with my pacing.

Wearing a groove in my brain going over and over everything Mal said to me before we left for town.

He knew I'd insist on coming with him. He also knew I'd insist on not staying in the truck at the market. He could predict exactly what I'd do at every turn, and now I'm pissed at myself for being so damn obvious.

I'm more pissed at him for not telling me what happened with Pakhan.

What was so horrible that he had to send me away?

"Come in."

Sloane opens the door, comes inside, and closes the door behind her. She leans against it, staring at me as I continue to pace back and forth at the end of the bed.

"Hey, Smalls."

"Hollywood."

"You look . . . different."

"It's the contacts."

"It's everything."

"Really? That's where we're starting? With my looks?"

She throws her hands in the air. "Where am I supposed to start?"

I stop pacing and look at her. Dark circles nest in the hollows under her eyes. Her hair is lank and disheveled. I've never seen her appear anything less than perfectly groomed before. Even when she was fifteen years old and sporting a black mohawk, it was artfully gelled.

That she's obviously been worried sick about me melts some of the ice off the tip of the iceberg I feel for her.

In a softer voice, I say, "I'm okay. Mal took very good care of me. And thank you for sending Spider to rescue me, even though I didn't need rescuing."

She considers me in silence for a moment, then murmurs, "No, you don't seem like you do."

We gaze at each other across the room until she says, "You're missing a kidney?"

I nod. "And my spleen."

She whispers, "Jesus."

"Yeah, getting shot is a barrel of laughs."

She rubs a hand over her face, sighing. "Spider's a wreck about it."

"He doesn't need to be. Except for the stupid lightning bolt scar and the occasional nightmare, I'm fine."

"Lightning bolt scar?"

I lift my shirt and pull down the waistband of my trousers. Sloane's eyes widen. Her face pales. She puts a hand over her mouth and stares at my stomach like she's trying not to puke.

Remembering how Mal described it, I mutter, "Not bad, my ass."

"Oh my god, Riley."

Lowering my shirt, I wave a hand. "It looks worse than it was." That's a lie, but she doesn't seem like she can handle the truth at the moment, so I'm going with fibbing.

Feeling like a caged animal, I start to pace again.

"So . . . this Malek person."

"Don't say his name like it tastes bad."

"I'm sorry, it's just that all I've heard the past three months is what a monster he is and what a—"

"Wait. *Three months?* I haven't been gone that long."

"Yes, you have."

I think for a minute, trying to piece together a timetable. "What month is it?"

"June. It's June eighteenth."

"Holy shit."

"Yeah."

"And Spider was in Moscow that whole time?"

She pauses for a beat. "Against Declan's wishes, yes."

"What do you mean?"

"I mean Declan forbade him to go. Spider went anyway."

If Spider went against his boss's orders, that can mean only one thing: Mal was right about him having feelings for me.

This is a giant clusterfuck.

I stop pacing and sit on the edge of the bed, dropping my head into my hands. Sloane comes over and sits beside me. She rests a hand lightly on my back. We stay like that for a while until something occurs to me.

"What did you mean by that comment about Stockholm syndrome?"

She clears her throat. Then she emits a small, embarrassed laugh. "Declan kidnapped me. That's how we fell in love."

Shocked, I sit up and stare at her. "No way."

"Swear to god."

"Seriously?"

"Yep."

"I'd say holy shit again, but it would be redundant."

"I know. It's remarkably bizarre."

After a moment spent readjusting my brain, I chuckle. "Look on the bright side. We finally have something in common."

When her eyes fill with tears, I'm horrified. "I swear I didn't say that to be mean."

"I know." She sniffles, looking down. "But it's true. And for the past few months, I've been crucifying myself for all the ways I've failed you as a big sister."

Lord, this drama queen. My sigh is heavy. "Dude. The only time you ever failed me was when you stole my boyfriend."

She jerks her head up and stares at me. "*What?* I did no such thing!"

"Yes, you did."

"No, I didn't!"

I scoff. "I don't know what kind of revisionist history you've created in your head, sis, but you definitely did."

Indignant, she leaps from the bed and glares at me. "Who? When?"

"Really? You really want to get into this now?"

"Yes! Right fucking now! Start talking!"

Okay, *here's* the Sloane I know. The bossy, impulsive, confident Sloane who once seriously considered getting the words "Pussy Power" tattooed above her cooch.

In a way, I'm relieved. That other, weepy Sloane creeps me out.

"Chris. My twenty-first birthday party."

Frowning, she thinks. "Your twenty-first birthday party was at that club in San Francisco. Chris was that tall guy you were dating who had that weird lazy eye."

I say sourly, "I see it's all coming back to you now."

"I never dated that guy."

I lose my temper and bark at her. "For fuck's sake, Sloane, you *told* me you were dating him!"

She folds her arms over her chest and looks down her nose at me. "Baloney. You must've been high at the time."

"Uh, *no,* I was on the phone with you after hearing from my girlfriend that she thought she saw the two of you together. You admitted it."

"That's ridiculous! I'd never date a guy with a lazy eye!"

"Man, I really wonder about your priorities."

Ignoring that, she insists, "Do you have any idea how many guys named Chris I've dated?"

I mutter, "I'm guessing the number is in the thousands."

"Exactly! Jesus Christ, Riley, I'd never do that to you! *Never!*"

We glare at each other until her face crumples. "You don't believe me."

I warn, "Don't you dare start crying on me, you frickin' wimp. I'm the one who should be bawling here, not you."

She bites her lip and blinks a lot. I want to jump up and smack her. A knock on the door distracts me.

"Can I come in?"

It's Declan. My heartbeat goes into overdrive. I jump from the bed and yank open the door to find him standing there with a pained look on his face, like he's constipated.

"Did you arrange the flight? When am I leaving?"

He glances at Sloane. When he looks back at me, he says, "I need to tell you something, lass. You should take a seat for this."

I wave him off. "I think better on my feet. Just tell me what's happening."

He glances at Sloane again. It makes me nervous. "What?"

"You two are so much alike."

Crap, not this broken record again. "Yeah, I keep hearing that. What's happening?"

"May I come in?"

I step aside and let him into the room. He goes straight to Sloane and gives her a hug and a kiss, then brushes a thumb over her cheek, gazing tenderly down at her. It looks like he's about to start spouting poetry.

I throw my arms into the air. "Any day now!"

He turns to me with Sloane tucked under his arm. "Do you want the good news or the bad news first?"

I look at Sloane. "Does he not know his life is in danger?"

She wraps her arms around his waist and gazes up at him. "You should probably just get straight to it, honey. I like you better without stab marks all over your body."

He shrugs. "All right, if you insist. Malek is the new head of the Russian Bratva."

That leaves me breathless.

So there it is. The reason Mal wanted me out of Russia.

I recall his hypothetical question about keeping something

precious close though it would be dangerous and wish I'd bashed a pan over his head to force him to talk to me.

A mistake I'll never make again.

Shaking off the tidal wave of emotion that's threatening to overpower me, I say, "What happened to Pakhan?"

Declan lifts a brow. "What do you know about Pakhan?"

"That he makes questionable fashion choices, including wearing real fur and pinkie rings. What happened to him?"

Declan lifts his other brow, so now he's staring at me in open astonishment. "You met him?"

"Yeah. We had dinner together. He's really sweet. *What happened to him?*"

"He has cancer. He's decided to make Malek his protégé."

Cancer. Oh, no. He was so nice to me. Thinking of our dinner, I say absently, "You mean successor."

"Excuse me?"

"A protégé is in the process of training. A successor takes over where someone leaves off."

Sloane says, "She has a thing for words. Just keep going."

"That's it."

Pulling myself together, I say, "What's the good news?"

He gets a mysterious glint in his eye, like he has a secret. "How do you know that wasn't the good news?"

I look at Sloane.

She says, "Seriously, honey. Look at that face. You're taking your life in your hands."

"Thank you, sis."

She smiles at me. "You're welcome."

"All right . . . let's just say Malek and I now have a mutual friend."

I frown. "You mean the guy Mal visited in New York to get information about how to find you?"

Declan goes very still. He says slowly, "What guy?"

"Some guy named Kazimir. I heard Mal say the name over dinner with Pakhan and asked him about it later."

His stillness turns to stiffness. Murder flares in his eyes. Through a clenched jaw, he says, "Kazimir told Malek how to find me? *So he could kill me?*"

Sloane whistles. "Oh, he's gonna be in so much trouble."

"What am I missing?"

Grimacing, she glances at me. "That's Nat's fiancé."

"Whoa! Hold on! What the fucking-fuckedy-fuck?"

"Kage—Kazimir—is the head of the Bratva here in the U.S."

I can feel my eyes bulging out like a cartoon. *"And Nat's engaged to him?"*

"It's a long story. I'll fill you in later. Right now, I think the three of us need to get on a conference call."

Declan roars, "I'm not getting on the phone with that bloody arsewipe!"

Sloane pats his chest. "I meant us three girls, honey."

Sputtering in fury, he says, "You're not talking to Natalie! I forbid it!"

Sloane kisses his cheek. "That's cute." She holds her hand out to me. "Come on. The sooner we can sort this out, the sooner his blood pressure can get back to normal."

We leave Declan behind in the room, shouting something in Gaelic that doesn't sound like it has anything to do with his blood pressure.

FORTY-FIVE

RILEY

I spend two hours on the phone with Nat and Sloane, starting off by saying, "Okay, explain this all to me like I'm a toddler."

I get a story that makes my eyes cross.

Nat's former fiancé, David, who went missing on the day of their wedding years ago and who everyone presumed was dead, was actually a Bratva accountant named Damon who embezzled money, turned on his bosses, and went into the witness protection program. With a new identity, he moved to Lake Tahoe, where he met Nat. Fast-forward a bunch of years, he's gone missing, and Nat is still in mourning.

Except then this hot stranger, Kage, moves in next door, and Nat's dormant mourning ovaries jolt to life like reanimated zombies starving for brains.

"Brains" being a euphemism for the exceptionally hot dick Kage is packing.

But Kage, being cagey, hides the fact from Nat that he's really the assassin sent to locate Damon and all the money he stole from the Bratva, then kill her.

I mean, it's understandable he omitted that pesky detail, right? It would be a deal breaker for most girls.

But Nat, also being cagey, figures out who Kage and her ex really are—wait, there's another assassin in there somewhere who shows up to kill her because Kage failed to do it—and she heads off to Panama to find Damon, who was never really dead in the first place, just waiting for her to find him from a secret message he left in a painting. He skipped town on their wedding day because the FBI told him the Bratva had discovered where he'd been hiding.

Except by the time Nat finds him, he's married to some other lady.

Who also doesn't know his real name or that he was in the mafia.

Anyway, Kage and Nat get past all the thorny I-was-sent-to-kill-you business and move to New York together. Then, of course, Sloane has to go visit her bestie Nat in Manhattan, because the number of millionaires per capita is higher there than anywhere else in the U.S.

When I ask Sloane how she knew that, she says she looked it up. Shocker.

So Kage sends a private jet for Sloane—I swear, these gangsters and their private jets—and Sloane heads to New York. Just as she steps out of the car at Nat and Kage's building, however, Declan roars up with the Irish cavalry to kidnap her on orders from then-boss Diego, who wanted information about Kage and a shootout that went down at some Mexican restaurant in Tahoe where both Irish and Russians were killed and Sloane was the cause.

Then Diego dies—supposedly but not really—and Declan becomes the new Mob boss.

I know. I could hardly follow it, either.

But I did follow the part where Declan got a lot more than he bargained for in a kidnappee, because within a few days, Sloane had his whole crew eating out of her manicured hands and him wrapped around her pinkie finger.

There was a side story about some guy named Stavros and another jet, but I'd zoned out by then.

The bottom line being that Sloane fell in love with Declan, turned over a new leaf as a human being (I tried very hard not to snort when she said that), and wanted to mend fences with the little sister she'd never been that close to, partly because the little sister—wrongly—thought she'd once stolen her boyfriend.

By the end of all that, I'm exhausted.

We hang up with Nat—who, from the sound of it, is about to go do something violent to her man Kage for giving Mal intel about Declan—and I lie down on the floor.

To the ceiling, I say, "So to wrap it all up, the three of us are in love with a trio of powerful mobsters."

Sloane says, "Who are all enemies. Yes."

"Why would Mal and Kage be enemies?"

"Maybe 'enemies' isn't the right word, but those boys don't like to share their toys."

"So they don't hate each other as much as they hate Declan."

She lies down on the floor beside me and takes my hand. "Right. Though I don't understand what Declan meant when he said he and Malek have a mutual friend now. I'll have to ask him about it later."

Whatever it means, I know she'll get it out of him. The woman was born to dissolve a man's independent will.

"Circling back. How did Spider know I was in Moscow from the beginning?"

"Kage told Declan in return for a marker."

"Is that some kind of mobster slang I should know?"

"It's a favor. A big one. That can be called in at any time, and Declan can't refuse."

"Yikes."

"Exactly."

I feel bad about that angry speech I made to Declan when I first came in, until I get confused again. "Wait, so Kage and Declan are enemies, but they work together?"

"Sometimes. Other times they try to kill each other."

That makes me smile. "Sounds like sisters."

"Ha."

"What about Diego? Is he still in the hospital?"

"He went to live with his sister in New York. He still can't remember a thing that happened. He's working at a diner as a short-order cook."

"Poor guy."

"I dunno, I think he might be better off."

"What makes you say that?"

"There probably aren't too many people trying to kill short-order cooks."

"Good point. And Kieran? I've been worrying about him."

"He's a tank, that guy. Three shots to the torso and he lived! Declan put him on leave for a while, but he's back on the job." She turns her head and smiles at me. "He's almost as tough as you."

"Yeah, we mouse deer with the tiny fang-like tusks are super badass."

When she makes a confused face, I say, "Forget it. Inside joke."

Then I'm depressed. Abruptly, completely depressed, and longing for Mal with such a fierce ache, I can hardly draw a breath.

I whisper, "He let me go. *He let me go.*"

"It sounds like he was trying to protect you."

"I know he was, but what an asshole!"

"You don't think he's an asshole."

"Yes, I really do!"

She quirks her lips and looks at me sideways. "Remember in *Twilight* when Edward left Bella to protect her even though it killed him to do it, and you thought that was the most romantic thing you'd ever heard?"

"No!"

"Shut up. Yes, you do."

"I hated that movie!"

"Yeah, but you loved all the books. And you *loooved* Edward, Mr. Broody Telepathic Vampire who would sacrifice anything for his dumb-as-rocks human girlfriend, including his own life."

I think of Mal's self-sacrificing tendencies and his love of bitey sex, and have to admit she might have a point. "So you're saying I'm the dumb-as-rocks human girlfriend in this scenario."

"No, I'm saying you don't really think Mal's an asshole. You think he's the bee's knees."

"Who says that? What are you, eighty?"

Breezing past that, she muses, "You know what's funny? Nobody ever mentions that Edward was like a hundred years old and Bella was only seventeen. Talk about perving on a baby."

I grimace at the image of my dear Edward Cullen as a child molester. "Thanks for ruining my favorite book series for me."

"Ha! I knew you loved *Twilight*!"

I grumble, "Whatever. And he didn't leave Bella until *New Moon*."

We lie there in companionable silence for a long time, until I sit up and scrub my hands over my face. "God, this is a fucked-up situation."

Sloane props herself up on her elbows and gazes at me thoughtfully. "We might be looking at this the wrong way."

"What do you mean?"

"Well, between you, me, and Nat, we have the three most powerful men in the U.S. and Russia totally pussy whipped."

I say drily, "Always the incurable romantic."

"I mean, think what we could accomplish!"

I see the mad glint in her eye and know she's planning something. Like overthrowing all the governments of the world and becoming Supreme Ruler of Earth.

I can already see her throne, a massive structure made of all the souls of the men whose hearts she's crushed.

"First things first. I need to get back to Russia."

"There might be a little hiccup with that."

Sloane and I turn at the sound of Declan's voice. He stands in the doorway, gazing down at us with his hand on the doorknob and an inscrutable expression on his face.

I say, "Such as?"

"Malek has put the word out. Anyone who assists you in attempting to return to him dies."

Shocked, I shout, *"What?"*

"Apparently, he knows you well."

I leap to my feet and stare at him, vibrating with anger. "Apparently, he doesn't! Because I'll swim there if I have to!"

He says gently, "Maybe it's for the best, lass. You'd never be safe with him now, not with what he's doing."

"You mean the way Sloane isn't safe with you, but she's still here? You mean the way Nat's not safe with Kage, but they're still together?"

He gazes at me for a beat with a million unspoken words spiraling behind his eyes. "Not exactly."

When he doesn't continue, I say, "I'll throat punch you, gangster."

"Honey, just tell us what's going on," says Sloane, standing.

He looks back and forth between us, then looks heavenward and sighs.

"Stop praying and spit it out!"

"There's this group called the Thirteen," he starts, but gets interrupted by Sloane, who says, "Group? Like a band?"

Declan mutters, "I told him that name was shite." Then, louder: "They're not a band."

He goes on to describe the plot of a James Bond movie. Bad guys disguised as good guys, good guys disguised as bad guys, international espionage, corrupt governments, I don't even know what else because I stop listening halfway through.

Sloane says, "Are you in this group?"

"We help each other out from time to time, but I'm not a member."

"What about Kazimir?"

He looks offended. "No!"

"Don't get your panties in a wad. I'm just asking."

I say loudly, "Everybody shut up. I have an important question."

Sloane and Declan look at me.

"Whoever else is in this stupid international spy-band-whatever group, do any of them have girlfriends or wives?"

Declan says instantly, "Of course."

He realizes his mistake when I glare at him. Then he raises his hands like he's in a holdup. "I don't make the rules, lass."

"You know what? This is bullshit. Get Mal on the phone."

"You say that like you think I have his number."

"Whoever *you* know that *he* knows, this mutual friend, call *that* guy and get his number!"

He's beginning to look like he's regretting this entire conversation. "He's not the bloody telephone directory."

"I have your boyfriend's number."

We all turn. Behind Declan in the hallway stands Spider, staring at me from under lowered brows.

"You want it?" He crooks a finger, then turns around and walks away without another word.

After he's out of earshot, Sloane says uneasily, "Why do I get the feeling there's going to be a price attached?"

I mutter, "Blackmail's popular for a reason," then follow Spider out the door.

FORTY-SIX

RILEY

*S*pider leads me down the hallway to another bedroom and closes the door behind us. He stands with his hand on the knob, facing away from me, then says quietly, "Make me understand this."

"There's nothing to understand."

He turns to me. What I see in his eyes makes me take a step back.

We stare at each other in tense silence, until he says gruffly, "Three months. I searched for you for almost three fucking months."

I can already tell this is going to be a drama-filled conversation and brace myself for the worst. I moisten my lips and say, "I know."

Wound tight as a spring, he steps away from the door and closer to me. His intense gaze never leaves my face.

"You know? You know what I went through? How I couldn't eat? I couldn't sleep? I couldn't even close my eyes without seeing the look on your face after I shot you?"

I say gently, "It was an accident."

His voice rises. "An accident that never would've happened if that son of a bitch hadn't been in the room with you."

A vein throbs in his neck. His breathing is erratic. He's upset, visibly so, and part of me wants to hug him.

I know if I did, it would be a disaster.

He says bitterly, "And now you think you're in love with him. The assassin who came to kill Declan. The man who kidnapped you and took you to another country."

"Please, Spider—"

"The man who threw you out like trash when he was finished with you."

That feels like a punch to the stomach.

When he sees the expression on my face, he closes his eyes and mutters, "Fuck."

I turn away, wrap my arms around myself, and take a steadying breath.

He says, "I'm sorry."

"It's okay."

"No, it's not. Look at me, lass. Please."

When I don't turn around, he comes to stand in front of me. He looks at my posture, how I've got my arms around my body, and sighs heavily, dragging a hand over his hair.

"Now you're afraid of me. That's bloody wonderful."

"I'm not afraid of you. But I can't understand why you didn't listen to me when I begged you, over and over, not to put me on that plane. To take me back to the market. I didn't exactly mince words."

He pauses, then says in a gravelly voice, "You know why." When I don't reply, he prompts, "Don't you, lass?"

I hesitate. Chewing my lip, I nod.

My silence makes him bolder. "Why? Say it."

Burning with mortification, I blurt, "Please don't make this harder for me than it already is."

He steps closer. His voice drops. "Say it. Tell me you know what I feel. What I want. Say it, and I'll give you his number."

When I remain silent and he takes one more step toward me,

his energy borderline threatening, I flatten a hand over his chest. Looking into his eyes, I say, "That's enough."

Under my palm, his heart beats like crazy.

Keeping my voice gentle though I'm angry, I say, "You're my friend, and I care for you. I hate that you've put yourself through hell with guilt—"

"You don't know the half of it."

"—and I hate that you won't accept that I don't blame you for anything. That I know you didn't mean it. And thank you, honestly, thank you for trying to find me, for spending all that time looking. I'll never forget you did that.

"But please don't think you can back me into a corner and make me say something I don't want to say or do something I don't want to do, because I've spent the last three months growing into a person who knows her own strength. I looked Death in the face and told him to go fuck himself. Nobody can push me around anymore."

He stands staring at me with his jaw working and his nostrils flared.

"Please, Spider. Please can we just be friends and put this behind us?"

After a long moment, he says flatly, "Sure. We'll be friends."

He steps back and heads to the door. I watch him go in dismay.

"I take it this means you won't give me Mal's number."

Over his shoulder he says, "I never fucking had it."

He walks out, throwing the door open so hard it slams against the wall.

The next week is the longest of my life.

I stay with Declan and Sloane in their new place in Boston, wandering listlessly up and down the hallways, sighing, until Sloane shouts that I'm driving her crazy. I retreat to the bedroom they gave me to brood by myself.

Declan agreed to pass a message to his mysterious friend to try to get to Mal for me, but wouldn't promise it would make it.

The message was simply, *"Mouse deer never give up."* I hear nothing back.

I spend hours at a time on the computer, poring over maps of Russia, plotting routes in every direction that would take me to a small town a two-hour flight plus a one-hour drive away from Moscow.

There are hundreds of them.

Even if I did somehow get to Russia, I could spend years trying to find the little cabin in the woods. The country is huge.

If I could only recall the word Mal said when I first woke up in the cabin. I asked him where he'd taken me, and he said a Russian word that I think was the name of his town, but my memory refuses to produce it.

I could start in Moscow, look for the tall glass building Mal's apartment was in, but I doubt I'd recognize it. I only saw it once, in the middle of the night. And Moscow's huge, too. I didn't drive, so I don't know what the building is near. And I couldn't ask anyone, because I don't speak the language. And anyone who helps me get there would be risking his life.

I have nightmares every night. I can't wake myself up from them. Or maybe I don't want to wake up, because they're so vivid and include Mal.

It's always the same. His face receding through the van window as Spider sped me away from him. His anguished expression.

His beautiful, haunted eyes.

I cycle through almost all the five stages of grief, except I never make it to acceptance. I just start over at denial, spend a lot of time in anger, then bargaining, finally ending up in depression, where I wallow until I get pissed again.

I make myself sick with it. Literally sick. At least once a day, I throw up.

Spider disappears. Declan makes a vague reference to him need-
ing time off, and I don't ask for specifics.

Then nothing.

Another week passes. And another. June becomes July. Sloane
asks if I want to go back to San Francisco, because they paid the rent
on my apartment while I was gone, but I say no. That's not home
now.

Home is a cabin in the woods with a man who'd rather see me in
the arms of his enemy than keep me with him if it meant I'd be safe.

God, how I hate him for that. Chivalry is bullshit.

Then Fate decides to throw me a curve ball.

And man, if I thought it had been screwing with me before, this
time takes the cake.

"You look like shit."

"Thanks for that," I say drily. "Your support is always so helpful."

"No, I mean it," says Sloane, watching me from across the kitchen
table. "You don't look healthy, Smalls. Your color isn't good. You're
always barfing. And I think you've lost weight since you got here."

With my fork, I poke at the pancakes on the plate in front of
me. The sickly-sweet smell of maple syrup makes my stomach roll
over. "It's probably a tumor."

Showing great forbearance, she refrains from smacking me. "It's
not a tumor."

"Then it's Lyme disease. Bugs have always found me tasty."

"Can you be serious for a second? I'm really worried about
you."

When I glance up, I find her watching me with concern in her
eyes. Sighing, I say, "I'm fine. Pinkie swear. It's just . . . you know."
I make a vague gesture to encompass the general fuckery of my life.
"The situation."

When she makes a scrunchy face, I say offhandedly, "I'm not pregnant, if that's what you're thinking."

"How do you know?"

"I'm on the birth control shot."

It's only when she narrows her eyes at me that my heart skips a beat.

Wait. How long ago did I have my last shot?

Swallowing back the acid taste of the bile rising in my throat, I start frantically calculating dates in my head.

I was with Mal for three months. It's been three weeks since I got back.

How long before I went to Russia did I get the shot?

My brain, which has been so unhelpful to me lately, cheerfully provides the precise answer: six weeks.

It was the week before Valentine's Day, which means that the shot would have been effective until about the beginning or middle of May.

I was with Mal until the middle of June. It's now the second week of July.

And I haven't had a period yet.

Oh, fuck.

Sloane says sharply, "Riley?"

"Yep." Avoiding her eyes, I stare at my pancakes as if the winning lottery numbers are in the syrup. *Oh fuck oh fuck oh fuck.*

"So you're covered?"

"Yep. I'm due for another shot, but seeing as how I won't be having sex with anyone but myself for the rest of my life, I might not bother."

Shitfuckpisscrap. Fucktrumpet cumbubble!

She exhales. "We should get you to a doctor for a checkup, anyway. This isn't normal."

"I'm fine. I promise. It's just depression, that's all."

After a moment of silence, she stands up, rounds the table, and hugs me.

"It's gonna be okay," she whispers. "Don't forget that I love you."

This bitch is trying to kill me. She's never told me she loves me before. Not ever that I can remember in our whole lives.

My voice breaks when I say it back.

Then a hot wave of nausea hits me. I run to the kitchen sink and throw up.

Panting, eyes watering, leaning over the sink staring at the contents of my stomach, I wonder how the hell I'm going to smuggle a pregnancy test into a safe house.

As it turns out, I don't have to. I find three unopened boxes of pregnancy tests in a drawer in Sloane's bathroom when I'm rummaging around for a bottle of shampoo.

It only takes one of them to deliver the news.

My heart thudding, I stare at the two little pink lines in the window on the white plastic stick and whisper, "Your daddy's a jerk, kiddo."

Then I do the only reasonable thing left to do. I burst into tears.

FORTY-SEVEN

RILEY

I spend the rest of that day in a haze. I go to bed, pull the covers over my head, and try to think clearly about what I should do next.

It's useless. My brain is broken.

To match the other broken organ inside my chest.

Now, Mal will have another reason to want to keep me away.

An even more powerful reason. It isn't only my safety at stake. I've got a baby gangster on board.

And if Mal is so protective that he'd keep me at arm's length for my own safety, I can imagine exactly what a nutcase he'd be if he discovered I'm pregnant.

He'd probably move to another planet. He'd set up shop on Mercury and run the Russian Bratva from there.

I don't sleep at all that night. By the next morning, I've decided I just need to put one foot in front of the other and deal with the most obvious thing first.

I have to tell my sister that I'm pregnant with the child of the assassin who swore vengeance on the man she loves for the murder of his brother.

Jesus on a cracker. How does that conversation start?

As it turns out, it doesn't, because Sloane has her own important news to share.

She knocks on my door, poking her head in when I don't answer. "You awake?"

From under the covers, I exhale a leaden breath. "Bright-eyed and bushy-tailed. Come on in."

The mattress dips with her weight. The covers slide down over my face because she's pulling at them.

"Good morning, Little Miss Sunshine."

"Ew. Don't smile like that. People will think you're a cult leader."

"Don't be crabby. I need to tell you something, and I want you to be happy about it."

"Wait, let me guess." I inspect her disturbing megawatt smile. "There's a huge sale at Bergdorf's."

Instead of answering, she lifts her left hand. On her ring finger sparkles a piece of ice that could double as a children's skating rink.

I gasp, sitting up on my elbows. "It's a ring!"

"It is!"

"You finally said yes!"

"I did!"

"You're officially engaged!"

"I know! Isn't it amazing?"

My voice choked and my eyes watering, I nod enthusiastically.

"Oh, shit," she says, her eyes wide. "I'm such an idiot."

"No, you're not. I'm so h-happy for you!" Then I start to cry, because it's my new default setting.

I'm blaming it on the hormones.

She grabs me and hugs me so hard, it leaves me breathless.

"God, my timing. I've always had terrible timing! You can punch me in the face if it will make you feel better."

I consider it for a moment but toss the idea aside. I can't be throwing swings at my kid's auntie. Between all the warring mafia factions, we'll have enough family strife.

"No, I'm glad you told me." I pull away, wiping my eyes. "I'm very, very happy for you guys. Did you set a date yet?"

"The day after tomorrow."

That makes me blink in surprise. "Oh. Wow. Carpe diem."

"Exactly. While you were gone, I realized that life is short and full of random assholery. You have to seize the good while it's there for the seizing."

"Wait, you know carpe diem means seize the *day* right?"

"No, it's seize the good. I know a guy who has it tattooed on his forearm. He explained it to me."

"Uh-huh. And did this Ph.D. have any idea he had a Latin phrase derived from Horace's eleventh ode inked on his skin, or did he just think it was a cool Instagram meme?"

She sighs. "You could give a person a stroke."

"No wonder people keep telling me we're so much alike. Back to this wedding of yours. Where will it be happening?"

"The Old North Church. It's Declan's home parish."

I find it interesting that the head of the Irish Mob goes to church, but I guess he probably has lots of confessing to do. "Is Dad coming?"

A cloud passes over her face. "I didn't invite him. And before you ask why, there's a story I need to tell you, but I'm in too good a mood to discuss it now."

I know they haven't been close since she was a teenager and that she and our stepmother never got along, but it sounds like things are worse than that. Best to leave it alone until she feels like talking about it. "Okay, next question. Nat?"

"She'll be there."

"With what's-his-face?"

Sloane smiles. "As if he'd let her out of his sight."

"I feel like I'm missing some behind-the-scenes logistics."

"I told Declan I'm not getting married without my best friend in attendance. And Nat told Kage she would *consider* not castrating him for giving Mal information about Declan if he showed up to the wedding to apologize."

She squeezes my hand. "Sorry, sweetie. I don't mean to make it sound like Mal is the bad guy."

I wave it off, too interested in the developing drama to care about that. "So Nat *and* Kage are coming to the wedding?"

"Yep."

"And Declan is okay with Kage being there?"

She laughs. "Not even a little bit. But those are the rules the boys are working with. And it's not like they've never been in a room together before." She pauses to think. "Although, I'm pretty sure every time that's happened, somebody's gotten shot."

"Wow. Should be a fun wedding."

She seems unconcerned about the possibility of a massacre breaking out during her nuptials, saying airily, "There'll be security up the yin-yang. Everybody will be searched and their weapons removed before going into the church. I'm sure they can manage to play nice for thirty minutes."

I'm not sure about that at all, but I admire her confidence. "What am I wearing? I can't borrow another one of your outfits to wear to your wedding. That seems like it would be bad luck. The bride is supposed to wear something borrowed, not the guests."

"I've got a dress ordered for you. The seamstress will be here to fit it tomorrow morning."

That surprises me, but not too much, considering my gift from Pakhan. "It's amazing how you mobster folk can just order up custom gowns on a moment's notice."

"I can't have my maid of honor walking down the aisle in a pair of camouflage hunting pants, now, can I?"

Now I'm not only surprised, I'm flabbergasted. "Maid . . . maid of honor? *Me?*"

"You and Nat both."

My voice is strangled with emotion. "You're having two maids of honor?"

Her eyes shining, she says softly, "You're my sister, dumbass. Of course I'm having you as one of my maids of honor."

When she sees the tears gathering in my eyes, she takes pity on me. She sits up straighter and says haughtily, "Everyone would think I'm a dick if I didn't."

Trying to hide how overwhelmed I am, I say, "Everyone already does think you're a dick."

Her smile is self-indulgent. "Don't be ridiculous. Everybody loves me."

I fall flat onto the mattress and pull the covers over my face again. Only this time, I'm laughing.

I keep forgetting that this is Sloane's world. The rest of us mere mortals are just living in it.

I get fitted for the dress. It's long, silk, sleeveless, and hugs my body like a glove.

It's also black, so it can double as funeral attire when the wedding with warring Irish and Russian gangsters in attendance hits the inevitable bumps and the bullets start flying.

I'm trying to be optimistic, but seriously. This seems like a bigger mistake than the twelve publishing houses made that turned down J. K. Rowling before *Harry Potter* was finally published.

The day of the wedding, what seems like five hundred Irish gangsters in tuxedos show up at the house.

Spider's there, too. He looks great in a tux. He also won't look at me, which hurts but might be for the best.

I help Sloane into her dress, an insanely gorgeous floor-length chiffon gown with a plunging neckline that shows off her cleavage. It also has a split in the front of the billowing skirt that shows off her legs when she walks.

It's not white, because this is my sister we're talking about.

Every bride wears white.

Sloane's dress is vivid, bold, blood red.

Dripping in diamonds, with her hair cascading down her back and a real freaking tiara on her head, she looks like a goddess. I've never seen anything so beautiful in my life.

When I tell her that, she smiles. "Right? Declan is so lucky. He doesn't deserve me."

I say drily, "If zombies ever take over, you'll be safe."

"What do you mean?"

"They only eat brains."

We ride together in a limo to the church. We're surrounded front, back, and sides by black Escalades filled with heavily armed gangsters in tuxedos, who Sloane keeps waving at like she's the queen of England in a Christmas parade.

When we get to the beautiful old stone church, I'm shocked to see the front steps swarming with people.

Looking out the window of the limo as we drive into the parking lot, I say, "Um. Sloane?"

"Yeah, babe?"

"Why are there four thousand people here?"

"Because this is Boston, and the head of the Irish Mob is getting married. It's an important event. People are here from all over the country, plus overseas."

I turn to her, goggle-eyed. "I thought you said you were planning a small ceremony?"

"I was." She gestures smugly to her diamonds and dress. "But then all this glory would've been wasted."

"Do you know all those people?"

"No. They're mostly Declan's work friends."

"His *work* friends? You mean those are all gangsters?"

"And the affiliates, yes. Oh, don't look at me like that. It'll be fine."

"Hair is fine. A Catholic church stuffed with armed mafiosi is a *True Crime* docuseries about to happen!"

She pats my hand reassuringly. "Listen. Declan is handling it. The security is top-notch. There are even snipers. All we have to do is look stunning and enjoy the attention. And if anything happens—which it won't—just duck."

I stare at her. "*Duck?* That's your survival advice?"

She shrugs. "Always works for me."

Dear god. She's actually serious.

I blow out a shaky breath, wondering if I can steal a gun off one of the goodfellas milling around in front of the church before they're confiscated by security.

We're hustled from the limo into the church by a circle of body-guards three deep. I keep expecting a bomb to go off, but we make it inside without incident and settle into a room in the back reserved for the bride's quarters.

Our bouquets are waiting there, nestled in white boxes with tissue paper and cotton. Mine is a perfect sphere of pearl-dotted stephanotis. It smells heavenly.

Sloane's bouquet is a dramatic cascade of hot-pink orchids studded with Swarovski crystals. It's glamorous and over the top, just like her.

Two minutes after we arrive, so does Nat.

The moment she comes through the door and spots Sloane in her dress, her face crumples, and she starts crying. "You look like a princess."

Sloane smiles. "Bitch, I'm a queen. Get your butt over here."

She opens her arms. Nat runs to her. The two of them stand hugging in the middle of the room for so long, I wonder if the wedding will have to be delayed.

Then Nat turns to me. Her watering eyes widen as she looks me up and down. "Riley? Little Riley? Holy cow."

I smile. "I'll take that as a compliment."

She comes over and gives me a big hug, too. I haven't seen her in so long, I'd almost forgotten what she looks like. Black hair, blue-gray eyes, scarlet lips . . . she's gorgeous.

She whispers, "Are you okay?"

"Ugh. Yes and no. We'll talk about it later. There's way too much to go over right now."

"Okay, sweetie. I'm glad to see you."

"You, too."

Sloane says warmly, "Look at my girls. This church will be full of boners. Even that sad statue we passed on the way in will be sprouting wood."

I say over Nat's shoulder, "That was a statue of the Virgin Mary."

"So she'll get a lady boner."

"You're going to hell."

"Ha! They *wish*."

Nat pulls away and smiles at me. "The queen is proud of her handmaidens."

"We do look pretty good, though. And you're glowing."

Sloane says, "That's because she's getting the big Bratva bratwurst on the regular."

Nat's cheeks turn faintly pink. "She really has a way with words, doesn't she?"

"She missed her true calling writing love songs."

Sloane chuckles. "Nat, your gown is hanging on the back of the bathroom door. We've got about ten minutes before the coordinator will come get us and we start down the aisle."

As Nat goes into the bathroom to change, I say, "Which reminds me. Are there groomsmen we'll be walking with?"

"No. Kieran and Spider will be waiting at the altar with Declan."

"Oh. So what's the order?"

"The order of what?"

"Like does Nat go in front of me, then I go, then you go?"

Sloane walks over to me and rests her hand on my cheek.

"No, silly," she says, smiling. "The bride is supposed to walk down the aisle with the most important people in her life. So the three of us are walking down together, arm in arm."

My chin quivers. My eyes well. I have to swallow around the rock in my throat. "If you make me cry, I'll rip that tiara right off your head."

"For a girl who showed up at my house looking like something out of the *Backwoods Survival Guide,* you're a big softie."

"I would've thought you'd think it was an improvement over all the gray fleece."

"Honey, you went from sweatpants sloth to *G.I. Jane.* It was a lateral move, not an upward one."

Looking stunning, Nat emerges from the restroom in her dress. We make a few last-minute adjustments to our hair and makeup, pick up our bouquets, and head out when the coordinator knocks.

And believe it or not, the ceremony goes off without a hitch.

Declan is glorious in his tux. Sloane is a fairy tale. They exchange vows and kiss to thundering applause.

Wisely, they omit the part of the vows where the priest asks if anyone objects.

There's a small moment of awkwardness during the photographs afterward, when Spider does nothing but stare at me with such searing intensity, my ears burn. But it's a momentary hiccup in an otherwise perfect event.

It isn't until the reception that everything falls apart.

FORTY-EIGHT

RILEY

The reception is held at the Four Seasons Hotel in a magnificent ballroom. It has floor-to-ceiling windows, grand glittering chandeliers, and expansive views of the lush green Boston Public Garden.

Every guest has to pass through a metal detector on their way in and also undergo a pat-down by hand, performed by glowering Irishmen.

I'm surprised there isn't a cavity search, these guys are that intense.

Sloane chose to forego a head table of the entire wedding party—another wise move—opting instead for a sweetheart table she and Declan sit at alone.

Marveling that she pulled all this together in a matter of days, I sit at a table with Nat, Kage, and five swarthy Sicilians wearing so much cologne, I can taste it.

Kieran and Spider sit at a table directly across the dance floor.

Every time I happen to glance in their direction, Spider is staring at me.

After everyone is seated, Nat introduces me to her fiancé.

He's ruggedly handsome. With tousled dark hair, an unshaven jaw, and massive shoulders, he emits the kind of big dick energy every woman and man in the room can feel.

Though he's wearing a tux, he seems like he'd be far more comfortable in a leather bomber jacket and combat boots, a handkerchief knotted around his neck. Chunky silver rings decorate the thumb and middle fingers of his right hand. One of them is a skull.

He's what I picture the swashbuckling pirates of the Caribbean looked like.

"It's nice to meet you, Kage. I've heard a lot about you."

He has the kind of gaze Mal does, that same penetrating, laser beam intensity that could slice you in two. But his eyes are dark instead of pale green.

"Bet you have," he drawls, slinging an arm over the back of Nat's chair. "Must be some interesting conversations that go on in that household."

I smile at him. "Don't worry, I didn't believe a word of it. If Nat likes you, you're good in my book."

He tilts his head and considers me. After a moment, he says, "You okay?"

He packs so much into those two words, it's amazing. My heartbeat ticks up a notch.

I know he's the one who gave Mal information about Declan when all this started, but I also remember Sloane saying the Russian Bratva and the Bratva in the U.S. aren't that friendly.

What I don't know is if Kage and Mal are still talking.

On the off chance they are, I'm not missing the opportunity to send a message.

"If you mean physically, yes. If you mean mentally, spiritually, emotionally . . . I'm dying."

He inclines his head. "Yeah. Heard you caught feelings while you were away."

"It's much worse than that."

He looks at me more closely.

"Do you think we could talk after dinner? Somewhere not so . . ." I glance at the Sicilians. "Loud?"

"You got something you want to pass along?"

I nod, starting to tremble.

"Declan won't like it." He glances at Nat. His tone becomes wry. "I'm already in enough trouble as it is."

Nat squeezes his thigh. "It's okay, honey. This is different."

He sends her a look that's equal parts hot and sour.

"I don't want to get anyone into trouble. I won't say anything to Declan, but I doubt he'd mind anyway, considering he tried to get a message to Mal for me, too."

Kage narrows his eyes. "He tried to send a message from you to the man who wants to kill him?"

"Mal isn't going to kill Declan."

"Since when?"

"Since I asked him not to."

He's silent with astonishment for a second, then he shakes his head and chuckles. "Talk about a self-fulfilling prophecy."

"I don't get it."

"Never mind. It's just something Malek said to me once. Sure, we'll talk after dinner."

"Thank you."

Then, somehow, I'm conversing with the Sicilians. They're so eager to know if I'm single, I'm worried they want to sell me on the black market. It becomes apparent after a few minutes, however, that what they're really after is an alliance with Declan.

One of the men has a son he'd very much like to see married to someone in Declan's family. The other has a daughter around my age, who he casually mentions is still a virgin and comes from excellent stock.

He says it as if he's a farmer discussing his breeding mares.

I guess the whole arranged-marriage thing is still alive and well in the mafia.

Dinner is served, followed by dancing. From what I can tell, Kage is the only Bratva in the room. Everyone else seems to be either Irish or Italian, though I do hear a few accents I can't place.

When I feel a hand on my shoulder and turn to see who it is, I freeze.

Spider stands behind my chair, gazing down at me. "Care to dance?"

I hesitate, but he's relaxed and smiling, so I smile back and nod. "Sure."

He pulls out my chair for me, then leads me onto the dance floor and takes me into his arms.

Because of course the fucking music changed from pop to a ballad, didn't it?

It's like Fate hates me.

We sway in silence, listening to the music and not looking at each other, until he says, "You look beautiful tonight."

"Thank you. And you're very handsome in that tux."

He glances down at me. A muscle flexes in his jaw. "I remember you called me that the day we met. 'Handsome.'"

"And I remember how red your face turned."

"It was the first time I've ever blushed."

He spins me around. I see Declan and Sloane at the sweetheart table, watching us, but then Spider spins me again, and they're gone.

"I owe you an apology for the way I acted a few weeks ago. I was an idiot."

He sounds sincere. I'm relieved, but don't want to make a big deal about it, so I keep my voice light. "It's over. Let's forget it."

"I can't. I've tried." His arm tightens around my waist. His voice drops, turning husky. "I can't forget anything that happened between us."

My relief vanishes. Butterflies explode into panic in my stomach.

We dance for the rest of the song in silence. As soon as it ends, I break away, murmur a thank you, and head to the ladies' room to hide.

I lock myself into a stall, lean against the door, and close my eyes while I try to come up with a solution to the Spider situation. Short of a kick to the balls, he doesn't seem like he's going to be deterred.

Just get through tonight. Then talk to Declan and Sloane, and let them take care of it. Spider will listen to them.

Except he might not, considering he followed you to another country against Declan's wishes.

Heaving a sigh, I use the toilet, then go to the sink to wash my hands.

When I turn off the water and reach for a paper towel, I happen to glance into the mirror above the sinks.

I freeze.

A man is directly behind me. He's huge.

Frighteningly tall and broad, he stands with his legs spread open and his massive hands hanging by his sides. He's all in black, including a heavy wool overcoat with the collar turned up against his tattooed neck.

His hair and beard are thick and dark. A small silver hoop earring glints in one earlobe. Beneath lowered brows, his eyes are a startling shade of pale green.

He's the most beautiful man I've ever seen.

"You're here." It comes out choked, on a sob.

Mal says softly, "Did you think I'd let you attend a Mob wedding without my protection?"

God, his voice. That lovely voice, deep, rich, and hypnotic. All the hair on my arms prickles. So do all my nerve endings. A dangerous current of electricity crackles through my body. I feel like I stepped on a live wire.

I whisper, "Yes."

"You know better."

"Do I? You didn't even want to be in the same country as me."

His voice drops an octave. "You know exactly what I want."

"I know that you're an obstinate fool who should have a little more confidence in me."

In the mirror, our gazes are locked. I'd turn around, but I can't move my legs. I can't move anything.

"Confidence in you?" he repeats. "I have every confidence in you."

"Pakhan had more."

His eyes spark. "What does that mean?"

"Remember what he said to me at our dinner? 'Empires aren't run by the meek.' I get what that means now. He wasn't talking about you. He was talking about me. He assumed I'd be by your side when you took over."

My voice breaks. "But you decided to give me away instead."

The spark in Mal's eyes flares into fire. He steps closer, bringing with him that scent I know so well. Pine trees and moonlight, fog caressing the branches of towering evergreens in an ancient woods.

My woods, the one where I learned how to be happy.

He growls, "I didn't give you away, *malyutka*."

"You sure as hell didn't keep me."

"Didn't I?"

The emotion making me misty-eyed and weak-kneed evaporates abruptly, leaving me furious. I whirl around and glare at him.

"I have no interest in playing word games with you. Or mind games, for that matter. The answer is *no*, you didn't fucking keep me. You put me onto a plane and shipped me off like cargo!"

His gaze rakes over me, as hot as coals. He takes in my expression and my dress in one swift, hungry look, then reaches out and grabs me.

He drags me against his chest and crushes his mouth to mine. All the fight drains out of me like somebody pulled a plug.

I sag against him, kissing him back with desperation. His smell, his taste, his heat—how did I ever survive even a day without all this?

"I never let you go," he says gruffly, his mouth moving against my bruised lips. "Not for a goddamn second. You were with me all the time, haunting me with that smart mouth and those beautiful eyes and that heartbreaking smile that kills me every time I see it. I didn't last a week before I made the first trip here."

"Wait, what?" I blink up at him, confused. "You were here? I never saw you."

"That's because you were asleep."

After a moment of astonishment, I start to laugh. "You broke into my bedroom again?"

"The last time that will ever happen."

The voice, low and lethal, comes from our right. We look over and see Spider standing at the door. He's holding a gun.

I freeze in horror. I taste ashes in my mouth. Beneath my dress, my scar tingles and turns hot, like it just caught fire.

I wonder for a split second how he has a gun when everyone else was searched, realizing just as quickly that not only would security have cleared Declan's personal bodyguard, but he probably carried extra weapons for the occasion.

Mal's entire body has fallen perfectly still.

Spider gestures with the gun. "Riley, move away from him."

"No."

His furious gaze never moves from Mal's face. "Do it. Now. I don't want a repeat of last time."

Shaking all over, I still manage to keep my voice even. "You're not going to shoot him. Put the gun down and walk out."

His laugh is short and hard. "He might've promised you he

wouldn't kill me, but the reverse isn't true. Get your ass away from him right now."

In a low, deadly rumble, Mal says, "Speak to her like that again, and I'll happily break my promise."

"Fuck you."

Spider's voice is loud and full of hatred. It echoes off the tile walls.

In the ballroom, the music is still going strong. A cheer goes up. Passing by the hallway outside, a woman laughs. She sounds drunk.

Mal releases me, moving carefully. He pushes me behind him and stands facing Spider, holding me back when I try to move to get between them.

Panic claws its way up my throat. "Spider, please! Please don't do this! You can't do this! I'm—"

"I don't want to hear how you're in love with him," he snaps.

"No, listen to me—"

"Get the fuck away from her. Walk toward the door. We're going to do this outside, for everyone to see. You deserve a public execution. The Hangman should die with an audience."

Pushing me back, Mal takes a step forward.

Red pulses at the edges of my vision. My panic is so total, I can see the blood flowing through my own veins.

I don't understand why he's listening to Spider, why he's following him out the bathroom door. I stumble after them, shouting for them to stop. The music drowns out my cries.

Then we're pushing through the crowd on the dance floor. People pull away, startled. Someone sees Spider's gun and screams.

The band stops playing. The guy on bass guitar realizes it last, plucking away until finally he notices he's the only one jamming and looks up, blinking in surprise.

Then, except for the roar of my pulse in my ears, there's silence.

I don't know where Sloane or Declan are. I don't know what anyone else is doing. I can only focus on Spider standing ten feet away from Mal in the middle of the dance floor, pointing the gun at his head.

I gather myself, take a deep breath, and say forcefully, "Spider, put that gun down right this minute!"

"Give me one good reason I shouldn't shoot this Russian pig, Riley!"

Okay, if you insist. "Because I'm carrying his child!"

Surprise ripples through the crowd. Several people gasp.

Spider jerks his head around and gapes at me.

I can't look at Mal. I channel all my energy into staring Spider down, willing him to back off.

"Do you know what that means? We're family now. Me, Mal, Declan, Sloane . . . and you, too. We're all a family. This baby links us together. The Mob and the Bratva now have blood ties."

A quiet cheer rises from somewhere in the room. I'm pretty sure it's Nat.

With a hand held out and my pulse throbbing, I walk slowly toward Spider. Frozen in shock, he watches me approach. He's breathing hard, and his color is high. Any sudden movement might make him pull the trigger.

When I get close enough, I rest my hand gently on his wrist. Holding his wild gaze, I say softly, "Just put it down. It's over."

He swallows. After a pause that feels like forever, he drops his arm to his side and bows his head.

Declan appears from nowhere. He grabs the weapon from Spider's hand and shoves him into a group of Irishmen who are waiting to one side. As a murmur begins to spread throughout the room, they hustle him away.

I'm grabbed and engulfed in a bear hug.

Mal lifts me clear off the floor so my feet dangle in the air as he holds me. Into my ear, he says hoarsely, "You're pregnant?"

"Yes."

"You're having my child?"

"Yes. And if you move to Mercury to try to protect us, your unkempt homeless deer mouse will hunt you down and kill you."

He groans, crushing me against his chest. One of my heels falls off.

We stay like that, locked in a tight embrace, oblivious to the murmuring crowd, until someone clears his throat.

When I look up, I see Declan and Sloane standing arm in arm behind Mal.

Sloane is beaming. Declan looks like he needs a stiff drink.

"Set me down, sweetie," I whisper. "The bride and groom would like a word."

He growls, "The bride and groom can wait their fucking turn. I need a word with my woman first."

He flips me up into his arms and strides off the dance floor. Over his shoulder, I watch Nat and Sloane embrace as Kage and Declan square off and glare at one another.

The band breaks into a rousing rendition of "We Are Family."

As if nothing happened, the guests flood back onto the dance floor and start gyrating.

Wow. So that was a gangster wedding. All in all, I think it went pretty well.

FORTY-NINE

RILEY

I don't know where he takes me. There's a short car trip, followed by a short elevator trip, both of which I spend with my face buried in the crook of his neck and my eyes closed, dragging his scent into my nose and clinging to him.

Then he's lowering me onto a bed.

Without a word, he tears off my dress, ripping the silk apart like a tissue. He removes my bra and panties and my remaining shoe. Then he kneels beside the bed between my spread legs and presses his burning cheek against my bare belly.

My heart swelling like a balloon, I dig my hands into his thick hair and sigh in happiness.

"You're going to have my child," he whispers, wonder in his voice.

"If it's a boy, let's name him Mik. Actually, that would be a cute name for a girl, too."

He exhales. Wrapping his hands around my hips, he reverently kisses my stomach. "I have to admit, I'm thrilled your birth control shot was no match for my super sperm."

"Don't break your arm patting yourself on the back, stud. My shot expired while I was in Russia. Funny how time flies when you're having fun." I glance around the unfamiliar dark room. "Where are we?"

"Hotel. Now hush. I need to fuck you."

My laugh is soft. "I missed you, too."

He gets his clothing off in record speed, impatiently tossing it all to the floor, then lowers himself on top of me. He kisses me, cradling my head in his hands, giving me his weight and every ounce of his passion.

When he breaks away, he's breathing hard. He stares down at me with adoration shining in his eyes, murmuring something in Russian.

I shake my head. "No, say it so I can understand it this time."

He says gently, "It's the same thing I've been telling you since the beginning, *malyutka*. You're beautiful. You make me crazy. I can't remember my life before you. I'd give anything to be able to love you for all time."

My throat gets tight. Tears well in my eyes. I inhale a ragged breath, feeling like I'm flying. "So you like me, huh?"

Against my lips, he whispers, "I worship you, my sweet, mouthy little queen."

"Prove it. I'm still mad at you."

He grins then kisses me again, this time harder. His hard cock throbs against my thigh.

When he slides inside me, I gasp and arch. A lone tear slides down my temple.

In a husky voice, he says into my ear, "Daddy's home."

I laugh, but it quickly turns to a groan as he starts to thrust, lowering his head to kiss my throat then bite it. I wrap my legs around his waist and my arms around his shoulders, holding on to him as he fills me, body and soul.

I know he always wanted to keep me safe. To protect me, no

matter what it might cost him. But what he didn't know was that I never needed a white knight to save me.

I need the dragon.

I need him, forever, and that's all.

Later, sweaty and sated, I lie in his arms with my cheek resting on his chest and my heart glowing.

Into the darkness of the hotel room, I whisper, "What happens now?"

He stirs, rousing to press a kiss to the top of my head. "What do you want to happen now?"

My reply is instant. "I want to go back to your cabin in the woods."

His chuckle is a low rumble under my ear. "*Our* cabin, you mean."

My toes curl with happiness.

"Poe misses you, by the way."

"I miss him, too, that big dumb cocky bird."

"Don't let him hear you call him dumb. He'll steal all your shoe-laces and make a cape for himself out of them."

"I bet he would. You know what else I miss?"

"What?"

I smile. "Bath time."

I hear the smile in his voice when he replies. "I found it interesting that the heroine in your book took a lot of baths also. Strange thing for a ghost to do."

The thought of him in the cabin reading through my yellow legal pads while we were apart makes my heart sing. "That was in her memory. From before she died."

He says thoughtfully, "That's right, she didn't know she was dead."

"Judging by your tone, I feel like I might need to make some revisions."

He slides his open palm up my back and cups my chin, tilting my head up for a kiss. He whispers, "No. It's perfect. Except that man she was in love with when she was alive sounds like a gorilla."

"He's not a gorilla! He's macho!"

He looks at me pointedly. "Please tell me you didn't base his character on anyone you know."

My smile is sweet. "I would never. That's probably illegal, anyway."

"What's illegal is the size of his dick. I bet that's how she died, right? Punctured lungs?"

"Okay, you know what? You're not reading any more of my works in progress."

He presses his lips together. I can tell he's trying not to laugh at me.

I poke him in the ribs and tuck my head under his chin, sighing.

When he speaks again, his voice has turned serious. "It's going to be dangerous."

His life, he means. As if I didn't already know it.

"If you can break in undetected to safe houses all over the world surrounded by armed guards and crash a mobster wedding, you can keep me protected. I trust you. Plus, look on the bright side. I know how to shoot guns!"

"But with a baby—"

"Mal," I say in a warning tone. "Tread carefully. I don't want to hear any more nonsense out of you about us not being together because it's too dangerous. That subject is closed."

He chuckles. "And you say I'm bossy."

"Look, I know the Thirteen isn't a bachelor party, okay? Those guys have wives and girlfriends and manage to keep them breathing. So can you."

After a short silence, he says, "Who told you about the Thirteen?"

"Declan."

He rolls me onto my back and stares down at me. His voice is deadly soft. "Did you just say another man's name in my bed?"

Oh, shit. Commence backpedaling. "Um. You sort of asked. And unless you own this hotel, technically this isn't your bed."

He growls, "Nice try, baby. I do own this hotel."

"What?"

"I own a lot of real estate all over the world. Pakhan compensated me very well for what I did for him."

"Not well enough to hire an interior decorator, obviously."

"Excuse me?"

"That apartment of yours in Moscow isn't what you'd call cozy, sweetie. I think skeletons would like it, but for people with flesh, it's a little cold."

His eyes glitter. His nostrils flare. He doesn't know whether to laugh or spank me.

I snuggle closer to him, grinning.

"You're trouble, little bird, you know that?"

"Yeah, but you like trouble."

His eyes soften. He kisses me like I'm the most precious thing in the world, then says gruffly, "Actually, I love trouble. I love it more than anything."

That settles it. My next tattoo is going to be the word *"Trouble."* I'll let him choose where on my body I should get it.

I say innocently, "You know what I love more than anything?"

"No, what?"

"This gorilla I met. Once you get past the scary exterior and all the grunting, he's really sweet."

His smile is as brilliant as the love shining in his eyes. "I've heard that about gorillas."

He kisses me again, this time more deeply, his tongue delving into my mouth and his hand wrapped lightly around my throat.

I put my hand over his and make him squeeze tighter.

He chuckles against my lips and whispers something in Russian that sounds filthy. Then he says in English, "You're going to have my baby. You're going to be my wife. You'll be the center of my universe and the queen who stands by my side."

His voice drops. "But first, I'm gonna fuck you again and show you who your king is."

He flips me onto my belly, drags me up onto my knees, and spanks my ass five times.

I bury my face in the covers, laughing.

Yes, Daddy's home. Oh, yes, he is.

EPILOGUE

SPIDER

TWO WEEKS LATER

*I*t's just the two of us in Declan's office, sitting on opposite sides of his desk with whiskeys in our hands.

It's the night of his first day back from his honeymoon in Greece. He's tan and relaxed, leaning back in his chair in a white dress shirt and black slacks, looking like what he is.

A man who has everything he's ever wanted.

If I looked in a mirror, what I'd see would be the opposite of that.

He doesn't bother with small talk. Neither of us has ever been good at it. He simply opens with, "I'm promoting you to second-in-command."

When he sees my shocked expression, he says, "Did you think I'd fire you?"

"For ruining your wedding? Aye."

"Don't be dramatic. You didn't ruin anything. All you did was put on a wee show."

"Is that your wife's attitude, too?"

His expression sours. "It would be grand if anyone around here would pretend it's my opinion that matters for once."

I glance down at the glass in my hand. I'm gripping it so tightly, my knuckles are white.

I haven't been able to get the night of the wedding out of my mind. It plays on a loop inside my head, taunting me.

That bloody Russian bastard. I should've shot him in the bathroom when I had the chance.

Now he's family. Fucking *family*. What a nightmare.

Through clenched teeth, I say, "They've gone back to Russia?"

He hesitates. "Aye. And you'd be well-advised to forget all about it."

An impossibility, but I bite my tongue.

"Spider. Look at me."

I glance up.

He says, "You're a good man. Loyal and brave. The situation is less than ideal, but it's what we've got to deal with."

"How can you be so calm about this? He wanted to kill you!"

"Aye. Can't really blame him, though, can I? If he killed my brother, I'd want to kill him, too."

I say bitterly, "How very magnanimous."

"Get your head back on business, mate. I need you focused. We've got a bloody shit show to deal with. Between Kage and the Italians alone, I'll lose my ever-loving mind."

"What's going on with Kage? Considering he attended your wedding, I assumed you two had made an accord."

He rises and walks to the window, folding his arms over his chest and staring out into the evening sky. "I owe him a marker. He called it in."

I frown in confusion. "He called in a marker for an invitation to your wedding?"

Declan's laugh is dark. "No, that was simply politics."

I make a sound of understanding. "Your wife and his."

"Aye."

"So what does he want for the marker?"

"For me to kill one of his men."

Brutal, but it doesn't surprise me. The Russians are animals. They'd eat their own young if they were hungry enough. "For?"

"Disloyalty."

"Why doesn't he kill the lad himself?"

"Because it's a man I promised my wife I would never harm." He turns and gazes at me. "Which makes it excellent sport for Kage."

When I say, "Stavros," Declan nods. "Oy. If Sloane finds out . . ."

"I'll lose my balls. I have to admit, the son of a bitch knows how to play dirty."

"What will you do?"

He turns to the window again. A faint smile lifts the corners of his mouth. "What I always do when the only two options are shite. Create a third."

He doesn't explain that, and I don't ask. If he wanted me to know, he'd tell me.

"What's going on with the Italians?"

He sighs heavily, passing a hand over his face. "They're bloody mad, that lot. Do you know they still have arranged marriages?"

"They can't want you to marry one of their lasses now!"

"No, not me, obviously. But Caruso's got it in his head to marry his daughter into the Mob."

Gianni Caruso is the head of one of the Five Families. Since the capo of the Cosa Nostra was killed a while back, the Sicilians have been jockeying each other for position. No one has come out on top yet.

"Why us?"

He says drily, "Because we're so handsome and charming."

"Or because we have something they want."

"Exactly."

"Do they have anything we want?"

"Aye. Territory. Distribution. Trade routes. Cash. We had a tentative accord when Diego was in charge, but it dissolved when his memory did. But it hardly matters, considering I don't have any male family members to sell into slavery."

My mind starts to turn. I say slowly, "What if you did?"

Declan looks at me sharply.

"Second-in-command is about as close to a son or brother as you have."

When he understands what I'm suggesting, he says flatly, "You've lost your bloody mind."

"You said you wanted me focused. Nothing like new pussy to get your mind off the old."

He lifts his brows. "Now you're scaring me. Also, watch your mouth, mate. Riley's my sister-in-law."

"Do you have a picture of Caruso's daughter?"

"Spider! Knock it off!"

I down the rest of my whiskey, set the glass on his desk, and stand. "Show me her picture."

"You can't be bloody serious!"

"Look at my face. Does it look serious to you?"

"This isn't like adopting a puppy. You can't take it back if it doesn't work out. This is a bloody *lifelong* commitment we're talking about!"

"You just made one. Why can't I?"

He roars, "Because you're not in love!"

"This wouldn't be about love. It would be about business. And frankly—I mean this with no disrespect to you or your wife—from what I can tell, a business arrangement with no feelings involved would be a helluva lot easier."

"I'll pretend you didn't say that."

"Just show me a picture of the lass."

He walks over to his desk, flattens his hands on the top, and leans over it, glaring at me.

"You don't understand. You could *never* walk away. If she grows warts or has the laugh of a hyena, you'd be tied to her for the rest of your life. If she slept with every bloody man she saw, you'd be tied to her. Forever! Her family would kill you if you tried to leave. And I couldn't stop it, because you'd have agreed to it beforehand!"

I hold his infuriated gaze and say calmly, "Just show me a bloody picture. If the lass has warts, I won't mention it again."

He stares at me for a few moments longer, then curses and drops into his chair. Muttering oaths under his breath, he opens his laptop, clicks around for a while, then sits back and silently stares at the screen.

"So? Warts?"

He looks at me then back at the screen.

"Not exactly." He turns the laptop so the screen is facing me. I'm looking at a picture of a young woman with long dark hair, dark eyes, and a sweet, heart-shaped face. She looks all of twenty and innocent as a doe.

I say gruffly, "Not exactly is right."

Declan groans. "Jesus Christ."

"Set it up."

"You're fucking insane."

"Set it up, boss. Talk to Caruso. See if he'll bite."

I turn and walk toward the door, listening to Declan piss and moan behind me, but knowing he'll consider it once I'm gone.

Kings have to move the pawns at their disposal. It's just what kings do.

As for the pawns, well, they might not have a king's power, but they can still make themselves useful.

And, if given the right opportunity, they can have a little fun while they're at it.

Being the good guy hasn't gotten me anything so far except heartache.

It's time to be bad and break something innocent.

BONUS CHAPTER

MAL

*S*he twitches in her sleep like a puppy.

Fierce in reverse proportion to her size, the mouthy little she-devil in my bed is restless, moving her legs under the sheets and rolling her head on the pillow, every so often jerking with a small whine.

I know she's having a bad dream. Even if I hadn't studied her sleeping many times before, her distress would be obvious.

That she's in pain is obvious, too. It's all over her, in every move and expression. What's less obvious is why I feel so compelled to ease that pain. Why do I care so much about this demon waif with the big mouth and bad dye job? Why am I having to force myself to stay seated in this chair when every instinct I have is screaming at me to run over to the bed and comfort her?

She did take a bullet for me. There's that.

Me. The assassin. Friendless dispenser of death.

What she hasn't done is beg me to release her. She hasn't cried, either. Mostly, she's just argued and sassed the fuck out of me.

I don't understand this woman at all.

She looks as fragile as a bird, but when I broke into the safe house and threatened to snap her neck, instead of begging for her life, she growled like a bear and promised she'd come back as a ghost and haunt me forever.

I hate to admit how endearing that was.

From the first moment I saw her, I wanted to protect her. To keep her safe. I was drawn to her before I knew a single thing about her, and now she's in my bed, suffering from a bullet wound that still might end her life, and I'm sitting in this chair across from her struggling with my feelings.

Feelings! What has she *done* to me?

Those sweet brown eyes might have something to do with it. So might that stubborn streak. That she looks like a mouse but stands her ground like a Rottweiler is oddly compelling.

And she thanks me for everything. She even thanked me for not killing her!

Most inexplicable of all . . . she's attracted to me.

She responded when I kissed her at the safe house. Arched into me with a small moan of pleasure, dug her fingernails into my skin, and pressed her breasts against my chest. Then today, when I took my shirt off because it was covered in blood, her eyes bulged and her face turned red as she examined my body.

It was obvious that blush wasn't from disgust.

And let's not forget that when I asked her why she took a bullet for me, she replied, "Because I didn't want you to die."

There's definitely something wrong with her head.

Maybe if I keep telling myself that, it will ease the strange ache in my chest.

She emits a soft cry, yanking me from the chaos of my thoughts. I frown, studying her pale face in concern, until she suddenly jerks upright, screaming.

I'm across the room and pulling her into my arms before my

brain registers what I'm doing. "It's okay," I murmur. "You're safe. I'm here."

Trembling, she clings to me and hides her face in my chest. I rock her and reassure her that I'll never let any harm come to her. That I'll always be watching over her, protecting her, even when she doesn't know I'm there.

I say all that in Russian because it doesn't make any sense that I should feel protective of someone who's supposed to be my enemy. I wouldn't know how to explain if she asked me why. But she needs some kind of reassurance to stop all this shaking and gasping, so I try to provide it. In English this time.

"Next time you have a nightmare, remind yourself that you're dreaming. It's not real. Then tell yourself to wake up."

"That makes no sense," she says crossly. "How can I tell myself anything if I'm asleep?"

I should have known she'd be argumentative. Riley loves nothing more than to challenge me, even straight out of a nightmare. That tongue of hers is honed as sharp as a knife.

It's a good thing she's not looking at my face or I'd have to hide this smile.

"Your subconscious will remember I told you. From now on, you'll be able to wake yourself up from a bad dream. It won't stop you from having them, but it will help."

She's quiet for a moment, no doubt thinking of some snappy comeback to take me down a notch. Before she can, I tell her I'm going to run a bath.

"Didn't you just take a shower?"

"It's not for me. It's for you." I pull away and smooth a hand over her tangled hair, forcing my face to remain expressionless so she won't guess how badly I want to kiss her. Just to make sure that doesn't happen, I add, "You stink."

Her look could melt steel. "That is *so* not helpful."

"Helpful or not, it's the truth."

It isn't, but I'm not telling her that I think she smells like what heaven must smell like because I'm being ridiculous enough as it is.

"Drink some water."

I take the glass from the nightstand, hand it to her, and watch carefully as she gulps the water down. When the urge to pull her into my arms again gets too strong, I stand and go into the bathroom, where I take a moment to steady myself before turning on the faucets in the bathtub. I test the temperature until it's just right, then plug the drain and return to the bedroom.

Riley is sitting where I left her in bed, but now she has her glasses on and is staring in dissatisfaction at the wall above my head. She points to it.

"Wasn't there a moose there?"

"No."

She blinks rapidly, looking confused and a little frightened, as if maybe she imagined it altogether, so I hurry to reassure her that she didn't.

"It was an elk."

Apparently, that was the wrong thing to say. She rolls her eyes.

"Oh, for fuck's sake."

Why the hell does it have to be so adorable when she sasses me? It's not enough that I feel protective of her, I have to actually *enjoy* it when she's disrespectful? If it were anybody else, they'd already have a bullet in their skull!

But it's not anybody else. It's Riley Rose. The only person in the world who makes me feel things.

My voice unintentionally gruff because there's a rock in my throat, I say, "I took it down."

She considers that with her head cocked to one side. "You took the elk head off the wall after I went to sleep?"

"Yes."

"Why?"

I could be headed into a minefield, but I tell her the truth anyway. I don't know when it happened, but lying to her is no longer a possibility. "Because you didn't like it."

Blinking, she lifts her brows and says archly, "So in addition to being able to walk through walls, you can read minds."

"No, but I can read faces. Yours is unusually expressive."

Like it is now, for instance, with the color rising in her cheeks and panic shining in her eyes. She's worried how much she's given away already.

She should be. Because I know she wants me. If I were another sort of man, I'd already have taken her, injured or not.

I cross to her, pull the covers off her legs, and pick her up in my arms. She weighs virtually nothing, which makes me deeply uneasy.

I need to feed her. I need to make sure she's eating enough so she can get her strength back. Why haven't I forced her to eat more?

She distracts me from being angry with myself by saying, "I'm supposed to be walking."

As if I'd let you. "You will be. Let's get you clean first."

I carry her into the bathroom and set her on her feet. When I tug at the hem of the nightgown she's wearing, she jerks back so hard, she loses her balance.

"Whoa! What're you doing?"

I grip her upper arm to steady her and keep my voice gentle because it's obvious she's horrified at the thought of me seeing her naked. "You're feeling shy. There's no need to be. I've already seen all of you there is to see, inside and out."

She stares at me in open-mouthed shock.

Looks like an explanation is in order.

"I stood at the head of your bed when they opened your stomach to get the bullet and your damaged organs out. I gave you sponge baths while you were drugged. I changed your clothes, changed your bedsheets, and helped the nurse change your catheter when it got plugged. There isn't an inch of your body I'm not already familiar with."

Her face is white. She might actually pass out.

She closes her eyes and whispers, "Wake up. Wake up. Wake up."

"You're not dreaming."

"This has to be a dream. There's no universe in which this can possibly be real."

I need to take care of her, and she's not letting me. Impatience makes my tone sharper than I intended. "Don't be dramatic. Bodies are just meat."

Again, it's the wrong thing to say. She glares at me with the heat of a thousand burning suns.

I'm sick for thinking how cute it is.

"Excuse me for not being deadened to all sense of humanity, Mr. International Assassin, but *my* body is not meat to *me*."

What am I missing here? She's not afraid to jump in front of a bullet for me, but she doesn't want me to see her naked? "Are you angry because you think I might have touched you inappropriately?"

"Jesus!"

"Because I didn't. I would never take advantage like that. I'm a psychopath, not a pervert. I believe strongly in consent."

Her face turns beet red. She snaps, "Well that's tremendous news! I feel so much better now!"

Withering sarcasm aside, she's genuinely embarrassed. I realize it's not fear that I did something to her while she's unconscious that's driving this, it's simple vanity.

Awake, asleep, or under anesthesia, she knows I wouldn't harm her.

She trusts me.

A seismic shift occurs inside my body. Volcanoes erupt. Mountains crumble. The sky turns to ashes, and the earth shudders under my feet.

When the dust settles, all that's left is her.

My voice thick and my body on fire, I say, "And there are many things I'd like to get your specific consent for, Riley Rose, but touching you while you're unconscious isn't one of them."

Her lips part as she stares at me, but she's not the only one surprised by the tone in my voice. I sounded like the besotted caveman I am.

Don't just stand here like a fool. Do something!

I test the bathwater again. That seems reasonable. Like something a man in control of himself would do. Then I shut off the faucets and turn back to her, determined to act calm and rational and keep my shit together.

If I believed in any gods, this is when I'd start praying to them for help.

"You can't get your sutures wet, so the water will only cover your legs. I'll wash your hair first." I point at the metal bucket at one end of the bathtub. "Tip your head over the edge of the tub."

When I tug on her hem again, she makes a face and stops me.

"Mal, I can't. I can't get naked in front of you. If this wound doesn't kill me, the embarrassment will."

"Embarrassment over what?"

"You seeing me naked!"

"I've already seen you naked. I just explained that." *And all of you is beautiful, Riley Rose, inside and out, wounded or not.*

"You haven't seen me naked while I was awake!"

Don't think about it. Don't picture her sweet naked body underneath yours. Keep your game face on! Say something to convince her she needs this. "You want to smell like a pigpen, is that it?"

Insulted, she curls her lip and huffs. "No!"

If there were a contest for the most wrong things said in a single conversation, I would fucking win.

"Then let me give you a bath."

"You say that like *I'm* the unreasonable one!"

You are. You're not afraid of me, which is completely unreasonable.

And I'm the fool trying desperately not to fall at your feet. "The faster you get over your useless modesty, the faster this will be done."

"Mal—"

"I promise I won't look at anything. How's that?"

There's that lip curl again. It's becoming my new favorite thing.

"Right. You won't look at anything while you're busy washing my hair and all my naked parts. I'm sure that will be very easy for you."

Why does she have to keep saying the word "naked"? Is she trying to kill me?

I manage to say calmly, "Easier than living with your stench."

She sends me one of her signature glares and pronounces, "You know what? I just decided I hate you."

That makes two of us. "Hate me all you want in the bathtub."

We stand staring at each other in silence while I fight the urge to kiss her and she plots my murder and dismemberment, until finally she relents and switches tactics.

She says pleadingly, "Can't you understand what this must be like for me?"

"Yes, I can. And I'm sorry. I don't want to make you uncomfortable. But you're not steady enough to get in and out of the tub by yourself or lift the pitcher to rinse your hair. I doubt you have the strength to lift a bar of soap."

She narrows her eyes at me, calculating if I'm lying or telling the truth. I wait patiently, silently willing her to understand that this is for her, that it will make her feel good, and that along with protecting her, making her happy is now my sole purpose in life.

Holding her doubtful gaze, I say as gently as possible, "I won't force you. It's your choice. I just want to help you feel better. I think a bath will do that."

"So I could ask you to take me back to bed, and you will?"

"Yes."

A shade of hostility fades from her posture when she realizes I'm being truthful. Chewing her lip, she gazes longingly at the water in the tub. Impatience nettles me, but I keep my mouth shut and let her come to her own decision.

Finally she mutters, "Fuck it." She turns back to me and commands, "But don't make it weird!"

That train has already left the station, but I wisely choose silence again and turn my back to her.

After a moment, she says, "What are you doing?"

"Would you prefer I stare at you while you take off your nightgown?"

I knew that would do the trick. She heaves a beleaguered sigh and begins to undress. Shocked by the sheer force of will I have to exert over myself not to turn and help her, I listen to her small sounds of frustration as she struggles to get the nightgown over her head.

Finally, she murmurs, "Okay."

I turn and pick her up, keeping my gaze averted so as not to make her feel insecure or embarrassed. Then I lower her carefully into the tub, kneeling and setting her down gently. She has her arms crossed over her chest and her head bowed, and I've never seen her look so fragile.

Tenderness seizes me. The emotion is so strong, it's almost overpowering. My heart thuds against my rib cage, and my throat constricts. I've never felt anything like it.

I hope I never will again because I can hardly breathe.

I cup my hand around the back of her head and slowly lean her back. She has her eyes squeezed shut now. I ask if she wants a towel to support her neck. Cheeks burning, she timidly says yes.

I quickly roll up a hand towel and place it under her neck, then take the pitcher from the floor and dip it into the bathwater, still keeping my gaze averted from her body. Then I wet her hair, grab a bottle of shampoo, squeeze a dollop into my hand, and start to clean her hair.

The moment I press my fingers into her scalp, she relaxes and exhales a soft sigh.

I've never heard a sound so sweet. Just when I thought I had myself together, that little sigh of pleasure unravels me all over again.

Her arms slide off her chest, exposing her breasts. She's relaxed now, her embarrassment gone. I concentrate on gently massaging her head and neck, hoping she won't notice how my hands tremble.

All these years, I was dead inside. Sleepwalking through life. Now, because of her, I'm awake again.

"I can't say this in your language, little bird, because I'm still trying to work out what it all means. But I've never met anyone like you. Before you, my life made sense. I knew my purpose. I knew my place, which was alone. I liked it that way. My days and nights had a predictable rhythm. Nothing upset that rhythm. I didn't think anything could."

I rinse the shampoo from her hair, then wet a washcloth and start to gently wash her body. She's slack and pliant, allowing me to tend to her as I continue to speak softly in Russian.

"Then I saw you, and everything changed. I can't explain why. Something . . . woke up inside of me. It feels like being possessed. My mind is consumed by thoughts of you. It's as if time has split into halves: before you and after you. The time where nothing much mattered and the time where *all* that matters is a smidgeon of a girl with a smile like an angel's and the personality of a hellhound.

"You wouldn't think that's a compliment, but it is. Here's another one: you make me crazy. I don't know what to do with myself, I'm so crazy. I've never felt so lost. It's awful, if I'm being honest. What's even worse is that I've had you here with me for only a short while now, and already, I can't imagine *not* having you here. How is that possible?

"I'm not a man who ever thought of the future because I assumed I wouldn't have one. Or at least, a different one. Day in, day out, it was kill or be killed. And I'm very good at my job, little bird. The best, actually. But now, when I think about tomorrow and the next day and the day after that . . . you're here with me. Talk about insane. Men like me don't get happily ever afters. We don't ride off into the sunset and live to old age. And women like you shouldn't be anywhere near me.

"But . . . I'd give anything to keep you. Anything. Not only is that stupid of me, but it's dangerous, too. For both of us, but mostly for you. This life I lead is ugly, but it's what I chose. I know the risks. I couldn't live with myself if I were selfish enough to force you to stay here. You'd hate me for it, anyway. In the end, you'd hate me. I don't think I could stand that. You took a bullet for me, after all. You saved my life. I don't understand *why*, but you did."

Her expression is one of bliss and pure trust, and the tenderness I feel as I wash her sweet face is huge and painful. I've endured multiple stab wounds less agonizing than this.

In English, I say, "Open your eyes, little bird."

Her lashes flutter, then her lids lift. Examining my face, she frowns. "Are you okay?"

Her voice is faint, but the concern in it flattens me. She's the one who's injured, but it's *me* she's worried about.

I shake my head, but don't answer because I can't trust what might come out of my mouth. I swallow it down, all the burning bright longing and feverish need, then tell her I'm going to lift her out of the tub.

"Do you think you can stand up?"

Eyes hazy, she considers it for a moment, then nods. "Not for long, though."

I lift her, set her onto her feet, and gently towel dry her skin. Then I wrap the towel around her body, lift her in my arms, and carry her back to my bed. She rests her head on my shoulder and snuggles into me, and I know that no matter what happens, I'll remember this night for the rest of my life.

I lay her on the mattress and move the towel around so I can change the dressing on her wound without exposing her breasts or the panties she kept on in the tub. As I work, I'm aware of her curious gaze on me, but I ignore it and concentrate on cleaning her sutures.

"Mal?"

"Hmm?"

"Thank you."

That feels like a kick to the gut.

I stalked her. I kidnapped her. I took her away from everything she's ever known, and still she's *grateful*? She should be punching me in the face!

Glowering, I look into her eyes. "Don't thank me."

Innocent as a lamb, she says, "Why not?"

"You were shot because of me."

"I'm alive because of you."

Her sweet brown eyes are soft, and I have to close my own eyes for a moment because the guilt is too fucking much.

I realize then, in those few beats of silence, that what I'm feeling has a name. All these powerful, confusing emotions so mercilessly battering my body and soul can be distilled down into one simple four-letter word fools like me have been struck down by since the dawn of the human race.

Love.

I've fallen in love with a girl who's related to my worst enemy. A girl who's better than me in every conceivable way. A girl who doesn't come from my world, who'd never fit into it, and who deserves so much more than what this monster could possibly give.

A girl, in short, who I can never call my own.

In a life full of bad moments, this one is the absolute worst.

I open my eyes and glower at her. "No," I say, my voice hard. "*I'm* alive because of *you*. Because you took a bullet meant for me. Don't get it confused in your head. And don't thank me."

I turn my attention back to her sutures, my heart filled with the tortured song of a thousand howling wolves.

But Riley, stubborn smartass that she is, doesn't let my glower intimidate her.

In a voice both innocent and tart, she says, "Am I allowed to thank you for taking away the big scary moose?"

I've met hardened killers less confident than this. And definitely less annoying.

Whatever she sees on my face when I glance up at her makes her smile.

"I mean elk."

"Be. Quiet."

Eyes dancing with mischief, she whispers, "Because I really hated that thing."

In Russian, I tell her she's a giant pain in my ass, then tape a fresh bandage to her stomach. Finished with that, I go to the closet to get her something to wear. Without asking myself why, I choose a shirt identical to the one I'm wearing, then help her sit up and put it on.

It's enormous on her, like a tent. She doesn't seem to mind, because she's too busy sniffing the sleeve and looking heartbreakingly happy about something.

That expression is instantaneously seared onto my mind's eye. I know I'll come back to it again and again after she's gone, taking comfort in the memory.

That alone will be able to sustain me to the end of my days.

"Lie back."

Miraculously, she does as I command without argument, then watches me in silence as I pull the shirt down over her hips. I pull the towel out from beneath her, hesitating only briefly before asking, "Panties on or off?"

She answers by lifting her hips.

I reach under the hem of the shirt and gently pull her wet panties down her legs, then go into the bathroom with them and the wet towel and lay both over the edge of the tub.

Then I brace my arms against the sink, bow my head, and struggle to get my breathing under control.

I'm in love with her. I'd burn down entire cities for her. I'll follow her to the ends of the earth and kill anyone who dares to upset her and spend the rest of my life with her ghost inside my head.

And I can never let her know any of it.

Inhaling slowly, I raise my head and stare at myself in the mirror. My eyes stare back at me, and though I expected them to be empty as they usually are, now I see an odd, unnerving glint.

It takes a moment for me to realize what the glint is. When I do, I'm afraid for the first time I can remember.

That strange spark reflected back at me is something maybe even more powerful than love. Something that makes people do even more foolish things, take even greater risks, keep fighting when all is lost and oblivion is not only possible, it's inevitable.

Hope.

When Riley took a bullet meant for me, she also set something else into motion. Something I've only heard about in fairy tales or storybooks, a thing only prophets or sorcerers can do.

She resurrected me from the dead.

Not only that, but she also gave me a reason to live.

Dazed, I return to the bedroom. My little resurrectionist is yawning, so I kiss her on the forehead and tuck the blankets around her body, making sure she's snug. Then I retreat to a safe space—the chair in the corner—sit down, and close my eyes.

Just when I think she's drifted off, she murmurs my name.

"What?"

"Were you really going to kill me?"

Never. Never, malyutka. I've been yours since the very beginning.

I don't say that. I simply wait until her breathing deepens and she's asleep, then I pace the floors until dawn breaks, understanding that this fight inside me is one I can't win.

I can't keep her here. No matter how much I want it, she can't be mine.

The only problem is that I know myself well . . .

And *can't*s have never stopped Malek Antonov from getting what he wants.

PLAYLIST

"Sit Still, Look Pretty" Daya

"Fantasy" Sofi Tukker

"Supermassive Black Hole" Muse

"Reviver" Lane 8

"Boss Bitch" Doja Cat

"Breathe" Télépopmusik

"Damn It Feels Good to Be a Gangsta" Geto Boys

"We Are Family" Sister Sledge

"You're Mine" Charlotte de Witte, Oscar and the Wolf

ACKNOWLEDGMENTS

Thank you to Sarah Ferguson; Letitia Hasser; Linda Ingmanson; Shannon Smith; Stephenie Meyer; Eleni Caminis; my husband, Jay; all the wonderful members of Geissinger's Gang; and you, my readers. Plus everyone else I'm sure to remember as soon as this goes to press.

If you haven't yet read the Dangerous Beauty series, that's where Pakhan and Killian are originally found. Killian also appears in the Beautifully Cruel series.

A full book list and suggested reading order can be found on my website.

ABOUT THE AUTHOR

J.T. GEISSINGER is a #1 international and indie bestselling author of thirty-one novels. Ranging from funny, feisty rom-coms to intense erotic thrillers, her books have sold more than fifteen million copies worldwide and have been translated into more than twenty languages.

She is a three-time finalist in both contemporary and paranormal romance for the RITA Award, the highest distinction in romance fiction from the Romance Writers of America. She is also a recipient of the PRISM Award for Best First Book, the Golden Quill Award for Best Paranormal/Urban Fantasy, and the HOLT Medallion for Best Erotic Romance.

Find her online at www.jtgeissinger.com